It was just supposed to be a murder investigation, but I soon discovered I was the one likely to be murdered...

Nelson was the first to turn to face the security police. "Oh shit," he said.

McGarvey, Granger, and I then turned. The security police all wore NWO guard uniforms, and the insignia on the panel trucks bore the NWO logo. I heard the tinted glass rear window on the side of the squad car slowly descend. I looked briefly in that direction.

A blonde woman with black sunglasses shrugged. "Take them to Interrogation."

Behind her, I could see the shape of a reptilian face.

"We're in some deep shit," I said aloud.

"Maybe deeper," Nelson replied.

"We're gonna be in the soup," Granger told us.

I leaned toward Granger. "Granger, no matter what happens, we kidnapped you at gunpoint to show us the way out of the underground facilities. Understand?"

"But, Mr. Arrow—"

"No buts. We forced you to show us how to get out of the facility."

The shortest of the NWO guards saw that we were whispering. "Shaddup!" he ordered. I winked at him. He strode over to me like a DI approaching a new recruit. "Are you some kind of wise guy?"

"Are you some kind of pretend law officer?" I asked

He hit me in the gut with the butt of his TEC-DC9. As he did, I grabbed its long clip with my right hand. "Hey, bucko," I wheezed. "This assault weapon is banned under federal law."

"Fuck the federal government and fuck you," he told me.

I released my grip on the clip, which was a mistake because it enabled him to swing the butt of his weapon into my temple. The last thing I remember was my cheek frying on the gritty tarmac.

Dan Arrow is a private detective who's catapulted into a world he never imagined when a guy named Billy Powers dies the night before their first meeting. In the mail the next morning, Dan receives Powers's notebook, which is full of handwritten comments and clipped articles about seemingly unrelated events. Initially dismissing the notebook's contents as the work of a crackpot, Dan soon meets Powers's wife and discovers that there's more truth than fiction about aliens cooperating with international governments to achieve covert agendas.

Dan wouldn't have called his ex-girlfriend, FBI Special Agent Mona Casola, except that his client is dead and Mona's employer has classified it as a suicide. Thrown together again, the duo's investigation takes them into deep underground military bases, where alien species are working with several governments to establish a New World Order. Then, when Mona is taken captive by a reptilian leader, Dan must choose between rescuing the love of his life or stopping the coronation of an evil leader and the unleashing of a global pandemic as the NWO agenda is set into motion...

KUDOS for *Dan Arrow and the New World Order*

In *Dan Arrow and the New World Order* by Edward S. Baker, Dan Arrow is a private detective. When a new client dies before he can meet with Dan, but a notebook from him shows up in the mail the next morning, Dan assumes the guy was murdered, even though the FBI claims it's a suicide. The client's wife doesn't believe it and hires Dan to investigate. Thinking there is something fishy about the FBI investigation, Dan calls his former lover, FBI Special Agent Mona Casola, and, together, the two dodge the NSA, CIA, and FBI, as well as some strange-looking aliens, as they try to uncover the truth. Well written with fast-paced action, lots of suspense, and an intriguing mystery, this is one that will catch and hold your interest from beginning to end. ~ *Taylor Jones, The Review Team of Taylor Jones & Regan Murphy*

Dan Arrow and the New World Order by Edward Baker is the story of a secret group of rogue government agents working with aliens to bring about a new world order and one world government. Private detective Dan Arrow gets a phone call from a prospective client who claims that his life is in danger. He's being threatened because he has been talking about a UFO encounter he was told not to talk about. When the man turns up dead a few days later, and his notebook arrives in the mail, Dan is sure the client was murdered. Then he gets a call from the man's wife who hires Dan to find the killer. The FBI is claiming it's a suicide. But the wife doesn't believe it. She wants to know what happened. Dan takes the case, thinking it will be a simple murder investigation, maybe a mistake by the FBI, or maybe even a cover-up. But he is not prepared for what he uncovers—and, even if he lives to tell the tale, who would ever believe him? *Dan Arrow and New World Order* is clever, fun, and intriguing. With fascinating characters, fast-paced action, plenty of surprises, and a lot of humor, whether you are into conspiracy theories or not, this is one you won't want to miss. ~ *Regan Murphy, The Review Team of Taylor Jones & Regan Murphy*

ACKNOWLEDGMENTS

Many thanks to Lauri Wellington, Acquisitions Editor at Black Opal Books, for believing in this work and making its publication possible. Thanks, as well, to Susan who ushered me through the first round of editing, and to Faith who truly helped to polish this novel into its final form. And thanks to Jack, whose work on the cover design was tireless. And finally, thanks to Dan Barrett, whose experience with the publishing process and positive encouragement have been greatly appreciated.

I would be remiss, as well, if I did not thank the pilots of those mysterious reddish-orange globes which were being chased by Strategic Air Command jets above Green Lakes State Park back in 1966. Their ninety-degree-angle turns and rapid acceleration made me sit up and take note that the laws of physics, as I knew them, had just been violated.

DAN ARROW

AND THE
NEW WORLD ORDER

Edward S. Baker

Edward F. Baker (signature)

A Black Opal Books Publication

GENRE: SCIENCE FICTION/THRILLER/MYSTERY-DETECTIVE

DAN ARROW AND THE NEW WORLD ORDER
Copyright © 2018 by Edward S. Baker
Cover Design by Jackson Cover Designs
All cover art copyright © 2018
All Rights Reserved
Print ISBN: 978-1-62694849-5

First Publication: JANUARY 2018

Published by Black Opal Books **http://www.blackopalbooks.com**

DEDICATION

To my wife Edna, who sat beside me at the lake while I read each word of this novel to her in the warmth of the morning sun. And to our children, Aura, Lauren, and Ed.

"Since I entered politics, I have chiefly had men's views confided to me privately. Some of the biggest men in the US, in the field of commerce and manufacture, are afraid of somebody, are afraid of something. They know that there is a power somewhere so organized, so subtle, so watchful, so interlocked, so complete, so pervasive, that they had better not speak above their breath when they speak in condemnation of it." ~ *Woodrow Wilson*

Prologue

I am one of only three remaining survivors of an underground battle that occurred at level seven of a large subterranean facility located near Dulce, New Mexico. It was a battle between alien Greys and American black ops troops. There were more of us, ten survivors in total, but some have died from exposure to a form of radiation from the alien weapons. Others have died mysteriously, with all cases being classified as suicide by federal authorities," said William G. Powers at the Newport Beach UFO Conference on June 24, 2012.

"I was a mole operator. Moles are large machines that drill holes in the Earth, creating tunnels and large caverns that become living spaces. Clandestine factions within our government are in the process of digging more than a hundred of these facilities across our country, as part of a larger conspiracy to permit the New World Order to assume control of the globe. These facilities are interconnected by high-speed shuttle systems and will be home to a select few who will live underground while a pandemic is unleashed on the surface.

"In 1979, while digging horizontally at level seven, my mole broke into a pre-existing facility that should not have been there. It was full of gray aliens, who fired liquid light at us. We called for reinforcements, and a firefight ensued. In total, sixty-six Americans died. We pulled two dead

Greys and two dead lizards from the facility when we escaped. Their bodies were shipped to Edwards Air Force Base. On the orders of our commander, the seventh level was nuked with a small device, causing the sixth floor to collapse upon it.

"I have been silent for too long, fearing for my life under the threat of death. However, I am here today to reveal to you now that factions of the most powerful governments around the globe are conspiring with reptilian space aliens to seize control of our planet and to rule it through a single New World Order. Our president called for the creation of a New World Order several times during his many campaign speeches. Check it out, and you will see that I am not lying. The time of the emergence of the New World Order is rapidly approaching."

ᘓᘓᘓ

William "Billy" Powers was found dead in a motel room on April 27, 2014. He had been strangled from behind with a length of surgical tubing. The FBI classified it as a suicide.

Chapter 1

I was looking at the picture that Hal had taped to the wall when the office door opened, pinning me behind it.

"Halina, this package was overnighted to Mr. Arrow. Can you sign for it?"

It was Wally, our mail carrier. He usually brought the mail at two, but special deliveries caused him to come earlier.

"Why don't you just shut the door and ask him to sign for it himself?" Hal replied.

Wally walked into my office. He came back out two seconds later saying, "He ain't in there, sweetheart." Then he saw me through the glass in the office door, still facing the wall and looking at the photo of Hal's boyfriend's new Fat Boy. "Oh, hi, Mr. Arrow," he stammered. "Was you there the whole time?"

"I guess I was," I replied. I stepped from behind the door and took the package from him. It was a large manila envelope with both ends heavily sealed with brown reinforced packing tape. I signed the USPS form where Wally had made an X, and then he left the office as quickly as he had entered. "I guess he has a lot to do," I muttered to Hal.

"Well, he's trying to finish his route by four, so he can catch the end of a pool tournament at Barney's," Hal told me. Barney's was our local sports bar. You could always find a game or two to watch on one of Barney's seven flat screens, or you could try your luck at a game of pool against the best local boys who were always hanging around there, playing for money. For a local dive, it was okay, but the beer choice was limited to anything Barney could buy for under $25 a keg. It was really cheap shit.

"Are we expecting anything from a client today?" I asked Hal, showing her the package.

"Give me that," she said. "Let me open it, so we don't have blood all over the contents like we did with the Myers documents."

I dropped my head in shame. The Myers documents were legal papers that I needed to sign and have notarized a couple of years ago, but while opening the package, I ripped my forefinger on a staple and bled all over the paperwork. Hal had to call for new copies, which pissed off the lawyers because it delayed their settlement of a big lawsuit by two days. I felt like a real schlep about that. Hal likes to rub it in from time to time.

"Oh," Hal said, "it's from that dead guy!"

"What dead guy?"

"That guy who was supposed to meet with you this afternoon."

"Is he dead?"

"Well, if you'd read the paper, you'd already know he isn't going to make the meeting."

I gave her a look of annoyance. "Why didn't you tell me he canceled the appointment?" I asked.

"Well, he didn't exactly cancel it," Hal replied, "but he made the front page. Apparently, it was a suicide. He strangled himself with surgical tubing." I took the package from Hal and walked toward my office to look at its contents. As I walked away, Hal asked, "I'm going for coffee. Do you want your usual?"

"Yeah, that would be nice," I said.

I heard the outer office door shut as I sat down at my desk. The package was from Bill Powers. He had called me two days ago to set up a meeting to discuss something that he said was top secret, involving every level of our government. When I asked why he hadn't gone to the FBI, he reminded me that the FBI *is* our government and, in fact, that the FBI was implicated in this cover-up. "What cover-up?" I asked.

"You won't believe it," he said. "You'll think I'm nuts, but you're the best person to help me figure this out."

"Why's that?" I asked.

"Because you figured out that Ponzi scheme that Madoff was operating."

"That was just dumb luck," I replied. "My client asked for assistance in getting Mr. Madoff to return the money he had invested. I didn't expect anything so large. And, besides, it really pissed off the DA that I didn't go to him before I turned that info over to the Justice Department."

"Yeah," Powers said, "but if you hadn't uncovered it, there'd still be plenty of people thinking they have money when all that they have is an empty savings account."

"Well, I didn't get anything for my efforts. My client had no money left, and he did the bankruptcy thing, so I'm out all my expenses."

"Well, you can write the expenses off and then write a book about it," he said.

"Yeah, sure."

"Well, Mr. Arrow, you're the man I need. Can I come on Wednesday at one?"

"Yeah, I'll have my secretary squeeze you in." Shit, business had been slow, and I knew there was nobody else scheduled for the rest of the week.

"Listen, Mr. Arrow, you've got to know that there are some guys trying to find me about this cover-up. Bad guys. If, for some reason, I don't make that appointment, will you call my wife? She'll fill you in on what I've been up to. Between her and my notebook, I think you'll be intrigued."

"Notebook?"

"Yeah, it's all in there—events, dates, and people. I just haven't been able to put it all together. That's why I need you." He gave me his wife's cell phone number.

"Okay, Mr. Powers. I'll see you on Wednesday at one."

So, the poor sap hung himself last night, I thought. Funny, though, he didn't sound suicidal when we spoke on Monday morning.

I pulled the contents out of the envelope. It was a one-inch thick spiral notebook, stuffed with loose photos and photocopied documents. I saw them but didn't look at any of them at first. Paper clipped to the cover was a handwritten note:

Mr. Arrow:

I've been followed since Monday afternoon by two tall men in black suits. I'm not sure if I will make the meeting on Wednesday. If anything happens to me, it isn't suicide. This is a matter of national security. My wife will fill you in. This is the notebook that I mentioned when we spoke. Thanks for your help.

Bill Powers

I flopped the notebook open to the middle and started browsing. This guy looked like a whack-o. Neatly printed in super-small letters, so correctly shaped that they appeared to be typed instead of written by hand, were pages of dates and events. Many were UFO sightings. Some were earthquakes and volcanic eruptions. The photos were of military bases, some taken from the air, and of UFOs. Most were in black and white.

Some notes detailed reports from *Earthfiles.com*, which I later learned is a web-based newsletter detailing strange events involving UFOs, cattle mutilations, crop circles, and government cover-ups. Others were from less rational web sites. "God save me," I muttered as I closed the notebook.

I picked up the phone and called Powers's wife. I owed him that much, but this didn't look like something I was going to get involved in.

Her phone rang three times before Mrs. Powers answered. "This is Dan Arrow," I told her. "I'm sorry for your loss. Your husband contacted me two days ago and asked to meet with me this afternoon to discuss something that was top secret."

"Thanks for your condolences, Mr. Arrow. I received a brief letter from him yesterday, telling me that he had contacted you and that I should expect a call if it happened."

"It?" I asked.

"Yeah, his murder," she said matter-of-factly. "He prepared me for this eventuality about two years ago. He's been living on borrowed time. I guess I wasn't surprised when the police called me last night. It was bound to happen to Billy sooner or later."

"When can we meet, Mrs. Powers? Maybe after the funeral?"

"Are you available this afternoon, Mr. Arrow?"

"Yeah, but—"

"I'll come around three if that's okay. Billy's body is already at the mortician's. There's nothing I can do for him, except to get you on the trail of who murdered him. The police have classified it as a suicide, so they won't be investigating anything."

"Well, Mrs. Powers, I don't want to interfere with your mourning."

"Mr. Arrow, I've been in mourning for the past two years. I've barely seen Billy in all that time, because he's been in hiding. There's no more mourning to do. It's almost a relief that it's finally over. I'll be at your office around three." She hung up.

Hal came back in with my coffee, one inch of high-test and the rest all decaf. If I had too much caffeine, I couldn't think straight. I offered her three dollars to pay for both of our coffees, but she refused them. "I'd rather you sprang for a coffee pot so we could make our own. That guy who sells this stuff gives me the willies." He was a Middle Easterner with one glass eye that didn't move but stared straight ahead as his other eye moved around in its socket. I felt sorry for the guy, but it did look weird.

"Hey," I told her, "not everybody is as cute as you are. It's not his fault that he can't keep his eye off of you!" Hal muttered something I couldn't understand, but I got the message from the tone of her voice.

I picked up the package that I had received from Powers and took it to Hal. "Would you mind reviewing this for me and letting me know what you think—by two this afternoon?"

Hal was good at analyzing paperwork. Probably better than I was.

"Thank God," she said. "I was hoping you'd find me something to do! You know, the days get boring when there's nothing to do but read the paper."

She was kidding, I thought.

I went back into my office and called my friend Nick, a detective with the homicide unit of the Alexandria police department, to see what he could tell me about Powers's death.

"Don't you read the papers?" Nick asked. "The department has classified it as a suicide. Case closed."

"Yeah, but did he leave a note or anything?" I asked.

"What's got you interested in the Powers case?" he asked.

"His wife called me. She thinks it was a murder."

"Look, Danny, I wasn't directly involved with the examination of the motel room, so I only know the hearsay. Apparently, he was alone and left no note. Griswold was there. I'll talk to him and get back to you, but I think this is a waste of time. He was a loner and some kind of nut job. Suicide is an expected outcome for a guy like him."

"What do you mean, nut job?" I asked,

"The guys here say that he was into weird shit, you know, conspiracy and end of the world stuff."

"Well, let me know what you find out, would you?"

"Yeah, but you're wasting your time."

අංංඅ

A little after two, Hal walked into my office. She dropped Powers's notebook onto my desk. "You ought to read this thing from cover to cover. At first, I thought he was some kind of cuckoo, but after a while, it's like the stuff sort of makes sense."

"What do you mean?" I asked.

"Well, there's a lot of stuff going on with UFO sightings and people going missing after seeing them, and animal mutilations, and it's like somebody is doing things to people, and we don't even know it."

"You mean little green men are doing it to us?"

"Well, maybe," she replied, "but maybe it's our military. It's not clear."

"Thanks, Hal, I'll try to read it before Mrs. Powers gets here."

"Well, you'd better hurry. She came in a minute ago."

"Shit. Well, you'd better show her in."

Hal left my office and returned with Mrs. Powers in less than ten seconds. Mrs. Powers was wearing a tight-fitting red skirt and a flowery blouse. Her brunette hair was pulled back into a bun like a school teacher, and her make-up was positive.

She certainly wasn't in mourning.

"Nice to meet you, Mrs. Powers," I said.

"Call me Marlene, Mr. Arrow. Billy would want it that way. He wasn't into formality."

"Fine, Marlene. You can call me Mr. Arrow. I prefer to keep a professional relationship with people who are paying me for services."

"You can still call me Marlene, Mr. Arrow."

"Listen, Marlene. I've checked with a contact in the police department. They've closed the case on your husband's death. It was a suicide. So, why do you feel that your husband was murdered?"

"Have you read my husband's notebook, Mr. Arrow?"

"It just came in this morning. I've skimmed it, but I'll read it in depth tonight. It's full of weird stuff. "

"My husband was a survivor of the Dulce Firefight, Mr. Arrow. Have you ever heard of it?"

"No ma'am," I replied.

"It happened in 1979. Sixty-six Americans were killed by aliens in a tunnel more than two miles beneath the surface of the Earth."

"Where?" I asked.

"In Dulce," she replied. "Dulce, New Mexico."

"Oh."

"The Americans were black ops military and a few contract workers who were digging tunnels and caverns for the military. The complex had seven levels, starting a quarter of a mile below the surface and descending a couple of hundred feet per level. Each level of the complex spread out horizontally and consisted of dozens of large rooms with electricity, plumbing, and air purification systems. We're talking several hundred thousand square feet of space at each level."

"Like building a warehouse at each level?" I asked.

"Yes, maybe several warehouses at each level, but instead of going upward like a skyscraper, the structure goes straight down. Well, at least once you hit the first level."

"So, when did the alleged aliens attack?"

"They were space aliens, Mr. Arrow. They were not alleged. They were the real thing."

"Okay. So when did they attack?"

"Billy said that when the workers were drilling out the seventh level, they broke through a wall of rock and exposed a pre-existing cavern. It was lighted and full of equipment. He and a few men entered the cavern to see what they had found. They were worried that they had broken into another top secret military facility of some kind. There are hundreds of them across the country, you know."

"I didn't know that," I told her.

"It's all in the notebook, Mr. Arrow."

"So go on. Marlene. What happened next?"

"The workers weren't inside very long, maybe thirty seconds, when they encountered a squad of gray aliens. The aliens set off some sort of alarm, and they were quickly joined by taller aliens, probably soldiers of some kind, who shot laser-type weapons at the workers. A couple of men were killed, but most managed to escape. The men quickly closed off the hole that they had bored into the wall, and then they went to the surface for support."

"What was your husband's job, Marlene?"

"He was a heavy equipment technician, specifically a drill operator."

"I thought you said that sixty-six workers were killed."

"Yes, I did. Most of the dead were military. You know, Green Berets and black ops. But workers were killed, too."

"Black ops?"

"Yes, black operatives are military who don't work for the armed forces. Nobody knows exactly who they work for, but they're paid from the federal black operations budget. It's a trillion dollar budget that's hidden in the regular federal budget. Nobody who isn't part of the black ops really knows what it exists for. Billy was working on getting that information, but most of the federal documents that he FOIAed came back all blacked-out because of their top secret nature."

"Okay, we have a couple of dead Americans so far. When did the rest die?"

"Well, when Billy and the workers evacuated from the seventh level, he and a few specialists were sent back down with several platoons of heavily armed military and black ops to try to determine exactly what they had exposed. Billy's job was to drill the wall open again. The one he had sealed before evacuating."

"I see," I told her, stroking my jaw with my thumb.

"When they got back down to the seventh level, it was obvious that somebody had already been there. The wall he had closed had been melted so that the rock was fused shut. He said the rock was welded shut, sort of like glass. Billy moved the drill over about thirty feet to the left and drilled a new hole. It was a big hole, Mr. Arrow, about fifteen feet in diameter."

"That's pretty damn big, Marlene."

"Well, when he broke through, some of the larger aliens came through the hole into the seventh level, shooting their laser guns. The military men fought back, killing several aliens and driving them back into their own side of the hole. Then the military went through the hole and into the aliens' side. More shooting ensued. Eventually, a few of our fighters came back into our side, shooting as they came, and dragging some wounded men with them. Most of the dead were left on the aliens' side. The commander of the American forces ordered Billy to close the hole, which he did. Billy was wounded in the arm during the fight. He had a scar that ran from his elbow to his shoulder on his left arm. When he went to the hospital, they cleaned it, but it didn't need any stitches. It was a perfectly cauterized wound. It was very painful for several months."

"Was that the end to the firefight?"

"Well, yes. Except that a couple of the dead aliens were brought back to the surface and the military ordered the seventh level to be destroyed. They did that with a small nuclear device that collapsed the sixth floor onto the seventh. They didn't bring any of the dead Americans to the surface before they blasted it."

"What happened to the dead aliens?"

"They were put into body bags and taken away. Billy never saw them again."

"So this firefight is why your husband was murdered?"

"Yes, Mr. Arrow. Not because of the fight, but because he started talking about it. They don't like that."

"The military?"

"Yes, and maybe the CIA or the FBI. A day after Billy came home from the hospital, two very tall gentlemen in black suits came to see him and told him that he was never to speak to anyone about the Dulce incident. Not even me. They were anything but friendly. They weren't concerned about his wound. They just told him that he was to forget that the incident ever happened. They threatened that if he told anyone, he would simply disappear in the desert and never be heard from again."

"But Billy told you about the incident?"

"Yes. We hadn't been married a year yet when the incident happened. I remember the men coming to see Billy. I was intimidated by them because they were so tall and menacing, but Billy spoke to them in private, and he didn't tell me what they told him until about fifteen years later, maybe 1994."

"What caused him to tell you?"

"Well, right after the incident, Billy bought that notebook and began keeping records about all sorts of things that he said were related to what happened at Dulce. He wasn't sure how they all fit together, but something big is going on right under the noses of our politicians. He was trying to figure it out so he could blow the whistle. Eventually, he was invited to make a presentation at a national UFO conference in Reno. When he agreed to make that presentation, he thought he should tell me what he had experienced so I could tell someone about it if he disappeared."

"That, in itself, should have frightened you."

"Oh, it did. I was terribly frightened at first. But, I attended that conference with Billy and heard what he had to say. You know, at first, I thought he might have lost his mind or something, but as I listened to what he told the audience, I became very proud of him. Proud that he was standing up and telling the truth. He was hoping that some of the other survivors would come forward to tell their side of the story."

"Did they?"

"No, but about a year later, one man, Gary Mitchell,

agreed to accompany Billy to another conference, but Gary committed suicide two nights before they were supposed to make their presentation. Another survivor wrote a letter to be published in a MUFON newsletter, but he, too, committed suicide before it could be published, and his letter disappeared from the MUFON office that same night. The best that the MUFON staff could do was to swear that they had seen the letter, but they couldn't produce it."

"MUFON?" I asked?

"The Mutual UFO Network. It's a bunch of civilians who are organized to formally study UFO incidents."

"This is a wild story, Marlene."

"I know, and I don't blame you for being skeptical of it, Mr. Arrow. But I assure you that Billy was telling the truth."

"How can you be so sure?"

"Well, first, that scar on his arm. He went to work one day and came home two days later with that horrible burn and loss of muscle. His tattoo of a skull with red eyes was ruined, not that I cared much for it. And then, two years ago, when Billy wasn't at home, I was visited by two of those tall men. They said that they were looking for Billy. They said that it was a matter of national security. I told them that when he came home, I would have him call them. They said not to bother. They told me that they would monitor the house and intercept him when he came home."

"Tall men? Were they the same men you saw back in 1979?"

"No, that couldn't be. They looked much the same as the men in 1979, but those men would have been much older by now. These were young men, maybe near thirty years old and tall—you know, like professional basketball players. Maybe seven feet tall."

"That's very tall, Marlene."

"Billy called them Nordics."

"What does that mean? Scandinavians?"

"I'm not sure, Mr. Arrow. He just called them Nordics."

"So that was two years ago?"

"Yes, and Billy never came home after that. He called me the next day on my cell phone and spoke very briefly. He said that he was going into hiding and that he had to turn his phone off when he wasn't using it, so he couldn't be triangulated. I was never to try to call him, but he would call me from time to time to tell me where to meet him."

"Did he call?"

"Yes. He was very good about that. He called me every few days, but at varying times of the day and night. Each time he called, we spoke for only two minutes. Twice a year he would surprise me by approaching me on the street and taking me to a hotel, where we would...well, you know, catch up."

"You said that he prepped you that he might commit suicide."

"Yes. Because of the suicides of those two men who had agreed to come forward, and because of the mysterious disappearances and deaths of a series of others who had been involved in the Dulce Firefight, Billy was sure that he had been targeted for termination. He was in the process of writing a book about the incident, including the identities of those involved, and he hoped to finish it before they found him. I guess his work will never be completed. I can't even find his working draft. It has simply disappeared."

"And how about you? How are you handling his death?"

"Like I told you on the phone this morning, I've been mourning Billy for two years now. I am through mourning. I want you to find his killer and bring him to justice."

"Aren't you still afraid, Marlene?"

"I don't think so, Mr. Arrow. I suppose I do check the rearview mirror when I'm driving, just in case I see any more of those tall blond men. But now that Billy is gone, I have nothing to fear."

"Blond?"

"Yes, the four I've seen all had blond hair. Maybe that's why Billy called them Nordics. You know, like Swedes."

"Well, I'll take this case, Marlene, but I'm not sure if I'm going to be able to find his murderer."

"I guess you'll want a retainer? Would ten thousand dollars do for now? I've brought a bank check."

Marlene handed me the check, we shook hands, and I told Hal to have her sign the usual contract before leaving the office. At $50 per hour, I had about 200 hours to devote to this case. I hoped it would take at least that long for me to discover that Bill Powers had actually committed suicide. I didn't want to have to refund any of Marlene's retainer.

Chapter 2

Hal was in the hallway yelling at nobody when I arrived for work the next morning. "Who are you upset with?" I asked.

"Don't you expect me to clean up this mess," she yelled in my general direction. "I didn't sign up for this!"

The door to my office was ajar, and I peered in. Papers were strewn everywhere. The drawers to Hal's desk were scattered about the room, and the contents of her two filing cabinets were dumped onto the floor.

"What in the Sam Hill is this about?" I asked aloud.

"Somebody decided to make our lives miserable for the next few weeks, Danny-boy!" Hal proclaimed. "Who did you piss off, anyway?"

"Come on, Hal, you know better than that."

"Well, I'm taking a couple of days off so you can clean this place up before I come back. Just you make sure that the stuff in those filing cabinets is all back in the correct folders and that those folders are back in alpha order!" Hal turned and marched out of the office, slamming the doors as she left.

"Nice fucking way to be, Hal!" I shouted at the office door.

I stepped carefully through the mess on Hal's office floor and made my way to my office. It was in the same condition as Hal's. What a goddamn mess!

I called the cops and reported a break-in and probable theft, although I couldn't be sure what had been taken. That would take three or four days to determine, and I needed Hal's assistance to be sure. It was nice that she was planning to be such great help!

Sergeant O'Hare filled out the police report. "Who did you piss off?" he asked.

I wondered if he was related to Hal. "Nobody that I know of," I replied.

"Well, they was either just messing this place up to screw with you, or they was looking for something. Got any ideas?"

"Nothing comes to mind," I told him, but I immediately thought of Bill Powers's notebook.

"Well," the sergeant said, "I'll turn in the report when you tell me what's missing, okay?"

I told him he'd have a list from me in a couple of days. After he left, I locked the office door and went down to the garage to check my car. Powers's notebook was still on the passenger seat. I opened the trunk and put the notebook into a special pocket that I'd had welded onto the underside of the trunk's lid. It was a great place to hide stuff, because most people tend to look down when they open a trunk. They never think to look up. It was also a great place to stow some of the firearms that I hadn't found time to license.

I drove home to check out my apartment. As I was parking my car on the street, I saw two very tall men in gray jumpsuits and baseball caps leave the front of the building. They climbed into a shiny black Hummer and drove away. What I would find when I opened the door to apartment 615 was a no-brainer. My place had been trashed. I called Sergeant O'Hare and reported the second break-in. "You'd better figure out who you pissed off," he told me. "If they find you alone, you might need some dental work!"

I thanked him for the advice and called Nick down at Homicide. "Do you have any news for me?" I asked.

"Yeah, I tried your office, but nobody answered."

"I am having some redecorating done. Use my cell phone from now on." I gave him my number.

"Apparently, we didn't make the call on the suicide," he told me. "It came from the FBI."

"Did they do the investigation? I thought this was your jurisdiction."

"We did, but I guess the FBI came in during the middle of it. They said that they had been looking for this guy Powers on some national security issue."

"And so they determined that it was a suicide?"

"Yeah, that's what Griswold said. He told me in confidence that it looked like a murder to him. The surgical tubing was twisted from behind the neck. Nobody could do that to himself. But it wasn't a robbery. All of Powers's personal effects were in the room, including his money and credit cards."

"So, the FBI is covering something up?"

"Well, maybe. Remember that this is a national security thing. Maybe they have to keep his murder under wraps for some reason."

"In the meantime, I'll bet his insurance policy doesn't pay off for a suicide, and his widow will be left high and dry."

"Well, that's her problem. My problem is that my hands are tied. I can't move to reopen this investigation because it has already been turned over to the feds, and they've determined that it was a suicide."

"Yeah, I understand what you're up against," I told him.

"You know anybody with the FBI? Maybe they can give you some inside information."

"Yeah, I do. Thanks, Nick."

Now I was intrigued. Somebody must have tipped off the feds that Powers was dead. And what would they want with him, anyway? But it was clear as the nose on my face that Powers had made somebody uncomfortable, and that it was probably murder. His notebook held the key.

I took a deep breath and then dialed my ex-girlfriend, Mona. She was an agent with the FBI. The last time I spoke with her, she was really pissed at me. But it was worth a shot.

"Mona, it's Danny."

"Hey, you slime ball. How've you been?"

"I'm all right. How long has it been?" I asked. I should have known.

"It's been two years, Danny, and you've never even sent a card."

"I'm sorry, Mona. Time has a way of slipping by, especially when you've got unfinished business with somebody."

"Hey, you dropped me like a hot brick the moment I told you how I felt about you."

"Yeah, I know it was my fault. I have—"

"Yeah, I know—a problem with commitment."

"Yeah."

"So why did you call? You got a longing to see me again?"

"Well, maybe…but I need your help with a case."

"Sure, you expect me to drop what I'm doing and come to your beck and call. Don't you know anybody else at the Bureau—somebody who isn't still pissed at you?"

"Yeah, I do, but nobody I can trust the way I trust you."

"If you mean that I should have cut off your nuts and I haven't, I guess I couldn't find a dull knife at the time. But I'm still looking—"

"Mona, I've got a client whose husband was murdered. I got an inside tip from the local PD that it looked like murder to them, but they say that you guys showed up, took over the case, and determined that it was a suicide. It was maybe some sort of national security thing. Can you get me any info on it? I'll keep it confidential."

"Hey, we don't interfere in local investigations until we're called in by the locals."

"Well, according to my source, the locals had just begun

the investigation when your guys showed up."

"I don't think that's likely, but I'll check it out."

"Thanks, Mona."

"But it's going to cost you a dinner," she replied. "Maybe after we're finished discussing what I find out, you can try to help me figure out why I'm even willing to help you at all."

"Okay, I'll spring for dinner. I guess I owe you an explanation, anyway. I'm a little older and wiser, now."

"I'll agree that you're older—"

"Yeah, you're probably right." I gave her Powers's name and the location of the crime. Then I said, "Call me on my cell phone when you know something, and I'll make the reservation. Little Italy?"

"Yeah... maybe Pizza Hut." Mona hung up before I could tell her how nice it was to hear her voice again.

My cell phone rang about an hour later. It was Hal, and she sounded concerned. "Listen, Danny, I don't think you should go home tonight."

"Why?" I asked.

"Well, two of the tallest men I have ever seen just left my apartment. They were looking for you."

"I asked them what kind of slut they thought I was that you would be here in my apartment when we aren't married. I told them to go find you at your office because you were busy cleaning the place after somebody made a mess of it."

"How did they react?"

"They asked me if you had given me anything special to keep—anything like a notebook. They were pretty insistent. So I told them that you check the mail and that I hadn't seen anything like a notebook in the office."

"What did they look like, Hal?"

"They were tall like professional basketball players. Maybe taller. They wore sunglasses, and they had blond hair. And they were dressed like undertakers."

"Any accents?"

"Maybe a little like Cousin Clyde's, but otherwise nothing out of the ordinary."

"I didn't know you had a cousin Clyde," I replied.

"Well, I don't. Cousin Clyde was a character in a movie I saw once. It was a western starring Red Ryder. The men who were looking for you had a sort of Western accent, maybe like an old time cowboy."

"Did they say anything else?"

"Yeah, they told me not to tell anyone that they had been here, especially you, or I would live to regret it."

"They sound like they were nice guys."

"Yeah, like some of the guys I dated back in high school. Listen, Danny, if you're still at the office, you'd better get out. I'll clean it tomorrow. And maybe you ought to check into a motel for a few days."

"I think I'll do that, Hal. Thanks for the warning."

I stuffed a few things into a ripstop duffel bag and went back to my car. As I pulled away from the curb, I saw a black Hummer pull out about two hundred yards behind me. I hit the accelerator, ran a few red lights, made a few unanticipated turns, and lost them in the heavy traffic heading into Washington, DC. But now I knew how Billy Powers must have felt every minute of the past two years. I probably needed to ditch my car someplace, just in case they'd put a bug or a homing device on it. So, I removed Powers's notebook from inside the trunk lid and left my old Accord in public parking at the docks near the Watergate, with the keys in the ignition. Either someone would steal it, or it would get towed, and I could get it out of the impound lot sometime in the future.

I hailed a cab and told the driver to take me to Bethesda. I had him drop me at a corner near the town line, and then I took a Connecticut Avenue bus southbound, toward DC. I got out at the northern border of Georgetown and walked to the Georgetown Inn. On the way, my phone rang. It was Mona.

"What did you find out?" I asked.

"Well, I'm probably going to kick your ass when I see you, Danny. It seems Powers was some sort of national security risk, and now I'm on the radar for even asking about him. The FBI and the CIA have been looking for him for the last eighteen months."

"Well, I guess they finally got their man. The Canadian Mounties would have gotten him sooner, and he still would have been breathing when they found him."

"Listen," Mona continued, "when my boss found out that I was interested in this case, he called me into his office and gave me the third degree. He wanted to know my interest in Powers and if I was working for the Alexandria PD or anybody else. He told me that persons high above him were interested in Powers and that anyone—he stressed anyone—who expressed even the slightest interest in Powers was to be suspected of high treason."

"What did you tell him?" I asked.

"I told him that I got a tip from an anonymous source, telling me that Powers was murdered and that the FBI had made a mistake in classifying it as a suicide. My interest was piqued by the call, but, hey, if it's a closed case, it's a closed case."

"Then he doesn't suspect anything, and he doesn't have my name?"

"Actually, he asked me to help him find you. He remembered that we used to be a number. Remember, he met you that time at the City Tavern after we buried Sal DeVito."

Sal was an FBI agent who was killed during a routine drug bust in Annandale, Virginia.

"What does he want with me?"

"He said that you're wanted for illegal weapons possession and interstate transportation of stolen property. I told him that you ditched me two years ago and that I hadn't seen you since. I asked him if I could cut off your nuts if he found you. He laughed at that."

"Are you back with the dull knife thing again?" I asked.

"Listen, Mack's a good guy. He thought I should make myself scarce for a few days, until people forget that I had asked about Powers. I'm going to my sister's wedding in Boca Raton in five days, so this extra time off is good for me."

"So, little Wendy is getting married! I remember that she was the ugly one of you three girls. Is she pregnant?"

Mona didn't acknowledge my last question. Instead, she said, "Well, Wendy's the youngest one, too, and my father didn't really want her to get married at all until Melissa and I got married first. You screwed that one up for me and almost screwed it up for Wendy, too."

"Sorry," I said. And, I really meant it.

"Well, you still owe me dinner. Where are we going?"

"Take a cab to the front entrance of the zoo. Be there at seven sharp. I'll pick you up."

"Where are we going, Danny?"

"I don't know yet, and I don't think you should know, just in case you're being tailed."

"Do you really think that's going to happen? You aren't into anything criminal, are you? Are you really transporting stolen property?"

"Mack was too generous with your time for a public official, Mona. I think he's setting you up to help them find me. I guess I'm on the lamb until I figure this Powers thing out. See you at the zoo at seven." I hung up my cell phone, turned it off, and took the battery out so I couldn't be triangulated.

I walked another two blocks and checked in at the Georgetown Inn. The room was more expensive than I had anticipated, but at the moment I didn't have a choice. I also had to get a vehicle, and I had to figure out where I was taking Mona for dinner. Life sometimes got complicated.

I hated riding buses, but cabbies had to keep a log of their fares, and I didn't want to leave any sort of trail that would lead to me. So I took a bus to Reagan International Airport, where I bought a ticket on an evening flight to

Mexico City, using my Visa card. That would probably set off some alarms at the Bureau, and while they were looking for me in Alexandria, I would be in Baltimore with Mona. Before I left Reagan, I used a fake driver's license and a matching American Express card to rent a Camry for two weeks. As cars go, I figured it was non-descript enough not to draw attention.

At seven, I called Mona and asked her to hail a cab from the zoo and tell the driver to go north on Massachusetts Avenue. From a distance, I watched her get into the cab and waited to see if anybody appeared to be following her. Nothing seemed out of the ordinary, so I tailed her cab for five blocks, called her again, and told her to get out at the next intersection. When she did, I honked my horn, and she saw me.

"Jesus Christ, Danny!" she complained as she climbed into my Camry. "This is my fourth cab ride this evening!"

"So, you suspected a tail, too?" I asked.

"No, I just wanted to be sure. You gave me the heebie-jeebies with this idea that they're using me to find you."

I pulled away from the curb and made several quick turns to see if we were being followed. Then, I found the beltway and headed north on I-95 toward Baltimore. "You look really beautiful tonight, Mona," I told her once we settled into a steady speed. "It's great to see you."

"Sure it is," she replied. "That's why you've called me so often in the past two years."

"There hasn't been anybody since you," I told her. I was lying, but not really. I'd had a short fling with a redhead, but as a group, they tend to be crazy, and that one certainly was. After we dated six times, she had "Danny" tattooed on her neck in blue ink adorned with green four-leaf clovers. I saw her at a bar a couple of months after we broke up, and she had added "Oh" in front of it and "Boy" after it. I guess you have to be Irish to understand why a pretty girl would do that sort of thing. Or maybe you just have to be a redhead.

"So tell me what you know about Powers," Mona said.

I told Mona about the Dulce Firefight and how Powers claimed that many of the survivors were committing suicide if they even thought about coming forward to tell the story. I also told her about Powers's notebook, and how it contained an accounting of many events that Powers felt were related to the Dulce incident.

"So when do I get to see it?" she asked.

"I'm not sure I want you to get involved in this, Mona. I'm already being hassled by tall, intimidating blond men in black suits."

"Maybe they'd know how to show a girl a good time," she replied.

"What I mean, Mona, is that getting interested in this case could mean your job or even your life."

"They already have me connected to you. How do you think that's going to play when they discuss promotions? I'm already done, Danny. I'm as high as I'm going to go."

"Maybe later, Mona."

About forty-five minutes north of Washington, I turned off the highway and found the Valley Inn, just west of Baltimore.

Nobody would look for us there, and we could have a quiet conversation about the past. I wasn't looking forward to being humble, but I anticipated some really fine crab cakes to soothe the pain.

We ordered drinks, and then Mona got right down to business. "You're a creep, you know. All I did was tell you that I loved you and you never called me again. Do you remember what you told me?"

"I think—"

She cut me off. "You said that I shouldn't go there. That it was against the rules to say 'I love you.' What kind of man says that to a woman he cares about? You didn't give a rat's ass about me, Danny, and you didn't have the guts to just tell me straight out."

"That's where you're wrong, Mona. I cared a lot about

you. It was just too soon to be talking about love and marriage."

"Who said anything about marriage? All I said was that I loved you."

"Yeah, but I wasn't ready to settle down, and the moment you said what you said, I saw a wedding coming at me like a freight train."

"You know, we could have talked about that. This isn't the fifties, Danny. Lots of people love each other, but nowadays they don't necessarily get married because of it."

"I'm really sorry, Mona. You know I'm not well skilled in the gentilities of life. I never had a woman's hand in my upbringing. I didn't know how to handle the situation."

"What situation? Is it a situation when somebody actually cares about you?"

"I didn't mean it that way, Mona. Telling me that you loved me sent fear through my body. Maybe it's because my mom left when I was four. I'm not sure I have a lot of confidence in marriage. Not even in long-term relationships."

"You didn't even give us a chance, Danny."

"I know, Mona. I'm truly sorry. I did care about you back then. Seeing you now, and hearing your voice on the phone this morning—I know now that I still care about you."

"Oh, please! You just need me for information about this case. And, when you're done with it, you'll cast me aside like last week's meatloaf."

"You're making me feel really low, Mona."

"Good. I mean to."

Thank God that the waitress interrupted our conversation. We put in our orders and asked for a second round of drinks. Mona could pound down double Scotches like a Marine. I stuck with beer. Well, it was a nice place, so I drank brown ale.

After dinner, a combo started playing mood music. I asked Mona to dance. She refused the first time I asked, but when they played Moon River, she acquiesced. God, the perfume on her neck smelled wonderful, and it felt great when she pressed into my body. She was a perfect fit, and she could follow me on the dance floor, which was something most women complained about. When the song ended, I saw that she had tears in her eyes. That did me in. "Mona," I asked, "would you consider giving me a second chance?"

"I'm seeing somebody," she told me.

I felt my heart fall into my stomach. "Oh," I said. "I guess a woman as pretty as you are should be seeing somebody."

"It's not like that," she replied. "I've been seeing a shrink since you left me. He would probably disapprove of my seeing you again."

"Maybe not," I replied, "at least if we're finishing some unfinished business."

"Let me think about it, Danny."

"So, you're not telling me 'No'?"

She pulled down on my neck and kissed me. It wasn't a passionate kiss, but it held promise. "No," she said, "I'm not telling you 'No.' I just want to consider the ramifications."

"Thanks, Mona."

The band started playing "The Twist," so we went back to our table, called for our check, and headed back to DC. When we got to the Georgetown Inn, Mona asked, "You aren't trying to play with my heart, are you, Danny? You aren't planning to fuck me tonight and then dump me again, are you?"

"No, baby, this is business. I want you to see Powers's notebook."

"Oh," she said, getting out of the car, "this ought to be interesting."

When we got back to the room, I ordered two more rounds of drinks from room service and cleared a pile of my stuff off of the small round table near the window. Then I used my pocketknife to remove the cover from the heating duct and pulled out the notebook. "You really are expecting visitors, aren't you?" Mona said.

"You never know."

I handed Mona the notebook and then sat down beside her so we could look at it together. She turned the pages quickly to see how Powers had organized the material, and then she turned back to the beginning and we began reading it from page one. Room service brought our drinks, and I set them on the table. Neither of us took a sip. Powers's notebook was simply too interesting.

The first section dealt with the Dulce Firefight, listing the names of most of the people who had survived. Beside the names of those who had died, Powers had listed the causes. Three were suicides, two were auto crashes, one was a plane crash, and three were heart attacks. Powers noted that the heart attacks were "alleged myocardial infarctions." Three survivors were not deceased. Well, when you counted Powers, it was only two.

The second section dealt with the alleged capture of aliens by the USA in 1948, but also by Germany in 1939, Russia in 1948, and China in 1961. Stuffed into a gallon-sized food storage bag, marked "Section 2" in indelible ink, were pictures purportedly of captured aliens. Some appeared dead, but others seemed to be alive. Two pictures had them standing with humans, who towered over them. One picture had them standing with humans, who were only half the height of the aliens

The third section dealt with reverse engineering of captured UFO technology. Much of this was photocopied testimony from a variety of sources, again stuffed into a marked food storage bag. In addition to US efforts, there were clear inferences to German, Russian, and Chinese initiatives. Names and addresses of engineers and scientists involved in the projects were printed legibly in the notebook.

The fourth section dealt with UFO literature, citing

events reported by various authors, quotes, the titles of their works, dates, and ISBN numbers. The bag of photos included examples of types of UFOs, from cigar-shaped objects, triangles, shape-shifting craft, various probes, and traditional bell-shaped flying saucers, all clipped or photocopied from the books and magazines. Powers had starred several events about the Ummites and the reptilians in several articles.

The fifth section dealt with bizarre weather, atmospheric anomalies, the Skunk Ape, strange dead animals—perhaps hybrids—that had washed ashore, the Sasquatch, the Chupacabra, and ape-men and dog-men from around the globe.

The sixth section introduced fourteen different species of aliens possibly living among us and most likely experimenting upon us, according to Powers. Among them were little gray aliens, Nordics, reptilians, and some that looked very much like everyday humans.

The seventh section listed the names of known members of the Bilderbergs and suspected financiers of world crises, such as the collapse of governments and the devaluation of currencies. This drew Mona's interest because of the recent collapse of Wall Street and the bailout of the banks.

The eighth section he simply called "Other." There he named twenty-one interesting people, including George Adamski, T. Lobsong Rampa, and Princess Marni Koski, all of whom claimed to have ridden in flying saucers and purportedly brought special messages back to Earthlings from our space brothers. It also contained a list of political events, seemingly disconnected, such as eight times that the President mentioned "New World Order" in his campaign speeches, governmental actions that Powers claimed devalued the US dollar, and recent "takeovers" of private corporations by the federal government, including General Motors, various banks, the student loan program, and the new farm bill.

At three in the morning, Mona got up and stretched.

Then she chugged her room-temperature Scotch. "Watery," she muttered. "I've had enough. I'm sleeping in the bed."

I found an extra blanket in the closet and looked around for a place on the floor, but Mona saved me from a sore back by inviting me to join her under the covers. "Keep your clothes on," she told me. "You should have gotten a room with twin beds."

I stripped down to my skivvies and climbed in between the sheets, only to discover that Mona was sleeping between the blanket and the sheet, just to keep me at bay. But, honestly, I was too tired at this point to try anything, and I wanted her to still like me in the morning so we could talk about what we had just read in Powers's notebook. She was better at analyzing paperwork than Hal was, and I could use her skills to help me find Powers's killer.

Chapter 3

When I rolled out of bed at eight in the morning, Mona was sitting at the table going back through Powers's notebook. I shuffled over to her, bent down, and asked her what she thought. "Jesus H! Please go brush your teeth, Danny!" she complained. I did what she asked. I'd found it was better that way. But, I didn't have a toothbrush, so I used the hotel's small tube of toothpaste and my finger. It would have to do.

I came out of the bathroom about two minutes later. "So what do you think?" I asked her with empty tanks and a minty-fresh mouth.

"At first, I thought he was a typical whack job, but the more I look at this stuff, the more it seems to fit some sort of pattern. I just can't piece it all together."

"That's what Hal thought. What did you write on that hotel letterhead?"

"These are the people we're going to go see," she replied.

I looked at her list. It included the two remaining survivors of the Dulce Firefight and a couple of engineers. "Well, if Powers is right, we need to get to these folks before they have heart attacks or commit suicide," I told her, pointing to the Firefight survivors.

"Yeah, you're thinking along the same line as I am," she replied. "I say we get started right after breakfast and a shower. Order me scrambled eggs, sausage, wheat toast, and coffee. Lots of coffee." She went into the bathroom and locked the door. I heard the shower come on.

When breakfast arrived, Mona was out of the shower and drying her shoulder-length brunette locks with the hotel's wall-mounted hair dryer. "I'm at a disadvantage this morning," she told me. "I don't have a toothbrush or my styling brush. I also don't have any fresh clothes."

"I think you ought to go home and get what you need to last for a couple of days. We should be back in time for you to catch the flight for your sister's wedding."

We ate, I showered, and then we checked out of the Georgetown Inn. Then, I drove Mona home. At her suggestion, I dropped her off two blocks from her apartment, and she walked the rest of the way as part of the usual early morning pedestrian traffic. I put the battery back in and turned my phone on in case she needed me. We agreed to meet around the corner from the main entrance to her apartment building in thirty minutes. As she walked away from my car, I couldn't keep my eyes off of her back end. She had an easy, appealing gait, if you know what I mean.

I turned right and drove past her. Two blocks later, I turned right again and actually found a parking space alongside the curb. As I was parallel parking, I saw a dark Hummer coming from the opposite direction. I froze for a moment and then realized that it was actually navy blue and being piloted by a woman in a white jacket with red piping. False alarm. I finished parking.

Mona arrived sooner than expected. "You'll like this, Danny," she told me when she climbed into the Camry. "The desk clerk told me that a couple of men were asking for me last night. They got testy, but he rang for the security guard, and they backed down and left." At Mona's place, you needed a special card to access the elevator, and the clerk wouldn't give one to anyone who wasn't a resident. It was a good thing.

"I guess you *are* on the radar screen," I told her.

"Yeah, let's get out of here. It's a long way to Lima, Ohio."

"Is that where the first survivor lives?"

"Yeah. His name is Melvin Wouck."

"He sounds like some kind of geek," I said.

"It says here in Powers's notebook that Wouck was a Green Beret at Dulce in 1979. He earned a bronze star for valor, and a purple heart for wounds received—get this—during an incident involving friendly fire."

"Did you happen to bring a laptop, Mona? Maybe we can Google him tonight and learn a little more about him."

"It's in my suitcase in the back seat. I'm a step ahead of you."

"You always have been," I replied.

The drive to Lima took us across southwest Pennsylvania and through Columbus before we veered northwest for the last leg of the trip. We switched drivers every two hours, which meant that Mona was driving when we arrived. That also meant that she got to pick the motel, in this case, a Hampton Inn. I would have picked an economy place, but at least the Hampton would give us a free breakfast in the morning. After we checked into our room, Mona called Melvin Wouck to ask if he would receive a couple of visitors tomorrow. "We're friends of Billy Powers, and we're just trying to help his widow answer a few unsettled questions," she told him.

"How did Billy die? Heart attack?" Melvin asked.

"The local authorities say it was suicide," Mona replied.

"That poor fuck!" Melvin told her. Then he apologized for his language.

"That's okay, Mr. Wouck. I think I said the same thing when I learned that it was probably murder."

They set a nine o'clock meeting time at Melvin's home. Mona told him that she would be bringing me and that I would spring for doughnuts and coffee. Melvin asked for decaf.

We cleaned up and then drove to a Chinese place for

dinner. The interior was red and gold, which was no surprise, but their prices were lower than what we pay in DC. Mona ordered a double Scotch and a combination plate with chicken and black bean sauce. I ordered a Manhattan and two appetizers. Mona rolled her eyes at me as I gave my order to the waitress but, hey, I like Chinese spare ribs and fried dumplings.

"What are you expecting to find tomorrow, Danny?" Mona asked me.

"Probably nothing. Even if Wouck experienced everything that Powers said happened, he's probably been well trained and won't tell us anything other than that Powers was out there on the fringe of reality and all by himself. Military types seldom tell the truth if they've been told not to talk. They protect the unit and the mission at all costs."

"Well, you didn't hear his voice, but I think he knows that his days are numbered, and he's wondering how he's going to die and when. Living like that has to be an awful existence."

"I hope you're right, Mona. Maybe facing that kind of future will help loosen his tongue. Maybe we can even get a signed deposition."

"Would you let me do the primary interviewing, Danny?" she asked. "I mean, I spoke to him today, and I think that means we've established some sort of preliminary rapport."

"Yeah, baby, I'm fine with that. But if I see some questions that need to be asked, I'm going to jump in."

"That's okay. Just don't threaten him and make him clam up."

"I'll try not to. Mrs. Powers is counting on me to identify Powers's killer. I'll need every scrap of information that I can get if I ever hope to find the bastard."

We ate and reminisced about our childhoods. I remembered some of Mona's youthful past from previous talks we'd had two years ago, but I think she told me more than ever before. It must have been the Scotch. After dinner, we

took in the new Harry Potter movie. The posters inside the
theater called it the first half of the final movie. It was one
long ass movie, and I wasn't sure I'd see the second half
next year. But maybe I would, especially if Mona asked me
to see it with her.

Our room was a double, meaning it had two double beds,
and when we got back to the hotel, Mona bounced on them
both before selecting which one she would sleep in. "That
one is yours," she said pointing to the one farthest from the
bathroom. I got the message. We shut the lights off at elev-
en-thirty. At midnight, I thought I felt the covers on my bed
open and even thought that I felt Mona's feet rub against
mine. "I still love you, Danny," I thought I heard her say. In
my sleep, I realized that it was a dream, but I let it play out.
I started to say something, but she covered my mouth with
her hand and said, "Shhh." Then she kissed me.

Her breasts brushed against my chest. "You're naked," I
told her. I was always good about stating the obvious.

"Yeah," she replied. "I'm the lucky one. Come on, let
me help you out of your skivvies."

She undressed me and then explored my body with her
hands. When I tried to return the touch, she pushed my
hands away and told me not to be in a rush. With Mona,
sometimes it had to be her way or the highway. It wasn't a
hill to die on. I waited my turn, and when I was given the
green light, I spent my time making sure she was ready before we joined bodies.

As I began to feel her warmth, I woke up from my
dream, rolled over and, in the light from the room's clock
radio, saw the outline of Mona's body in the other bed. I got
up and relieved myself to get rid of my erection. But I knew
then that I still had it bad for Mona, and until our unsettled
relationship came to some sort of conclusion, I was going to
be vulnerable to her whims.

Chapter 4

S
o Billy Powers is dead," Melvin Wouck said matter-of-factly. "That leaves two of us."

Mona was right about Wouck. He knew that it was just a matter of time before he'd be a headline in the local section of the Lima News. "How did he die?" he asked.

"He was strangled with a piece of surgical tubing. It didn't look like there was a scuffle. He appears that he just took it," Mona told him.

"Yeah," Wouck said, "he was probably resolved that it was going to happen and that there was nothing he could do about it anyway. If he fought it, he would have just made the experience more painful."

"You sound as though you've been expecting a similar fate," Mona replied.

"Well, when you look at those of us who survived the action at Dulce, and you see what's happened to us, you don't have to think too long before you start looking over your shoulder."

"What exactly happened at Dulce?" I asked.

"If you want the official version…"

Mona interrupted him. "We're trying to put an end to these murders. We know the official version is a pile of crap. So, what really happened? Was Powers telling the truth?"

Wouck cleared his throat. "You know, my telling you

this could be putting the bullet in the assassin's gun, but I think my number is on it anyway. I was surprised to learn that Powers was making presentations about the firefight at Dulce. When I found out about it, I figured he was a dead man. He actually lived longer than I thought he would."

"Why is that?" I asked.

"They threatened all of us. Told us to forget it ever happened. They said that if we said anything, our bodies would disappear into the desert. They even threatened the same for our families."

"Who is 'they'?" Mona asked.

"You've heard them called the 'Men in Black.'"

"You mean the tall blond guys who wear black suits, sunglasses, and sport a bad attitude?"

"That would be them. Have you ever met one? They can be intimidating, even for a Green Beret." Wouck took a long sip of the decaf coffee we'd brought him. I noted that his biceps were impressive for a man in his mid-fifties. He took a breath and then began spilling the beans. "We knew there was some kind of trouble when the panic alarm sounded and the workers came up from the seventh level. The commander ordered two platoons to go down and engage whoever it was who was shooting at us. We were to assess the situation and secure the area."

"Who was the commander?" Mona asked.

"Ma'am, I'd rather not say. It isn't important, anyway."

"Go on," she replied.

"Powers and two engineers went down with us. One engineer was a subterranean facility specialist, probably a geologist, and one a chemical specialist. It took four trips down the shaft from the first to the seventh level to get both platoons down."

"How many men are we talking about?" I asked.

"Close to eighty. Eighty-three if you include the civilians."

"Go on," Mona said.

"Well, we got down there and our platoon leader, Capt.

Markel, broke us down into squads so we could spread out and secure the area quickly. Powers showed us the spot where the workers had accidentally drilled into the other facility. It was welded shut."

"Welded?" I asked.

"I don't have a better word. Have you ever seen obsidian? It's like black glass. That's what it was like. Kind of like somebody melted the rock and fused it completely shut."

"You gave us your platoon leader's name," Mona noted. "Any reason for that?"

"Yeah, she's the only other survivor. You're probably going to want to talk to her, too."

"I have the name as Jerri Fontaine," Mona told him.

"It's Geraldine, and she got married a few years after the incident. Before that, she was Jerri Markel."

"So what happened?" I asked.

"Well, Powers moved the mole to the left and started drilling a new hole on Capt. Markel's orders. She had us stand on both sides of the mole so that when it broke through, we could enter the other facility in combat status. When the mole broke through, it had to be withdrawn before we could enter. As it withdrew, we were assaulted by troops from the other side, firing bolts of liquid light. It cut through a man in Kevlar like he was butter. We threw hand grenades, which surprised them and took a lot of them down. Then two of the guys had flame throwers, which we used to clear them out of the tunnel so we could counterattack."

"It sounds gruesome," Mona said.

"The noise was incredible," Wouck told her. "Our weapons made loud blasts, and theirs made high-pitched whining sounds, like bottle rockets. The smell was awful, too."

"You mean the napalm?" I asked.

"No, I like the smell of napalm. It was the smell of their burning bodies. They smelled like burning snakes. It wasn't human flesh. I smelled that in Nam. This was different—just like burning snakes."

"So did you go through to the other side?" I asked.

"Yeah. That's when the fighting got really bad. They were clustered to the right side of the hole in the wall. We were able to take cover behind some of their machines and engage them more like guerilla fighters. We managed to drive them back to the cages before they were reinforced by the tall ones and pushed us back through the hole."

"How many of you got back safely?"

"About fifteen of us initially, and about four wounded. The wounded all died by nightfall. And five of us contracted lung cancer and died within a year, which left an even dozen, if you include the civilians."

"You mentioned cages?" Mona asked.

"That was horrible," Wouck replied. "There were humans down there. Well, they looked like humans, but some had animal parts, like claws or hooves instead of hands or feet. They begged us to help them, but we couldn't cut the metal or force open the locks. It was some kind of metal we had never seen before. When we were driven backward, we had to leave them. Some begged us to shoot them, but we didn't."

"Are you serious? You didn't dream any of this?"

"No, we reported this to the commander, but he told us to remain silent about it and that he would send word about it up the chain of command."

"Did he ever do it?" Mona asked.

"I wouldn't know, ma'am. I was only a sergeant. I just carried out orders."

"So, then what happened?" Mona asked.

"Well, when we got back through the hole, we kept firing until Powers could auger the walls down and close it off again. He got hit in the arm by one of their weapons, but he kept working until he was finished. Jerri helped him out of the facility and onto the elevator."

"Did you bring any of the dead aliens up in the elevator with you when you retreated?"

"No, we figured we needed to get the fuck out of there. We could get our troops and some of those aliens out of there later. But it never happened."

"What did they do?"

"The commander sent a nuke squad down the shaft, and they set off a suitcase nuke that sealed off the seventh floor permanently."

"When did the 'Men in Black' come to see you?" I asked.

"About two days later. I was at home. They were two of the biggest men I have ever seen. I opened the door, and they pushed their way in. They told me what I was to say, and they threatened me, like I already told you."

"Did you ever talk to anybody about the incident?"

"Just with some of the other survivors. We used to get together every few years at somebody's home to celebrate our survival, so to speak. The military gave us all medals and pay raises for our efforts on behalf of the United States. We all knew that something bigger was going on, but we didn't know what. Mostly, it was those people and half-humans that bothered us the most. We never went back down to get them."

"What did the aliens look like?" Mona asked.

"There were two sizes. Most of them were dressed in combat uniforms of some type with full face helmets. The short ones were our size, like maybe five and a half to six feet tall. The reinforcements were huge, like seven or eight feet tall. Maybe they were in deep-soled boots, or they were made up to look bigger in some way to intimidate the enemy, but they appeared huge to us."

"What about their faces? Were they human?"

"Like I said, they wore full face helmets, so I never saw their faces. Cpl. Wiegert told me that he saw the arm of a dead one—one of the smaller ones—and it looked like lizard skin."

"When did he tell you this?" I asked.

"He was one of the ones who contracted cancer. He told me about that when I went to see him before he died. He said that he hoped he was going to heaven because he had already been to hell and had seen what the Devil's minions look like."

"It must have been one hell of an action. I heard you were wounded," I told him.

He said, "Pardon me ma'am for dropping trous in front of you, but the scar is on my upper thigh." He unbuckled his belt, dropped his pants to the floor, and pulled down the waistband of his boxers until we could see the missing flesh on his hip. "They grazed me," he told us. "It might have been a ricochet. The flesh just melted away, but there was no blood because the wound self-cauterized. Whatever hit me was white hot. Maybe as hot as the sun."

Before we left, we asked Wouck if he had any idea who might have been killing off the survivors and why. He said that he thought it was probably the Men in Black, or else some kind of contract killers paid by whomever it was that didn't want the information about the Dulce Firefight to go public. He asked, "If you were our military and you knew those bastards were down there and you didn't have the technology to take them out, would you want John Q. Public to know about it?" He had a point.

Mona and I left Wouck's home at eleven in the morning. He dead-bolted the door after he closed it behind us. I guess I couldn't blame him, although he was an easy target just being at home. Mona told me that she hoped we wouldn't read about him in the paper anytime soon. He was a nice guy. Too bad he was carrying such a large burden.

On our way out of town, Mona asked me if we could stop for a bite to eat. I pulled into a joint called Kewpee Hamburgers. Mona ordered a burger with fries, and I ordered a cheeseburger with onion rings. Then, Mona changed her order to rings, too. "Self-protection," she told me.

I had never had a square burger until then, not even at Wendy's. There's something un-American about a square burger. But it was good. We got coffees to go, and I took one last look at the giant Kewpee doll that stood over the counter watching the diners. It was bizarre.

In the car, we set our GPS for Bluefield, Virginia, where Jerri Fontaine made her home after leaving the military. It was a six-hour drive, so we figured to be there in time to call her after dinner and make an appointment for tomorrow.

On the road, Mona and I talked about Powers and Wouck and the commonalities in their stories about the Dulce incident. It was either a mass hallucination or the real thing. I voted for the real thing. Mona asked me if maybe the memory could have been planted in each man's mind separately. "Maybe by some sub-culture of the CIA. They've been known to do that sort of thing," she told me. I shrugged it off as being too difficult to pull off, and then, what would be their purpose in doing it? Would it be part of some disinformation scheme? I didn't think so.

Well, as the day wore on, I kept checking the GPS to see how much farther it was to Bluefield. It was after dark when we finally reached the green *WELCOME TO BLUEFIELD* sign. We were a couple of hours behind schedule because of road construction on the West Virginia Turnpike, if you could really call it that and not laugh. And it was just too damn late to call Mrs. Fontaine. So, we found a Holiday Inn high up on the side of a mountain and called it an evening. The bar was closed due to lack of interest on the part of the natives, and there sure as hell weren't any tourists in Bluefield.

Mona and I drove into town to find a liquor store, but they all were closed, too. We turned in to a quick market of some local variety and settled for a six-pack of Blue Ribbon and a bag of pretzels. I could see that it was going to be one of those boring evenings in a hotel with three channels on the tube. I was wrong. There were six channels, but one of them was the hotel channel, and one was a televangelist, so we got to choose from TNT, ABC, NBC, and FOX. I had the clicker and opted for FOX, where Greta Van Susteren was interviewing some experts on the collapsing American dollar. One of them kept going on about recent revelations that the USA was spending a trillion of our tax dollars bailing out European countries to keep the European Union from collapsing. It actually piqued my interest because Powers had made some notes about that in his notebook. I made notes of my own and put them in my duffel bag.

I wanted Mona to ask me to shut the tube off and make love to her so I could tell her that she would have to wait until Greta was over. She didn't ask. She fell asleep, instead, and I let her sleep. It had been a long day. I listened to her breathing for a while and saw how beautiful she was when she was not playing FBI agent. Then I blew her a kiss, turned off the light, and hoped that a good night's rest would get the kinks out of my back.

Chapter 5

Mona and I pulled up to the Fontaine's house on Pearl Street Extension, only to see a FOR SALE sign in the front yard. This couldn't be a good omen. Fortunately, a neighbor was puttering in her front yard, so Mona did the girl thing and asked her about Jerri Fontaine. When she got back into the car, she said, "Head back down the hill and take the first right. She's just gone into the local nursing home."

"God, I hope she's still got her synapses," I replied.

"Yeah," agreed Mona.

The nursing home wasn't the most secure place I'd ever been. They must not have had many senior citizens beaten and robbed in Bluefield, because the automatic front door opened when we approached and we walked freely into the hallway. A couple of attendants greeted us as they walked by, but nobody asked why we were there. Finally, we found a nurse's station and asked where we would find Jerri. A heavyset woman with a bad dye job told us, "Mrs. Fontaine is in the residential end, back the other way." We thanked her and hiked back the way we'd come.

At the other end, we found another nurse's station, where Gomer Pyle's sister directed us to room 31, bed A. We knocked on the door and then walked in. Nobody was there.

As we were about to leave, we heard a toilet flush, so we

backed out of the room and stood outside the door until a little old lady in a pink robe made her way from the bathroom to her lounge chair and turned on the television, using a clicker.

Mona knocked on the door again, and called out, "Mrs. Fontaine? Are you accepting visitors?"

"Why, yes!" came the reply. The television clicked off as we entered the room, Mona first and me following behind.

"Do I know you?" Jerri Fontaine asked.

"No, Mrs. Fontaine," Mona replied. "I'm Special Agent Mona Casola with the FBI, and this is Daniel Arrow, a private detective."

"Oh my, then this is official business." Mrs. Fontaine repositioned herself to be more erect. "So what brings you here? I know it isn't about my taxes."

Mona laughed and said, "No, actually we're here investigating a recent homicide. You may remember the gentleman—William Powers. You served with him in a Green Beret unit in Dulce, New Mexico."

The smile left Mrs. Fontaine's face. "Bill Powers was a good man. He visited me less than a year ago. I'm sorry they got to him."

"They?" I asked.

"If you're looking for his killer, you should give up now and go home. Whoever he is, he is buried deep in the clandestine world of governmental security, and he is protected by many levels of secrecy."

"We've learned that you were a platoon leader during the Dulce Firefight," I told her. "You know, you are one of only two remaining survivors of that incident. We're hoping that you're free to tell us about it."

"Look where I am," she replied, gesturing to her room with both hands. "The average life span of a person in a nursing home is two years on the outside. My husband died in 'oh-six, and our only child was killed in Afghanistan last year by an IED. Why shouldn't somebody know? What can they do to me now?"

"You seem way too young to be here, Mrs. Fontaine," I said.

"It's all about finances," she replied. "I'm here on my attorney's advice." She shrugged her shoulders. "Let's get down to business."

Mona reviewed the succession of events of the Dulce Firefight, as we had learned them from Powers and Wouck, and asked Mrs. Fontaine to fill in any missing information.

"Well, you're correct about the dead Americans. They were all buried when we nuked the seventh level. But you are wrong about the aliens. I went back down with the nuke squad, and while three of the team prepped the device, the rest of us moved three aliens to the level three, so that they could be examined by medical and technical specialists. One was still alive, but barely. We tied his arms so he couldn't touch his chest and kill us with one of his weapons."

"Touch his chest?"

"Yes, the breast plate on their combat uniforms contained a series of buttons. When they touched one or more of them in combination, death rays shot out at us from their helmets, near their foreheads. They were pretty accurate."

"What happened to the aliens?"

"I told the commander what we'd done, and he had the bodies removed. A team of four medics went down to perform triage on the one that was still alive. After that, I don't know. The bodies were removed that night and were sent to some military installation in Montana."

"Anything else we should know?"

"You know, I got the distinct impression from the wounded alien that he was trying to communicate with me. It was like I got a series of pictures in my mind whenever our eyes met. He let me know that they're working with us humans in underground facilities. They're giving us technology, and we're giving them life, crazy as that sounds."

"So you saw his eyes. What did he look like?"

"I could only see them through the protective shield on his helmet. They were larger than ours and were like cat's eyes."

"Like a snake's or a lizard's?" I asked.

"Yes, but more like a cat's," she replied.

"Why is that?"

"A cat is more intelligent, and it has an element of nurturing in its personality. Snakes and lizards don't raise their young. They just lay eggs and go away. I got the impression that the aliens nurture their young."

"Thanks so much, Mrs. Fontaine," Mona told her. "We'll keep what you told us confidential. Is there anything we can do for you or get you before we leave Bluefield?"

"Why, yes," she replied. "Would you mind going to Bob Evan's and getting me a bowl of their French onion soup? I used to get it to go. The food they serve here is enough to keep you alive, but it has no flavor. I have a real hankering for French onion soup."

We said goodbye and got directions to Bob Evan's Restaurant from the nurse. It was only a half-mile away, so we shot down there, got the soup, and returned in about ten minutes. While Mrs. Fontaine opened the lid on the Styrofoam container, Mona asked, "Is there anything else you can remember or anyone else you think we should talk to?"

"Yes, go talk to some of the engineers."

"The engineers?"

"In that notebook he kept, Powers included a short list of engineers who were back-engineering alien technology for major corporations under contract with the CIA and the black ops sections of our government."

"Do you mean trying to make a flying saucer?" I asked.

"Oh, for sure, but more than that. They were working on what the death rays are and how to work them, invisibility, microelectronics, and medical things, all compliments of captured alien technology. You don't think we conceived of the laser beam or the microcomputer by ourselves, do you?!"

"I guess that would make sense, wouldn't it?" Mona replied.

I nodded and thought that Mrs. Fontaine would probably be able to tell us a lot more, if we had the time to pick her brain. But I had to get Mona back to DC so she could catch tomorrow's flight to Florida for her sister's wedding. I thanked Mrs. Fontaine and walked into the hallway. When I noticed that Mona wasn't standing beside me, I turned to see Mrs. Fontaine giving Mona a small piece of paper. Mona squeezed her hand and gave Mrs. Fontaine a kiss on the cheek before saying goodbye.

When we got back into the car, Mona opened Powers's notebook and added another name to our list. "Who's that?" I asked.

"Jonathan Alden."

"Like the pilgrim?"

"Yeah, exactly. Only this guy is an electrical engineer who just retired from Parker-Andersen."

"Who is Parker-Andersen?" I asked.

"One of the largest defense contractors in the nation. They're big into electronic guidance systems for aircraft and missiles, and they've got a large presence at Sandia and Dulce. I have a hunch he knows a lot."

"Well, be sure I have his address, and I'll go see him while you're at Wendy's wedding."

"You're not going to see Alden without me," Mona replied. "This is the most compelling story I've ever investigated. I'm going to have to call my sister and beg out of the wedding on the pretense of national security. She'll be disappointed, but she'll understand."

"And your father?"

"If he finds out that I'm with you instead of being with the family at the wedding, he'll disown me. That's a risk I'll have to take."

I set the GPS for Alden's address in New Mexico and settled in for a very long ride. Along the way, in Beckley, WV, Mona had me stop at a Barnes & Noble so she could buy *Mass Contacts,* a book by some Italian professor who claims to have been in contact with subterranean aliens from the planet Ummo over a ten-year period back in the fifties. After an hour of reading, she said it was a difficult book to follow because the original was in Italian and the translator wasn't completely fluent in English, but she stuck at it for the day. However, from time to time she said, "Listen to this..." and then would tell me interesting things, such as the fact that Ummite aliens were nine feet tall on average and that, because they were a gentle race, they eventually were driven from their facilities by a hostile reptilian race from the Pleiades star system. The reptilians had evil plans to take control of the Earth, and the Ummites promised eventually to return with reinforcements to help save the Earth from them. I had to admit that after what Wouck and Mrs. Fontaine told us about the aliens that they had encountered at the seventh level, the concept of hostile reptilians sounded plausible.

It was a twenty-eight hour trip to New Mexico, not including stops, so we divided it into two days, spending the night at a truck stop in Jonesburg, Missouri. Mona had tried to get me to pull over at a couple of mom and pop motels after we passed St. Louis, but I pressed on. When it got to be one in the morning, even Mona was willing to sleep in a truck stop, so I pulled over at a place where they rented rooms by the hour to interstate truckers and highway hookers.

The bed was bowed in the middle, lengthwise like a hammock, so after trying to sleep side by side, Mona finally climbed on top of me, and we slept like a sandwich. She complained that I wasn't treating her like a lady, so I promised her a nice place the next night and a good hot meal instead of the fast food we were living on. It was the least I could do.

The next evening, when we arrived at Lumberton, New Mexico, we found a clean motel on the main drag, but it wasn't the kind of place Mona had been hoping for. It was run by a nice Native American family and was decorated in Navajo colors. They didn't serve breakfast but offered fifty-percent-off coupons for the diner that was on the corner three doors down the street.

Mona and I ate dinner at El Ranchero, a Mexican food place that I wish they'd relocate to DC. I had a combo plate was simply fantastic, especially the chili rellenos. After dinner, we drove a few miles west of town to a local bar called The Apache House of Liquor, where a country music band was playing. Inside, the cowboys, oil men, and government workers were pounding down beers like there was no tomorrow. I thought they might be right about that, especially the workers who might know what's going on two miles below Dulce, just a few miles away.

All the tables were taken, so Mona and I found two stools at the bar and ordered a couple of beers. It seemed to be the drink of choice in the place. Mona really liked country music, so she enjoyed singing along with the band whenever they played something she knew. Her favorite was *Up Against the Wall You Redneck Mother*, by Jerry Jeff somebody.

It was hard to hear her tell me things when the band was playing, and I felt like I was going to be hoarse in the morning, like what happens at a wedding reception when the music is played too loud.

I went to the john, and when I came back, Mona was talking with a guy in work boots who I thought was looking too friendly toward her. "Hi, I'm Dan," I said, sticking out my hand.

He shook it. "I'm Nelson. I hope y'all don't mind my talking with your lady."

Mona said, "Nelson works at Dulce. He's an HVAC drilling technician, and he's helped build a lot of the facility."

"Even the underground stuff?" I asked.

"I've built underground facilities in Dulce, Jefferson Mountain, and Sandia. That's my specialty," Nelson said with a smile.

"Awesome!" I replied. "Can I buy you a drink?"

Nelson asked for a Lone Star, which told me that he needed to wash the dirt out of his throat. I went to the bar and came back with two, as well as refills for Mona and me. As I sat down, I said, "We have a friend who used to operate a mole. He helped build one of the facilities at Dulce."

"Hey, mole drivers are cool. That's the fun job. My specialty is air exchangers. I drill the shafts for fresh air to be pumped down and for bad air to be pumped up. I do most of my work from up top, but sometimes I get to go down to see if the hole I'm drilling is where it needs to be to ensure that the fans don't take up critical facility space down below."

"My friend's mole made a fifteen-foot hole. How big are your air shafts?" I asked.

"They're about four feet in diameter, and then we line them with aluminum. When you figure in the emergency repair ladder, the holes are probably three feet in diameter. It's a little tight for a guy my size, but I've been up and down every shaft I've ever drilled. It's part of the inspection process."

Mona gave me a raised-eyebrow and asked Nelson if he would show her how to two-step. He was eager, so they left me alone for fifteen minutes. I bought him another beer and left it beside the one he was working on. As I watched Mona dancing, I realized that I was going to have to gain an appreciation for country music and line dancing if I carried our relationship along any further. She was good at it for a beginner.

When they came back to the table, I applauded and thanked Nelson for teaching Mona how to shuffle her feet. Mona stuck her tongue out at me, and Nelson laughed.

Then I asked, "Hey, Nelson, you said you've worked on all of the underground facilities..."

He cut me off. "I said I've worked on three. Shoot, Dan, there's at least twenty that I can think of, and probably more. The government is building them like hotcakes. I don't know why they need so many, but they seem to like them. And, of course, I don't mind, because I'm never out of work and I like the money!"

"Have you ever heard of the Dulce Firefight?" Mona asked.

"Yeah, but I don't know that I hold much stock in that story. It sounds like a good piece of science fiction," Nelson replied.

"What if I told you that we've already spoken with two survivors of that incident and they swear that it's true?" Mona asked.

"Well, like I said, I've worked on three similar facilities, and I've never had a problem."

"When you're working, do they have armed guards or troops down there with you?" I asked.

"Yeah, but that's just security."

"Security from what?" Mona asked. "Nobody can get onto the grounds without top secret security clearance. I mean, I'm sure you have it." Nelson nodded thoughtfully. Mona pressed him further, "So who's going to break into the facility, find his way down to whatever level you are on, and start some sort of gunfight?"

Nelson just looked at her. Then he said, "You know, Mona, I never gave it any thought. I just figured the government has all those armed units as a precaution against..."

"Against who?" I asked. Nelson just stared through me.

Mona sighed. "Tomorrow we're going to meet with another guy who maybe can shed some light on the Dulce Firefight and what's going on down in those caves. We'll take you along..."

"Oh, I can't go tomorrow. I have to work. Would y'all

mind meeting me here tomorrow night to tell me what you learned?"

"Maybe," I said. "But how do I know you won't report us and have us detained for some stupid kind of security questioning?"

"Well, who are y'all, anyway? And why are you interested in those underground facilities?" Nelson asked.

Mona showed him her badge. "Mona Casola, FBI. Dan is a private detective. We're working on a murder case, and it involves national security. Whatever is going on in those underground facilities is the reason that more than four people have been murdered. We need to get to the bottom of it."

"I'll do y'all one better," Nelson said. "Not all of the air shafts are inside the security fences of the Dulce facility. If y'all will trust me enough to meet me here tomorrow night and tell me what's going on, I'll take y'all to one of the air shafts that go down into the original site of the Dulce Fire-fight."

"You actually know where the shaft is?" Mona asked excitedly.

"Yes. I already told y'all that's my area of expertise. I inspect all of them on the base, and I have complete access to maps that show the locations of all the air shafts, including the ones that are outside of the fence."

I stuck out my hand and said, "You've got a deal, Nelson. Nine o'clock tomorrow night, right here."

As we got up to leave, Mona gave Nelson a kiss on the cheek and said, "Thank you, Nelson. Dan's client is going to be especially grateful. Her husband was murdered just a few days ago. And, speaking on behalf of the FBI, I can assure you that your country is grateful as well."

Nelson blushed at the kiss and smiled. He walked out with us, climbed into his new four-door Ford F-350, and drove west toward Dulce. We went in the opposite direction to find our hotel. On the way, I told Mona that she was really a quick learner with that two-step. "I already knew how to two-step," she said. "I just wanted to get a little friendlier with him."

"Well, I guess you did that. I think he has a crush on you."

"It doesn't hurt," she replied with a smile. "In fact, that little kiss on his cheek may have bought you a ticket into the air shaft at Dulce."

"If he doesn't show up with the CIA or the black ops tomorrow night," I reminded her.

Chapter 6

We called Jonathan Alden the next morning at nine o'clock. He was out playing golf, but his wife said she'd have him return the call when he got back, around ten. At ten sharp, the phone in the hotel room rang. "This is Alden," the voice said when I answered. "What can I do for you?"

"My name is Dan Arrow. I'm a private detective working on a murder case. I have an FBI escort with me. I'm hoping that we can speak with you about the case."

"I'm not a suspect, am I?" he asked.

"No," I replied, "but you may have some information pertinent to helping us find the murderer. It has some national security implications."

"Ah, that explains the FBI."

"Yes, it does. The Bureau has some interest in this case."

"Well, we can't meet at my house. It would upset the wife. How about we meet at the public library, in the study room...say, in forty-five minutes. I need to catch a shower."

"Thank you, Mr. Alden. We'll be there waiting for you."

Mona and I got some eggs and a quick cup of coffee at the diner, and then we found the library on the outskirts of Lumberton. It was an old cinder block ranch house with a flat roof, maybe a total of 1500 square feet on a good day. But I'd bet the town didn't have a thousand residents, so having a library was actually a luxury for its citizens.

Alden arrived at ten-fifteen, but before then, Mona had already begun worrying that he wouldn't show up. He apologized for being late, but he told us that he'd been sitting outside waiting for a while to see if anybody strange came in, thinking that he was already inside with us. We assured him that we had no accomplices and no intention of harming him or his family in any way. Mona showed him her credentials, and that helped ease his concerns.

"We're here investigating the death of William Powers, you may have heard of him, possibly also as Billy Powers," Mona said.

"No, I can't say that I know him," Alden replied.

"Well," I started, "he worked at Dulce during the construction of one of the early underground facilities. The one where they collapsed the sixth floor onto the seventh to avoid further conflict with some form of alien life."

"Oh, that one," Alden said with a sigh. "So, you believe the stories about it?"

"More than believe," I replied. "We have eye witness accounts, and we've talked with two survivors."

"Well, the military has some conjecture about mass hallucination, caused by poisonous gases on the seventh level."

"That's a bullshit cover up, and we all know it, Mr. Alden," Mona said. "We aren't here to crucify or indict anyone. We're simply trying to find Powers's murderer, and we're hoping that you can give us some details that might shed some light on the subject."

"Well, I won't sit here and fabricate some long story for you," Alden said, "but I'll answer any questions you have to the best of my ability."

I asked, "So, how many underground facilities does the military operate?"

"The military operates only about eight. However, there are another twenty operated by defense contractors for the Department of Homeland Security, approximately a dozen operated by the CIA, approximately fifteen run by black ops, and four overseen by the Office of the President. At least ten more are under construction as we speak, and half of those in existence are being expanded, both horizontally and vertically."

"Why the hell do we need so many?" Mona asked.

"It depends upon who you talk to. The military is preparing for some sort of doomsday scenario. Their facilities are used to store vital munitions and chemical and biological weapons, as well as all sorts of military history and sensitive documents which, of course, are on various forms of electronic media."

"And what about the CIA?"

"Again, there is some concern about doomsday. It's the same with the ones operated by the Office of the President. The President's facilities are escape and safety dwellings for the cabinet and key members of Congress and their families."

"Like the one under the Greenbrier in West Virginia?" Mona asked.

"Yes, and the ones at Cheyenne Mountain, Colorado; Raven Rock, Pennsylvania; Mount Weather, Virginia; and Sedona, Arizona," Alden told her.

"That's five," I told him. "You said there were four."

"The one in Sedona may or may not be managed by the President's Office. You'll note that the others are all a short commute from Washington, DC."

"Well, the Congress would have to get several hours of advanced notice if they were to drive to one of those locations in time to avoid a missile strike."

"Who said they'd drive?" Alden asked. "They'd take the shuttle."

"The space shuttle?" Mona asked.

"No," Alden replied, giving Mona a look that asked, "what planet are you from, lady?" He shook his head. "The underground shuttle. There are high speed underground trains that run between DC and those facilities. They operate on Maglev." Alden saw the puzzled look on our faces, so he said, "...magnetic levitation. With no friction, they can attain very high speeds and move two hundred congressmen from DC to West Virginia in less than twenty minutes."

"You're shitting me!" I said.

"No, it's common knowledge. You need to Google it on your computer. Its location and how it operates were figured out years ago by interested civilians."

"You said we're preparing for some sort of doomsday scenario. Would that be an atomic bomb attack?" Mona asked.

"That was the fear in the fifties when the federal government started building the first of the major underground facilities. Nowadays, it depends on who you talk to. Some still fear nuclear bombardment by foreign or domestic terrorists, some expect a large, natural event, like the earthquake that will send California into the ocean and cause huge tidal waves to sweep across the coastlines of America, and others fear the return of Planet X."

"What the fuck is Planet X?" I asked.

"Some call it Niburu, the tenth planet in our solar system. It supposedly circles the sun once every twelve thousand years, and, as it passes by the Earth, it slows our rotation and causes our poles to shift. That will bring wide scale destruction and death to most humans on Earth. At that point, we will have to rebuild."

"So, we would be building these huge facilities to be places for people to hide until it is over," I conjectured.

"Well, in some cases. But in others, they would simply be mass tombs, especially if they were built beneath places where new oceans would form. Some say that if you put on a welding helmet and look toward the rising sun, you'll see Planet X at about four o'clock, coming straight at us, and the populace is totally unaware."

"Do you buy into that crap?" I asked.

"Maybe some of it, but I haven't looked through a welding mask yet."

"Are there other scenarios?" Mona asked.

"A few. One that might interest you is that the New World Order is building those shelters to protect its own from annihilation when it unleashes a mass epidemic to reduce the world's population."

"New World Order?" Mona asked.

"Yeah, it's the height of conspiracy theories, where we need to eliminate all nations, all religions, and all currencies and move to a single global government. We also need to reduce the human population by eighty percent or more. Such a move would end all wars. Some believe that it would make for a fairer and more just world."

I asked, "And who would lead the new government? Would it be a democracy or some form of socialism or communism."

"Probably one of the latter. However, if they kill off all the poor and sickly and all those who don't want to be controlled by the NWO, there would be no opposition to any form of government that provided food and shelter to the survivors."

"Kind of like the killing fields of Cambodia, isn't it?" I told him. "Or maybe like China after Mao took over."

"I can see which side you stand on, Mr. Arrow," Alden said. "If the NWO comes into existence, I wouldn't be so bold with my comments against it."

"Is that a threat?" I asked.

"No, I like you, Mr. Arrow. I meant it as a word of caution."

"Well, thank you, then."

Mona changed the subject. "What about our client, Mr. Powers? Why would anyone want to kill a mole operator?"

"First, moles are old technology. They aren't used any more. Nowadays we use laser drills that melt their way through the rock as they drill. The melted rock flows back into the ground around it and, as it cools, it creates an impermeable enclosure around the tunnel or wall. These devices can cut four miles of new tunnel per day.

"As for the second part of your question, my guess is

that your Mr. Powers has disclosed military or black ops secrets to someone. The penalty for that has always been life in solitary or death. The latter is cheaper and more permanent, especially from the point of view of the CIA."

"Yeah, I'd say Billy Powers was spreading secrets," Mona replied. "So you think his death was at the hand of the CIA?"

"Yup, or the black ops. Either way, you'll never get the individual who did it, unless you get them to give that person up in order to cover-up the person who ordered the hit."

"You seem to know a lot about clandestine operations for an engineer," I told him.

"I'm a West Point grad, and after my obligatory four years in the military, I was with a black ops team for ten years before moving into contract work for the Department of Defense. If I don't know it from doing it, I know it from conversations with others. You know how that stuff spreads."

"Exactly who do you work for?" I asked.

"I get my paycheck from Parker-Andersen."

"Who gives you your orders?" Mona asked astutely.

"Miss Casola, I get my orders from my supervisor with Parker-Andersen."

"And what is it that you do?" she continued.

"I conduct the planning teams that develop the scope of work for each of the underground projects. Then, I do site visits during the construction phase, and I do final inspections before turning the finished project over to the customer."

"And how many of these projects have you been involved with?" Mona asked.

"Since 1996, all of them."

"Shit!" I said. "Then you're the mother lode of information."

"Oh, I'm far from it. I can only make conjectures about what is being done in those facilities, based on the needs of the infrastructure. You know, if they're storing nukes, then the walls and caps are thicker, and the doors are super strong. If they're housing troops or other beings, they need cooking, sleeping, and recreation facilities, as well as restrooms and quality airflow. And if they're doing experimentation, they usually need refrigeration, incineration, and lots of electricity."

"And in which of these facilities are space aliens housed?" I asked.

"I didn't say there were space aliens housed below."

"You said, if I may quote you, 'troops or other beings.' "

"I meant people, troops or other people."

"Mr. Alden," if you were to point us at a facility where other beings might be housed, where would you suggest we look?" Mona asked.

"You can't be serious!" Alden replied. "You know, if you stick your nose into this sort of stuff, you'll probably join Powers in pushing up daisies!"

"Where would somebody look, Mr. Powers?" Mona reiterated.

"You didn't hear it from me, okay? I am totally off the record and will deny ever meeting you two loonies, do you understand?" Mona nodded. Alden looked at me, and I gave him the okay nod. "Rumors have it, and they are only rumors, that what you're looking for might be found in Dulce or Sandia or under the Denver Airport."

"Thank you, Mr. Alden," Mona said.

"But even with help from your FBI higher ups, you guys will find it very difficult to gain access to those bases, and you will probably be killed if you try to sneak into or force your way into any of the subterranean facilities. It just can't be done."

"Is there anything else that we should know?" I asked.

"You already know too much, and I'm a dead man if they ever find out that I met with you."

"Thanks, Mr. Alden," Mona said. "Here's my email address in case you can think of anything else that we ought to know. I would prefer that you not call me. The email address is a new one, it's personal, and I just created it this morning. I think it's untraceable."

"Sure," he replied. He left without shaking our hands. After he drove away, Mona and I looked at each other in disbelief. "He as much as admitted that space aliens are working with our government in some of those underground facilities," I said.

"He also told us that Nelson was lying to us last night," Mona added. "Nelson didn't say anything about the laser melting drills. I'll bet he knows plenty and he has already turned us in to the CIA."

"I hope you're wrong, but there's only one way to find out."

"Yeah, we're going back to the Apache House of Liquor tonight."

Chapter 7

Before we went back to the hotel, Mona and I drove from Lumberton to Dulce, about five minutes away. The main highway was a two-lane, and it was bordered on both sides by desert. It would have been a great place to live if you were a rattlesnake or a sand flea.

After twenty minutes of driving in circles, we found the road to the top of Archuleta Mesa. As we approached the summit, we saw a sign that read *ENTERING JICARILLA APACHE RESERVATION*. Great. Now we had to deal with questions of trespassing on tribal lands. We drove for about a mile and then turned around. I parked the car, and Mona and I walked to the edge of the mesa and looked southward over Dulce and into the desert beyond. We saw nothing that looked like a military base, but the view was magnificent. Mona took my hand, looked me in the eyes, and kissed me. For a moment I forgot all about Billy Powers, but Mona said, "Come on, cowboy, let's go get some vittles and then see if we can rustle up Nelson the bullshitter."

I found the way back to Lumberton. After a quick dip in the pool and another round of Mexican food at El Ranchero, we took a cab back to the Apache House of Liquor. I thought it might be good if our car wasn't parked outside the bar, just in case it might be used to identify us. Instead of going inside, we sat on a bench across the street and drank a couple of beers while we waited for Nelson to arrive. A few minutes before nine o'clock he showed up, right on time. We waited for another half-hour before following him inside, just to be sure that he wasn't bringing a posse. "There y'all are!" Nelson said when we walked up to him, sitting alone in a booth. "What did y'all find out?"

As we sat down, Nelson snapped his fingers at a waitress who came over and asked if we wanted drinks. We ordered two Blues. "Put them on my tab," Nelson told her. Then he turned to us and asked, "How did it go for y'all today?"

"Nelson, we learned some things that made us question your veracity," I told him bluntly.

"Like what?" he asked with a puzzled expression.

"Like you told us that mole drivers are cool, and that mole driving is the best job."

"And?" he asked.

"You guys don't use regular moles any more. You use laser drills that melt the rocks away," I told him.

"Well, yes they do use those laser moles, especially when they're down around two-thousand meters. But the standard moles are still used when we expand caverns horizontally. That's where I come in. I drill the shafts for the air exchange systems. Those laser babies are used for drilling tunnels, mostly, because they're super-fast. They can do maybe five miles per day."

"Four," I told him.

"Okay, four, then," he replied. "But they still use them."

"Well, we learned again that the Dulce Firefight was a real incident, and that Dulce may not be the only place where space aliens are working in underground facilities with our military personnel and some scientists. Have you ever seen a space alien?"

"I've heard of people who've seen them, but I can't just go down to any level without proper clearance first. They usually give me an escort."

"Is he armed?"

"Oh yes, usually with an Uzi or an AR-Fifteen," Nelson replied.

"Then you were straight with us last night?" I asked him.
"One hundred percent," he replied.

"Well, I guess there are a hell of a lot more underground facilities than you know about. I think our source counted something in the neighborhood of seventy, if you include the new ones being constructed. Were you aware of that?"

"No, just the ones I've worked at, plus a few more. But, damn, that's a lot of money being spent on underground places that nobody can enter without the highest level of security clearance. No wonder the government is so damn broke!"

Mona finished her beer and asked if she could buy us another round. Nelson replied, "Sure, Mona, but get them to go. Remember, I promised to take y'all to one of the air ducts that was outside of the security fences. I'm all set to go."

"Are you riding with us, or are we taking two vehicles?" I asked.

"We're riding with Nelson," Mona replied. "He's got a truck, and if we need to hightail it across the desert, it's the only vehicle we have that can handle the ride."

"I'm with you on that, Mona!" Nelson replied. "Besides, I put some flashlights and ropes and stuff in the bed, just in case we need them."

Mona got a six-pack of Pearl, and we headed west toward Dulce. In town, we turned north and climbed the same road that Mona and I'd traveled earlier in the day. "We're heading into the Indian Reservation," I told Nelson.

"Yeah," he replied, "that's where the facility is located. The government pays rent to the Indians for the use of the land. They make out pretty good. Each one gets almost five thousand dollars per year. That's ten thousand for a married couple. I wish I got that, 'cause I'd lease me a Corvette."

Mona and I laughed, and then Mona asked, "How far into the reservation is the facility?"

"Y'all will start to see warning signs, and that's the clue that we're close."

When the first warning sign appeared, *NEARING RE-STRICTED FEDERAL PROPERTY. TURN AROUND*, Nelson killed his lights, and we drove by the light of the moon for another mile. Then he pulled off the road and bounced a quarter of a mile across small rocks and sage brush before drifting to a slow stop. "No sense using my brakes and alerting the sentries that we're here," Nelson told us.

We climbed out of the F-350 and stood silently for almost a minute before Nelson said, "Okay, I don't hear anybody coming. I think we're safe, so far. The sound of tires on a gravel road can be heard a long way in the cool desert air."

He pointed at a lone tree in the distance and told us that the tree was our destination. "The shaft is right beside it," he told us. We walked the one hundred yards to the tree and found a concrete cylinder with an iron grate on top, which was protected by a hood, just as Nelson had explained on the way up the mountain. He and I struggled, but we managed to lift the grate and pull it off. "This is an inspection shaft for the Dulce Firefight Facility. There are six others, and almost thirty other smaller shafts for air transfer. An inspection shaft is about three feet wide, like I told y'all last night."

"Can we go down?" Mona asked.

"Yup. That's why we're here," Nelson replied. "There are no civilian workers here at night, so it should be pretty safe down there, but I have to warn y'all that it's a very long way down. Can y'all climb a ladder that is a quarter of a mile tall? It's over a thousand rungs down, and a thousand back up. When we get down, we'll be at the first level. and we can look around."

"Can we go deeper?" I asked.

"Yeah, but I worry about Mona," Nelson replied. "She isn't wearing the right kind of shoes for climbing." I looked, and sure enough, Mona was in tennis shoes, which would leave her with very sore arches in the morning.

"I didn't think about how far we would be climbing

down a ladder," Mona said. "I thought it would be just a hundred feet or so."

I rolled my eyes. "Maybe you should stay up here this time. If the military security forces find our truck, you can make up some excuse about getting lost after a fight with your boyfriend Nelson and ask them to help you find your way back out of the desert."

"You always give me the dumb blonde jobs," Mona replied. But she knew I was right this time.

Nelson went back to the truck and brought two flashlights and two baseball caps with visor lights. "You think of everything!" I told him.

"Well, I didn't bring a gun because I figured y'all probably have one."

I patted under my left arm. "Colt Nineteen Eleven, forty-five caliber."

But just in case he tried any funny stuff while we were in the tunnels or if he had arranged for security to surprise us down there, I didn't let him know that also I carried a Beretta Jetfire .25 ACP strapped to my ankle. I was really good with that weapon at close range.

I let Nelson start down first, so he could alert me to anything out of the ordinary, such as a loose or slippery rung. As I descended below the rim of the opening, I felt a rush of claustrophobia, much like I had when I'd crawled through a culvert when I was a kid. We stopped three times to rest and, when we did, I would grab the step closest to my shoulder with the crook of my arm, taking the strain off of my hands, and then I would take the weight off of one foot and then the other to let the blood circulate. After what seemed like an hour, we finally reached the bottom.

"We're at level one," Nelson told me. It was pitch black, except for the light coming from our caps. I was glad that he had brought them along. I kept my flashlight off just in case our cap batteries went dead, but Nelson had his on. As I moved my head, I could see the ramp leading from level one back toward the surface. It came down diagonally, at maybe a thirty degree angle. Surprisingly, it was two lanes wide.

Nelson waved me forward, and we began walking down the ramp toward level two. He said, "After level two, no vehicles are permitted except those with special authorization. Otherwise, access is only possible by elevator or stairs." Stairs? They would have been easier to climb than the ladder we just came down, but using them would have been like climbing to the top of the Empire State Building, because each level of the facility was separated from the others by six hundred feet of solid rock.

"Nelson, do you have any sort of diagram of this facility, maybe something that would show me how the chambers and tunnels are connected?" I asked.

"Yeah, but I left it back in the truck. Sorry."

We were walking down the ramp, when suddenly a loud banging noise broke the silence.

"Shit!" Nelson whispered. "Somebody's down here."

Then we heard the sound of a propane motor. It was distinctly different from a gasoline engine. White light reflected off of the distant wall in front of us. We pressed against the shaded side of the tunnel and didn't make a sound. After a tense moment or two, the light diminished, and we heard the loud bang again.

"Whoever it is has gone back inside level two with a Tow Motor or forklift," Nelson said. "Do we want to keep on going or go back up?"

"Let's keep on," I said. "But if you want to go back, you can."

We quietly continued downhill until we reached a mammoth door, which apparently had caused us the anxiety when it had been opened and closed by someone on the other side.

Along the wall beyond its swing range were three Tow Motors with the keys in their ignitions.

"Is there another way in?" I asked.

Nelson replied, "Yeah, but it would only be another ventilation shaft, and we'd have to get inside the restricted area to gain access to it. From where we are, I think this is the only way in."

I pressed my ear against the door but could hear nothing moving on the other side. "Well, here goes," I said. I spun the wheel on the door counterclockwise until it stopped. It was well lubricated and probably heavily utilized. I struggled to pull the door open, so Nelson grabbed the handle, too, and we both pulled until the door cracked open. Light streamed into the darkness on our side of the door, so we shut off our cap lights. When we had opened the door about eighteen inches, we slipped through. A similar wheel was on the other side, so we slowly pulled the door closed behind us. It made a dull thud as we closed it, and we did not turn the wheel to lock the door.

Along the wall to our right were government issued crates and miscellaneous machines. We quickly moved behind them to hide until we could figure out where we were and what was going on. In the distance, there were sounds of people working, an occasional clang and the whirring of small machines. As we crouched and listened, a giant shadow appeared in motion on the wall to our right. Someone was approaching.

"Shit!" Nelson whispered.

"Shhh!" I told him.

The shadow stopped moving for a moment, as though the individual stopped to listen to some unexpected noise— probably us. After a moment, the shadow began moving again, growing larger and more ominous. Then, the individual came into view. At first, I thought it was a child, but then I realized that I was watching a short gray alien coming in my direction. It was skinny, stood no more than four feet tall, and had the large head I would have expected from the movies, although its chin was more pointed and protruding and its eyes were perhaps rounder. It must have been wearing a stretch suit of some kind, because nothing in the manner of genitalia was visible. I wasn't sure.

The alien stopped about forty feet from me and opened the lid to a wooden crate. It moved some unseen items about, retrieved a standard roll of gray duct tape with its three long fingers, and dropped the lid with a whack. Nelson flinched at the sudden sound. The alien turned and stared in his direction, but Nelson was securely crouched behind a crate. Then a voice cried out, "Where's that damn tape?" The alien turned and walked back into the distance.

I motioned for Nelson to come forward toward me. He was visibly shaking. "We're dead men," he whispered in my ear. I shook my head and motioned that we should go onward into the tunnel. I figured that we could continue to hide behind large objects until we could see was going on. But, just as I was about to move forward, a group of moving shadows began to appear on the wall, meaning several individuals were coming our way. "Shit!" Nelson whispered. "There's several of them coming our way!" We hunched down and watched. Walking toward us were three little gray aliens and two taller ones, maybe six feet in height. They were wearing uniforms and helmets. This meant trouble.

I pushed Nelson in the direction of the door. It only took him a split second to realize we were bailing out of level two.

We quickly reached the door and pushed it open far enough to get out. Nelson went first. In my head, I heard the phrase, "Stop where you are!" But I didn't stop. Then I heard a high-pitched whine, and a ball of light burst off the edge of the door above my hand. They were shooting something at us. As I dived quickly out the door, I heard another near-miss shot. Sparks spewed out the door above my head. Nelson helped me to my feet and, together, we pushed the door shut. Nelson turned the wheel to lock the door. While he did that, I started a Tow Motor and drove it up against the door. These babies were heavy, and I thought blocking the door would buy us some time.

I grabbed Nelson's arm and pulled him toward the two remaining Tow Motors. "Get in and start it up."

As he got into one, I took the key from the remaining one and put it into my pocket. Nelson hit the gas as I hopped in beside him, and we sped up the ramp toward level one. When we got to the air shaft opening, I sent Nelson upward. He didn't mind going first. Then I drove the Tow Motor to the base of the ramp toward the surface and killed its motor. I saw a small stack of broken shipping-crate wood against the wall and used a piece of it to jam the accelerator of the Tow Motor down. Then I turned the key, and the Tow Motor accelerated up the ramp. I ran back to the air shaft and started climbing.

The climb was exhausting, but my adrenalin output was on overdrive, so I climbed quickly. We were about a third of the way up the shaft, when Nelson and I heard a faint noise below. We stopped climbing and shut off our cap lights. I looked down at the small circle of dim light below me. Suddenly, I could see a pear-shaped head look up the shaft, but the being couldn't see me because of my distance into the darkness of the narrow cylinder. He should have brought a better flashlight. When the head disappeared from view, Nelson started climbing again. I was right behind him.

Twenty minutes later, Nelson popped out of the concrete cylinder at the surface. Mona exclaimed, "God, you missed it! Where's Danny?"

"He's right behind me. We have to get out of here," Nelson told her, gasping for air.

I climbed out of the shaft a moment later and surprised Mona when I shouted, "Go! Go! Go!"

The three of us hopped into Nelson's truck, and he started speeding away before I could close the door. "Jesus, Nelson, give me a second," I shouted at him. He took his foot off of the accelerator long enough for me to close the truck's door and snap my seatbelt, and then he jammed his foot down again. We lurched forward, fishtailing on the sandy desert floor.

When we reached the paved road, Nelson turned toward

Dulce, but continued driving without his headlights on.

"We're going to die!" Mona screamed. "Put on your damn lights!"

"No way, Mona! Tell her why not, Dan," Nelson shouted at me.

"Mona, we're being chased by aliens! Big ones and little ones! They shot their ray guns at us. We almost started a second Dulce Firefight!"

"You should have seen it, Danny!" Mona blurted. "About five minutes before you came out of the shaft, a giant disk came up out of nowhere. It was maybe fifty feet in diameter and dull aluminum in color, except that its edges had pulsating white lights, and a circle at the center of its bottom glowed in translucent reddish orange. It was simply beautiful. It hovered over me for maybe a minute and then it flew off toward Dulce so fast that it disappeared in less than five seconds."

"Fuck!" cried Nelson. "They've probably already identified my truck. I'm a dead man."

"Cool it, Nelson," I told him in a loud voice. "They've got enough fire power to have melted Mona and your truck into a cinder. Maybe they scanned Mona and simply decided that she was no threat."

"They could be monitoring where we're going, Dan," Nelson replied forcefully. "They'll just come get us tonight and bury our bodies out in the desert somewhere."

"You'll be fine," I told him. "Let's go back to the Apache House of Liquor and get a stiff drink."

"It was beautiful, Danny!" Mona said again.

Chapter 8

We hurried from Nelson's truck and into the Apache House of Liquor. The Native American host said, "Welcome back, Folks," as we passed by him and found an empty booth. *Good memory*, I thought. Hell, we had been gone for almost three hours.

"Fuck, we're dead men!" Nelson repeated for the umpteenth time since we climbed out of the air shaft.

"Howdy, and what can I get you folks?" the waitress asked, interrupting us at the moment that I was going to let Nelson have it.

"I'll take a boilermaker," I told her. Nelson ordered a Scotch, straight-up, and Mona asked for a glass of their best merlot.

"Wine?" I asked her when the waitress left the table.

"I think this may be the last drink of my life, Danny, so I want something I can say a little blessing over and make my peace with God," Mona replied. She sounded serious.

The waitress was back with our drinks in record time. As she set them on the table, she said to Mona, "You've been out in the sun today, ain't you? You'd better put some aloe on that sunburn tonight, or you're going to be hurtin' tomorrow."

The waitress was right. Mona clearly had a sunburned face, which was something that I hadn't noticed earlier.

"Must have been that UFO, Mona," Nelson told her,

"like in that movie *Close Encounters*, where he gets a burned face from looking at that UFO over his truck."

Mona excused herself and went to the ladies room to check her face. So, I looked at Nelson. "Listen, bucko, you have to get a hold of yourself and quit saying that we're all dead. I'm thinking that if they wanted us dead, they'd have sent some kind of death ray at us from outer space and obliterated all three of us and your truck before we got back into town."

"How can I go back to work tomorrow, Dan?" Nelson asked. "If they traced my plates or figured out who owns my truck, I'm never coming home."

"Well, maybe you have a point, and maybe not. Why don't you use my cell phone and call-in your truck as stolen? That ought to throw them off."

"Good thinking," Nelson replied.

I handed him my phone and Nelson called it in. He gave the deputy the story that his truck had been stolen from outside his home while he was napping. He explained that he'd had a few beers and was sleeping them off. When he woke up ten minutes ago, he discovered that the truck was gone. The deputy said he would send a squad car over to Nelson's home to take his complaint, but that it would be about an hour before the officer would be able to get there because they were handling a rash of calls about a UFO sighting. Nelson thanked the deputy and handed back my phone.

Mona came back and complained that her face was starting to hurt a little.

"It's psychosomatic, baby," I told her. "If that waitress hadn't said anything, you wouldn't even have noticed."

"My face is starting to hurt, Danny," she replied. "If it was your face hurting, you'd be blubbering like a baby."

She had a point. I suggested that we find a ride back to the hotel and that we could then hop in our car and drive Nelson home.

"What about my truck? I can't leave it here," Nelson said.

"It's stolen, isn't it?" I replied. "The cops will find it here and call you as soon as they do. In the meantime, you don't want to be caught behind the wheel, either by the cops or the aliens."

We found our way to the door and asked three different guys for a ride before we found one who wasn't heading back toward Dulce. He was a nice-looking man with a pocked face and dark hair. Probably a Native American.

"I'm a Nez Perce Indian," he told me when I asked. "We don't like being called Native Americans. Call us by our tribe—you know, like Apache Indian, Navajo Indian, and like that."

"I thought you Nez Perce were from Michigan or something," I replied.

"No, man, we're from along the Columbia River in the northwest. I'm down here because of work."

"What line of work are you in?" Mona asked him from the back seat of his Bronco.

"I sell refrigerators," he told her with a laugh, "like to the Eskimos, except I sell them to white women at Sears in Dulce. I also sell dishwashers and washer/dryer combos."

When Thomas Red Raven dropped us off in front of our motel, we offered him a couple of bucks for gas, but he waved us off. He was headed down the road to pick up his girlfriend, who was just finishing her shift at the lasso factory.

"Lassos like the cowboys use?" I asked.

He laughed again. "No, they're small bows that are sewn onto women's lingerie. That's what she does all night. She ties little bows and tacks them with a single knot of thread so they won't come apart. They get shipped to China, where somebody else sews them onto panties and bras. Some job, ain't it?"

We laughed and waved goodbye as he drove away. Then we hopped into our rental and quickly took Nelson home. We were just in time, because as we pulled up to the curb by his condo, a Dulce Sheriff's car pulled in behind us. Nelson got out, greeted the deputy, and gave the cheap excuse that we had been out looking for his truck. As I pressed down gently on the accelerator, Mona rolled down her window and shouted, "Good luck finding your truck, man. See you after work tomorrow."

Nelson waved goodbye. He had a worried look on his face.

Chapter 9

Mona kept me up most of the night, sending me outside for ice cubes from the machine in the vending area. Each time I returned, she would wrap a couple of handfuls of cubes in a washcloth and press it against her face. That burn was pretty bad, something akin to the aftermath of falling asleep on the beach at noon in mid-August and not waking up until dinnertime. At one point, I even woke the desk clerk to get her a couple of aspirins to ease the pain.

In the morning, she looked at herself in the mirror and remarked, "I'm as red as an orangutan's ass, Danny!"

She might have been understating the obvious.

"Pack up," I told her. "We need to touch base with Nelson and then figure out our next move."

I thought Mona ought to make the call because Nelson would probably be more willing to hear from her than me. He seemed to like her, as I recalled from our first meeting. She sat on the edge of the bed and direct dialed his number, following the directions on a plastic-coated card which was attached by a key chain to the nightstand.

When he didn't answer, Mona said, "He's probably gone to work." It was already eight, so I figured that she had a good point.

"How about we call that guy Alden and ask if he'll meet with us again for ten minutes," I suggested. "I'd like to share last night's events with him to see if it helps him remember anything else."

Mona asked me for his number and punched the keys on the phone. While she waited for the phone to make the connection, she crossed her legs and rubbed her right ankle.

A man answered. "So what did you learn, knucklehead? And why didn't you use my cell phone?" he asked.

"Excuse me?" Mona asked.

"Oh, sorry, lady," he replied when he heard a woman's voice. "I thought you were my deputy."

"Is Jonathan there?" Mona asked.

"Yeah, but he can't come to the phone right now. How did you know him, lady?"

"Is he deceased?" Mona replied. "This is the FBI."

"This is bullshit, lady. You called him 'Jonathan.'"

"This is Mona Casola, special agent with the FBI. I'm from the DC office."

"And this is Sheriff Perry. If you are who you say you are, come to Alden's home and show me your badge. Otherwise, I've got business to attend to."

"We'll see you shortly."

"I'll bet."

Mona hung up the receiver. "Danny, something's happened to Alden. We need to go talk to the sheriff. I think Alden is dead."

"The death tally seems to be rising, Mona," I replied.

We quickly threw our stuff into the car, checked out of the motel, and drove toward Alden's place. Along the way, we stopped at a drug store so Mona could buy some aloe cream for her face, and a bottle of buffered aspirin.

Finding Alden's home wasn't difficult. It was the only place on his street that was decorated in yellow crime scene ribbon. As we approached, an ambulance was arriving to take the body to the county coroner's for an autopsy. We parked next door, and Mona showed her badge to gain us entry to the crime scene.

Sheriff Perry acknowledged Mona with a nod. "Nice face. It's gotta hurt."

"Tell me about it," Mona replied. "I'm Special Agent Casola, FBI, DC office. We spoke a few minutes ago."

"You ought to know that your buddies from Santa Fe are on their way here by chopper. I suppose you want to see the body?"

Mona nodded.

"Who's your friend?" the sheriff asked.

"Detective Arrow," I replied, extending my hand.

"He's a private detective," Mona said, "on special contract with the DC office. We're following the trail of an unknown killer who has left a string of bodies across the country. They've all been staged to look like suicides."

"Same MO here," Perry said, "except this ain't no suicide. The victim's tongue has been cut out."

"No shit?" I asked.

"Strange, though…"

"Why's that?" Mona asked.

"There ain't no blood. Whoever did it, he used something really hot. Maybe a knife blade that had been heated to white hot," the sheriff replied. "The body's in there."

Mona and I walked into the bedroom. Perry followed us in. Alden was lying on his back staring straight up at the ceiling from his bed. His eyes were bulging, and his mouth was open. A length of surgical tubing was tightly twisted around his neck.

"Same way my client died," I muttered.

"Thought you are under contract with the FBI," Sheriff Perry remarked.

"I am. My *former* client," I replied. "He was with NASA." It was a lie, but it was close to the truth.

"So where's Alden's wife?" Mona asked. "Who found the body?"

"She's currently a suspect. She called in the homicide, saying that it was all her fault."

"Her fault?" I asked.

"Yeah, that's what she kept saying. It was all her fault. She said that she saw an official looking sedan pull up and opened the front door to see who it was. Three tall men got out. When she called out his name, her husband slammed the front door shut, leaving her outside with the men. That's all she remembers. She says that when she came to, she was on the sofa in the living room, and her husband was in here. Dead."

"Can we interrogate her?" Mona asked.

"Nope. Not unless your Santa Fe bureau claims authority over this case."

"Can we speak with her?" I asked.

"Not until we've finished processing her, and then only if her lawyer gives you permission and if we can have an officer present," the sheriff replied. "She had a couple of feet of surgical tubing in the pocket of her bathrobe. The cut on one end appears to match that on the victim."

"She didn't do it," Mona said matter-of-factly.

"So who did?" the sheriff asked.

"Space aliens," I replied.

"Sure they did," the sheriff said, rolling his eyes, "and they took his tongue to make sandwiches for their flight back to Mars!"

"Maybe," Mona said, looking at Alden's body. "Maybe."

We scheduled an appointment with Sheriff Perry to meet him back at the county jail at four p.m., under the pretense that we wanted to chat with Mrs. Alden. He told us that he would try to get permission from whatever attorney was assigned to represent her.

He also told us that we might have to stand in line behind the Santa Fe Bureau. We thanked him and walked to back to our rental.

"You're not really planning to hang around here all day, are you, Danny?" Mona asked as we ducked under the crime scene tape.

"I think we should blow town and head for Colorado," I replied. "Alden told us that there is a large underground complex below the airport. I think we ought to check it out."

"What about Nelson?" Mona asked. "Don't you think we owe it to him to let him know what we're doing?"

"He didn't show us the courtesy of answering his phone this morning. Maybe he was at work, but I smell something fishy. I don't think we should hang around Dulce any longer. In fact, maybe we should have left last night. Besides, we can call him again tonight, after he's home from work."

The car was already packed, so we drove west on Route 64 until it intersected Route 84, where we turned north toward Colorado. Denver was less than a day's drive, so we stopped in Pueblo for lunch. It was a relatively large town, and we thought it might be easy for us to disappear into the crowd, especially if anyone was looking for us.

I turned off of the main drag and told Mona to look for a restaurant that served something she was in the mood for. In the Goat Hill section of Pueblo, she pointed to the Bingo Burger. "I'm always in the mood for a cheeseburger," she said. I pulled in. On the window, a sign claimed that the joint was "the only game in town." I knew it was going to be memorable.

"Whatcha want, ma'am?" the bleach-blonde waitress asked after we scooted into our booth.

She was in her forties, probably a single mom with three kids who were employed as blue collar workers.

I figured that would make her a grandmother, several times over.

"A cheeseburger," Mona replied, "and fries."

"To drink?" the waitress asked.

"A root beer."

The waitress looked at me and readied her pencil.

"I'd like something special. What do you recommend?" I asked.

"You aren't from around here, are you?"

"What gave us away?"

"Your lady's sunburn, for one," she replied. "Nobody from around here does that to herself. It causes deep wrinkles by the time you're forty."

"I can see that," I replied, noting the lines on her face.

"Thanks for the warning," Mona said.

"I recommend the lamb burger," the waitress continued without acknowledging Mona. "It's greasy good, especially with jack cheese and a milkshake."

"Six bucks for a milkshake seems kind of steep," I told her.

"They're made from ice cream from the local creamery. It's the best you'll get anywhere."

"Shit, why not?" I replied, handing her my menu. "Make it chocolate, and I'll try that lamb burger. Make it medium well."

When she left, Mona opened her purse and removed the small tube of aloe that I bought her on the way out of Lumberton. She squeezed some onto her fingers, crossed her leg, and rubbed the cream onto her right ankle. As she massaged it into her skin, she asked how I expected to find an underground facility near an airport. "We don't have any leads in Denver," she told me, "so how are you expecting to find an entrance. You know it'll be well-protected."

"Didn't Powers's notebook have some stuff about Denver?" I asked.

"Yeah, I think so," Mona replied.

"Well, why don't you check it out for leads when we get back in the car?"

"I guess that's a start. Maybe I can find something that will lead us in the right direction."

"What's with your ankle?" I asked.

"Small scratch, and it's really itchy," Mona replied. "I think I got it out in the desert last night. I probably brushed up against a cactus or something."

"What about your sister's wedding?" I reminded her. "Have you talked to her since you called in an excuse?"

Mona's expression turned to one of distress. "No," she replied, "not until she gets back from her honeymoon."

"Are you going to call your folks and see how it went?" I asked.

"I probably should," Mona confessed, "but I don't want to face them. Not even over the phone." Mona rubbed the side of her face and sighed. "I feel like a real shit for not having gone to my sister's wedding. You know, I should have been there, because it was a once in a lifetime opportunity. If you look at the odds, she may get married again, but she'll never have another wedding."

"It's okay, baby," I told her. "Seeing that UFO was a once in a lifetime opportunity, too."

"It *was* beautiful," Mona replied.

Lunch arrived. The lamb burger didn't look as good as Mona's cheeseburger because it was light gray in color. But it tasted pretty good. And I guessed I was used to the fast food places because the french fries were darker than I would have liked. I didn't eat many. Neither did Mona. However, my milkshake was "to die for," if I could borrow Mona's expression.

After lunch, we climbed back into the rental sedan, and Mona pulled out Powers's notebook. While she read, I got us back onto the main drag and headed north out of town.

Before we reached Colorado Springs, Mona had it all figured out. She was really good that way. "Danny, Powers pasted a newspaper article in here about the Denver airport. We have to go see it. There are all sorts of symbols in the airport that refer directly to the New World Order. That's that government takeover thing that Alden talked about."

"Are the symbols actually inside the airport in plain view?" I asked.

"Yes. That's what it says."

"Incredible. What else?"

"Handwritten in the margin is the name E-N-G-R Weiner. Odd name."

"Sounds German, maybe Austrian Jewish," I replied,

applying the brakes gently because we were entering a construction zone.

"Why would the first name be in all caps?—Oh, I know," Mona exclaimed, "E-N-G-R is an abbreviation for engineer!" She flipped the pages in the book until she came to Powers's list of individuals and their roles in the underground facilities conspiracy. "Here it is," she said. "Weiner... Fritz Weiner. Powers connects him to the Denver project. He even gives us an address. The guy lives in Centennial, Colorado."

"Where's that?"

Mona pulled her cell phone from her purse. "Shit!" she exclaimed, "My mother texted me last night."

"Did you find Centennial yet?" I asked. "You can deal with your mother later."

"Hold your fucking horses, Danny. This is no laptop computer."

I decided to keep my mouth shut until she collected herself and found Centennial.

"Here it is. Hey, we're almost there. It's a suburb of Denver!"

"Of all the dumb luck," I exclaimed.

"It's on the south end. We'll have to watch the exits as we enter the Denver area, and we can pull off in Centennial and ask directions." Mona seemed excited about getting back on the trail. Maybe coming to Denver wasn't such a bad idea, after all.

An hour later, we passed Meridian and saw the first of three exit signs for Centennial. I decided to get off in the middle of town and see if we could find Weiner, maybe in a phone book. So, we exited at Dry Creek Road, found the first gas station, and pulled in. Mona discovered that there was no phone book, so while I relieved myself, she used her cell phone to call information and get Weiner's address. It was easy. There were only three Weiners in Centennial. One was a dentist, one was a woman, and one was named

Fritz. "Could I confirm that address?" Mona asked the operator.

"Fourteen Thirty-Five Hunter's Hill Drive," the virtual operator told her. "Hold while I make the connection."

Mona canceled the call and jotted down Weiner's address and phone number. She went back into the service station where a map of Centennial could be purchased for $7.95. She opened the map, checked the index of streets, and found the location of Hunter's Hill Drive. We were only three blocks away, which was more dumb luck. Mona then took a Diet Dr. Pepper from the cooler and approached the man behind the counter.

"Do you want that map you were reading, ma'am?" he asked.

"No thank you. It doesn't include Denver," Mona told him. She paid him for the soda and came back out to me.

"Any luck?" I asked as she opened the car door and slid onto the seat.

"It's right around the corner. Maybe we ought to call him, first."

"Naw," I replied. "Let's just go see if he's home. If he isn't, we can call tonight before you call Nelson again. And before you call your mother."

Mona winced at the thought.

Chapter 10

W hen will this container be ready?"
"We estimate one million clicks, Your Excellency," replied the draconian scientist. His onyx
reptilian eyes reflected the greenish light from the monitor
he was observing.

"In Earth time, please."

The reptilian's snake-like tongue darted quickly as he
turned his attention to the aged human who stood beside
him. "Approximately eleven days, Excellency."

"I am anxious, you know, Doctor. It has been a very
long time since I have enjoyed the flexibility of a youthful
body." She pulled at the loose flesh on her neck. "These
temporary containers have all been abused by their former
occupants. I have tired of them. It will be good to be back in
my own again."

"The growth process has taken us much longer than expected, Excellency. Your human containers are different
from ours. Humans mature very slowly. But it appears that
we have finally mastered the process of growing the space
your fundamental essence must occupy. We had not expected to encounter such an entity. What do you call it? "

"The soul."

"Yes," the reptilian hissed. "When the hybrid project is
completed, we will be able to move all humans and their
souls into containers that can be directed as you wish, and

our own destiny will finally be achieved. The queen has long awaited the achievement of this phase."

"You have taught me much about our species, Doctor Modo. Your advanced sciences and studies of life forms across the galaxies have been most interesting to explore these past years."

"As you know, Your Excellency, your species evolved through several forms before you developed the delicate body that protects you from your sun's PN-twenty-five radiation. It is amusing that you call that protective body a soul, and that you named it after your sun, the very thing that shortens your lifespans so." The reptilian closed a notebook and smiled at the woman. "Those rays are so destructive to our containers that they have driven our species underground for two thousand years. But soon, when we enter hybrid containers, we, too, should find modest protection from the PN-twenty-five. The lifespans of the new containers will be less than thirty percent of our own natural containers, but we find comfort in our ability to create new containers as we need them, such that we may continue to live until our termination."

"Have you yet been able to create a soul for your species," the aged woman asked.

"No, Your Excellency. That is our final quest. We think that the hybrid containers are the best answer, but we have yet to unlock that riddle."

"It is unfortunate, Dr. Modo. I know it has been your dream."

"But we are close. And when we achieve that goal, we will be able to emerge from these caverns and live on the surface among humans, even if only as a hybrid species." Dr. Modo removed his glasses and put them in the pocket of his lab coat. "The bovine DNA is promising, as well as the lip and uterine tissues we have been using for accelerating the growth of clones and hybrids."

"I am anxious to learn of your success with this container," the woman said, returning her attention to the male body that was floating in clear liquid. "It looks so much like I did during those years of greatness. My return will be perceived as a second coming, and the human masses will throng to hear my words."

Dr. Modo hissed. "And with our advanced technology, you will be perceived both as a healer and seer. You will then pave the way for our emergence from the depths."

"Yes, and your queen and I shall rule this blue ball together."

"She intends it so, Excellency," Dr. Modo said, nodding his head.

Chapter 11

Hal called my cell phone while we were in the car. I put it on speaker. "Don't tell me where you are," she started, "in case the office phone is tapped."

"Thanks, Hal. How are things in DC?"

"You've got to stop whatever it is that you're doing, Danny. There's been a line of people wanting to get to you."

"Like who?"

"FBI, CIA, Homeland Security, and those tall goons again. Whatever you're up to is rattling the wrong people."

"Just tell them I'm on a case, Hal. Tell them I'll check in with you, but it will be sporadic. Nothing regular. Okay?"

"Okay. But when will I really hear from you?"

"It'll be at least a week. Don't call me again because they can triangulate my location."

"What about my paycheck, Danny? I've got to pay my bills and eat."

"Call Willie the bookie. His number is in my Rolodex. He owes me two grand. Tell him you're under orders to get it or turn him in."

"This really sucks, Danny."

"Yeah, I know, Hal."

"You take care, and don't take any stray bullets."

"Thanks for caring, Hal."

ↄ৵ↄ

Four cars were parked in front of Weiner's house when we got there. "Must be a party going on," Mona said. Nevertheless, I parked so that our car blocked the driveway and nobody could back out unless they drove through our rental. I would never have parked my own car in that sort of harm's way. As Mona walked toward the front door, the sound of a screen door slamming shut came from the right side of the house, and suddenly a skinny man in his late thirties appeared. He fumbled as he tried to retrieve his car keys from his pants pocket. I caught him by the arm. "Hold it, Hondo! You aren't leaving the scene of the crime just yet!"

"Please don't hurt me," he begged, pulling at my fingers. I tightened my grip on his puny bicep. "I'm not part of it anyway. I'm just offering support to my friends."

"Part of what?" I asked, intentionally raising an eyebrow.

"I'm not part of it, mister, honest!"

I pulled him to the concrete front porch and held on while Mona rang the doorbell. We could hear commotion and hushed talking inside, so I figured Weiner was in some sort of trouble.

"Take this sucker," I told Mona. She flashed her badge and snapped one cuff on the little guy and the other onto a wrought iron post that supported the overhanging porch roof. I tried the door knob. It was locked, so I did the movie thing and kicked at the door. Surprisingly, it took very little force to break the door frame. *Cheap wood*, I thought. *Probably Philippine mahogany*. I pulled my 1911 from its shoulder holster and slowly entered Weiner's home.

A frightened voice rang out, "Hold it, mister, unless you want to die!"

"Agents Arrow and Casola from the FBI," I replied. "We're looking for Fritz Weiner. We only want to ask a few questions. Nobody needs to get hurt!"

"Hold your gun in the air and come in slowly!"

I did as directed. As I entered the darkness of the room, I

could see the tops of three heads huddled behind a green-plaid sofa. One held a shotgun. It looked like a twenty-gauge side by side, and it was pointed in my general direction. I would have been happier if he were holding a .22 pistol because I knew that if I rolled to my left, there was a ninety percent chance that he'd miss with the first shot or two. The problem with a shotgun is that it scatters pellets in a sphere, so even if his aim was off, I could still get hurt. Even if he was using number nine bird shot.

"Look," I told him. "I'll put my gun away." Slowly, and I mean very slowly, I returned my piece to its holster and raised both hands. "See?" I said, "I'm not going to hurt you." *Not yet anyway*, I thought.

The man with the shotgun was the first to stand up. He looked like some kind of a geek, maybe computers. "Show me your credentials," he ordered. Slowly I pulled my wallet from my trousers and threw it on the sofa in front of him. As he reached for it, the barrel of his shotgun descended toward the floor.

Another voice surprised us all. "Drop the shotgun, meathead!" it commanded. It was Mona, and her command surprised us all. She stepped from behind me with her FBI-issued nine-millimeter poised at full ready. "Don't make me make your mother cry tonight!" Her words sounded like some poorly written scene from a B-rated cop show. But they worked. The shotgun made a soft whump as it hit the beige carpet. These guys were amateurs.

I picked up the K-Mart special shotgun, opened the breach, and removed the two shells. They were home de-fense rounds, so I was glad he never pulled the trigger. The disks and BBs would have ripped my lungs to shreds, and I'd never have had the chance to show Mona how I truly feel about her. If she'd ever let me.

"So which one of you is Weiner?" I asked, dropping the shotgun back onto the carpet.

"That would be me," replied an older man who struggled to get to his feet. He appeared to be in his mid-fifties, salt and pepper hair, and still in pretty good shape, except for knee strength. "Are you really from the FBI?" he asked.

Mona flashed her badge with one hand, but she kept her pistol pointed at the three men with the other.

"Are you with the detachment at the airport?" he asked.

"No, we're from Washington," Mona told him. "We're in Colorado on a murder case, and we're hoping you can help us."

"If you'll put down your weapon, I'll be happy to answer anything that I can."

Mona glanced at me and then back at Weiner, who pointed at the shotgun on the floor. "That was our only firearm. It's of no use to us now, and we have no other weapons."

Mona relaxed a little and holstered her pistol. I twisted the shotgun, pressed the button at the top of its forearm and removed it. Then I pushed the lever on the receiver and broke the shotgun down into its two remaining pieces. I laid them on top of the papers which were scattered on the glass-topped coffee table.

"Watch out for those papers!" warned Weiner. "Don't soil them!"

I dropped the shotgun pieces back to the floor. "So what are you guys doing here?"

"We're just talking," said one of the two other men from behind the sofa.

"What about the guy on the porch?" I asked.

"He came to try to talk us out of it," replied Weiner. "Let him go. He's of no value to you."

"You don't even know what we want," I told him. "We may need that guy."

"He's not part of what we're doing," Weiner said. "Just let him go. He's got a bad heart, and you're going to make him sick."

I nodded to Mona, and she stepped outside. While she was gone, I kept the evil eye on the three inside. I'd learned that relentless stare from my grandmother. It worked well.

Soon, we heard a car door shut, an engine start, and a car drive away. Mona had released the guy on the porch.

When Mona reappeared, she opened her jacket, showing that her piece was still in its holster. "Okay, is there any chance we all can have a peaceful conversation?"

Everyone nodded.

I dragged a straight-backed chair from the dining room and sat down. Mona gave me a dirty look, so I relinquished the chair to her and dragged over another one for myself. Weiner and his two friends sat on the sofa.

Mona started the conversation. "We're here because we're investigating a murder. The clues thus far have led us to Denver. We're hoping you can help us fill in some of the missing pieces so we can solve the mystery."

"So you aren't here to arrest or detain us? " Weiner asked.

"No," I said. Then I got right to the point. "Did you know Billy Powers?"

"I saw him give a presentation in San Diego a couple of years ago, but I don't know him," Weiner replied

"How about either of you?" I asked, pointing to the two other men.

"Who are you?" the taller one asked.

"Dan Arrow," I replied, extending my hand. "This is Mona Casola. She's an FBI agent, and I'm a private detective."

"Will Martin," the taller one said, shaking my hand and then looking at Mona.

"Arthur McGarvey," the other one said. He rose, shook Mona's hand, sat down, and extended his hand to shake mine.

"Did either of you know William Powers?" I asked.

"Never heard of him," Martin replied.

"Saw him on a YouTube video," McGarvey said, "but I don't know him."

"What's this about?" Weiner asked.

"Powers is dead, recently deceased," Mona said. "His is

one of a string of deaths related to the Dulce Firefight. We're looking for his killer."

"You'll need to go underground to do that," Weiner told us.

"Been there once," I replied, "but I didn't get anyone to confess. Can you be a little more black and white?"

Weiner pointed at Mona. "You mentioned the Dulce firefight. Was Powers there? How did he die?"

"Yeah, he was there," Mona replied. "They say he strangled himself with rubber medical tubing. Death by strangulation seems to be highly contagious recently."

"I've read about similar suicides and strange accidents in the tabloids," Weiner said, "but, you know, they're actually executions. The NWO snuffs out people who get too close."

"Like we said, we're here investigating his murder," Mona said.

"We thought you were NWO."

"What can you tell us about the New World Order?" I asked him.

"They're here. And they're bold. Have you been to the airport yet?"

"That's one of our primary destinations after we talk to you."

"I'll take you to see it, if you'd like. We were planning on going in tonight, but maybe we'll wait a day or two since you're here."

"Going in?" Mona asked.

"Yeah," replied McGarvey. "One of our members, Charlie Bobbin, has disappeared. We think they have him in one of their cages."

"Unless they've made soup out of him," Martin blurted out.

"Whoa, slow down," I said. "You're *waaay* ahead of us. What do you mean by soup, and what about those cages?"

Weiner put both hands up, as though he was pushing a car. "Let me frame it out for you," he said. "Beneath the airport is a large underground facility. All levels of state and federal government deny its existence, but I'll take you out there and show you evidence that it does, indeed, exist. I know it's there because I did some of the structural engineering on the first three levels. But there are more levels, and it goes deep, maybe ten or twelve levels by now. Whenever I was on site, all security was provided by heavily armed black ops people whose insignias clearly said *New World Order* on them. They were not regular army or special forces, or marines."

"So what is the soup that you mentioned?" Mona asked.

"I'm getting there. When I worked in the facility, we were allowed to intermingle with the other engineers and workers on our level only. There was no intermingling with those who were working on other levels."

"How did they manage to keep you apart?" I asked.

"We were all assigned to secure parking areas in the desert, and we were bused back and forth in shuttles that served our specific parking areas. We also were assigned specific arrival and departure times. They checked our IDs at the entrance to the parking lot, and they scanned our irises as we got on the buses, both coming and going. Security was pretty intense."

"So what about the cages and the soup?" Mona asked again. She seemed to be getting annoyed with how long it was taking Weiner to get to the point.

"I was out to dinner in Denver one night, and my table was next to a table with three men. They were discussing work on some of the other levels, the deeper ones. One talked about a friend who had disappeared. He told the others that his friend had confided in him that he had been escorted down to do electrical repair work on the eighth level and that it was full of cages with humans and half-humans. The cages were all numbered and operated electronically. He said that it looked like an experimentation center of some sort. Most of the people and the creatures in the cages seemed to be suffering."

"What else did he say?" Mona asked.

"The friend disappeared shortly after confiding that information, as though somebody knew that he had broken the pledge to remain silent."

"Or maybe eliminating him after he finished his work was part of the overall plan of secrecy," Martin added.

"Pledge?" I asked.

"Yes," Weiner continued, "it's a non-disclosure agreement you have to sign before you go to work there. Everybody has to sign it. But it's more than that. They tell you that you cannot tell anyone anything that goes on there, or that you do so under penalty of death. It's above top secret, national security work."

"Have you seen the cages?" Mona asked.

"No, but I've read about them in some of the tabloids. It is like somebody is leaking information, but the sources are never revealed. I'm convinced they're there."

"So what about the soup?"

"This may be hard for you to swallow, but when those three men were talking, one kept referring to his Grey."

"Grey?" I asked.

"Yes, gray alien. From what I could gather, he was assigned a Grey to assist him with the project he was working on. The Grey had the ability to perform certain tasks that he couldn't do himself because he didn't have the technical knowledge to do it. The Grey shared some of the knowledge with him, but not all of it. Just enough to help him get it done. It was some sort of device that can be controlled mentally by the Greys, and he was trying to adapt it so that humans can operate it the same way, by their thoughts."

"Back to the soup," Mona said.

"Well, he said that his Grey had to go bathe in some kind of liquid every six hours, or else it got weak and didn't function well. He said it was like the Grey was some sort of robot, but it was made of flesh and didn't run on electricity or need batteries. Instead, it bathed in a soup of organic materials, like chopped up animal parts and fluids. He thought it absorbed the liquid through its skin, like maybe that's how it ate or recharged itself."

"I think they use humans," McGarvey said. "I think they grind up human flesh and mix it with other chemicals and nutrients to feed the Greys."

"Have you ever seen a Grey?" I asked.

"No, but I am pretty sure they're real."

"I've seen some," I told them. "They're the little guys. It's the big ones who have the weapons."

"You've actually seen a Grey?" Weiner asked excitedly.

"Wow! Then we're right," exclaimed Martin.

I looked at Weiner. "Did those guys know you overheard what they were talking about?"

"I don't think so. I had my back to them and tried not to react to what they were saying. You never know who is who in Denver. They certainly didn't know that I also worked at the airport facility."

"I guess that explains why you haven't disappeared yet," I told him. McGarvey and Martin agreed.

"So were you planning to go find your friend?" Mona asked. "You said that he was part of your group."

"We were planning it when you guys arrived," Weiner replied. "Maybe you can help us. You've got guns and FBI credentials."

"Who's your group?" I asked.

"We're a small group, originally five, but we're now down to three. Bobbin disappeared, and now Fraley, the guy you let go, just wished us luck, but backed out. The three of us are convinced that something big is going on down in the facility. We think the president, the military, the FBI, CIA, and big business are running it, maybe with participation by some influential foreign governments. The news media appears to be part of it, like keeping the NWO hidden from the general public, even though there are signs and symbols of it everywhere," Weiner said.

"So who is your leader?" I asked.

Martin and McGarvey pointed at Weiner.

"And how were you planning to get into the facility?" I asked him.

"I know the location of an air shaft that will take us down to the first level," Weiner said. Because I worked on levels one, two, and three, I can guide us through there. After that, it's going to be touch and go."

"And what roles are you two dweebs playing?" I asked, wiggling my pointer finger between McGarvey and Martin.

"My specialization is cartography," Martin replied. "My job is to map our way into the lower levels so we can get back without becoming lost."

"I am the photographer," McGarvey said. "My task is to make video and photographic records of our exploration of the facility, so we can show what we discover to the proper authorities when we get back, especially if we see aliens or, God forbid, people or creatures in cages."

"Who would the proper authorities be?" Mona asked. "If the FBI and CIA are part of this, where can you go to show your evidence without risking immediate disappearance?"

"We were thinking Jesse Ventura," McGarvey replied.

"Or maybe Fox News," added Martin.

Mona rolled her eyes.

"Here's what we have to go on," Weiner continued, pointing at the first two layers of papers which were on the coffee table. "These are commercially available topographical maps of the region. Beneath them are aerial shots of the region, obtained via Google Maps and Zillow. Look at this area beside Gold Bug Street, just east of the Swastika. That's where they piled the dirt from the early tunneling. It used to be mounds of dirt, but it's been bulldozed into a small plateau."

"Swastika?" I asked.

"Yeah, look the shape of the airport," Weiner said, outlining its basic shape with his finger. "See how it resembles a swastika?"

He was right. It did look like a swastika. "So are they still piling dirt there?" I asked.

"No, they stopped removing dirt once the first level was completed and they were into solid rock. That's when they brought in the laser drills. Those babies can melt a mile or more of tunnel in a day."

"Did you see them in action?" I asked.

"Yeah, but only on the second and third levels. Each level is the size of a neighborhood on the surface. You know, like at least a mile square. Maybe bigger on the lower levels. I know they used the laser drills on the subsequent levels, but I retired before they started drilling them."

"So where's the entrance to the facility?" Mona asked, rubbing her ankle again.

"See this white building on East Eighty-Eighth?" Weiner said, pointing to a Google map. "It's out of the way and inconspicuous. That's it. It doesn't look like anything but an old warehouse, does it? You drive inside and immediately begin descending. After you're two hundred feet down, you pass through a huge vault door. Once you've passed that, you're officially inside."

"If you're right, it's in full public view, but nobody suspects anything, do they?" I said.

"That's definitely the idea," Weiner continued. "I told you that I used to come and go from there every day. In the beginning, we would be dropped off in front of that building, but once the first level was finished, they simply drove the shuttle in the door and down there to drop us off. It was almost door to door service."

"You called us dweebs, Mr. Arrow," Martin said with drooping shoulders.

"Danny meant it in a complimentary way," Mona lied. "You're like Spiderman. You're little guys, but you have special powers that make you superheroes. And because you aren't all bulked up like the Hulk or Batman, nobody would suspect you."

"Gee, yeah, when you say it that way, I guess we are dweebs!" McGarvey exclaimed. "I kind of like it."

"Yeah, we're the Dweeb Squad," Martin added. "Maybe

we should get ourselves some custom tee shirts with a
Dweeb Squad logo!"

"I like that," I told them. "I meant it like Mona told you.
Your special skills in map making and videotaping will help
us on this mission." I was lying. I wasn't sure they'd be anything but trouble.

 ප⁄පප⁄ප

About ten minutes later, the Dweeb Squad piled into the
back seat of our rental sedan and directed us to Route 470-
N toward the Denver International Airport. Before we got to
the main terminal, Weiner had us head west on East Eighty-
Eighth Avenue. About half a mile down the road, Weiner
made me slow down. "See the dirt on your right, Mr. Arrow," he said. "Last year, it was a series of huge piles, each
maybe three stories high, but they bulldozed it down into
that plateau."

I could see that the dirt rose to a height approximately
four feet higher than the road. Its top had been flattened, so
to the casual observer it would look like a new runway was
under construction. "Yeah, I can see the difference in color
that you mentioned. The regular desert is light tan, but this
is much darker," I told the dweebs.

"Imagine how much space that dirt would occupy if it
was underground," McGarvey said.

"How long does this plateau go?" Mona asked.

"It's about a mile and a half long, but it is almost two
miles wide," Weiner told her. "My guess is that if the first
level of the underground facility is twenty feet high" this
amount of dirt would mean that that level is about a third of
a mile square, "Weiner replied.

"Make that point-four-six-five square miles," Martin
said, "but remember that some of the dirt has been hauled to
Bennett."

"Bennett is a small town about ten miles east of the airport," Weiner continued. "They store a lot of the heavy equipment and construction supplies there. For most people around here, Bennett is the last place they'd ever go for a visit."

"Yeah," added Martin, "There's nothing there but a gas station and a redneck bar."

"Sounds like it's right up your alley, Danny," Mona told me. "Maybe we could go dancing there."

"Whatever you say, sweetheart," I replied.

When we reached the end of the new plateau of dirt, a large white building came into view on the left, about one hundred yards off the road. "That's the main entrance to the underground facility," Weiner said. "Don't slow down, or you'll look suspicious." As we drove by, an army-green eighteen wheeler was pulling out of the main door, with its headlights on. It was pulling a flatbed with three military jeeps strapped to it.

"There are no military bases around here, Mr. Arrow, and why would there be jeeps in a commercial facility?" McGarvey asked.

"Maybe they needed tune-ups," I replied sarcastically.

"Quick, Mr. Arrow," Weiner exclaimed when we were a couple of hundred yards past the building, "turn around and drive back by the facility. One of the shuttles just came out!"

I slammed on the brakes and drifted our sedan into a spin. Then I steered us back toward the white building. As we passed by the gravel road that led from the building to East Eighty-Eighth, a twenty foot shuttle, the type used to carry the handicapped in many small cities, stopped at the hardtop to let us pass by. It was full of dweebs. Behind it, another one was emerging from the building's single garage style door.

"That place tunes up all sorts of vehicles, doesn't it?" I said, turning to look backward at the building.

"Watch out, Danny!" Mona squealed.

I looked back toward the front of our car, quickly

swerved to the right onto the shoulder of the road, and slammed on the brakes. As the car stopped, a cloud of brown dust engulfed us.

"Jesus fucking Christ, Danny, keep your fucking eyes on the road!" Mona screamed at me. "You nearly killed us all!"

"I guess I came up on the rear end of that eighteen-wheeler pretty fast. Sorry, baby," I said. "Are you guys back there okay?"

"My heart's in my throat," Weiner said, "but Martin blew his lunch, Mr. Arrow."

Mona handed her box of tissues over the seat to Martin. "Here," she said, "use these to wipe your mouth and to get that mess off your shorts." The acidic smell of vomit began to fill the car. I rolled down the windows, letting the heat and dust pour in. A few seconds later, the first shuttle bus passed by. The dweebs inside looked down at us as they passed.

Martin opened the back door, stepped outside, and began wiping the vomit off of the carpet in the back seat. "I'm so sorry, Miss Mona," he said. "Sudden turns do that to me."

"That's okay, honey," Mona said. She could be motherly when she needed to be.

"He didn't barf when we stopped," McGarvey said. "He barfed when you did that four-wheel drift back on the road."

"I guess I owe you dinner," I told him.

"That's okay, Mr. Arrow. I just need a shower."

രൗരൗ

It was getting late in the afternoon, and Mona and I needed to find a place to spend the night, so we drove the Dweeb Squad back to Weiner's house in Centennial.

"Tomorrow morning, let me take you to the main terminal, Mr. Arrow," Weiner said as I pulled up to the curb in front of his house. "Then we can talk about going down the air shaft."

"Sounds like a plan," I replied. We exchanged cell phone numbers and made plans to meet at Weiner's home at ten a.m.

Martin got into his car and started its motor. He was shower bound.

"It was nice meeting you all," McGarvey said, extending his hand.

"You, too," Mona replied, shaking it.

"Miss Mona," he said. "I noticed that you keep rubbing that scratch on your ankle."

"Yeah, I got it the other night. It's itchy."

"Before you go to bed tonight, I suggest that you stop by a drug store and get one of those magnetic bandages that they sell for people with arthritis. Wrap it so that the magnet is over the scratch. If it stops itching, then you've got a bug."

"What kind of bug? Like a tick?" she asked.

"No, ma'am," he continued, "like a homing device that has been inserted under your skin. Aliens and the government do that if they want to monitor your movements. There's a doctor in Denver who can remove it, if you've got one, but the magnet will disrupt its ability to transmit your location."

"Fuck!" Mona said. "All we need is to be found by those guys who shot at you and Nelson, Danny!"

"It's okay, Miss Mona," McGarvey told her. "It may just be a scratch, but go buy a magnet wrap just to be sure."

"Come on, Mona," I said, "let's go find a CVS and then a motel. I could use a hot meal and a good night's sleep."

"Do you ever think of anybody but yourself?" she asked.

"Yeah," I replied, "I plan to go to the drug store first."

Chapter 12

A t ten in the morning, Mona and I pulled up in front of Weiner's house in our new jet-black wheels. McGarvey and Martin were already there. Martin had a video camera hanging around his neck and a fanny pack with a liter bottle of water attached.

"Hey, nice Expedition, man," McGarvey said. "When did you get it?"

"Last night. I returned the barf mobile, and picked up something that has some off-road capabilities," I replied. "And Mona is wearing her magnet."

"Hi, Miss Mona," McGarvey said to my sidekick. The look on his face gave away the fact that he had a schoolboy crush on Mona. "How's the itching?" he asked.

"It's stopped," Mona replied. "I don't suppose that's good news?"

"Well, it might be. Maybe this afternoon we'll go see Dr. Rogers and let him X-ray that spot. In the meantime, you'd best keep that magnet on."

"Thanks for the advice, Mac."

The front door of the house opened, and Weiner appeared. He was wearing sunglasses and a Hawaiian shirt that made him look like some kind of tourist. I guessed that was his plan.

"Are you all ready to ride?" he asked. There was a general consensus that we ought to get going, so the Dweeb

Squad took the backseat, and Mona turned to greet everyone while I put the transmission into drive.

We headed out Route 470N again, but this time we just
followed the signs to the main terminal. As we approached,
a giant statue of a blue horse with glowing red eyes captured our attention.

"Bizarre," Mona remarked. "What kind of sick-o would
have commissioned that as a greeter?" she asked.

"Many of the locals call him 'Blucifer,'" Weiner told us.
"He freaks us out."

"I'll admit that he draws your immediate attention," I replied.

I parked in short-term parking at $4.00 per hour, and we
headed toward the revolving doors at the front of the terminal. To our right stood a tall statue of an Egyptian man with
a dog's head. "Another bizarre piece of art," I said, pointing
to it.

"Tell me about it," Weiner replied. "He's Anubis, Egyptian God of the Dead."

"So why didn't they put up a statue of a bighorn sheep?"
Mona asked. "Isn't that the Colorado state animal?"

"I'll show you. The answer is inside," Weiner replied.

We walked through the revolving doors, and once everyone was inside, Weiner directed us to the dedication
monument. "I call it a 'headstone,' because I think it fore-
tells the death of the human race, at least death for most of
us."

I couldn't believe what I read on the stone: *New World
Airport Commission.* It was boldly carved just below a Ma-
sonic emblem. "Looks like the New World Order has made
its presence known," Mona said.

"There is no such commission! But there's a lot more,"
Martin chimed. "Let's show them, Fritz."

Weiner instructed us to follow the main concourse and to
look at the murals on the walls. One showed what looked
like a German soldier in a gas mask, carrying an AK-47 and
stabbing a white dove with a sword. I thought it would be

really cheerful, if you were a Nazi. "Aren't white doves supposed to be a Christian symbol of peace?" I muttered. "Eerie."

"What do the bombed out buildings signify, Danny?" Mona asked.

"War, maybe. WW Two? I don't know. I've never been one for understanding this kind of stuff, baby."

"Look at this one, Mr. Arrow," said Weiner, pulling at my sleeve. "This one portends the end of the world."

"What do you see in this one?" I asked

"There are three caskets, one with a black, one with an American Indian, and one with a little white girl clutching a Bible." I nodded. "And look in the background. The forest is on fire, and a penguin, a bison, and a parrot are all on display as though they're extinct. Elephant tusks are stacked on the right, and a sea turtle and a dolphin are on the left."

"Yeah," I said. "Like it predicts which animals will be extinct."

"And which races," Weiner told me. "And the death of Christianity."

That one caught me by surprise.

We walked a few yards, and Weiner stopped beneath a sculpture which was positioned on the wall. "What does that look like, Miss Mona?" he asked.

"It's like one of those gargoyles you see on a medieval church, like Notre Dame in Paris," Mona replied.

"So what is it doing?"

"Like clutching its face and—oh, it's coming out of a suitcase!" Mona said with surprise.

"I like to think of it as the horror of travel," Weiner said. He took Mona and me both by our forearms. "Come on, I have one more thing to show you…"

We walked back toward the mural of the guy in the gas mask. Weiner stopped and asked, "What do you see?"

"That ugly mural and lots of people," I replied, looking around. "Some with little kids. I don't think I'd bring little kids in here to see this bizarre artwork. It would give them nightmares."

"Look down, Mr. Arrow."

We did as Weiner told us. "It's a mining cart," Mona remarked. "One of those things that you use to haul ore out of a mine."

"And?" Weiner asked. After we pondered for a few seconds, he continued, "Well, I'll tell you. The AU is the element symbol for gold, and the AG is the symbol for silver."

"Does it relate to the world economy?" I asked.

"Maybe," Weiner replied. "But AUAG is also the abbreviation for 'Australia Antigen,' which is a deadly virus."

"Oh," Mona gasped.

"Have you ever heard of the Georgia Guidestones?" Weiner asked.

"Do we look like we have?" I asked. I knew he was going to tell me about them, anyway.

"They were erected almost thirty years ago, but nobody knows who commissioned the work. The guy used a fake name: R.C. Christian."

"We think R. C. stands for Rosicrucian," Martin said.

"It's all related to the NWO, Mr. Arrow," McGarvey added.

Weiner continued, "It's a monument which consists of four huge slabs of granite. Each stone has the same message, but each one is written in one of four different languages. The message is basically a new set of Ten Commandments. The first one says to limit the Earth's population to five hundred million humans. The second one says to reproduce wisely, getting rid of those who are not perfect. And the third says to unite humanity with a single language. I can't remember all of the others, but you can check it out on the internet."

"Wow," Mona said, "how could we reduce the population of the world to five hundred million people? Isn't that like the population of the USA alone?"

"With AUAG, Miss Mona," replied McGarvey, pointing

to the mural above. "See how the guy in that mural is wearing a gas mask. We think that the NWO plans to release the AUAG virus on humanity and kill ninety percent of the human population!"

"You're shitting me," Mona exclaimed.

"I'm afraid not," Weiner told us. "It's all here. You just have to decipher the symbols and messages in the murals."

Mona looked at me and said, "Powers might have been onto this, so they snuffed him out."

"I'm seeing a slightly different picture, Mona. Don't forget the aliens. I think that the NWO and the aliens may be working in collaboration to do the deed. Maybe they'll distribute the virus from their fleet of UFOs."

"That also explains the underground fortresses, Mr. Arrow," Weiner said. "They're working down below to perfect the virus. They're testing it on abductees. They're also making mutants who are resistant to the viral strain, and antidotes for themselves. Worse yet, they have already identified who they plan to save. Before they release the virus, they will shepherd those to be saved into the underground facilities, where they'll be safe from the chaos that will happen on the surface. When the rest of humanity is dead and has rotted away, they will emerge and begin the New World Order."

"And because all the destruction will be done by a virus, all the buildings, highways, and technology will be in perfect working order. There just won't be any people other than the chosen few," Mona suggested.

"I hope you're wrong," I replied. "It's really a sick plan. A sick idea."

❧❧❧

On the way back to Centennial, Weiner told us, "We've got to go inside and take pictures and videos. If we're right about all of this, we have to blow the lid off of it and expose the New World Order for what it is."

"So when do you want to go in?" I asked. "You can count me in."

"We were planning to go last night, but you guys sort of interrupted our planning."

"Sorry about that."

"How about tonight?"

"Yeah, that sounds good. What time?" Mona asked.

"After dark. Maybe tenish, after the guards have settled down to watch late night television."

"Okay," I said, "We'll be here about nine to pick you up."

"Dress warm, and be sure Miss Mona wears jeans," McGarvey said.

"You can count on it," I replied.

On the way back to our motel, Mona turned her cell phone on and tried reaching Nelson. He didn't answer again. "I don't like this, Danny," she told me,

I nodded in agreement, but I didn't have much to add to the obvious. Nelson either was avoiding us, he was working, or he was dead.

As we passed by a small shopping center, I stopped at an army-navy store to get some black jeans and black sweatshirts for our trip into the underground. We also bought some black golf gloves and new batteries for our flashlights. We didn't need any more ammo, but I didn't think we could get any, anyway, because of the new laws requiring a state driver's license. I hadn't had time to get a fake license for Colorado from my friend Eddie yet. Actually, I hadn't needed one. I put it on my mental shopping list for some time in the future.

Chapter 13

The security commander had a look of concern on his face. Commissar Nargas disliked trouble, and he had come in person to assess the situation. "I assure you, sir," the commander told the commissar, "that we expect nothing to interrupt or delay his excellency's migration into the special container."

"Have you been able to reestablish a location on the woman?" the commissar asked. "Where you find her, you will find the man."

"Not yet, sir. We know that she has entered Denver, but the signal has experienced disruption of some sort."

"So they are here," the commissar hissed in anger. His eyes blinked from the sides. "I thought these new devices were almost flawless, Commander Beadle."

"Personally, I prefer the older tracers that were inserted into the sinus cavity on humans, but the high command has provided us only with the newer subdermic models. They can be inserted into any muscle tissue below the skin."

"So is this one defective, Commander?"

"No, sir. We tested it twice before we inserted it beneath her skin. She may be near a primitive electrical device of some kind. Small magnetic fields will sometimes interfere with the transmission of the signal on these new models. I am confident that the signal will be located shortly, sir, and when it is, we will send a squad to terminate both of them."

"Be sure you terminate the male, but take the female alive. The queen has waited almost seventy Earth years for this moment, and she will not be happy if the migration does not go well."

"And what of the other?"

"He is detained on the level above, sir. He is in one of the enclosures, awaiting migration into a recycled container in two days."

"The sooner, the better, Commander. He needs to be migrated, and his own container must be destroyed as quickly as possible."

"Yes, sir, I understand your concern. We will drain his memory banks once he has been migrated. We will then know with whom he has shared information about his work in our subterranean shelters."

"Keep me apprised, Commander. I want to know the moment that you have located her. She is not to be terminated. You are to bring her to me. She carries my seed."

"Did you—" the commander asked with surprise.

"Never with a human, Commander!" the commissar hissed. "A fertilized ovum was implanted by our technicians less than a week ago, Earth time. I was surprised that you found her near the Dulce facility a few days later and inserted the tracer. That was disturbing news."

"I am sorry, sir. We were simply following protocol with possible intruders."

"I mean you no criticism. You did as you were supposed to do. This one is just special to me."

"Yes, sir," the commander said. "I will bring her to you myself."

Chapter 14

Weiner directed me to the location of the air shaft. We had to park a hundred yards away and crawl under an eight foot tall chain link fence, but finding the shaft was a snap. "Who'd have guessed they'd put an air shaft beside the instrument landing system beacon!" I exclaimed. I thought we'd be out in the desert like we were in Dulce.

"Just stay in the shadows, and we'll be virtually invisible from the conning tower," Weiner told us.

"All ILS systems have a single power unit at the beacon station," McGarvey said. "You'll notice that this one has two, Miss Mona." McGarvey was obviously attempting to win Mona's affection with his knowledge. He hadn't figured out that she wasn't into dweebs. "The one with the louvers on all four sides is our gateway to the subterranean facility."

"Oh, I see," Mona replied.

At least I didn't think she was into dweebs.

Martin had the bolt cutters hanging opposite the water bottle on his tool belt. It was his job to cut the large padlock. He seemed to be struggling, so Mona took the cutters, repositioned them, and severed the shackle at its heel. Martin looked despondent about being emasculated by a woman. "Thanks for doing the hard part, Will," she said. "You already had it cut halfway through." I was impressed that she remembered his first name, especially since I forgot it about five seconds after he told us. Maybe sooner.

Mona handed the bolt cutters back to Martin while McGarvey removed the lock and opened the cover. The air coming from the shaft smelled slightly like diesel, or maybe like the french fries back at the Bingo Burger in Pueblo. "I'm going first," said Martin. "Will and Art will follow me, then you, and then Miss Mona."

"That's fine," I said smugly, "she likes being on top, anyway."

The expression on Mona's face turned sour. "I'm going in last because I want the dog shit from my shoes to fall on your face, fuckhead!" Mona replied in annoyance. Sometimes she had a colorful way with words, but I didn't think she really meant it. Maybe. I made a mental note not to look up for the first fifty rungs as we descended.

Before he entered the shaft, Weiner said, "Miss Mona, please be sure to lower the cover behind you once you're on the ladder. That way it won't be sticking up and look unusual to any security guards who might happen by."

"Sure thing," Mona replied.

Weiner gave a salute with his pointer finger, turned, and then began climbing down into the darkness. The rest of the dweeb squad followed, and then it was my turn. The rungs were made from round bars, which made it tough on the balls of my feet. As I entered the darkness, the LED brim lights from the caps worn by the Dweeb Squad members below me flickered on the walls. I was glad I was wearing golf gloves, because the brown dust that appeared on my palms indicated that the rungs were showing signs of rust. The bang from above me let me know that Mona had closed the cover and was on her way down. Analyzing all these clues made me feel like a scientist, or maybe like a struggling private investigator.

For what felt like an hour we climbed downward, and then I felt McGarvey's hand tap my ankle, which was the signal that I had reached the bottom. Unlike Dulce, the rungs went all the way down to the floor. I figured this was an upscale snake's den. As I stepped away from the shaft onto the concrete floor, McGarvey reached up and touched Mona's ankle. I now knew for sure that he had a thing for her. "Get your hand off of me, Danny!" she snapped.

"It's me, Miss Mona," McGarvey told her. "You've reached the bottom. Welcome to the first level."

"Thanks, Arthur," she replied. As far as I was concerned, she was being *waaay* too nice to him. If she was trying to make me jealous, it was working.

Once Mona was down, we all turned to look around. It looked like nobody was home, at least on level one. The Dweeb Squad shut off their headlamps because the ceiling level emergency spots gave us enough light to see clearly. They reminded me a little of the afterhours lights that I saw in a WalMart when I did an investigation there about two in the morning a few years back. You just didn't need anything else to find your way around.

"If I remember correctly, we need to go this way," Weiner said, pointing to his right. "There won't be anything of national interest on this level. The stairs to level two are about two hundred yards down and on our left. They'll be near the vehicle ramp."

So, we headed in that general direction, walking two abreast along the concrete wall. In the first two hundred feet, we passed two security cameras, mounted about fifteen feet above the floor. Neither appeared to be turned on because their telltale red and green lights were simply off. *Interesting*, I thought. *They certainly don't expect anyone to be down here.* I would have thought that the cameras would have been motion activated, but they weren't. It seemed odd.

Almost to the yard, we came to a ramp along the left wall. A red-on-yellow sign was painted on the wall of the ramp, with an arrow indicating level two: that-a-way. Fifteen feet past the ramp was a door with a glass window. Painted on the door was the word STAIRWAY. It appeared to me that we had found the way down, but Weiner whispered, "No, not here. We'll go down in the maintenance elevator. The stairs will probably be guarded at the lower levels."

"Okay, you're the expert when it comes to this place," I told him.

"Isn't the noise going to raise the alarm?" Mona asked.

"Probably not if we use the maintenance elevator," Weiner replied. "Only engineering and maintenance staff have keys, and I kept mine when I left. I don't know why they forgot to take it from me, but they did."

We walked another fifty feet and found a small alcove with an elevator large enough to hold a pickup truck. "Here we are!" declared Weiner. The door was open, so we all walked in, and Weiner closed the door with a pulley chain that hung to the left.

"Kind of low tech for a place that cost a billion dollars," I said.

"Two and a half billion," McGarvey replied.

I blew out a lung full of air. I think I was stressed that my tax dollars were being used for clandestine stuff like this. Then I noticed that Martin was drawing on a digital tablet of some kind. "What are you doing?" I asked.

"Making sure we can get out of here. I traced our way in, making sure that we know how many steps to take in each direction before we make a turn. It's in case the lights go out, or the batteries in our headlamps fail, or maybe they fill the cavern with smoke or something."

"Nothing like being prepared!" I replied.

"If nothing else, I can get a good sense of size when I create a scaled map at home."

He was right. It was good that he came along.

Weiner inserted his key into the control panel on the elevator wall. The panel lit up in white and yellow numbers, all the way down to level five.

"I thought there would be more levels," Mona said to Weiner.

"There probably are more. We'll have to see what we can find when we get to level five." He turned to me and asked, "What do you think? Should we stop at each level and see what we find, or just go to level five and chance it?"

I opted for the former and said, "If you guys want to know what's down here, we ought to stop at each level and take a tour. Maybe McGarvey should shoot some photos of each level for the audience at home."

"Good idea," McGarvey said, nodding at Weiner.

Weiner hit the button for level two. The elevator gave us almost no sensation of motion, except for a little jiggle when we stopped at level two.

"Just a minute," McGarvey said. He pulled a stethoscope from his fanny pack and listened to the door. "I think it's okay. There doesn't seem to be any noise outside."

Weiner pulled on the chain, and the hoist slowly lifted the door. We all stepped out. This portion of level two was lined with heavy equipment. Bulldozers, backhoes, tow motors, and several large dump trucks could be seen in the dim light from the security spots.

"Nothing worthy of a picture," McGarvey told us.

He was right. It just looked like something you'd see in a service lot inside the Baltimore Harbor Tunnel, DOT stuff, mostly painted in bright yellow, but some were painted in camouflage, desert style. But then, Martin pointed to a decal on the door of the dump truck closest to us. *New World Construction* was emblazoned in a circle of red letters. In the middle of the circle was a bird of some kind with its wings outstretched. Its feet were clutching the globe.

"It looks like an eagle with a long neck, but it's a phoenix," he told us. "It's the symbol of the NWO."

"I've seen something like that before," Mona said. "Some of the women on Capitol Hill wear them, except the globe is a large pearl."

"That would be Hillary Clinton, Barbara Bush, and a few other elitists. For the most part, there is little room for women in the NWO except as sexual objects."

"Then I think the NWO has already come into being," Mona replied. "I can't think of a time in my life when women haven't been sexual objects."

"You're probably right, Miss Mona," Martin told her. "If I could apologize for some men, I would."

"If you could apologize for Danny Arrow, I might thank you, but sometimes he's not worth your breath."

"What?" I asked. "Are you guys talking about me?"

"We're thinking that we should go down to the next level," Mona said to Weiner.

We walked back into the elevator and Weiner took us down to the third level. Again, McGarvey listened with his stethoscope before Weiner opened the door.

"This is the deepest I've ever gone," Weiner told us. "I helped plan this area as a bomb shelter for dignitaries. It has a cistern that holds enough water to feed and bathe two hundred people for a year. In the north end, we built twenty bedrooms that hold ten cots each, and there are video monitors and digital libraries with thousands of movies and sitcoms. The south end has an infirmary and a cafeteria."

"When you were building it, did you ever think that somebody would poison the Earth with a virus and use this facility to protect a chosen few?" Mona asked him.

"No, Miss Mona, I'm embarrassed to say that it was just a job. I never thought that our government would ever do anything to intentionally harm our own people."

When we stepped out of the elevator to look at level three, Weiner pointed to symbols painted on the wall. They were the same symbols used by the interstate highway authority to identify motels, restaurants, and restroom facilities as drivers approach exits. Under each symbol was an arrow pointing the proper direction. I told Weiner, "Wait for me. I have to take a leak." Mona sighed in disbelief.

I quietly walked in the direction of the restrooms, following the signs. As I walked, pallets of boxes began to appear along the concrete walls. At first, just a few dotted the floor along the walls, but then more, and then finally a warehouse full, lined the walls for as far as I could see. Using my penknife, I slit one of the unmarked boxes with an X and peeled the cardboard outward so I could see the contents. Whatever it was, it was stored in hard metal canisters, and its label was written in German. I copied the words that were stamped on the canisters onto my shirt tail with my gel pen. They can write on just about anything. I double-checked the spelling: *GIFTGASE! ZYKLON B.* Yeah, I didn't forget anything.

About fifty feet down the corridor, I found the men's room and went in. The used paper towels in the trashcan let me know that this floor is busy during the daytime. The smell from the unflushed toilet in one of the stalls also let me know that this place was used by Broncos fans... or maybe they were Yankee fans. I've seen the latter urinate in the bathroom sinks during a break in an important game. But, hey, I might have been one of them when I'd had a few beers, and the line for the urinals was just too long to wait any longer.

At any rate, I did my business, but I didn't flush. I thought it might make too much noise. Besides, a gentleman always leaves a calling card if nobody is home when he knocks.

I found my way back to the elevator, but not before checking the contents of a couple of other pallets along the way. It was the same stuff on all of them. A mountain of it, and all stored under the Denver Airport. Go figure.

"What took you so long, Danny?" Mona asked. It sounded like she really missed me.

"This whole level, at least down that way, is stacked full of pallets of some crap that I can't decipher. There's a shit-load of it. I checked three different pallets at different intervals, and it is all the same stuff." I pulled out my shirttail and read what I had written, "GIFTGASE! ZYKLON B. Does anybody know what that means?"

"I studied Latin," Martin said.

"Spanish," McGarvey said.

"Me, too," said Weiner.

"Mona?" I asked.

"Pig Latin," she told me.

"Oh, yeah," I remembered, "You took Italian."

"Grazie," she replied. "It's nice that you remember something about me after all these years."

Martin took out his cell phone and began tapping on the small keys. "I can actually access internet down here!" he exclaimed. "They must have wireless."

"Cool," McGarvey exclaimed. "See if you can find a German-English translator app."

"I'm already there. What's that first word, again?"

Mona grabbed my shirt tail and spelled the first word for him, "G-I-F-T-G-A-S-E."

"Whatever that stuff is, it is toxic. That's what giftgase means...toxic," Martin told us.

"The second word is Z-Y-K-L-O-N, space, B," Mona said.

"It doesn't translate," Martin replied.

"Try googling it," McGarvey instructed.

"Shit!" Martin said after a few seconds. "This isn't good."

"What is it?" Weiner asked.

"Zyklon B is a nerve gas. According to Wikipedia, it's the stuff the Germans used to gas the Jews in the concentration camps during World War Two. It's nasty stuff!"

"Why would the government have so much nerve gas stored down here?" Mona asked.

"It's not the government, Miss Mona," Weiner reminded her. "It's the NWO."

McGarvey rubbed his forehead and then told us, "There have been reports that a large number of train cars have been manufactured, double decker box cars with shackles. Supposedly they're stored in freight yards across the country. Some NWO conspiracy theorists think they'll be used to transport undesirables to death camps."

"You're shitting me," I replied.

"I wish I were, Mr. Arrow," Weiner said, "but all this Zyklon B makes me wonder if those reports might be true."

"Who are the undesirables?" Mona asked.

"Anybody who might pose a threat to the NWO's taking over. That would be us, but also gun owners, educators, and all individuals who have a blot on their health records."

"The NWO wants the human race to include only perfectly healthy specimens," McGarvey added. "Anybody with any type of physical disability, anybody with any type of learning disability, anybody who can't work, anyone with a history of retardation in the family, mental illness, or anything else that might be handed down genetically to the next generation. They will all be history."

"God, that's just about everybody," Mona replied.

"That's how they can reduce the world's population from seven billion to five hundred million," Weiner said. "Only one out of every fourteen people will be permitted into these underground caverns, and they'll all be hand-picked. Those of us remaining on the surface will be marked for extermination."

"This is bullshit," Mona replied.

We all nodded.

"That's why we have to stop them," I said, pointing my finger like a pistol.

"That's why we need to get irrefutable evidence and give it to the media," Weiner told us.

"So how do we get to the next level?" Mona asked.

"We ought to rethink using the elevator," Martin said. "There's too much risk of opening the door and finding a crowd."

"I agree," said Weiner. "I'm feeling spooked."

"And I'm feeling spooked that we've already come down three levels and we haven't seen anyone, not even a sentry," I said. "Where is everyone?"

"Good question, Mr. Arrow," Martin said. "I've been wondering the same thing."

"The bathroom has seen some use," I told them. "The

trashcan is full of used paper towels, and at least one of the commodes wasn't flushed."

"We'll need to be especially quiet and careful as we go to level four," Weiner replied. "I agree that all of this seems abnormal for a secure facility."

"Is there another way down?" I asked.

"Probably near the large ramp, which will be over that way," Weiner replied, pointing to our right. As he turned his back and began to walk in that direction, he muttered, "First one to see an alien is in the chowder."

The Dweeb Squad led, followed by me and then Mona. As we crept along, Martin could be heard counting his steps and then making a record of the way out on his tablet computer. McGarvey had yet to take a picture, at least that I know of. He may have taken one of Mona while I was relieving myself.

After what felt like a quarter mile, we found a down ramp. It was twenty feet high and two lanes wide, with a lane marker painted down the middle in reflective white. Like the caverns above, the walls were lit by spots, separated by about one hundred feet. You couldn't ask for better directions to the fourth floor.

"So are we going to use the ramp?" I asked Weiner.

"If we can't find a stairwell," he replied.

We broke into two groups. Weiner, McGarvey, and Mona crossed the cavern to check for stairs on the opposite wall. Martin and I continued past the ramp and kept checking the same wall we had been following from the elevator. After about five minutes, I heard motion behind me. I pulled my 1911 and spun around. It was Mona.

"Danny, put that down. If I had been the NWO, you'd have been dead ten seconds ago!"

I holstered my pistol.

"Come on," she continued, "Weiner thinks we've found a way down."

Martin and I followed Mona across the cavern to a dark shadow against the far wall. As we grew closer, we could see two forms emerge from the blackness—McGarvey and Weiner. They were bent over, struggling with something on the floor.

"What did you find?" I asked.

"It's a heavy grate, highway grade. I think it's another air shaft," Weiner replied.

I used my flashlight to inspect the shaft. Through the grating, I could see ladder rungs bolted to the concrete wall and descending as far as my puny light would illuminate. "This looks promising," I told Weiner.

"Yeah, that's what I thought," he replied. "It's just really heavy."

When Martin joined us, all four of us men grabbed the grate at one end and heaved it upward and to the right, toward the wall. It made a loud clang. We all froze. I thought I even stopped breathing for a few seconds. Fortunately, we heard nothing that made us suspect that our presence had been heard. Looking down at what we had accomplished, I felt puny when I realized that the four of us had managed to move the grate off of its concrete support and to the right, but barely five inches. As we considered our next move, Mona appeared with a six foot section of angle iron.

"Thanks, baby. Where did you find this?" I asked.

"It was against the wall, about fifty feet that way," she said motioning behind me.

"Awesome," I replied."

"You scared the shit out of me when you guys dropped that grate," Mona said. "You gotta be more careful."

"Sorry," Weiner replied, "but that thing must weigh a thousand pounds. You could drive a tank over it."

Weiner took the angle iron from Mona and slid it into the five inch gap we had created. He looked at me and said, "You have some weight, Mr. Arrow. Why don't you and I try to budge this thing together?"

I thought Mona was the only one to have something to say about my weight, but I guess I was wrong. "If you're saying that I have more muscle than your friends, then I guess you're probably right," I told him. So, I took the end, positioned myself, and pushed downward. As the grate rose, Weiner pulled against the angle iron, and we succeeded in moving the grate another six inches. Better than that, I was able to set it down quietly.

"Good boy, Danny," Mona said. "We've got it now!"

I love a little encouragement, so I looked at her and winked, thinking that she might keep it up instead of dissing me like she had been. But when I winked, she was looking the other way. I sighed, but then pushed down on the angle iron again so we could make an opening large enough to gain access to the air shaft. It took two more pushes to accomplish that feat, and when we finished, I was sweating.

After checking our gear, we climbed down the air shaft in the same order that we climbed down from the surface. Mona was last. This time, however, she couldn't close the hatch because it was just too damn heavy. And if it were closed, one man standing at the top of the rungs would never be able to open the grate alone.

About ten feet down, the Dweeb Squad began turning on their brim lights. I noticed that it was dark and cool in this shaft, and there was no scent of diesel. But coming from the distant cavern below, I thought I could hear an occasional noise. However, I wasn't sure. I was beginning to feel uneasy, like the way a field mouse must feel when he suspects that he's going to come across a snake in the depths of his burrow. Something—maybe the lack of sentries, maybe the lack of any activity on the first three levels—just wasn't right, but I had no way of knowing what it was. In my belly, I wished that Mona had not come with us. I loved her, yes I admitted to myself that I loved her, just too damn much to have anything bad happen to her, especially a thousand feet or more beneath the ground.

My arms were beginning to tire when word came up from below that we had come upon a diagonal vent that was labeled "4" in red paint. It led away from this main shaft in both directions, so we divided again to explore it. We formed the same groups: Martin and I headed to the right, and Mona, Weiner, and McGarvey headed to the left. We agreed to meet back at the main shaft in twenty minutes. I looked at my watch. It was nearly midnight. *No sleep tonight,* I thought.

The vent that Martin and I followed was about five feet high, so we could walk, as long as we were hunched over. Walking that way was crippling, especially since my legs were hurting from the two downward climbs I had already made tonight. Why couldn't we simply have taken the ramp? Well, I told myself, all we needed was to get shot at by tall guys with ray guns like Nelson and I had in Dulce. It was simply too risky, and who knows when the cameras along the ramps might be activated, and some security guard would discover us. At least in these vents, we stood a chance of not being discovered.

About one hundred fifty yards into the vent, Martin and I came upon a fan that was mounted perpendicular to the vent and was slowly turning. Through the moving fan blades and a louvered cover beyond it, we could look out into a chamber of some sort that must have been part of level four. In the dim light, there were rows of cots, laid out in military fashion, as far as we could see.

On the far wall hung two red flags. One bore the same gold NWO symbol we had seen on the truck a level above. The other was a shocker. "Nazis!" Martin whispered to me in surprise.

"Fuck!" I whispered back. "What the fuck are they doing down here? World War Two was over like seventy years ago."

"I don't like it, Mr. Arrow," Martin replied, "especially with all of those gas canisters upstairs. Something isn't right, down here."

"We have to get McGarvey over here so he can take some pictures!" I whispered.

"This will make national headlines, *won't it?*" Martin chimed.

We decided to follow the vent to the next fan to see what else might be down on level four. It was another hundred-yard hike, but I was feeling less bodily pain since discovering Nazis under the Denver Airport. When we looked out through the second vent, we saw more cots, all occupied. Occasionally one of the troopers would stir, but nobody knew we were there. From our vantage point, we could see light emanating from an office on the far wall. Someone was working, but we couldn't see who or what. My guess was that one of the Nazis was pulling night duty.

"How many Nazis do you think there are down here, Mr. Arrow?" Martin asked.

"Count the rows of cots from this wall to the far wall. Let's see if we get the same number." I counted about thirty cots, but I couldn't be certain.

"I think maybe twenty-five."

"Okay, we'll use your number. Each cot and the space between it and the next cot takes up about six feet. Let's guess that this chamber is an eighth of a mile long. So how many columns do we have?"

"That's six hundred sixty columns times twenty-five, which equals sixteen thousand, five hundred!"

Obviously, I figured, Martin was working things out on his digital pad. Nobody could multiply that fast in his head. "That's one hell of an attack force," I said, "especially if they do their business in the dark. Our civilian populace wouldn't stand a chance against such a force, at least not until a civilian militia is formed!"

"Maybe we should get back to the shaft so we can tell the others what we've found," Martin suggested.

"That's probably a good idea," I replied. "We have about ten minutes to get back. It should be a piece of cake."

The hike back would have been quicker, but we stopped twice to sit on the concrete floor of the vent and stretch our legs out straight. Martin complained about his neck and lower back being strained by walking stooped over. In my head, I thanked him for the two breaks. I really needed them as well, but I didn't share my misery because I didn't want him to think that I was a pantywaist.

When we got to the intersection of the shaft and the two vents, we sat on our knees and waited for the others to appear. It took longer than I had anticipated. Maybe Weiner hadn't checked his watch. It was a long five minutes before they appeared at the mouth of the vent.

Mona's face was the first to appear. "Danny," she whispered excitedly, "we saw Nazis. Can you believe that shit? Nazis!"

"So did we, all sleeping like little babies. I'd like to have set off a dozen canisters of that nerve gas!" I told her. "How many did you see?"

"Hundreds. It was hard to tell. They were sleeping in cots, lots of cots."

"We saw the same thing, Mona. Rows and rows of cots. We estimated maybe sixteen thousand Nazis."

"How is that possible?" Mona asked.

"NWO!" Weiner said, as he peeked around Mona and scooted beside her. "They have to be in league with the NWO."

"Did McGarvey do his thing?" Martin asked.

From behind Mona came McGarvey's voice in a loud whisper, "I took about twenty pics from two vantage points. Hopefully, they'll turn out okay. There wasn't much light, and I shut off my flash so I wouldn't draw anybody's attention."

"They're going to be just fine, Arthur," Mona said. "I have the utmost confidence in your camera skills."

I rolled my eyes at Mona's coddling of McGarvey. "How about we keep going," I suggested. "As long as we know what's happening on the fourth level, there's no use in hanging around in these vents. And, we certainly aren't going to go inside and ask those suckers to dance."

"I agree," said Weiner.

"Me, too," said Mona. I love it when she agrees with me.

We went down as we had before, with Mona taking the

last position on the rungs. At least it was some kind of protection for her against whatever lay below. This time, though, our brim lights were still on because there was simply no light in this shaft or the vents, except for the little bit that crept in wherever the fans were installed.

When we reached level five, we found the same type of red numbers painted above the openings to the vents that stretched out in opposite directions. From the mechanical noises, the clanging and squeaking of metal on metal and metal on concrete, we knew there was definitely activity on level five in the middle of the night. I was anxious to see what was causing it. This time, McGarvey and I went left, while Mona, Martin, and Weiner went right. As before, we had to hunch over if we intended to walk, and it was definitely tougher walking here than on level four because my legs weren't getting any younger and they had gotten quite a workout already.

When we reached the first fan unit, we discovered that it wasn't running. Instead, the large fan blades were motionless, giving us enough room to squeeze a torso between the blades for a close look between the louvers at what lay inside the level five cavern. Because he was the skinner of us, I gave McGarvey the first peek.

"Cages!" he told me. "Hundreds of cages!"

"What's in them?" I asked.

Without warning, McGarvey turned on his flashlight and aimed it through the louvers and onto the floor below. From below, there came a clatter of cage wire and commotion as the occupants of the cages reacted to the sudden appearance of light.

"Shit," he exclaimed. "Those cages have both humans and animals in them. Give me a second, and you can look."

Again, without warning, McGarvey put the lens of his digital camera to the louvers and pressed the shutter button. The flash of light was blinding. Instantly, the cages began rattling, but this time simian-like shrieks and screams burst into the darkness.

"Stop it with the flash," I snapped.

"I have to record this, Mr. Arrow," McGarvey replied. "Nobody will believe it if I don't!"

The loud bang of metal against metal rang out, as if someone had opened and slammed a metal door. Then the squealing sound of heavy metal on concrete pierced my ears. Again, the slamming of a metal door. The cages below rocked with commotion for a third time.

I pulled at McGarvey's sleeve and motioned for him to move back from the louvered panel.

"Just one more picture," he pleaded.

"Not now. Let's back away until things settle down again."

I could see the look of frustration on his face, but he agreed to pull himself back through the fan blades. As he did, we retreated into the darkness of the vent. It was none too soon.

The sound of footsteps and a man's voice let us know that we might have been discovered if McGarvey had remained to take another picture.

"Hush, now," the voice said. "What's got you boys on edge? You should be asleep."

"What's with the lights, Granger? Are they coming?" another voice asked.

"No lights tonight, Nelson. Get some sleep. You've got another day."

"Yes, there were lights, Granger. Something flashed, and it was bright. Y'all heard the commotion. I'm not the only one it woke."

"I'll look around. Maybe a light bulb blew. I can't fathom what else it might have been. Now go on and get some sleep."

I could hear the footsteps move away. As they did, a few more simian screams pierced the night. Then the creaking sound of a heavy door opening was followed by the clang of its being shut. The one called Granger had left the area.

I shuffled past McGarvey and pushed my torso through

the fan blades. "Pssst!" I whispered. "Hey, you!"

Silence.

"Pssst. Hey, Nelson! Are you from Dulce?" I asked.

"Who is it?" a voice replied from directly beneath the vent cover.

"Are you Nelson from Dulce? It's me, Dan Arrow!"

"Arrow! Is it really you?"

"Yes. I was with you just a couple of days ago in Dulce. Mona and I met you at that Apache bar."

"It *is* you, Arrow!" Nelson exclaimed. "How did y'all know where I was?"

"Dumb luck. Mona's been calling you every day, sometimes twice. We've been worried about you."

"I don't have my phone. They took it from me. They came for me about an hour after y'all left me with that cop."

"Who came?" I asked.

"Three really tall dudes. They all looked the same. Dark eyes, blond hair. They put me into a black Expedition and took me into the desert. I thought I was a dead man."

"How did you get here?"

"Some kind of underground transportation system. Very smooth. It was like a horizontal elevator ride, except no noise. Something electric that made my hair all full of static."

"You're shitting me. You went from Dulce to Denver underground! How long did it take?"

"Is that where I am? Denver? I was guessing somewhere else in New Mexico or Arizona. I was in that transport for maybe an hour."

"Mona is going to be glad we found you," I said.

"Is she here, too?"

"Yeah, we came with the Dweeb Squad to see what was down here. You're the last thing I expected to find."

"Can y'all get me out of here?" Nelson asked.

"I'll try. I'll have to figure out how to get inside without making a disturbance. Some of the dweebs may have a suggestion."

"It has to be no later than tomorrow night."

"Why's that?"

"They have me scheduled for migration the day after tomorrow."

"Migration?" I asked.

"From what I've gathered from Granger, the aliens have the technology to move a person from one body to another. Granger calls bodies 'containers.' They're going to move me into another container. That's what they mean by 'migration.' If y'all don't get me out of here, the next time y'all hear a stranger call you by your first name, it'll be me."

"Do you think they can put an alien into someone else's body?"

"Don't you mean to ask me if I think that it is possible that some of our leaders could be aliens who have been migrated into human bodies? I thought about that, too. Granger says they can't do that yet, but they're working on it."

"What's with this Granger guy? You two seem to have hit it off."

"Granger Taylor is his name. He's like me, a technical kind of guy. He says the aliens contacted him about thirty-five years ago. They promised him a forty-two day journey through the universe, but, instead, they gave him a ten minute ride around the planet and then took him to Dulce. He's been working for them since then, mostly taking care of captives. He says he has to work or they won't feed him."

"Do you think he'd tell you how to escape?"

"I don't know. I can ask him how someone might get out of here. Maybe he'll help me."

"Have you seen any more aliens?"

"They're like ants, Dan. The little guys all look the same, like they came off of the assembly line in a Chinese robot factory. They can send a man messages telepathically, but only if you have eye contact with them. If you ever see one again, don't look it in the eyes."

"What about the tall ones?"

"The tall blonds or the lizards?

"Tell me about both."

"The tall blonds are the ones that drove me into the desert. They don't talk much. They're like Mafia goons. They like to give orders. I don't think they're smart, they're just big and physical, and they get things done by intimidating a fella."

"And the lizards?"

"They're the smart ones, and they control everything. I think they invented the little guys. I've seen a couple of the scientist types and a couple of the soldiers from a distance, but they tend to stay away from this part of the facility. Granger says that they mostly stay in the lower levels."

"You're on level five," I told him.

"Granger calls this the holding area." Nelson became more serious. "Dan," he said with a hint of terror in his voice, "y'all have got to get me out of here! I don't want to be migrated. It sounds horrible, and Granger says that the new body often rejects a fella after a few weeks."

"I'll do what I can, but you have to get us some information about how to get out of this snake den from that guy Granger."

"Yeah," he replied. "I'll talk to him when he comes back."

I pulled myself from between the fan blades and said to McGarvey, "Go ahead and take a few more pictures. Maybe that guy Granger will come back."

McGarvey squeezed into the opening and started flashing his camera. Simian squeals and screeches erupted, as did the rattling and banging of cages. I imagined that the sound was similar to what would happen if somebody started playing Yoko Ono music in the middle of the night at the Washington Zoo.

When McGarvey was finished, we turned and headed back down the vent to meet the others at the shaft. We were last to arrive.

"Was that you guys causing all the commotion?" Mona asked when we got there.

"It was McGarvey and his camera flash," I replied. "The creatures in those cages don't like sudden bursts of light."

"They aren't creatures, Danny," Mona said. "They're people. We saw people through both fan ducts, but some of them were like movie monsters. Some had feathers growing out of their backs. Others had claws or hooves instead of hands. They are like the lab rats that we grow human ears on, Danny. It was horrible."

I wanted to hold Mona and comfort her, but she was across the shaft from me. I extended my hand, and she grabbed it. Her eyes were full of tears.

"Baby, I have some important news. Maybe good news," I told her.

"What is it?" Weiner asked, poking his head around Mona's shoulder.

I ignored him. "Nelson's here, Mona," I said.

"Nelson? Here?" she asked. "Where?"

"He's in one of the cages at the first fan vent on this side."

"Who is Nelson?" Weiner asked.

"Nelson is a friend who took us into a vent shaft in Dulce," Mona told him. "He was with Danny when they were shot at by the aliens." She turned to me and asked, "Is he okay?"

"He's scheduled to be moved the day after tomorrow. He's hoping we can help him escape." I didn't tell her that he was going to be moved from one physical body to another. I thought it would be too much information for her to swallow at the wrong time.

"Impossible, Mr. Arrow!" Weiner snapped. "We don't even know if we can get ourselves out of here. What will happen if we break into this cavern and try to free one of the captives? We'll have every Nazi in this place on us in no time!"

"Yeah, and the aliens, too!" I told him. "They're down on the next level."

"So they *are* here," he replied.

"You betcha," I said, "and I ain't leaving Nelson down here to be some kind of guinea pig. I owe the guy that much."

Chapter 15

McGarvey and I left Mona with the Dweeb Squad at the entrance to the shaft, and we went back to see if the commotion had caused Granger to come back out into the cavern.

I was hoping that Nelson had had a chance to talk with him, although no more than twenty minutes had elapsed since we had left Nelson.

When we got back to the fan vent, I once again pushed my torso between the fan blades and tried to raise Nelson.

"Pssst, Nelson! Are you there?"

"Dan, is that you? Did you bring Mona?" he replied.

I could see him looking up, trying to see my face through the louvers in the vent cover. "No," I replied. "It's better that she isn't here right now, in case we have any trouble."

"That's probably a smart move, Dan."

"Did you get a chance to talk to Granger," I asked.

"Better than that, Dan."

"What do you mean?"

Suddenly a face rose from the bottom of the louvered vent cover. I pulled backward in surprise, scratching my arm on a fan blade.

"Howdy, I'm Granger Taylor."

"Jesus, you scared the shit out of me," I said.

"Sorry," he said. "Are you Nelson's friend?"

"Yes, my name is Dan Arrow. Behind me is Art McGarvey."

"Hi," McGarvey said over my shoulder. "Pleased to meet you, Granger."

"Nelson told me that you've been down here awhile," I said.

"Yup. It's been a long time since I done seen the sun. I just sit under them sun lamps to get vitamin D."

Through the louvers, I could tell that Granger was in his mid-sixties. His white hair and wrinkles gave his age away. But he appeared tall and strong for a man of his years.

"Nelson tells me that they plan to migrate him into a new container in a couple of days. Is that so?"

"Yup. He's scheduled, not for tomorrow, but for the next day. They're preparing a special container for him. It's something experimental."

"Well, Granger, Nelson doesn't want to be migrated."

"You're damn right I don't!" Nelson added emphatically.

"Is there any way to get him out of that cage before they take him?" I asked.

"Nelson and I was talking about that before you came."

"And?" I asked.

"I figure the best way out is through that vent that you're in. He could go with you."

"Can you open his cage?"

"I'm not supposed to. I could get into trouble," he replied. "But the way I see it, they lied to me about seeing the universe thirty-five years ago, so I don't mind helping another fella."

"Do you want to come with us?" I asked.

"I don't rightly know," he said thoughtfully. "My parents are probably dead by now. Don't know if the house is still there for me to live in."

"Don't worry about houses and money, Granger," Nelson told him. "You'll make a fortune, telling your story about being deceived by the aliens, and telling everything you know about them and what they're doing down here. Besides, there's still time to spend many days out in the sun."

"I suppose it's past time, ain't it?"

"Great. It'll be good to have you come with us," I replied. "So how do we get Nelson out of that cage?" I asked. "And how do we get this vent hood off so you guys can climb in here?"

"It'll take a few minutes to find all the tools I need," Granger said. "I'll be back in about half an hour. Now, don't you go away or nothing, Mr. Arrow. I promised to help Nelson, and I am good to my word."

"I'll be right here when you get back, Granger. And please call me Dan."

"Okey-dokey," he replied. "I'll see you fellas in about half an hour, Mr. Arrow."

I told McGarvey to stay put and talk to Nelson, while I went back to the main shaft to speak with the others. He agreed. I think he wasn't interested in another hunched hike through the vent, anyway. At least not yet.

လာင်္လာ

When I got back to the others, I told them about our plan. "Nelson's found a friend down here who's going to help me get him out of the cage."

"Friend? Do you mean an alien?" Weiner asked.

"No, he's a guy who they impressed into service over thirty years ago. He wants to help, and he's coming out with us. His name is Granger."

"How do you know we can trust him?" Mona asked.

"I don't," I replied. "That's why you and the Dweebs are going to start back up the shaft. If he's going to double-cross us, I want you guys out of here, especially you, Mona."

"You're not saying that I'm too weak to handle anything we'd encounter, are you, Danny?" Mona asked, looking perturbed at me.

"No, baby, I'm saying that I love you, and I don't want anything bad to happen to you."

"You pick now to tell me that?" Mona replied. "Why now? Why not a day ago? Why not two years ago?" She pointed her finger at me. "You got some bad sense of timing, Dan Arrow. You've never known what time it is!"

"Mona, please listen to me. If this guy double-crosses us, this place will be swarming with aliens and Nazis. If you and the Dweebs get out now, you can tell the world what you've seen down here and maybe stop this NWO thing."

"Is that all, Danny?" she asked. "Isn't there something else?"

I reached across the shaft and took her by the hands. "Mona, I love you. If we get out of this alive, I want to marry you and make up for all the pain I've caused you."

Mona leaned forward to try to kiss me. The position was awkward, and I had to grab one of the rungs to keep us from falling down the shaft. When our lips met, it was wonderful. But then Weiner interrupted. "Come on, you two. There's plenty of time for that later. We've got to get your bride up to the surface."

Mona gave him one of her curt replies, "I never said I was going to marry him." Then, she climbed onto the rungs, leaned over and kissed me again. "I love you, Danny. Be sure to come back out to me alive!" she told me.

"You can count on it, baby."

I watched as she began climbing up into the darkness. Weiner was next. As he got onto the rungs, he asked, "What about McGarvey?"

"He's going to stay with me. When Granger and Nelson open the vent cover, McGarvey's going to have a heyday shooting pictures of what's in those cages. We need those pictures to prove what's down here."

Weiner agreed and then began his ascent. He was followed by Martin, who asked, "Do you think you can find your way out?"

"I've found my way out of worse places than this," I assured him. But, to be honest, I wasn't too sure. Besides that, we'd been underground for a long time, and I wasn't sure how long the batteries in our brim lights would last. I hadn't brought any extras.

Chapter 16

When the reptilian technician turned to the small gray alien who stood beside him, his serpentine scales were reflected as rainbow hues by the Grey's large onyx eyes. "Get the commander immediately!" he hissed. The Grey turned and hurried out of the dark room.

Within a minute, the Grey was back. When Security Commander Beadle entered the room behind him, a sentry at the door snapped to attention.

"I hope this is important, Corporal Zydo."

"Sir, see the small pulse on the monitor!" Zydo said excitedly as he pointed to the green monitor in front of him.

"Barely, Zydo. What do you think it is?"

"It is the signal that you have been asking about, the one in the female human. The one that might have been malfunctioning."

"Excellent, Corporal. Where is she?"

"Sir, the signal is weak, but it appears that she is here."

"What do you mean, here?"

"Inside the facility, Commander."

"Impossible," the commander hissed.

"Sir, because our receptors are on the surface in the surrounding mountains, the thick rock and concrete have diminished the strength of the signal, but I have double checked the vectors. She is inside the facility, between the fourth and third levels."

"Then she is in the tunnel! Is she descending?"

"Sir, she is not in the tunnel. It appears that she is in an air shaft and that she is ascending."

The commander looked closely at the monitor. "We will intercept her on level three. The male will be with her!" His tongue darted out in anticipation. Placing his three-fingered claw on the technician's shoulder, he said, "Good work, Sergeant."

"Sir, I am a corporal."

"No, you are now a sergeant, Zydo."

Chapter 17

Mona's arms were aching, but she pulled herself high enough to peer out of the grate that was still ajar from its resting position on the floor of level three. As before, there appeared to be no activity on this level. She looked below her and said, "It looks all clear."

Fritz Weiner, who was eight feet below her on the rungs, gave the thumbs-up sign and said, "Outstanding!" He then passed the word on to Martin, who was another few rungs below.

"Good!" Martin replied. "My palms have blisters on them."

Mona offered each man a hand as he climbed out of the air shaft and onto the concrete floor. Once they all were out of the shaft, she sat on the floor and rested her back against the rock wall of the cavern. Martin and Weiner joined her.

"Which way to the elevator?" Mona asked.

Martin looked at his digital tablet. "Across the cavern and then two hundred yards to the right along the wall," he replied. "The elevator will be in a small alcove."

"We should probably get going, Miss Mona," Weiner said. "As it gets closer to dawn, there's a greater possibility of activity down here."

The three struggled to their feet. Mona put her hands on the small of her back and stretched her shoulders backward.

"I thought Danny was the only guy who could show a girl such a good time," she said.

Because he had the tablet, Martin led the way. At the sound of something mechanical starting up, they froze for a moment but continued walking quietly when nothing else accompanied the humming. When they reached the wall across the cavern, they followed it to the right. After fifty yards, they discovered the ramp that descended to level four. "Just another hundred yards or so and we'll be at the elevator," Martin said in a tone that conveyed his joy at nearing the surface.

"I hope Danny and McGarvey are okay," Mona said, feeling the texture of the wall with her left hand.

"We'll wait for them in the Expedition. They may be as much as an hour behind us," Weiner replied.

"I left a thermos of coffee and some sandwiches in the back seat," Martin told them. "There is enough for all of us."

"Outstanding," Mona said. "Right now I could go for some Dweeb Squad rations!"

"Is peanut butter okay?" Martin asked.

"I love it," Mona told him.

"Shhh!" Weiner whispered. "I thought I heard something behind us!" The trio froze again. The humming of a mechanical system was the only audible sound.

Weiner took the lead as the small group continued along the wall in the semi-dark cavern. Soon, the wall made an abrupt turn to the left, and they were at the alcove. Peeking around the corner to ensure that all was safe, Weiner waved his comrades forward. "Everything still looks good," he said.

The three clustered in front of the closed elevator doors. Weiner pressed the call button, and the outer doors opened. Reaching above his head with both hands, he began pulling the chain to raise the heavy inner door. As the bottom of the door reached four feet high, a blinding flash of light ripped through Weiner, severing him in half at the waist. Mona and

Martin both covered their eyes, unsure of what had happened. Mona screamed as a second flash of light decapitated Martin, and his headless body fell against her, knocking her to the ground. Mona reached behind her back and pulled her nine-millimeter pistol from her waistband. But before she could aim at anything, a strong hand grabbed her wrist, and another wrenched the weapon from her hand.

"I should have known you lizards would be in there when the doors were closed," Mona said, still squinting from the bright flashes of light.

One reptilian soldier held her from behind by her elbows. Another turned her head toward the Security Commander so he could look her in the eyes. His lips did not move, but Mona clearly heard him say, "Commissar Nargas wants to see you." The giant lizard's tongue darted out, and Mona closed her eyes, repulsed by his appearance. The Commander placed a small round object against Mona's forehead and pressed down. It lit, and Mona fell unconscious into the arms of her captor.

"This is, indeed, a good morning!" Commander Beadle hissed. "Leave those containers for our allies to deal with."

Within a few moments, the wall across the alcove began to shimmer. Beadle and two reptilian soldiers, one carrying Mona, walked through the wall, as though it were only an illusion. Once inside a small crystalline room, Beadle touched a panel, and the room and its occupants descended through the rock to level six.

ళ⌒ళ⌒ళ

When Mona regained consciousness, she was lying on a metallic lounge chair. "Where am I?" she wondered. She blinked and then squinted her eyes, clearing her blurred vision. Her head ached, especially in the frontal lobes. "Like a serious migraine," she told herself. When she tried to sit up, she discovered that she could not make her muscles move, although she was not bound by any visible shackles. She tried to call out for help, but her mouth would not open. All motion was restricted to her eyes, which moved freely in their sockets. Above her, the ceiling appeared to be made from melted glass. Attached to the ceiling and running above her were multiple conduits and pipes. Soft white light emanated from the walls, which were made from the same material as the ceiling. She was not in an examination room but, rather, in something more like an outer office or waiting room. She heard a noise from behind her. "Who the fuck is here?" she wondered. "Am I going to be hurt?" A rush of fear shot through her body.

Mona moved her eyes upward, straining to see who was there. Two figures moved from her left and stood beside her. She recognized the taller one as the lizard who had captured her outside the elevator at level three. His face was covered with pale green scales which blended into creamy yellow near his neck. He wore a skin-tight, black-and-silver uniform of some sort. She didn't recognize the gold symbol on his collar. It was a circle with two diagonal bars crossing it. On his chest was a panel with several oval buttons. "Death ray!" she told herself, remembering Danny's story of his encounter below Dulce.

The other lizard was several inches shorter. His face was covered by small, grayish-blue scales. His iridescent black clothes were looser fitting. Crossing his chest, bold maroon and silver stripes denoted authority that even a human could sense. On his collar was a gold insignia that clearly resembled the phoenix she had seen in the NWO symbol that was painted on the doors of the trucks on the second level. He did not appear to have a weapon. This smaller lizard looked into Mona's eyes, and without moving his lips, she heard him say, '*Have no fear. I have ensured that you will not be harmed. It is nice to see you again.*'

Again? Mona thought. *What does he mean, again?*

'*We have met before,*' he told her. '*In my tureen.*'

Tureen? she wondered.

'*You would call it a ship, or saucer. We met above Dulce. Your container carries my seed.*'

What does he mean? Mona thought. *I don't understand.*

The alien heard her thoughts. '*Our child is within you,*' he told her.

Mona's thoughts turned to revulsion. She imagined this creature on top of her naked body, entering her privates with some hideous phallus. Her eyes filled with tears. *You raped me?* Mona thought. *If I'm pregnant, I will reject this monster inside me.*

'*It is done,*' he told her, '*but I find your body equally repulsive. We performed what you would call artificial insemination. It was brief and painless.*'

Mona searched her memory but could find no recollection of what this lizard told her. *That's bullshit*, she thought.

'*Your egg has been fertilized with a human sperm that has been modified with my DNA. The code has been modified to carry the intelligence and longevity of my species, but to carry the physical characteristics of your species.*'

Mona continued to feel revulsion, mixed with her natural anger. *You have no right to put an alien object into my body against my will. It is still rape, and rape is not condoned by mankind.*

'*We were given the right to interbreed with humans by the leaders of the atomic nations of Earth in your year 1958. The Great One has agreed to facilitate our peaceful emergence into a shared outer world. It is all according to the master plan. Your leaders are in agreement. Soon, this planet will be controlled by one government and wars will cease to exist.*'

You're speaking in bullshit riddles, Mona replied through her thoughts. *And when I can get free from this chair, I'm going to castrate your ugly pecker and abort this beast inside me!*

'*When it is time, you will see our child,*' he continued, '*and your fear will turn to affection for the little one.*'

I'll kill it, Mona thought, *and then I'll kill you!*

'*You Earth females never kill our offspring. Your maternal instincts are like none other in the galaxy. Your kind are nurturers. That is why your species has degenerated to its present status. Your maternal nurturing of the deformed has shortened your lifespan to less than a century, and your intelligence has been compromised by permitting the feeble and the unintelligent to breed.*'

Mona's eyes filled with tears again. She imagined that she could feel the entity within her and she wanted to rip it out of her belly. *I want it gone,* she thought.

'*Not yet,*' the lizard told her. '*When it is time.*'

"Commissar Nargas," the other alien interrupted. "She had two males with her."

"And what of them, Commander Beadle?" the commissar asked, turning his gaze away from Mona.

"Terminated."

"Excellent. Her male will not interfere with the migration of the Great One into his new container. The day of our emergence will soon be at hand. The queen will be pleased."

Commissar Nargas returned his gaze to Mona. '*Your male is dead,*' he told her. '*You are now a guest inside our facility. It is time for you to eat and to rest. Our offspring requires your container to fulfill its function.*'

Dead? Danny is dead?

'*Yes, your male is dead.*'

Tears gushed from Mona's eyes. Her thoughts rocketed back to kissing Danny, to passionately making love to him, to the depression she experienced when he left her, to being with him again so recently, and to wanting to feel him inside her again. She wanted to join him in death.

The commissar beckoned to his left. From across the room, two gray aliens appeared. They went about their business unemotionally, like vet med technicians preparing a dog for a vasectomy. One carried a small metallic cylinder in its three fingered hand. The other rubbed a solution on

Mona's neck. The first then inserted a needle into her wet flesh, while the second pressed a circular object upon her forehead. It lit briefly and, as she lost consciousness, Mona's last thoughts were of the unrequited love she held for Danny Arrow, now deceased.

Chapter 18

I'm back," I said. "The others are headed up the shaft."
"Good," McGarvey replied. "Granger is removing the
bolts that hold the louvered vent on the wall. I'm pulling back on it so it won't fall to the floor."

"Do you need a break?" I asked.

"Naw, I've got it. I fished my belt through it."

"Is that Mr. Arrow?" Granger asked.

"Yes, Granger," I replied. "What can I do to help?"

"Just hold your breath that this thing don't clang to the
floor. The last bolt is almost out."

Over McGarvey's shoulders and through the louvers I
could see Granger's face moving, and I could hear him issue a small grunt with each turn of the wrench. It must have
been a subconscious habit from years of performing manual
tasks for the aliens.

"There it is," he said, holding the last bolt up for
McGarvey to see. "Let loose of your hold on that cover. I
got it now."

McGarvey slowly loosened his grip on his belt, and
Granger lowered the vent cover to the floor. "What size are
them bolts that are holding the fan in place?" Granger
asked.

"They look like half inch heads," McGarvey replied.

Granger disappeared for a few moments and then returned with a smaller wrench. "These are easier," he said as

he began loosening the four smaller bolts that held the fan in place.

In less than five minutes, the fan was free from its anchors. Granger opened the small electrical box, unscrewed the caps that held the wires in place, and lowered the fan to the floor. McGarvey was the first to climb down onto the concrete floor, and then I followed. It felt good to stand erect again.

"Dan, it's damn good to see you," Nelson said, extending his hand through the grid on his cage. I shook it.

"How do we get you out of this thing?" I asked.

"It's on an electrical circuit. I'm not sure where the breaker panel is. Maybe Granger knows. Just get me out."

"Be patient a little longer, and we'll figure this out," I told him.

McGarvey and I followed Granger back to his shop area. Along the way, McGarvey stopped every few steps to take a picture of the beings inside the cages. As he did, the creatures nearby stirred, but it was the middle of the night, so none moved for long before drifting back to sleep. I couldn't help thinking that the rows of cages reminded me of a dog shelter. The area even smelled a bit like one. Sanitation didn't appear to be a concern. Like Mona told me, the beings inhabiting the cages were mostly people, and most were deformed in some way. It was grisly.

"Come on, Mr. Arrow," Granger said. "We have only two hours before they come to take a few of these people out of here to continue their experiments.

᎒Ꮛ᎒Ꮛ᎒

Granger's workshop was a mess and just the kind of place that seemed perfect for a man of his age to tinker with small mechanical devices.

"How do we get Nelson out of that cage, Granger?" I asked.

"The panel is on the wall. They open it whenever they need to take a specific person out of a cage. They have a device that they put on the door to open the breaker panel. I think it's sonic. When they push a button, the device beeps, and the panel opens."

McGarvey was the first to think of an alternative. "Can we short-circuit the electronics somewhere between this panel and the cage?" he asked.

"We'd have to be careful not to set off an alarm," Granger replied. "They have all sorts of back-up systems."

McGarvey began looking through Granger's work benches. Within a few minutes, he held up some alligator clips and loose wires. "These may do the trick."

"How so?" I asked.

"We scrape the insulation off of the wires, attach the alligator clips, and run a wire between them, creating a complete circuit. Then we cut the wires beyond the splice, and we should be home free."

"Ain't going to work," Granger told him. "They use printed circuits, like on computer motherboards."

"You got anything that we can use to short out the printed circuits?" McGarvey asked.

"Come to think of it, yeah, I do. I got a battery operated soldering iron. All I need is some gold. Their circuits are made of gold."

"Can you melt some off of my watch?" I asked. "My watchband is supposed to be plated with twenty-four-karat gold."

"It'll be a very thin layer if it's plate, but maybe I can get enough off of it to do the trick," Granger said.

I removed my watch and handed it to him. I hoped that the guy who sold me that watch wasn't bullshitting me about the band. I paid almost fifty bucks for it in a casino in Atlantic City. The guy was broke and claimed that his slot was going to pay off soon. Maybe I got ripped off.

Granger took the band from the watch, handed back the watch, and put the band in a metal cup, which he held over a Bunsen burner. "This ain't plate," he said after a minute. My hopes fell. "It might be pure gold," he exclaimed. "Look at it melt!"

Thank God for gambling addicts, I thought. Things were looking up!

When Granger was finished, he packed a few things into a small tool bag, and the three of us walked back through the dog shelter toward Nelson's cage. At the sound of our footsteps, some of the creatures began stirring. *It's definitely getting closer to breakfast time,* I thought.

As I passed one of the larger cages, without warning a hand grabbed my arm. I froze and turned my head to see what was holding me. McGarvey stopped as well to see what had happened. An older woman, maybe in her early seventies, had my arm. "Did I hear Granger call you 'Mr. Arrow' when you passed by earlier?" she asked me.

"Yeah. What's it to you?" I replied.

"Are you Dan Arrow, the detective?"

"Yeah, I guess so," I answered, wondering how she knew me.

"It's me, Mr. Arrow," she said with a look of hope in her eyes. "It's me, Billy Powers!"

I was so surprised by her claim that you could have knocked me over with a feather. "Come on, lady," I begged. "Please let go. I've got things to do." I guess I could have broken free from her grip, but she was an old lady, and I didn't want to hurt her. "I'll be back in a few days with the authorities, and all of you will get out of here."

"It may be too late for me, Mr. Arrow. You have to believe me. I am Billy Powers."

"Billy Powers is dead," I replied.

"I called you to make an appointment. I didn't get there, but I sent you a package with my notebook. You got it didn't you?" she asked.

"Yeah, I got a package from Powers," I said.

"It was from me. Did my wife come to see you? I called her and told her to go see you if I was found murdered."

I was still having trouble getting my head around the idea that Billy Powers might be a woman, but this alien stuff was sending me into all kinds of new territory. Nonetheless, she was telling me stuff about Powers that nobody other than Powers could have known.

"How did they leave my body?" she asked.

"Powers strangled himself with surgical tubing," I replied.

"No," she said, "they migrated me into the magnetic field of a superconductor battery. When my body stopped functioning, they staged it to look like a suicide. The real me, my electrical essence, was plenty alive inside the magnetic field. It was painless, but I couldn't see or hear anything. I simply was. It's hard to explain."

I didn't understand all this stuff about superconductors, so McGarvey filled me in. He sounded like an encyclopedia when he said, "Superconductors are metal matrix composites which, when frozen, conduct electricity with no resistance. By arranging a series of superconductors into a circular shape, a large magnetic field is created that is capable of storing megawatts of electricity, perhaps enough to light Miami for a few minutes."

When he had finished, I didn't know any more than when the old lady started trying to explain things to me.

"So, is this lady on the level?" I asked McGarvey.

"Yes, Mr. Arrow. I think she *is* Billy Powers."

"No shit?" I asked, surprised.

"It *is* me, Mr. Arrow," the old lady pleaded. "Honest!" I rolled my eyes. "You have to get me out of here tonight," she begged. "They moved me into this early model hybrid container. I have to bathe twice a week, and I'm due. But this container isn't working well, and I think I have only a short time to live. You have to get me out of here. I want to see my wife one more time!"

"Okay," I replied. "We'll try, but no guarantees."

McGarvey left us to chase down Granger Taylor, who was already beginning to work on the printed circuit panel outside of Nelson's cage. "Granger," he asked, "do we have enough gold to take someone else with us?"

"Got plenty of gold. Don't know if it will work until we try it on this here cage."

"Mr. Arrow found someone else who has to come with us."

"Who would that be?"

"It's a guy he knows who's in a woman's body."

"That would be Miss Powers," Granger said.

"That would be Billy Powers. They migrated him to a woman's body," McGarvey said. "He survived the Dulce Firefight. Have you ever heard of that?"

"I was there," Granger replied. "It was after that big explosion that they moved me and all these cages to here from Dulce. That was a while back."

"Did you come in a flying saucer?"

"I came by mag shuttle in one of them tunnels. Took about an hour. But I didn't come until most of the cages was already here. It was a big move that took a couple of days."

"You'll have to tell Mr. Arrow about it when we get out of here. He'll be really interested in your story."

"Container," Granger said, melting a thin line of gold onto a circuit board.

"What?" McGarvey asked.

"It's a container. He ain't in no woman's body. He's in a container. It looks like a woman's body, but it's a container. It's different."

"Well, we're going to take Miss Powers with us, too."

"I hope that there container can climb out of here. It's a long way up that shaft for an old container, even if it is being driven by a younger man." Granger lifted his safety glasses and said, "Well, hold your breath."

Granger used a penknife to scrape a small section of gold off of the circuit board. As he did, a dull metallic click let Nelson know he was free. He pushed open the cage door and stepped out.

"Thank you, man," Nelson told Granger. "I really owe you."

"Come on, Granger," McGarvey said, "Let's go let Powers out of his cage."

On the way back to Powers's cage, McGarvey praised Granger. "Good work, Granger. A man with your skills is highly prized in today's America. If you decide that you want a job, I know a couple of companies that will bid for your services."

"They put old men like me out in the field, don't they?" Granger asked.

"Not if they want to work. You're a mechanical genius!"

"Yeah, thanks for getting me out of that rabbit hutch," Nelson said. "I was afraid that I'd be dead tomorrow."

"You still might be, Nelson," Granger told him.

"Yeah, but on my own terms."

ↈↈ

When we got back to Powers's cage, Nelson gave me a big hug, like I was a fraternity brother that he hadn't seen in twenty years. "I don't know whether to kiss you or kick your ass for getting me into this, Dan. But right now, I'm leaning toward kissing you."

"Save it for Mona," I told him. "She always enjoys a sincere kiss."

Nelson laughed and hugged me again.

While Nelson and I were celebrating our reunion, Granger and McGarvey were busy at work on the circuit board outside of Powers's cage. It was an older model cage, but Granger's knowledge of cage mechanics was indomitable, and soon Powers was free.

He shook everyone's hand, but then suggested that we get out of the facility while the getting was good. We all concurred.

"I need to get my stuff," Granger said. "I'll meet you at the vent. You guys get started, though."

As we made our way back to the fan vent, McGarvey took a few more pictures. One thing that could have passed for a Sasquatch woke and let out a blood curdling yowl. Other creatures sprang to their feet and began shaking their cages. "Shit," McGarvey said, "we're making too much noise." He put his camera away.

We helped Miss Powers into the vent first, followed by Nelson. Then, I got on my hands and knees and let McGarvey use my back as a stepping stool. Nelson reached down and helped him up and inside the vent. I waited for Granger. He was taking a long time to get back, and I suspected that he would never be able to climb into the vent without using my back and being assisted by the others.

Finally, he appeared, carrying an old suitcase. "You'll never be able to carry that up the shaft," I told him.

"But it is everything that I brought with me when I went for a ride in the saucer thirty-five years ago. It has all my worldly possessions."

"Sort through it and take what you can carry, but you'll need two free hands for the climb up, Granger."

He laid the suitcase on the floor and opened it. It contained books and magazines, underwear, socks, a few sweaters, and several pairs of sunglasses. Everything was old. Granger seemed panicked at the thought of leaving anything behind. He put on one sweater, and then another over that one. He stuffed a few magazines under the sweaters and put a pair of underwear into each trousers pocket. "My books!" he cried. "How can I carry my books?"

"You may have to leave them behind," I said. "But believe me, you can get new copies of everything you have here. It's all still available today."

A loud bang broke our conversation.

"Someone is here!" Granger whispered. "There's no time. Quick! Get into the vent!"

"You first, Granger," I told him.

"Come on, Granger," McGarvey said to him, extending his hand from the vent. "It's time to go!"

"I've been here so long," he replied nervously. "I don't know how I'll live up there."

"You'll be fine, Granger," I said. "We'll all be there to help you settle in."

Granger shook his head. "No, you go without me, Mr. Arrow. I need to stay here and keep them from discovering you."

Granger got on all fours and let me use his back to step up into the shaft. McGarvey assisted in pulling me up and in.

Once inside, I turned and looked back at Granger. "Last chance, Granger. Come on."

Another loud bang broke through the cavern, alarming the creatures into screams and squeals. The ceiling lights came on.

"Hurry, they're coming!" Granger told me. He then picked up the fan and handed it to me. I passed it sideways to the men behind me. Then I watched as Granger gently placed the louvered vent cover into the hole in the wall. He took several steps, turned, raised his hand, and whispered, "Good luck, Mr. Arrow!" He walked to Nelson's cage and pulled the door shut. I was pretty certain that I'd never see him again.

"Come on Mr. Arrow, we have a long way to go and time is not on our side right now." It was McGarvey, and he was right about that.

Chapter 19

It took us longer to reach the vertical shaft than I had anticipated, mostly due to Miss Powers, whose aging container had difficulty with hunching over and moving at the pace that I tried to push. We stopped every thirty-five yards to let Powers rest. I had strong doubts about Powers's ability to move that female container up the rungs to level three.

When we finally arrived at the shaft, McGarvey gave me a piece of nylon rope from his fanny pack. I tied one end around my waist and the other end around Powers's chest, where the container's boobs should have been. They were lower, as you would expect on someone of advanced age. Powers was okay with the plan. I would go first, and as I climbed, I would help pull Miss Powers up, thus relieving some of the strain on her arms as we ascended.

Nelson followed Powers, and McGarvey took rear point. It was slow going. At first, I could pull Powers along just by my waist, but after a while, the thin nylon rope began cutting into my flesh. So, each time I ascended a step, I would grab the rope with my right hand and pull upward, helping Powers to the next step. It was a workout, and the sweat that formed on the small of my back and my brow was proof of the effort.

When we reached level four, I suggested that we move into the side vents to rest for a few minutes before continuing upward. I helped Powers into the vent and then sat beside her.

"I'm not sure I'm going to make it, Mr. Arrow," Powers told me, breathing heavily.

"You'll be okay, Powers," I said. "Only one more level, and then we ride an elevator."

"Listen, Mr. Arrow, you need to know some things, in case I fall or have a heart attack or something."

"Yeah, I know. What's a nice woman like you doing in a place like this?"

Powers chuckled. "I think you meant to ask, 'What's a nice man like you doing in a woman like that?'"

It was my turn to chuckle. "So what is it that's so important, Powers?"

"Something big is going down, Mr. Arrow. I haven't been able to piece it all together yet, but somebody important is being migrated into a new type of container, and it's scheduled to happen very soon."

"Yeah?" I asked.

"They call him 'The Great One.' I'm not sure who it is, but the NWO considers this person to be their supreme leader."

"An alien?" I asked.

"No, he's human. He's somebody who has been living in temporary containers for more than half a century. But, he has many followers. It might even be Jesus!"

"I don't think it's Jesus, Powers."

"Well, I remember the scriptures saying that Jesus would one day return to Earth. There will be a big battle between good and evil, and the Earth would live in peace for a millennium."

"Yeah, I remember some of that from Sunday school," I told him.

"Is it possible that the NWO is, in fact, preparing for the second coming of Jesus?" he speculated.

"Would Jesus need aliens to help prepare for his second coming?" I asked.

"Maybe Jesus was an alien, Mr. Arrow."

"Not hardly, Powers. The stuff that's going on down in this facility is more military. Do you think Jesus would approve of experimenting on people? Of sewing animal parts onto humans? Would he plan to use nerve gas on people in order to establish his millennium of peace?"

"Nerve gas?" Powers asked in disbelief.

"Yeah, the second level is full of it. Thousands of canisters!"

"Oh my! I knew the stuff I was researching was not good, but inflicting nerve gas on mankind is nothing that I had imagined. The NWO must be stopped."

Now, he's being rational, I thought. As he was speaking, I noticed something dangling on the fourth rung above the vent. I got up onto my knees, climbed onto the rungs, and took the material in my hand. As I lowered myself back into the vent beside Powers, I felt the round metallic disk that was sewn into the fabric. A shot of horror ran through my body. "Mona!" I said aloud.

From the other vent, McGarvey asked, "What did you find, Mr. Arrow?"

I didn't answer him at first, as my mind was racing with all of the possibilities. Finally, I said, "It's Mona. It's Mona's ankle magnet."

"Shit," McGarvey blurted. "I hope they aren't able to track her through this rock!"

I hoped for the same. Either they had taken her captive, or the magnet had simply fallen from her ankle and lodged on that rung. Or, maybe she left it as a message of some sort. I couldn't be certain. All I knew was that my beloved Mona was someplace without this magnet. Certainly, if the aliens were looking for her, they'd spot her the moment she emerged from the air shaft at the surface. This was not good.

Before we resumed our climb, McGarvey and Nelson moved down their vent to see if anything new was happening on level four. When they returned, McGarvey told me that the Nazis were beginning to rise. Nelson was excited because he had just seen them for the first time. "Nazis, Dan! This level is full of Nazis!"

Miss Powers looked at me in horror. "Nazis?" she asked.

"Yeah, this level is occupied by Nazis."

"Nazis and nerve gas go together like mosquitoes and malaria," Powers said. Before I could say what I was thinking, Powers beat me to the punch. "Mr. Arrow, the NWO is planning to establish a one world government. That's the same thing Hitler wanted to do. The Great One isn't Jesus, he's—"

"Hitler!" we both said in unison.

"It all makes sense now," Powers told me. "Do you remember the stuff in my notebook about the Nazi Bell?" he asked.

"Not exactly," I admitted.

"In the early 1940s, the Nazi's were working on a new type of propulsion system, one that worked on magnetism. Their project looked like some types of UFOs, the ones with the flat bottoms and the bell shaped tops. Obviously, they were working with the aliens to perfect a flying device that would transport humans without killing us when they make those abrupt directional changes at high speed."

"What's in it for the aliens?" I asked.

"Access to the Earth, especially to our gold. They need it for their technology. We know they're here, but they've been forced underground by our sun. I think if they're in it for too long a period, it shortens their lives. But, if they could create a hybrid species, a docile one that they could dominate, they could capture all of our gold, and create a safe harbor here against exploration by other alien species."

"It's all beyond me," I confessed. "All I want is to find Mona and to put an end to the NWO."

"I feel energized, now, Mr. Arrow. I think we should continue to the surface."

I asked McGarvey if he was ready to start back up. He nodded, so I crawled onto the rungs and waited until Miss

Powers was beneath me. Up we went, in the same order as before. As we climbed, my mind raced back and forth between thoughts of Hitler returning to power as head of the NWO, and thoughts of Mona. I hoped she was safe, but my guts told me that she was in trouble. I had to find her.

I was first to peek out of the air shaft at level three. The grate that we had removed was still ajar. That was a good sign. I heard no movement of any kind, not even the hum of the air transfer system. Cautiously, I climbed out of the shaft and then helped Miss Powers to her feet. My calves ached, so I presumed that Powers was probably in misery. Nelson and McGarvey were right behind. Both stretched their muscles. It had been a difficult climb. I pulled my watch case from my pants pocket and checked the time. It was four-twelve in the morning. We had to get moving, or else the sun would wake the roosters, and we'd get caught.

We hurried across the cavern to the far wall and followed it to the right. Then, we passed the ramp that led downhill to level four, and soon found the alcove where the elevator waited for us. When I peered around the corner, I wanted to barf. "Don't look, Powers!" I said, "and stay here!"

I told McGarvey to stay with Powers and pulled Nelson to me so I could whisper in his ear. "Nelson, listen to me carefully. McGarvey's two friends are lying dead in front of the elevator. One has been decapitated. The other is lying there in two pieces. It's grisly."

"What about Miss Mona?" he asked.

"I don't see her."

"This isn't good, Dan."

"No, but maybe she's still alive."

He nodded.

"Let's find another way out," I continued.

He nodded again.

I motioned for McGarvey and Powers to huddle with Nelson and me. "We can't use the elevator to get back. It isn't safe."

"What do you mean, Mr. Arrow?" McGarvey asked.

"I'll explain later. For now, though, we have to find another way out."

"I think it's either the ramp or the stairs," McGarvey said.

"I'll opt for the stairs," I told everybody. "Nobody is going to come down here using the stairs unless they're forced to, but the ramp is bound to have traffic this morning." They all agreed.

McGarvey led us back to the ramp, where the door to the stair tower was awaiting us. He led, followed by Miss Powers, me, and then Nelson. My calves continued to ache, but the stairs were much better than steel rungs on the balls of my feet. Compared to our time in the air shaft, we climbed the two flights to the first floor effortlessly, and in record time. Powers, of course, was huffing and puffing, but she made it without stopping too often.

Nelson self-selected to look out the glass window of the exit door. "It's still dark out there," he said. "I'm surprised by that."

But, just as he was about to open the door, a loud clanging sound echoed down the cavern. We all froze in our tracks. Soon, we could see the reflection of headlights strike the window of the stairwell. A vehicle was headed in our general direction. The motor sounded like a Jeep, and it needed a new muffler.

From the movement of the headlights on the window and the changing sound of the motor, it seemed as if the vehicle turned just outside our door, and its occupants headed down the ramp to level two.

"We have no choice, but to climb back out through the air shaft, Mr. Arrow," McGarvey said.

"I think you're right," I replied. I looked at Nelson and Powers and asked, "Do you two think you can handle one more flight of air shaft rungs?" They both look dismayed, but they nodded.

"If this hike doesn't kill me, nothing will, Mr. Arrow,"

said Powers. "But I am beginning to feel a little weak. I'm going to have to bathe soon."

Nelson opened the door slowly. I was amazed when it didn't squeak the way most steel doors do. Out we crept, all of us being as quiet as possible because each of us knew that this place was rising to life along with the sun outside.

"If I remember correctly, the air shaft is about two hundred yards that way," I said, pointing to the right. Nobody disagreed, so we headed in that direction, hugging the wall as if it offered some kind of protection from anything that might come at us from behind. There was simply no place to hide if anyone else came into the cavern, so we hurried along.

The shaft was exactly where I thought it would be. McGarvey went up first, followed by Nelson, Miss Powers, and me. As I entered the darkness, I heard a deep clang from below. Someone else was either entering the cavern, or the Jeep we'd heard earlier was now exiting. Either way, it was good that we were well hidden by the air shaft. About half an hour later, McGarvey passed the word down that we had reached the top and that the coast appeared to be clear. He pushed the cover up and exited.

Although I was still down in the shaft, I could hear McGarvey say, "Tell Mr. Arrow that his car is still here."

"Mr. Arrow, your—" Powers said.

"Yeah, I heard," I told her. "I hope Mona is curled up asleep in the back seat."

She wasn't. After we closed the lid on the air shaft, we walked to the rented Expedition. There were no signs to indicate that anybody had even been near it. My heart fell, because I knew that Mona was still below, probably in one of those cages, if she wasn't already dead.

"I wonder where Will and Fritz are," McGarvey said.

I intentionally ignored his question and made a statement that changed the subject. "I'm going back down tonight," I told everybody. "Mona is still down there, and she doesn't deserve anything that those sons of bitches plan to do to her."

Then McGarvey changed the subject. "Mr. Arrow," he said, "I think we need to take Powers and Nelson to Fritz's friend the doctor to see if they have implants. We don't want them to be easily recaptured."

I knew he was right, so after we all piled into the Expedition, I let him direct me to the doctor. We had to drive back into Denver, ultimately to a quiet street with modest homes and large leafy trees. "What the fuck is this?" I asked when I saw the doctor's sign. "He isn't a doctor, he's a chiropractor."

"He's nationally renowned for removing alien implants, Mr. Arrow," McGarvey said. "He's made numerous presentations at MUFON conferences."

We climbed the three steps to the porch, and McGarvey rang the bell. Even though it was not quite seven-thirty a.m., the door was opened by a young woman in a white smock. I thought that she probably was dressed up like a pretend nurse for this pretend doctor.

Is Dr. Cattrell in?" McGarvey asked.

"Yes, but it's early. Do you have an appointment?"

"No, but tell him it may be urgent. It's MUFON business."

She let us into the waiting room and then went back where the doctor practiced his bone snapping witchcraft. In a few minutes, Dr. Cattrell came into the waiting room.

"Hi, Dr. Cattrell," McGarvey began, "I'm an associate of Fritz Weiner. My name is Arthur McGarvey."

"Glad to meet you, Mr. McGarvey. How is Fritz?"

"Good, he is good," McGarvey replied.

I wasn't about to tell McGarvey that Weiner wasn't too good right now. In fact, he was dead and probably a head mount on some alien's wall.

"So, this is MUFON business?' the doctor asked.

"We have two abductees who need to be scanned for implants. As usual, you can keep the implants."

"Two?" Cattrell remarked with delight. "Well, let's get down to business, gentlemen."

Cattrell introduced himself to each of us, clarifying which ones were the abductees, and which were along for the experience. His handshake was feminine, almost limp, which I didn't care for, as you might guess. He then escorted us into his examination room, where he showed us the machinery he planned to use.

Speaking to Powers and Nelson, Cattrell said, "Rather than subject your entire bodies to X-rays, I'll use a wand to identify probable sites, and then we'll X-ray only those places on your bodies."

I'd seen wands before, not only at airports but also at prisons, where the guards look for specific metals if you set off bells and whistles when you walk through the large metal detectors. On me, the big detectors are always set off by my belt buckles and by the eyelets on my boots, when I wear them. Cattrell's wand looked like military surplus, but I didn't ask.

He went to work on Powers first, finding hot spots behind her left ear and in her left knee. He wrote her name and the date on the top of a sheet of paper that displayed the printed outline of a human being, and then he drew little black circles that corresponded to the hot spots that the wand found. Then, he followed the same process with Nelson, whose right leg and forehead set off the wand.

"That leg ain't nothing, Doc," Nelson said. "I got a pin there when I broke my leg in a motorcycle accident back when I was a teenager."

"We'll double check, anyway," Cattrell said. "If you have any implants, we'll want to get them all." Next, he used his big X-ray machine to take pictures of the hot spots on Nelson's and Powers's bodies. Fortunately, it was a digital model, so we didn't have to wait half an hour for the film to be developed. "You're both infected," Cattrell told them. "Nelson, yours is in your nasal cavity, where the bridge of the nose meets your forehead."

"No way!" Nelson said in disbelief. "When did they put it in there?"

"They do it with a machine. Most of the people who have implants have no recollection of going through the procedure."

Cattrell turned his attention to Miss Powers. "Yours is behind your ear. You must have been in an accident as well, because the metal in your knee is a screw. When did it happen?"

"I have no recollection of such an event, Doctor," Powers replied. "This isn't even my body."

The doctor raised his left eyebrow and turned to me. I motioned with my finger that Powers was a little crazy. He nodded.

Removal of the implants took about an hour of outpatient surgery, which Cattrell performed in his office with injected local anesthetic. Nelson's procedure took the longest because every time the doctor got near the implant, it actually moved away from his probe. "They do that sometimes," Cattrell told us matter-of-factly. Miss Powers's surgery required a single stitch. Nelson's required that his nostril be packed with gauze for a day. "Now, don't you go scuba diving for about two weeks," he told Nelson. "The pressure isn't good for healing."

We all looked at the implants under the doctor's microscope. They looked a little like splinters, except they were both the same size, shape, and color.

"We think they operate off of the electrical field produced by the body," Cattrell told us. "They give off a weak pulsing signal until they're removed. Once they're removed, they stop pulsating. They're made of something so hard that I haven't been able to cut one open to look at the microcircuits."

"Have you tried crushing one in a vise?" I asked.

"No, Mr. Arrow, I'd be afraid of destroying the circuits inside."

"Well, you have two more to add to your collection. I

don't think that sacrificing one in the name of scientific knowledge would be a bad thing," I replied.

కుఖు

I drove McGarvey back to his place, which was a boarding house, of all places. I left the others in the Expedition and went inside with him. Once in his first-floor room, I told him to sit down.

"What's wrong, Mr. Arrow?" he asked.

"Back at the elevator, I didn't let you and Miss Powers come around the corner for a reason. Your friends Weiner and Martin are dead. Their bodies were lying on the concrete outside the elevator at level three. That's what I didn't want you to see."

McGarvey burst into tears. He put his face into my chest and bawled like a little kid. It was out of character for me, but I stroked his head. After a few moments, he raised his head. "How are we ever going to have a funeral?"

"Maybe a memorial service," I suggested. "Their bodies will never be recovered, Artie." I paused while he composed himself, and then I asked, "Did Weiner and Martin have any next of kin?"

"Weiner has a daughter in Seattle. They're estranged. Martin was like me. I don't think Martin had anyone but our little group of ufologists."

"Maybe you ought to go to Weiner's house and see if you can find a number for his daughter. This is going to be a tough run for her."

"Why so?"

"How can she prove that her father is deceased?" I asked. "There is no body, no medical record of his death. Unless she has power of attorney, I don't think she can sell or even rent his house. She won't collect from his insurance company without proof of death. He is simply a missing person."

"I'll go over this afternoon."

I told him to get some sleep, because I planned to do so myself. We'd been up all night long, and none of us was thinking too clearly. As I left his room, I heard McGarvey begin sobbing again. The poor sap had lost his only friends, except maybe for the guy who hadn't hung around that day when Mona and I first arrived at Weiner's. "Mona," I whispered as I left McGarvey's house, "I'm coming for you. Don't worry, baby."

かかか

When we got back to the motel, I got separate rooms for Nelson and Powers, under aliases, of course. They were going to need everything—clothes, toiletries, and above all else, showers. The aliens didn't seem to care if their captives were clean and sweet smelling.

After Nelson and Powers were settled in, I went back to my room and collapsed on the bed. Mona's dirty socks and underwear were on the chair across the room. I pictured her and longed for her touch. I called out her name a few times but soon fell asleep from sheer exhaustion.

When the phone rang, it sounded like it was two rooms down the hall, rather than just a few inches from my head. I looked at the clock. It was four p.m., and I had been asleep for seven hours. It felt like five minutes. "Yeah, who's this?" I asked.

"It's Powers, Mr. Arrow."

"Yeah, what's up?"

"I need to feed, Mr. Arrow. I'm very weak."

"Call room service and have them put it on your tab."

"No, Mr. Arrow. It doesn't work that way. This container needs to absorb its nutrients through its skin. It needs a nutrient bath."

"How am I going to arrange that?" I asked.

"I've been thinking about it for days, Mr. Arrow. I think

that a mixture of Gatorade and raw meat might do it. It won't be exactly the same as the alien baths, but it might help keep this container alive."

"Okay, give me a few minutes, and I'll come down to your room."

I called Nelson and told him to meet me at Powers's room in fifteen minutes. Then, I took a shower and shaved. I wanted to look nice for Mona when I rescued her later. The clean underwear that I found in my duffel bag felt great when it touched my privates. There is nothing like clean sheets and clean underwear, I told myself. I made a mental note to buy some for Nelson and Powers.

When Powers answered my knock on his door, he looked older than before. His skin tone was gray, his cheeks were gaunt, and his eyes were yellow, almost jaundiced. I closed the door, and Powers collapsed onto his bed.

"This container is very weak, Mr. Arrow," Miss Powers told me. "Can you get me a few gallons of Gatorade and some raw chopped meat? That may be my only hope."

There was a knock on the door. I opened it. "Ugh," Nelson said when he entered the room and saw Powers.

"We've got to get her some nourishment, Nelson. Her container eats like an alien's. She has to absorb it through her skin. She thinks Gatorade and hamburger might do it."

"We passed a supermarket on our way here," Nelson replied. "We can get there in a couple of minutes."

"Don't go anywhere, Powers," I said. "We'll be right back."

"Don't worry, I'm not going anywhere unless I leave this container while you're gone." She closed her eyes and folded her hands across her belly. I didn't like the symbolism of that position.

☙❧❧

Nelson and I found our way to the supermarket, and

pushed two carts through the aisles. We stopped first at the New Age Beverages section, where we piled twenty half-gallon containers of Gatorade and a few gallons of some other knock-off stuff into our carts. Then we went to the Butcher Shoppe, where we took the last six packages of ground beef. "Will this do?" Nelson asked me. It was a meatloaf mix of beef, veal, and pork. I nodded. Nelson piled all the store had into the carts. Then I threw some ground chicken and ground sausage onto the piles. The bill exceeded two hundred dollars, but if it would keep Powers alive, I figured that it was worth it.

Back at the motel, we made five hurried trips to and from the Expedition with armfuls of our groceries. Together, we poured the Gatorade into the tub, and added the meat. It looked ugly. At least it wasn't too cold, because the Gatorade had not been refrigerated.

Powers was very weak, so I helped her undress. Her skin was wrinkled and sagged where a young woman wouldn't want it to sag. I suppose that Miss Powers didn't look too bad for a man in the body of a seventy-year-old woman. I was grateful that her container wasn't obese, because I had to carry it to the tub and place her into the mushy liquid. As I looked down at Powers, I silently hoped that Mona would never look like that. But, if she ever did, I felt like I would still love her. More than anything, I hoped she was still alive.

While we waited to see if Powers was going to get any sustenance from the makeshift nutrient bath, Nelson and I discussed my plans for going back into the Nazi and alien fortress that night.

"I want to go with you, Dan," Nelson said. "I'm not infected with one of those homing devices anymore, and I'd like to help with freeing Mona."

"How's your headache?" I asked.

"I never really got a headache from that surgery. It's just sore inside my sinus cavities. I think I'll be okay in another couple of hours."

"Well, frankly, I think it's a suicide mission, Nelson. I'm going all the way down to level six, where there is nothing except aliens. I'm not sure I want to watch you die. Those bastards cut Weiner in half, and they decapitated Martin. And the aliens left their bodies there as a warning to others, probably us. And they probably thought nothing of it, kind of like a farmer feels when he cuts the head off of a chicken. It's just another day's work."

"How about me, Dan? Those bastards took me from my home and transported me to Colorado, so I could live in a cage until they migrated me into something I wouldn't like, the way they did with that poor sap sitting in that bloody cocktail in the bathroom. I want to squeeze one of those lizards until its eyes pop out. Just one is all, before I die."

"Okay then," I said, "we're going in at ten o'clock tonight. Did you see that army/navy store next to the supermarket?"

"Yeah, boy, I did."

"Here are the keys to my Expedition. Go buy four gas masks, one for you, one for me, one for Mona, and a spare, just in case we need it."

"You got a plan?" he asked.

"I've got the basic concept, but I need to add some details. I'll fill you in when you get back. In the meanwhile, I'll stay here with Miss Powers, in case she runs into any complications. If she dies in that slop, somebody is going to have to wipe this place clean of fingerprints. That'll be my job."

Nelson left. And per my usual MO, I fell asleep in the chair.

Chapter 20

I t was Powers who woke me. She was standing in front of me with a towel wrapped around her waist, covering all the feminine parts of her body, including those parts that should have been higher on her chest. Pink-colored water was dripping from her legs onto the carpet.

"Mr. Arrow, it worked!" she exclaimed.

"Huh?" I asked, realizing that I had been asleep.

"It worked! I'm not sure whether it was the mixture of meats or the Gatorade, but that concoction worked. I feel like a new man!"

"Don't you mean a new woman, Powers?"

"I may look like a woman on the outside, but I'm all boy inside, Mr. Arrow!" She struck a pose like a body builder, both arms erect and showing her biceps. "Remember Bo Diddley, Mr. Arrow? One hundred percent more man! That's how I feel right now!"

"You still look and sound like a seventy-year-old woman, Powers," I replied. "Your biceps are sagging toward the floor, just like your boobs."

"It's not the container, Mr. Arrow. It's the person inside it. Right now I feel terrific!"

I suggested that we walk down to my room so that Powers could wash the meat scraps and juice off of her body. "Yeah, that might be a good idea," she agreed.

We shut the door to her room and walked down the car-

peted corridor toward my room. As we did, the elevator
door opened. A family with two girls in their early teens,
maybe not even quite that old, passed by. The mother was
horrified to see an old woman with only a towel around her
waist, walking down the corridor. Her daughters giggled
and snickered at Powers in her towel. Their father just kept
looking ahead, as though he didn't want to see anything. I
was sure the manager was going to hear about us from the
woman, so I waited until they entered their room before
identifying which room was mine by opening the door.

When Powers had showered, we walked back to his
room. As Powers was fumbling with the key, Nelson exited
the elevator, carrying a white plastic bag that screamed
ARMY/NAVY STORE in big blue letters. He gave me the
thumbs-up sign, meaning that he had the stuff. Color me
happy: my plan was coming together.

I gave Nelson the key to my room and asked him to wait
for me there. "I've got the masks, Dan," he said. I nodded
and pointed toward my room down the hall.

Before prepping for the trip back into "alienazi" land, I
thought I ought to give Marlene Powers a call to tell her
what my investigation had turned up. Hell, she was financ-
ing this adventure, wasn't she? I figured that she might be
surprised that her husband was still alive, but I also remembered that her reaction to Powers's death by strangulation
was different from most women's. I would have expected
tears and mourning, but she told me that she had already
passed that stage. In fact, judging by the bright colors that
she wore to my office that day, Powers's death might have
been a relief for her. It was going to be an interesting call,
and I wondered how she would react to Powers's being
alive in a woman's body—or, make that container.

Powers was getting dressed when I dialed Marlene's
number on my cell phone. After three rings, she picked up.
"And how is the investigation going, Mr. Arrow?" she
asked. Her greeting surprised me, but then I remembered
that I had forgotten to ask Hal to show me how to block

caller information on my new smart phone. It was something else to put on my list of things to do.

"Well," I told her, "I used your husband's notebook to identify a short string of people to interview."

"So it was useful?"

"Oh, yes. Actually, it is full of interesting stuff. But let me get back on point."

"Okay..."

"So, your husband's notebook led me to Dulce, New Mexico, where another guy and I climbed down an air shaft into the underground facility where your husband was involved in that firefight."

"Mr. Arrow, that level where my husband was injured was collapsed by the government many years ago."

"Yeah," I replied, "but the aliens are still there. We saw some and were shot at. Fortunately, the ones that shot at us were out of practice, and we escaped."

"Oh, dear, Mr. Arrow, I'm glad you're still alive!"

"Oh, but there is more, Marlene," I said. "Then I found my way to Denver, Colorado, where I enjoyed a spelunking adventure into another underground facility. I found an area in a lower level with people in cages. One of them was your husband."

There was dead silence on the phone.

After a few moments, I asked, "Marlene? Are you still there?"

"I'm not sure how to respond, Mr. Arrow. Billy is dead. I saw his body in the morgue. I went to his funeral. What are you trying to say?"

I could tell that she was crying. "Marlene, are you sitting down?" I asked.

"Yes, Mr. Arrow. I had to sit down a moment ago."

"The aliens have the technology to remove a person from his body. That's what they did to your husband. They didn't kill him. They simply removed him from his body and put him in some kind of storage battery or something. Then they put that surgical tubing around the neck of his empty body and made it look like he killed himself."

"This is all so bizarre, Mr. Arrow."

"You told me yourself that your husband would never kill himself, and he didn't."

"This is getting very complicated, Mr. Arrow. I have already accepted payment from the insurance company, and much of that money has been spent. If he's alive, they'll want it back. And, how will we explain this to our friends?"

"There's more, Marlene."

"Oh, please, Mr. Arrow, I'm not sure that I can bear any more."

"The aliens moved him from that battery into another body."

"So Billy is alive, but he doesn't look like himself. Is that what you are saying, Mr. Arrow."

"Oh, he definitely doesn't look like the Billy you married, Marlene, so I don't think you'll have to worry about repaying the life insurance company."

"Well, that's good, Mr. Arrow," she replied.

"But there's more, Marlene."

"God save me, Mr. Arrow, what else could there possibly be? Will you get to the point?"

"Marlene, the aliens put your husband into the empty body of a seventy-year-old woman." There, I said it, and I hoped that she could handle it.

There was dead silence on the end of the phone again. I decided to wait for her to speak.

"So," she finally said, "you're saying that if this person really is Billy Powers, and he expects to move back into his own house, it will look like I'm a widow who is caring for her aging mother."

"Yeah, that's one way of looking at it, Marlene, but Miss Powers—that's what I call her, Marlene—Miss Powers. She's feisty and does things that most seventy-year-old women wouldn't attempt. Hell, she climbed up an air shaft twice the height of the Washington Monument on ladder rungs!"

"Mr. Arrow, is Billy there with you now?"

"Yes, she is."

"Put him on, please. I want to be sure he *is* Billy Powers.

"She," I reminded her. Then I handed Powers the phone and told her, "It's your wife. She wants to say 'hi.'"

Miss Powers took the phone. "Hi, poopsie." There was a pause as Powers listened and then she said, "Yes, it's me." She nodded. "Yes, I know I don't sound the same. It's the way Mr. Arrow explained it." There was another pause as she listened again. "Red grraah bra and panties." Powers looked at me and signaled for me to leave the room. I guessed she wanted privacy, so I went into the hallway and sat on the floor to wait.

About ten minutes later, the door to the room opened, and Powers came out. She had tears in her eyes. "You can come back in now, Mr. Arrow," she said. As I entered the room, she continued, "Marlene wanted to ask me a few personal questions to be sure I really am Billy Powers."

"What is a graah bra?" I asked.

"It's the way I refer to animal prints like leopard or tiger skin. Whenever Marlene wears them, I growl like a dog. She wore a red graah bra and matching panties the first time we made love. Nobody would know that except for me."

"I get the picture, Powers," I said.

"She also asked me some very personal questions. That's when I asked you to leave."

"So is she convinced?"

"I think so. She's planning on coming out here to meet me in a couple of days. I wish I weren't in this blasted female container."

"Listen, Powers, I'm going to give you a credit card. The name on it is P.J. Brinks. I want you to go buy some new clothes and toiletries. When Marlene gets out here, take her to dinner and a show. Let her adjust slowly to the new you. That card is the only one I have with a name that could be a woman's. It's only got about two thousand dollars of credit left on it, so don't go too wild."

"That's really nice of you, Mr. Arrow."

"It's your money, anyway, Powers. It's part of the retainer that Marlene gave me to find your killer."

"If you do anything, Mr. Arrow, please find Hitler and be sure he doesn't get migrated into a new container. The New World Order has to be stopped."

"I'll do my best, Powers, but my primary concern is Mona. She is to me what Marlene is to you. I love her, and I don't want anything bad to happen to her."

"I know I'm in the body of an old woman, but if there is anything I can do to help you, Mr. Arrow, you just call on me."

"Thanks, Powers," I said, opening the door to her room. "Listen, I have to get back to my room and prep for going back into that facility tonight. I plan to bust Mona out of there."

"You go, boy! As for me, I've got to go get some new duds. Marlene is coming!"

"You go, girl!" I replied.

Chapter 21

I knocked twice, and Nelson opened the door to my room. "What took you so long, Dan?" he asked. "I was connecting Powers with his wife," I said. "She's flying out here in a couple of days to see him. I don't think there is anything he can do to prepare her for finding him in a woman's body, especially one that's so old. It's going to be an interesting reunion."

"Well, it's good that you did that. Now it's time to think of yourself."

"Yeah, it's time to go get Mona," I replied.

"Let me show you the gas masks," Nelson said, pointing to the small table near the room's window.

"These look older than shit," I said, picking up one of the four and inspecting it.

"Well, they are that old, but they're the only thing the guy had, except for spray painting respirators."

"Who made them?" I asked.

"They guy said they were 1939 World War Two Bulgarian. He called them Kingdom Royal DVF Gas Masks."

"I hope they're still functional."

"He said they were unused."

"Well, they're better than nothing, I guess. If they don't work, I don't guess we'll be able to get our money back, will we?"

Nelson looked at me kind of funny and then shrugged

his shoulders. "So are we still going in at ten?" he asked.

"Yeah," I replied. "Maybe we should get there by nine-thirty to scope things out. They may have sealed everything up by now."

My room phone rang. *That's odd*, I thought, but I picked it up and said my usual warm greeting, "Yeah?"

"Mr. Arrow, it's me, McGarvey."

"Hi, Artie," I replied, trying to be femininely sensitive. "How is everything going at Weiner's place?"

"I managed to find his daughter's telephone number, but she didn't answer. She's probably at work, so I left her a voice mail."

"How are you doing?" I asked more directly.

"I'm pissed!" he replied. "And the longer I sit here doing nothing, the angrier I get at those bastards."

"There's nothing you can do for Weiner and Martin, except to help their next of kin deal with their disappearance."

"That's where you're wrong, Mr. Arrow. I want to avenge their deaths in some way."

"Do you feel like going back underground tonight?" I asked. "I'm going back in to get Mona. I figure there's a good chance that I won't be coming out. But I could use a hand from you and Nelson."

"What do you have in mind?"

"Regardless of what happens to me, we need to expose what's going on down in that hole in the ground, and we need to cramp their style. That's where I need you. But you ought to know that you might die in the process."

"Count me in, Mr. Arrow. Do you need me to prepare anything?"

"Yeah, I need you to figure out how to make an industrial sized fan run backward. I want those fans at level four to blow into the facility instead of out of it."

"That's easy. You just reverse the polarity of the electric motors."

"Well, that's your job, McGarvey. You have to figure out a way to make those fans turn in the opposite direction."

"No problem. Any kid who's played with electric motors could do it. Do you want me to meet you at the hotel?"

"Yeah, maybe around eight-thirty tonight," I said.

"Good. That gives me time to do something else today." He let out a heavy puff of air. "Seeking revenge is better than sitting around mourning," he declared. "I'm feeling better already, Mr. Arrow. Thanks."

"No problem, McGarvey. I'll see you tonight." *This guy could turn into a hero,* I thought.

"It was McGarvey," I said to Nelson. "He's coming with us tonight."

"I heard," Nelson replied. "What's with reversing the fans?"

"It's just a little surprise for the Nazis. I'll fill you in when I have it all figured out."

Nelson nodded, although I know he wasn't too keen on agreeing to do something when he didn't know what he was agreeing to do. But he owed me for freeing him from that cage, and I knew that I could count on him. *He might turn into a lifelong buddy,* I thought. Well, maybe if we live that long.

Nelson asked if he could take a shower. "It's been kinda long."

"Make yourself at home," I replied. When Nelson closed the door, I lay down and closed my eyes. I pictured Mona in some cage, being an experimental subject for a couple of lizards that looked like Godzilla in hospital garb. I regretted ever letting her go down into that underground facility.

e⁄ɔe⁄ɔ

A loud ping from Mona's laptop woke me. She had an email message. I staggered sleepily to the small courtesy desk near the window and sat down in the chair. The seat was hard and uncomfortable against the sore muscles in my buttocks. Using my finger on the control pad, I moved the mouse over to the blinking icon and tapped on it twice. Rats! I needed her password to see the message. I remembered that she used to use Italian American Princess on her old laptop when we were first dating, so I typed in *IAP*. No go. Then I tried *IAP1*. Nope. So I tried lower case letters: *iap1*. Bingo!

I had hoped the message was from her mother, but it wasn't. It was from Dick Cheese—her boss at the FBI. Well, his real name was Special Agent Mack Smith, but I gave him that nickname because I had no respect for him, and I trusted him about as far as I could throw him with my left arm. You get the picture.

The message read, *Mona, you were supposed to check in this morning. Is everything okay? How was the wedding? Got some interesting skinny on your ex. Mack.*

I wanted to know who "ex" referred to, but I assumed it was me. I decided I needed to buy Mona some time, so I hit REPLY and typed a Mona-esque reply: *Dear Mack, The wedding was simply wonderful. I caught the bouquet! I need a couple of more days. Will explain when I get back. I know you'll understand. Mona*

I hit the *SEND* button. "That ought to do the trick," I said aloud. Then I found my way back to bed and waited for Nelson to finish his shower.

Chapter 22

McGarvey showed up at eight-thirty that evening. He had fashioned a small tool bag which he wore as a fanny pack, and he said it contained everything he would need to reverse the polarity of the air exchange fans down on level four. Nelson had purchased two small backpacks. Into his, he crammed the four gas masks that we'd need underground. I filled my backpack with several thousand yards of thin nylon rope and a couple of spare clips of ammo. After emptying our tanks, we synchronized our watches, climbed into the Expedition, and drove back out to the Denver International Airport.

About twenty minutes into our trip, the theme song from *The Godfather* began playing in the back seat. "That's Mona's phone," I told McGarvey. "She must have left it back there."

McGarvey tossed things around in the back seat as he searched for the source of the loud music. After a few moments, he plucked the iPhone out of the pocket behind the driver's seat. "Hello?" he said meekly.

"Jesus! I didn't want you to answer it!" I barked at him. "It's probably her mother!"

McGarvey handed the phone to Nelson and told him, "It's somebody from the FBI."

Nelson handed the phone to me. I shot him a dirty look and shook my head. I didn't want to speak to anybody from the FBI. Not now, anyway. But Nelson insisted.

I took the phone from him, lifted it to my ear, and said, "I'm sorry, but Special Agent Casola can't come to the phone at the moment. May I help you?"

"This is Special Agent Smith at the FBI. I insist that you put Agent Casola on the phone immediately.

"I'm sorry," I replied.

"Who is this anyway?" Dick Cheese asked angrily. "Where is Special Agent Casola?"

"I'm an innocent bystander. We're at the Southern Florida Reptile Farm. The lady who gave me this phone also gave me her purse and sweater to hold while she's wrestling with a big lizard."

"This is bullshit. Where is Special Agent Casola? Is she okay?"

"I already told you, mister, she's wrestling…"

"Arrow! Arrow, is that you?" he demanded.

I clicked the red icon on Mona's iPhone, abruptly ending the call. I handed the phone back to McGarvey and asked him to shut it off. "That bastard will keep calling," I said. "He's a persistent sucker."

A shot of "uh-oh" rushed through me. The last thing Mona would want to hear was that her boss might have deduced that she was with me.

୧ఌ୧

The sun had already set by the time we reached our destination, but a reddish-orange hue still hugged the tops of the mountains to our west. If I could have taken a picture of it, I would have, and I would have superimposed a photo of Mona in the center of it, running to me in a blowing skirt and with outstretched arms. It was a romantic image, but then I remembered that Mona wouldn't be running toward me, she'd be running at me, and, in her outstretched arms, she'd be wielding a baseball bat so she could show me how much she appreciated my placing her life into jeopardy. Really, she was that kind of girl. She told it like it was, and I guessed that was what always attracted me to her. She could swear like a man, drink like a man, and get pissed like a man. But once you got below the surface, she was all woman, if you know what I mean.

ᘓᘔᘓ

By the time I quit daydreaming and opened my car door, McGarvey was already at the entrance to the vent shaft, checking to see if it had been secured in some fashion. "It looks all clear," he shouted back to me and Nelson.

"Ssshhhh!" Nelson reminded him.

McGarvey hurried back toward the car. "It looks good, Mr. Arrow," he said in a hushed voice. "I don't think they know that we got out!"

Wanting to roll my eyes, I looked at Nelson, but he was busy peering up into the blackness of the sky. "What do you see, Nelson?" I asked.

"If you'll look up toward the Big Dipper," he said, pointing in the general direction, "you'll notice that some of the stars disappear."

"I don't understand," I replied.

"Look up there and watch the stars, Dan" he said emphatically.

McGarvey and I both stared up at the sky. It took a few moments before I realized what Nelson was observing. Something was moving in the sky. It must have been military black, because its surface was not shiny, and it had no running lights.

The only way you could tell it was there was that, as it passed between the ground and the stars, it blocked their light.

"What do you think it is?" I asked.

"It's a triangle, Mr. Arrow," McGarvey answered. "It's a

big triangle, and it's moving very slowly—and it's not making a sound."

Just then, the roar of a large commercial jet broke the silence as it charged down the runway in our direction, rose
into the sky, and vaulted over our heads. If that big triangle
was making any sound, I couldn't have heard it over the
racket made by the jetliner.

"Mr. Arrow?" McGarvey asked. "Have you ever seen a
triangle before?"

I shook my head.

"I have, Dan," Nelson said. "I saw one above Dulce a
couple of years ago. I think they might be some kind of ob-
servation drone."

"I disagree. I believe they're piloted," McGarvey said.
"There are lots of pictures of them on YouTube, and they
almost always have a cluster of five or six lights that outline
their shape."

"Are they theirs or ours?" I asked.

"Are you asking if they are military or alien?" Nelson
asked.

"Yeah," I replied.

"Probably both," McGarvey interjected. "I think it's
clear by now that the NWO is not a human venture only.
Either way, though, those triangles exist, and they're un-
conventional aircraft."

"How big would you say that it is?" I asked.

"Unless you have something of known size to use for
comparison, there's really no way of knowing, Mr. Arrow,"
McGarvey replied. "The higher it is, the smaller it appears
to be. That thing could be a small craft only a few hundred
feet in the air, or it could be a mile long and hovering at one
hundred thousand feet,"

"Do you think they know we're here?" I asked.

"There's only one way to find out," Nelson replied, giving me a damn-the-torpedoes look.

I pulled my model 1911 from the small of my back,
popped the clip to check that it was fully loaded, and then

slammed it home again. "Let's go get Mona!" I said.

McGarvey lifted the cover to the shaft and motioned that he would go last. I was the first to begin climbing down, followed by Nelson and then by McGarvey, who lowered the cover as he began descending the rungs. By the time I was thirty feet down, it was totally dark, so I flicked on my brim light. Shortly afterward, I saw that Nelson had done the same, as weak light suddenly appeared from above me, dancing around the narrow walls to the rhythm of Nelson's bobbing head.

The sounds of our breathing and the light tapping of our leather soles upon the steel rungs were the only noises in the shaft. No sounds or lights emanated from below. And, believe me, I kept checking.

After fifteen minutes had elapsed, I stopped descending and grabbed Nelson's foot to let him know that we had reached the opening to the first level. He flicked off his brim light. I followed suit and then climbed down onto the concrete floor of level one.

Once McGarvey was down, I let him catch his breath before we proceeded. My plan was to cross the open cavern to the far wall, and then follow the wall to the right, as we had done on our first visit. "I'm not in favor of using the elevator this time," I said.

"You can't anyway, Mr. Arrow," McGarvey told me. "Fritz had the only key and, well, he isn't here to loan it to you."

McGarvey had a point. "So, what do you think...stairs or ramp?" I asked.

"Stairs," they responded in unison.

We crossed the cavern and found the stairs. On our way, I noticed that, same as last time, the security cameras did not appear to be on, and nobody was guarding the first floor. If I owned this place, there would be a guard at every door. And now that I knew how to get in, I'd mount a locking grate on the bottom of each air exchange shaft.

McGarvey brought along his stethoscope, and he listened at the steel door on the stairwell before we opened it to find our way down to levels two and three. "Nobody is home," he announced. However, we entered cautiously and walked down the stairs the same way.

When we reached level two, McGarvey again listened through the door with his stethoscope. Hearing nothing suspicious, he gave the thumbs up sign. Nelson opened the door and took a two minute stroll around the trucks and tow motors that were still parked there.

"It appears that there's been no activity here since yesterday," he told us when he came back to the stairwell. "I find that truly amazing."

"Yeah," I replied. "Something doesn't smell right."

McGarvey just nodded.

The next flight of stairs went quickly. At least I was beginning to feel like I knew this place and that we were not going to encounter anything bad in the stairwell. Feeling that sort of comfort level is usually a sign of carelessness, so I redoubled my efforts to listen for anything out of the ordinary.

Level two had offered no surprises, but things were different on level three. I had anticipated an empty cavern with painted signage on the far wall directing visitors to the restroom. However, when we opened the door, instead of empty space, we were greeted by…

"Moles!" Nelson exclaimed. "There must be a dozen of them!"

"What's a mole?" McGarvey asked.

"They're tunnel excavators," Nelson told him. "Part of my job back in Dulce was to drive one of these. That's what they use for excavating these caverns and tunnels. One of these babies can move through solid rock at the rate of fifty feet per hour!"

"How about if the ground is sandstone?" McGarvey asked.

"They cut through sandstone like a hot knife through butter!"

I interrupted their conversation. "I am going to go check the stash of nerve gas. Why don't you guys go in the opposite direction and see if you can find anything of interest?"

"Let's meet back here in ten minutes," Nelson said.

I nodded, turned, and walked in the direction of the men's room, where I had first discovered the pallets of Zyklon B. As I had hoped, things had been moved around. Evidence of activity was a good sign, but it also meant that somebody or something could have heard us enter level three, so I proceeded cautiously.

There was no sense in walking into an armed guard, especially if his face resembled an iguana's.

But I was lucky. Whoever had been moving pallets was not here at the moment.

In fact, more of the Zyklon B was now stacked closer to the stairwell than it had been before, so my plan was going to be easier to pull off—I hoped.

When I found the alcove where Martin and Weiner were killed, I carefully peered around the corner before proceeding. Their bodies were gone. That meant that somebody had cleaned the area, and it also meant that Weiner's key to the elevator was not something I was going to find.

When I returned to the stairwell, Nelson and McGarvey were waiting for me. Nelson seemed excited. "So what did you guys find?" I asked,

"Two laser moles," Nelson said with wide eyes. "And the keys are in them!"

"Are those the ones that melt their way through rock?" I asked.

"Yeah!" he said with a grin. "Someday I'm going to drive one of those. They're supposed to be a fantastic ride!"

"And we found a couple of forklifts, too!" McGarvey said.

"Can you operate a forklift?" I asked McGarvey.

"No, but if you show me how, I'm sure I could learn quickly," he replied.

"I can, Dan," Nelson said. "I can run just about any piece of heavy equipment."

"Good," I said. "This floor looks empty of guards. Nelson, I want you to go get that forklift and drive it down toward the men's room. Get the first pallet that you come across and move it over there." I pointed across the cavern to the opposite wall. "That's where we'll find the shaft that leads to the fourth and fifth levels. McGarvey and I will meet you there."

"This is getting exciting!" McGarvey said.

"You ain't seen nothing yet," I told him, "but it's going to be hard work."

Nelson pointed his finger at me and said, "I'll be over there with the Zyklon in a couple of minutes."

McGarvey and I found our way across the cavern and looked for the grate that covered the air shaft. Luck wasn't in our favor because somebody had reset it into its proper position, which meant that we'd have to pry it open again. I looked for the length of angle iron that Mona had found, but it seemed to have disappeared. McGarvey figured it out quickly. "We'll have to wait for Nelson," he told me. "The forklift will make light work of removing the grate." He was right about that.

It wasn't long before we heard the motor on Nelson's forklift growl into action. If anyone else was down here, they wouldn't miss the deafening noise, either. I removed the 1911 from the small of my back and held it in the ready position while McGarvey and I watched for movement from anywhere across the cavern. The only signs of motion were shadows flitting up and down on the walls as Nelson drove to the gas canisters, picked up a palette and headed in our direction. The headlights on the forklift were surprisingly bright, forcing us to squint and turn away as he neared.

When Nelson arrived, we showed him that the grate had been moved back into place. "Not a problem," he remarked. He lowered the palette of Zyklon against the wall and then jumped from the forklift. He disappeared behind the round-ed back end of the machine and then reappeared with a length of chain that had a hook on both ends. "They must have left this on the bumper for us to use!" Nelson said.

I hoped he wasn't right about that.

Nelson inserted one hook into the middle of the vent grate and then wrapped the other end of the chain around one fork on the forklift. Jumping back into the driver's seat, he pulled backward on a lever, lifted the grate, and backed away from the vent. Modern machinery is nice like that, especially since nobody had to exert any effort to remove the grate, and nobody got hurt.

Then Nelson killed the motor on the forklift and joined us again. In the sudden and stark quiet of the cavern, I slid my backpack to the floor and removed three bundles of nylon cord.

"How many rungs down is it to level four?" I asked McGarvey.

"Two hundred fifty-six rungs," he replied. "It's about two hundred feet down."

"Can you measure out two hundred foot lengths of this cord?" I asked.

"Sure thing, Mr. Arrow. When I extend my arms in opposite directions, the distance is about six feet. So, if I do it thirty-four times with cord in my hands, each section should be two hundred feet long."

"Good, make as many lengths as you can with that cord. Use it all."

McGarvey tore open the plastic packaging and started his work, counting aloud as he measured each section. When he cut the first section and began the second, I tied one end of the first section of cord to the edge of the grating while Nelson tied the other end to the valve stem on a canister of Zyklon. When the canister was secure, Nelson slowly lowered it into the air shaft, letting the cord slip through his hands, several feet at a time. We continued this process, taking turns lowering the canisters, until we were out of cord and had lowered thirteen canisters into the shaft. If I had a concern, it was that so many canisters might block our passage to the horizontal shafts at level four if the sections of cord were too short. The only way to be sure that we had clear passage was to descend into the shaft and see what awaited us.

McGarvey reduced my fears a bit when he told us, "I varied the lengths a little, so no more than three canisters are hanging at the same depth."

"Good thinking!" Nelson told him. "You get an A for planning ahead!"

We put our backpacks back on and began our descent, Nelson first, then me, and then McGarvey. Occasionally my backpack would pull upward a little, especially if I leaned backward and let it rub against the thirteen taut cords. Overall, though, it was an easy trip down to level four. As before, our presence appeared to be undetected, even though the forklift motor had made so much noise on level three. Go figure.

e/ɔe/ɔ

Nelson grabbed my ankle, which was his signal to me that we had reached our destination. I paused while he maneuvered his body into the right hand tunnel. Then, I stepped down and into the left hand tunnel. As McGarvey joined Nelson across the shaft from me, I peered over the edge of the shaft at the canisters, which hung by their individual cords just below the entrances to the horizontal tunnels. We couldn't have planned it any better, and I have to credit McGarvey for that. Sometimes it is nice to have a nerd along on a mission.

"You guys know what to do, right?" I asked.

"Yes," McGarvey replied. "I'll reverse the polarity on the fan motors at each circulation vent. It should take me no more than ten minutes at each one."

"And I'll be the mule," Nelson added. "I'll carry the canisters to each vent and set them up in case we need them. I'll start with this side and then do that side. I'm not looking forward to this workout, Dan, but I'm doing it for Mona."

"I know," I replied. "And you can bet she'll give you a big hug and kiss when she sees you!"

Nelson smiled.

"I'll help you carry the first set of canisters," McGarvey said to Nelson. "And maybe we should pull them all into the tunnel before we go carry the first two to the first fan. It'll be a little help to you."

"Yeah, thanks," Nelson told him.

"Okay, then," I said, "I'm going to head down to level five and see if I can find Mona."

"Good Luck, Dan," Nelson said.

"And stay safe!" McGarvey added.

"Let's just hope that I don't step on any snakes," I replied, giving them the thumbs up sign. I began my descent. I had to press tightly against the first twelve rungs as I squeezed past the clusters of canisters that hung at different heights in the shaft. But once I was below them, it was smooth sailing into the darkness below. I froze once at the sound of a clang but realized that the sound came from above and not below. *Nelson or McGarvey must have knocked a canister over,* I thought. It was good to know that the guys were busy doing their work.

ᘓᘓᘓ

When I reached level five, I chucked my backpack into the tunnel on the left and climbed in after it. I knew that my best chance of saving Mona would be to find Granger and see if he knew of her whereabouts. I double-checked that the safety on my 1911 was off and that the clip was intact. Then, hunched over like Quasimodo, I made my way to the fan unit that opened to the cavern full of caged freaks. I felt like a mouse that was trying to sneak into a snake's lair, or maybe like that Hobbit guy who was trying to sneak past that dragon in the movie I saw last summer. Yeah, I only saw one movie. There I was, though, hunching along like a sacrificial victim in a B-rated drive-in flick. The hair on my neck was raised, and my nerves were on full alert.

When I reached the duct through which we had escaped just a few hours ago, I was surprised but relieved to discover that the fan had not been bolted back into place and that I could easily move it to the side and slip by it quietly. I approached the vent cover and found that it, too, was simply stuffed into the vent shaft opening, just the way that Granger had left it last night. Nothing had been reattached in any sort of permanent fashion. When I peered out the slits in the cover, it was dark and quiet on the other side. Across the cavern, a light on the wall near Granger's work room gave off the subtle glow of a night light, so it didn't brighten the space enough to let me see if a trap had been set.

I remembered that Granger had closed himself into the cage that sat directly below the vent opening, so I called out to him with a loud whisper. "Granger! Pssst, Granger! Are you there?" The sounds of restless movement came from the cage, as though its inhabitant had been disturbed briefly from sleep, but there was no response to a known name. "Granger, is that you?" I asked again. Nothing.

I removed my backpack and found the six-foot nylon strap I had brought along for one single purpose. Sitting on the floor of the shaft, I threaded the strap through the top slits of the vent cover and then gently pushed the cover out of the opening with my feet. "Ooof," I grunted, holding tightly onto the strap when it stopped the heavy cover's descent to the floor below. Then, I let it slip to the floor, where its metallic "clang" against the concrete floor brought a brief stirring of annoyed arousal from the cages around the cavern. I held my breath and waited for the door on the far side to open, but it didn't.

After a long thirty seconds, I turned off my cap light and

lowered myself to the floor. In the cage where I had last seen Granger stood a calf with an almost human face. Its eyes were larger than a human's but had an eerie stare that cut through me like a surgeon's scalpel. I had to turn away. To my left slept a child with three-fingered hands, sucking on its middle finger while it dreamed. I was reminded of the Nazi experiments on humans in the 1940s and wondered if those bastards on level four had anything to do with this child's disfigurement.

Thoughts of Mona filled my mind again. If some weirdo alien scientist would do this to a kid, what would he do to Mona? I had to find her, and to do that I had to find Granger. I looked in the direction of his work room and found my way through the maze of cages until I reached the steel door to the small space where he had puttered away forty years of his life in service to the aliens. I put my ear against the door and heard no activity, so I tried the latch. It was locked. Not having a clue what else to do, I knocked, like a kid hoping to sell magazine subscriptions to some stranger.

Instinctively, I pulled out my 1911 when the latch clicked and the door actually opened. It was Granger! And he was just as surprised to see me as I was to see him.

"Granger! You're safe," I exclaimed, giving him an un-expected hug while pointing my pistol at the work room behind him just in case he wasn't alone. "I thought you were a goner."

"When they found me, I told them that two men done locked me in that cage."

"And they believed you?"

"Yup. If they had captured you and your friend, my story would have done been nearly true. Besides, I been working for them for most of my life, and I ain't never tried to es-cape. Why wouldn't they believe me?"

"God, Granger," I reiterated, "it is just so good to see you alive and kicking!"

"Why did you come back, Mr. Arrow? Do you want me to go with you now?"

"There's always a place for you with me, Granger, but I came back because they have Mona."

"Who is Mona?" he asked.

"She's a woman I work with, Granger. But more than that, she's the woman I love. She and two other guys were leaving the complex when they were discovered at level three. The two men are dead, but I don't know about Mona. Do you know anything about her—maybe about a new woman who was brought here early this morning?"

"They ain't said anything to me about no new woman. She wouldn't be here, anyway, Mr. Arrow. She probably would be held on level six, where they do the breeding program."

I didn't like the sound of that. "Breeding program?" I asked.

"Hybrids, Mr. Arrow. They're trying to develop a better hybrid species, part human and part alien. They need our physical bodies because we's used to the Earth's environment, but they think we need their advanced smarts and mind powers."

"Why wouldn't they just come forward to suggest it to us, Granger? Lots of people would like telepathic powers, and God knows we could all benefit from more intelligence."

"They done been making hybrids for thousands of years, Mr. Arrow, and they ain't never asked permission."

"I don't understand, Granger."

"One of them done told me that when they develop a new hybrid, they kill off the remainder of the old ones. Remember the story of Noah? It ain't true the way they tell it in Sunday School. It's really about how they killed off one species of us, and the newer, smarter hybrid species took over. Our current type of mankind, Mr. Arrow, we are an experiment in making hybrids. They gave us greater mental power than the old type, but they also created the four races, just to see which one was a better survivor."

"No shit?" I asked. "Do you really believe that?"

"I ain't got no reason not to. They're busy developing Star Children and other hybrids right now. When the time is right, they'll kill off the rest of us and give the Earth to one of them new hybrids to populate."

"Only the strongest survive," I reminded Granger. "Didn't Darwin say that?"

"Only the smartest, Mr. Arrow. You and I will be toast."

I never was the smartest kid in school, but I could run circles around the nerds when it came to street smarts. I didn't know, but maybe there were different kinds of intelligence. Granger's commentary on the origin of mankind left me unsettled because it was somewhat likely that he was telling the truth. Well, perhaps he was telling me what some alien wanted him to believe was the truth. What's the truth anyway? To me, it was a bottle of Scotch, a loaded piece, and Mona in my arms. Nothing else mattered.

"I need to find Mona, Granger. How do you suggest that I get to level six without being seen?"

"You gotta go through the feeding baths to get to the ramp that goes down to level six. You follow me, and I'll take you there, but when we get to the ramp, you're on your own. I got work to do."

"Thanks, man," I said. "I'd be grateful for anything you can tell me about what I'll find or how to negotiate the sixth level."

Granger cleared a spot on a work table, found an electronic drawing pad of some type and began drawing a map with a stylus. "Level six ain't any different from the other levels, 'cept it ain't nothing but aliens. Only a few humans can go there, mostly NWO guards. And, of course, yours truly included. The breeding place is across this big central room. You'll probably find your lady friend in there. If she ain't there, you'll want to go to the transportation center, right over here, 'cause they might be moving her someplace."

"Where would they be likely to move her?" I asked.

"Could be most anyplace if they use the TAUSS...Sandia, Jefferson Mountain, Dulce, Yucca Mountain, Oakville Grade, or maybe even the Greenbrier."

"The TAUSS?" I asked

Granger opened a drawer, shuffled some papers, and then extracted a small pamphlet dated 1984 that bore the name Trans America Underground Subway System. "It's how they moved me here from Dulce, Mr. Arrow. That there booklet is like a bus schedule."

I looked at the pamphlet. On the left hand side was a listing of more than twenty-five locations with arrival and departure times, printed just like a New York City bus schedule. The commuting times were incredible: San Francisco to DC in four hours, Dulce to Denver in forty-five minutes. I couldn't read the ciphers on the right hand side, so I asked, "What's this, Granger?"

"That's the same thing as the English version, 'cept it's in alien."

"Damn, if they move her, it'll be like finding a needle in a haystack."

"You ain't got no time to waste, Mr. Arrow. She could already be gone to anywhere."

Granger had a way of boiling things down to the obvious.

Chapter 23

I followed Granger as he wound through the narrow pathways between dozens of cages in the cavern where Nelson and Miss Billy Powers had been held captive. I tried not to look at the creatures within the cages, because I was pretty sure that most of them were some sort of horrible crossbreed of human beings with God knows what. At one point, I thought I saw a college co-ed whose picture had come across my desk as a missing person a year or two ago. I hoped it was only my imagination. I remembered her mother crying into the television camera, begging that her captor release her daughter and let her come home. I wondered how many missing persons were not victims of human kidnapping, but had actually been abducted by aliens for these awful experiments. I shook that question out of my head, because it was too grisly to contemplate.

As we neared a doorway to somewhere, Granger stopped me and told me that I had to get into a wheeled cage, something like the circus wagons used in the 1800s to display lions, only it was much smaller.

"No way," I told him. "I'd be too easy a mark and would probably find myself in one of those experimental cages within five minutes."

"You can't simply walk beside me, Mr. Arrow. If they see you free, they'll know something is wrong."

"I'm not simply going to walk into a cage by myself,

Granger. That would be stupid and suicidal, and I'm not going down without a fight."

Granger sighed and then picked up a metallic device that looked like a single leg shackle and said, "Well, maybe if you wear one of these, we can avoid suspicion."

We were going into alien territory, and I knew that Granger was right about not raising suspicions, so I reluctantly agreed. Granger opened the device, but instead of putting it on my leg, he snapped it around my neck.

"What the fuck, Granger," I snapped. "I'm not wearing this fucking gorilla collar."

As I began to fumble with my fingers trying to remove the collar, Granger took my wrists in his large hands. "Mr. Arrow, when we go through that there door, you ain't nothing but a gorilla to them what's on the other side. You gotta act like you ain't angry or upset. You gotta pretend that you've been through this door a dozen times. You gotta react to nothing you see, like you're a zombie. Do you understand?"

I nodded. I figured that maybe he made sense, but I didn't like the restriction of the collar, much less the idea of being somebody's monkey on a leash. About the time I finished that thought, though, Granger did exactly what I feared. He snapped a wire rope onto a loop on the collar and started walking toward the doorway. At that point, I knew how a dog felt the first time he wore a collar, and his range of motion was restricted by a length of rope. Some dogs just gave in and complied, but if I were a dog, I'd be the one who kept tugging at the end of his leash, attempting to pull his master anywhere that his master didn't want to go, and always in the opposite direction. It was a matter of attitude. Walking like a compliant zombie was going to be against my basic nature. I was putting my life into Granger's hands, and I wasn't the kind of guy who trusted others in that sort of way.

Pulling me along, Granger pushed open the doorway, and we entered hell. Hell was highly structured and orga-

nized into long rows of glass tanks with reddish-brown fluids that contained decomposing body parts. I mean a school
kid could see feet with toes, segments of arms and legs, and
entrails that swam as the motion of the fluid swirled like a
hot tub in slow motion.

The cavern must have held a hundred of those tanks, and
maybe more. In many, but not all, tubs sat gray aliens, bathing in the fluids, like a bunch of women in a spa full of
bubble baths. There was no question that this was what
Miss Powers had been forced to do to keep that body of
hers alive.

These suckers are having dinner, I thought. I wanted to
pour in some gasoline, light it, and serve their meal flambé.

Several small Greys came toward us. They looked at me
quizzically. "C'mon, you!" Granger ordered, pulling me
along the concrete aisle. "Ain't no time to dawdle. You
need your DNA extracted." One Grey stopped as though he
wanted to ask Granger about me, but Granger pulled me
away from the Greys as though he had a mission to fulfill. I
remembered one of the dweebs telling me never to look the
Greys in the eye because they could read your thoughts. I
might have done that briefly, so I made a mental note to
look at the ground when their large eyes turned in my direction.

As we moved along, a corridor appeared on the left, and
I could see soldiers standing guard and a few people, men
and women, in lab coats with clip boards. But the soldiers
weren't Nazis, they were ours! They were dressed in American Army uniforms. Granger paused for a moment and
then turned to the right, pulling my neck as he quickened
his pace down an adjoining hallway to the right. After a few
yards, a uniformed guard stopped him. I noticed the insignia
on his chest. A green alien with red eyes was superimposed
over the Earth and around the perimeter was the phrase "A
Lifetime of Silence Behind the Green Door." A red dot was
sewn into the southwest of the USA. I figured it meant Dulce.

"Where are you taking this lab rat, Mr. Taylor?" he asked with authority.

"He needs his DNA extracted," Granger replied.

"DNA extraction has been relocated to corridor thirty-five, room G."

"When did they go and do that?" Granger asked.

"Three days ago. You were notified."

"Didn't read no updates yet. Been too busy."

"You're going to get yourself vaporized one day, Mr. Taylor."

"No need to be getting uppity. I'll take this'un back to corridor thirty-five, room G."

Granger turned around and pulled me back toward the feeding tubs. We took a left turn and passed at least twelve rows of feeding tubs before we came to another door. Granger pressed his eye against a panel to the right of the door, and the door popped open. This room was dimly lit and warm. Here, cylindrical glass containers glowed with a subtle yellow light. Each tube was about eight feet tall and contained a humanoid body suspended in some kind of liquid. As we passed the cylinders, I could see that each body was at a varying stage of growth.

"What is this room?" I whispered at Granger.

"Shhh!" Granger replied.

I grabbed the leash with my left arm and gave it a tug. "What's going on in here, Granger?" I asked firmly.

Granger stopped, looked around quickly, and replied, "They's growing clones. These is all hybrids of one kind or another."

"Are they alive?" I asked.

"Not really. They ain't alive until the aliens migrate somebody into them."

"They can really do that? Like they did to Billy Powers?"

"They can do it to anybody, so long as it suits their purposes. The problem is that the new body don't last too long, so them that's migrated gotta keep getting migrated."

"Oh," I said.

"Now shush!" Granger ordered, pulling me forward again.

We passed out of the growth chamber facility and entered what appeared to be a raw tunnel, sort of like entering into the maintenance section of a skyscraper. On the outside where business is conducted, everything is made of beautiful marble, brass, and polished mahogany, but in the belly, everything is raw concrete and exposed pipes, where dirty laundry and garbage wait for removal through some back door into an alley.

We walked about a hundred yards in the dim light of the tunnel until we came to a door with a strange hieroglyph that I thought might be Egyptian.

"This symbol means 'down' in alien, Mr. Arrow," Granger said, pointing to the inverted pyramid with a sword. "If you see one the other way, it means 'up.' Got it?"

I nodded as I removed the collar from my neck.

"You're on your own from here," Granger said. "This here door leads to another one that opens into the ramp that goes down to level six. You can expect a lot of traffic between levels five and six. It's been nice knowing you, Mr. Arrow. I hope you find your lady friend. I don't 'spect to see you again."

Granger knew he was pushing a blind man onto the freeway at rush hour. It was very likely that I'd be intercepted by the first alien or black ops soldier who figured out that I didn't belong down there.

I shook Granger's hand. "Thanks, buddy. You're one of the good guys, Granger." He patted my shoulder as our eyes met. Then I opened the door and closed it quietly behind me.

The narrow hallway led about thirty feet to a foyer which contained the exit door to the ramp, as well as a trash canister and a laundry cart that was overflowing with miscellaneous clothes. *Bonanza!* I thought. Rummaging through the laundry cart, I found a pair of coveralls that were about my size. They were spattered with a little blood, but I figured they would help me get into level six. When I put them on, however, I had no access to my 1911 which was not a good thing. So, I reached behind my back and pinched a crease into the coveralls where they covered my piece. Then I removed the coveralls and used my pocket knife to cut a six inch vertical slit along the crease that would let me pull out my defensive weaponry if necessary. I put the coveralls back on, reached behind my back and extracted my pistol. It was a little less efficient with the coveralls in the way, but the slit only added a fraction of a second to my quick draw. It would have to do.

I found a couple of plastic bags near the top of the trash canister. In the second one that I opened, I found a scratched pair of safety goggles, which I decided would add a little more identity protection to my disguise. So I put them on, took a deep breath, and exited the door to the ramp to level six with a devil-be-damned attitude.

The ramp was not unlike the ones in the Dulce facility. It was a full two-lane highway, with pedestrian walkways clearly marked along both sides. Industrial sconces mounted near the ceiling every 100 feet along the tunnel wall gave ample light for pedestrians. Vehicles, both those on wheels and those hovering a few feet above the ground, used head-lights to light their way. It was noisy, and I was in alien central. Beings of an assortment of sizes and shapes walked in both directions, Greys, reptilians, humans, and some hu-manoids that were at least eight feet tall. Humans, both male and female, wore lab coats or uniforms representing various branches, some US Army, US Navy, US Air Force, US Marines and even a few Nazis. I wanted to stare and to study each of them, but I remembered Granger's admoni-tion not to act as though I didn't belong. There was nothing to do except join the procession that was winding its way downhill.

I thought I might blend in better if I appeared to be part

of a group, so when two male humans in lab coats passed by, I fell in behind them and walked as casually as possible. They spoke in some language that I didn't understand, perhaps a Slovakian or Russian dialect. The man on the left carried a jacket over his shoulder, his identification card dangled from it on a lanyard. I removed the card as quickly as possible and put it into my pocket. When we reached the gate to level six, a tall reptilian stood watch as a single file line formed and individuals swiped their cards through a standard credit card reader to gain entry through a turnstile. The man in front of me panicked when he couldn't find his card. Protesting vehemently, he was quickly pulled aside and removed by alien guards, who wore green uniforms with the NWO symbol on their left breast plates. I swiped his card and simply entered as though I knew exactly what to do and where I was going.

Picturing the map that Granger had drawn on his electronic tablet, I moved through the giant cavern in the general direction of the transportation center. When I opened the door, the strong smell of snakes hit me in the face, as a wall of warm air rushed past me. *It's just like the subways in New York*, I thought. But when the cylindrical vehicle that pushed the air appeared, there was no sound at all until its doors were released and its passengers began to disembark. Both ends of the vehicle looked like the head of a blunt-nosed lead bullet. I walked close to the edge of the platform and saw no wheels. *So this is what a mag-lev transporter looks like*, I thought. Granger had told me about them only yesterday.

A reptilian guard approached me and gestured that I was to move away from the transporter. I saluted casually and walked toward the small waiting area. About a dozen or so beings sat on hard-backed metal benches inside the room, but Mona was not among them. "God, I pray that I am not too late to save her," I mumbled to myself. Then, I traced my steps back the way I had come and turned left toward the breeding rooms.

Granger had told me that there were two doors to the breeding area. The first was a double swinging door that anyone could enter, but to get into the areas where individuals were held in private rooms after surgery, one had to have proper credentials. I didn't know how I was going to negotiate that hurdle. However, when I pushed open the swinging door, a loud voice bellowed, "Finally you are here! The dead one in Four B needs to be prepared for the bathing pools!"

"I'm new," I replied to the seven foot tall woman with blond hair and jet black eyes who stood behind a control panel. "Where will I find the corpse?"

"They always send new guys on the ugly assignments," she complained. She touched a computer screen with one of her four long fingers, and a panel opened from the floor to the ceiling in the middle of the wall in front of me. "Down the corridor and on the right," she said pointing to the doorway. "And hurry! Commander Beadle has the new female waiting in Four J and wants her moved to better quarters immediately. The sooner you get the cadaver out of Four B, the sooner we can prep the room for Beadle's special one!"

I hurried into the opening and began looking for room numbers, but the only markings on the doors were alien hieroglyphs. So, I started counting A, B, C, D…until I got to J. I peered into the room and surprised the beings attending to a dark-skinned woman in the throes of labor. "Sorry," I said and closed the door.

Then I darted to the end of the corridor and began counting again, as though the numbers began at the end and ran backward. When I came to the tenth room, I quietly pressed open the door and peeked in. There she was! It was Mona, and she was alone!

I rushed to her side. When she saw me, her eyes filled with tears. "Mona, baby! It's me! I'm gonna get you out of here!" I said, holding her face with my hands and kissing her lips

Mona couldn't move her arms or legs. Her eyes, however, darted back and forth. "What is it, baby? What are you trying to tell me?" It was only through her eye motions that I realized that she was being held captive by the very gurney on which she appeared to be resting. "Which way, baby?" I asked excitedly. "Where are the controls?"

Mona looked upward toward the top of her head. "The wall?" I asked. "Are the controls behind you on the wall?" She blinked twice.

The wall behind Mona held an array of electronic devices, dials, gauges, tubes, and switches. I pushed and pulled at them, frantically trying to find the one that wirelessly held her captive. Nothing seemed to do the trick. Then I turned to her gurney. Attached to the end near her feet was a flat panel with blinking lights. I pushed a few buttons unsuccessfully and then kicked the panel sideways, causing it to fall onto the floor. Then I picked it up and smashed it against the wall panel several times.

"Danny! Danny, you're alive!" Mona suddenly exclaimed.

I turned just as she threw her arms around me, causing us both to fall backward against the wall. She planted kisses all over my face, neck, and lips. "Oh, Danny, they told me that you were dead! Oh God, how I love you!"

"Me, too, baby," I told her, "I love you so very much. I thought I'd never see you again! "

"Well, you took your goddamn time, you bastard!" she replied. "I expected you yesterday!"

I laughed. "Come on, Mona, we've got to get you out of here."

Mona wasn't dressed for traveling. She was in a gown made of some sort of strange material, and she was barefoot. It was important that we get her the things she would need to climb out of this den of lizards. More immediate and probably more important, we had to get out of the breeding area without drawing attention to ourselves.

"Listen, Mona, they think I'm here to remove a cadaver. You have to be that cadaver."

Mona agreed and hurried to a built-in cabinet, where she removed a bed sheet. "Cover me with this, and let's get going," she cried. "They're planning to ship me to Ada, Oklahoma sometime in the next few days."

"Never heard of it," I shrugged.

"We'll have to Google it. It's probably off of the radar screen," Mona replied. "From what I can gather, it may be a cloning facility and possibly a nursery."

"Are they growing flowers?" I asked.

"No, they're growing slaves and hybrids."

Mona climbed back onto the gurney while I shook the sheet open. Placing it over her, I said, "I'll try not to mess your hair, sweetie."

"Cut the shit, Danny. Just get me out of here!"

I loved a woman with moxie!

I opened the door and peered both ways down the corridor. The coast looked clear, so I pulled on the end of Mona's gurney and rolled it out of the room.

"Here we go," I whispered to Mona. "Wish us luck."

"Are you packing your forty-five?" Mona asked from under the sheet.

"Yeah, baby."

"That's all the luck you'll need." Then she added, "If you see a gray lizard called Nargas, put a couple of rounds in his face for me."

We came to the end of the corridor and into the foyer where the giant blonde woman had greeted me. She was speaking with a guy in a set of coveralls like mine when I rolled Mona by. I gave the woman a salute with my pointer finger and pushed the gurney into the swinging door. Immediately an alarm sounded and the woman shouted, "Halt! Stop! You there, halt!" I pushed through the door and entered the outer cavern.

The guy who had been talking with the incredible growing woman charged after us and grabbed my left arm. I pulled my pistol out of my belt and cold cocked him in the temple with the steel butt of my 1911. His legs buckled, and he went down like Marvis Frazier thirty seconds into round one with Mike Tyson. But I knew we were in trouble because the cavern had been bustling with business, and it all came to a grinding halt when Frazier hit the floor.

I quickly dashed toward the exit to the ramp but could see four lizard guards readying to stop me. Mona squealed when I suddenly pulled the gurney to a grinding halt. "Hold on, baby!" I shouted to her as I spun the gurney and pushed it quickly toward the far wall. "We're into some shit!"

"Shoot something!" Mona shouted at me.

"Stay under the sheet, baby. You're supposed to be dead!"

I could see a small squad of NWO guards running toward me from my left. I pushed a small gray alien to the floor in hopes that his body would delay their advance, and then I turned to the right and sprinted into the transportation center. The gurney lurched as its wheels abruptly hit the metal floor plate that divided the center from the main cavern. It careened on two wheels for a moment, and then it crashed onto its side, sending Mona tumbling onto the concrete floor. She was immediately jerked to her feet by a tall lizard in uniform, who touched his breast plate and sent a ball of white light whizzing from his helmet, just missing my left ear. I fired my .45 in his general direction, causing him to hold Mona in front of him as a shield. *At least he can't shoot me*, I thought. But Mona kicked herself free and punched him in the solar plexus, causing a volley of white light balls to leap from his helmet and ricochet around the room, breaking glass and making that peculiar whining sound that I first heard in the cavern in Dulce.

"Run, Danny!" Mona screamed. "Save yourself!"

The lizard grabbed Mona's wrist and handed her to two of the NWO guards who had entered the room in assault mode. I dived behind a row of metal benches to take out a few of the guards, but my 1911 spun from my hand as I hit the floor. As I reached for it, a size twenty-five black boot pressed down on my wrist like a Hummer had just parked on it. I froze, waiting for some sort of blow to my head. Instead, I felt large hands grasp my ankles and lift me into the air. Suspended upside down, I saw the NWO guards pop to attention.

Chapter 24

I s she injured?" Commander Beadle barked to the reptilian soldier who had captured Mona.

"She appears unharmed, Commander. The male discharged his weapons at her, but he was off target."

The commander's forked tongue darted out twice. He turned his gaze at Dan Arrow, held upside down by two ten foot tall Ummite renegades. "If that one had injured Commissar Nargas's issue, we all would have been nourishment for the Greys." He returned his gaze to the reptilian soldier. "You will accompany the Ummites to the feeding baths. You will personally cleave this male's container into one hundred parts and distribute a piece of it into every tub. Start with his extremities and make his death slow."

"It will be an honor to do your bidding, Commander," the reptilian hissed. "And what of the female, Sir?"

"She is mine."

Commotion at the entrance caused both Commander Beadle and the reptilian to look in that direction. "Greetings, Commissar!" Commander Beadle said when he saw Commissar Nargas stride through the entrance behind an entourage of his personal reptilian guard.

"I thought that the female was in good hands when I left her in yours, Commander," the commissar growled. He paused as he passed Mona, still in the grasp of two NWO guards, looked into her eyes and telepathically asked, '*Are you unharmed, my precious?'* Mona spit at his chest. *'Yes, you are well, and your spirit is unbroken.'*

"Commissar, the young guard who left her unattended has been vaporized," Beadle said. "It was indeed an unfortunate and unforeseeable circumstance. I could not have anticipated his disloyalty to our cause or to his oath of allegiance."

"And it is fortunate that the female has not been harmed, Commander," Nargas hissed. "Where is the male who tried to take her?"

Commander Beadle stepped aside, bowed slightly, and fanned his hand in Arrow's direction.

"You will dispose of his container, I assume."

"The order already has been issued, Commissar."

"Excellent. I want no further interference."

Commissar Nargas turned to his adjutant. "Commandeer the next shuttle to Dulce."

"It leaves momentarily, sir."

"I want no one else on board except my guard and the female."

"It will be done, sir.

The commissar's guard moved into the shuttle and removed its occupants. A human in a technician's garb protested that he was due in Dulce immediately and could not wait for the next shuttle. The commissar's adjutant looked at a guard member and flicked his pointer finger in the direction of the technician. The guard touched his breast plate, and the technician was cut in half by a ball of white light. Everyone left the shuttle quickly, and nobody else protested. The adjutant spoke into a device on his collar. Within a minute, a team of four Greys and two reptilian laborers appeared and cleaned up the mess.

Still hanging by his ankles, Dan Arrow watched as Mona was escorted onto the shuttle with the commissar and his personal guard. The shuttle door closed, and then with only a slight whooshing sound, disappeared into the darkness of its horizontal shaft.

Arrow looked at his watch. It was two-fifteen a.m., Mountain Time.

Commander Beadle looked at the reptilian soldier. "Dispose of his container immediately and painfully."

The reptilian pressed a small metal disk to Arrow's temple and tapped its center with his forefinger. The disk glowed brightly for an instant. Arrow's body arched and he lost consciousness.

Chapter 25

I was dreaming of snakes when the smell of ammonia roused me into consciousness. My head was pounding like the morning after a black-out drunk on cheap wine. I wasn't sure where I was or even who I was. Then I felt calloused hands grab my face. When I opened my eyes, two yellow snake eyes were peering into mine, and I heard a voice deep inside my head say, '*Feeding time, asshole.*'

I tried to move my hands to punch the reptilian face that was emitting a foul stench into my nose, but I couldn't move my arms.

'*I can read your thoughts, Earthling,*' the lizard told me. His eyes blinked sideways.

Aw, fuck me, I thought.

'*That's hitting the nail on the head, Earthdung. You've done enough damage by trying to kill Commissar Nargas's issue. But you failed your mission, and now you must pay the failed assassin's penalty.*'

What issue? I thought. *I don't have any issues, except how to get my hands free to squeeze your ugly neck.*

'*Your containers are weak. Their electro-nervous systems are simplistic. Did you know that a single sound wave renders you helpless against us? Look at how trapped you are in your container.*'

What the fuck is this bastard up to? I wondered.

'*I told you that I can read your thoughts, Earthling. Be-*

cause of your misdeeds, Commander Beadle has ordered the equal distribution of your container into the feeding baths. Your container will soon feed our slaves and clones.'

I pictured the feet and intestines that I'd seem floating in the feeding tanks at level five. *Container? Do you mean my body?* I thought.

'*It is only a container, Earthling. If you were worth the trouble, we would move you into a different container after we destroy this one. But Commander Beadle has ordered no such migration. You will simply cease.*'

Oh, fuck! I thought.

'*I understand your sentiment, Earthling. The commander also ordered your distribution to be slow and painful. I will enjoy watching you writhe in agony. And when you wish for death, I will ensure that your miserable existence is painfully extended.*'

The voice inside my head stopped abruptly when the lizard turned away. I saw movement to my right and glanced to see what he was doing. His long, scaly fingers placed a tray with instruments of obvious torture onto a table of some type which was positioned beside my body. I also noticed that one nail on his right hand was deformed. I hoped that it ripped the inside of his nostril whenever he picked his nose.

When the reptilian moved away, I looked above me and saw the reflection of my naked body in the polished chrome frame of the light which glared down at me. The vain side of me wished that I had paid more attention to staying fit, but then I realized that there wasn't anything that I could do about it at the moment, and I wondered if the Greys would mind the extra portion of fat that my love handles would add to their diet.

Motion to my right drew my attention again. The surgeon was selecting his first instrument of fun.

He looked at me, and the voice inside my head asked, '*Would you prefer me to start with your toes, fingers, or eyes?*'

How about cutting off that deformed finger of yours, you cocksucker, I thought. *Cut it off and shove it up your ass.*

The reptilian moved a bucket-looking container to a position near my feet. *'I guess we'll start here,'* he told me. *'If I remove your eyes, you won't be able to see what I will remove next. Your anticipation of pain will bring fear, and that is what is the most fun about this process.'*

He lifted a tool that looked like a cigar smoker's multi-tool and snapped it open and closed twice. He positioned it over the big toe on my left foot. *There goes my chance to win next year's Boston Marathon,* I thought and closed my eyes in anticipation of the shot of pain. The lizard hissed, and then I heard the sound of something heavy hitting flesh. As I opened my eyes, I felt four hundred pounds of iguana fall against my calves and then slide to the floor with a heavy thud.

"Mr. Arrow. You ain't dead, are you?"

It was Granger! He was holding a three-foot piece of iron pipe in his hand, and his eyes were wild with excitement.

"Mr. Arrow! Mr. Arrow!" he repeated, slapping my face with his free hand. Then he seemed to realize that I lay paralyzed by the alien sound technology. "Oh yeah," he said. He walked away from view. I heard him click a switch and suddenly I was free.

"Can you move now, Mr. Arrow?"

"Granger, I want to kiss you," I exclaimed. "You big hunk of hero! That lizard you cold-cocked was going to cut off my toes one by one!"

"You were right, Mr. Arrow," he said.

I nodded, not sure what he was trying to say.

"I forgot that I'm one of the good guys, Mr. Arrow. I forgot that a long time ago. There was lots of people that I done let the aliens experiment on without trying to help them. There ain't no way that I'm going to let them do it no more!"

"You *are* one of the good guys, Granger. Right now

you're the *best* one of them," I replied, giving him a bear hug.

"Where's your clothes, Mr. Arrow?" he asked. "I ain't never been hugged by a naked man before."

Granger's question made me suddenly aware of my nakedness, even though I had seen it in the reflection above me while I was on the chopping block. I felt stupidly self-conscious standing in front of him dangling in the breeze, and I had no idea where my clothes were.

"Your stuff is probably in the trash," Granger said matter-of-factly.

"Where would that be?"

"Probably out in the hallway."

I quickly stepped over to the large steel door, gently opened it, and peered out. Heaped on the floor against the wall were my clothes and shoes, waiting for maintenance to dispose of them. I scooped them up into my arms and backed quickly into the butcher shop.

While I dressed, Granger started telling me where we were and how we were going to get out. "You're back on level five," he began. "I heard you were in the food prep lab from a Grey that you knocked down outside of the transportation center."

"Yeah, I remember that little guy."

"You bruised his shoulder."

"It was only collateral damage, Granger. I hoped he would slow down some uniformed guys who were trying to catch me."

"They must have been NWO guards," Granger replied. "Anyway, this Grey told me all about the shootout in the transportation center. He was amazed that you didn't get yourself vaporized."

"Me, too, frankly," I said.

"So, after they done took your girlfriend away, they dragged you up here to the food prep lab. I figured I'd come see if you was dead or alive. When I saw you wasn't dead, I knew that if I was one of the good guys, I'd have to bust you out of here. So, I whumped that reticulan, and the rest is gonna have to be figured out as it happens."

"Reticulan?"

"From Zeta Reticuli. It's a bunch of stars a long way from here, Mr. Arrow."

"Do you know where they took Mona?" I asked, quickly tying my shoes.

"Nope. But it was a regularly scheduled shuttle, not one of the special ones. The commissar upset a bunch of folks when he booted them off of that shuttle."

"It was two-fifteen when that shuttle left. Where does the two-fifteen morning shuttle go?"

"Don't remember, but you can check the schedule back in my shop."

"Well, damn it, let's get going before Barney here wakes up!" I replied. "Which way out of here?"

"We gotta turn left down the hallway. At the end, take a right and then the first left through the feeding tanks. We gotta weave our way through the feeding tanks to the yellowish light on the far wall. That leads to the cavern with my office. Don't go to the whitish light, because that leads to the draconian sleeping quarters."

"You sound like you aren't coming with me," I told him.

"I am, but you never know what might happen. I just got this worrying feeling."

Granger opened the door and looked out. "Come on," he urged, "there's no telling who might come down this way. There's always somebody they's putting in the soup."

I took a sharp blade from the table of reticulan tools and stuck it in my belt. It looked a little like an Alaskan skinning knife that I was given by a client a couple of years ago, except that it had a hooked barb at the tip. At any rate, I didn't have my 1911 anymore, and I thought some kind of weapon for close combat was better than none at all.

Granger was still carrying his piece of pipe. His batting average was 1.00 at the moment, and I was sure he could hit a home run any time he needed to.

At Granger's nod, I exited the door and turned left, as directed.

We hustled to the end of the concrete corridor and turned right. At the first door on the left, we entered the feeding area. Most of the tanks were swirling away, nourishing Greys, who lay reclined with headsets on. God only knows what kind of shit they were listening to, maybe David Gray, or Joel Grey, or the theme song to Grey's Anatomy. Maybe they were listening to Grey Street by Dave Matthews, Grey Day by Guess Who, or Touch of Grey by the Grateful Dead. I shook my head to stop this train of stupid trivia from running through it. *Maybe I've been underground too long*, I thought. *Keep focused, Arrow!*

Granger stopped. "They done changed all the lights to the yellowish color, Mr. Arrow. I ain't sure now which one it is."

"Granger, you've lived down here for twenty years. Certainly, you know how to get back."

"Actually, I never come this way. I only did that today because that fella told us that the DNA extraction unit done been moved. I knew how to get there by looking on a site plan map, but getting back is a different story. I never thought you'd last so long, Mr. Arrow."

"Well, which wall is it, Granger?"

He pointed to two sconces that hung near a corner. "I'm pretty sure it is one of them two, but I'm a bit turned around."

"There's only one way to find out," I told him.

We weaved through the isles between the feeding tanks, zigzagging in the general direction of the sconces. Suddenly, three human NWO guards appeared in front of us.

One of them ordered, "Halt!"

We complied. As they approached us, Granger leaned toward me. "When I start swinging, you run to the sconces. I think it's the one on the right!"

"Granger..." I replied, hoping there was a better tactic.

"Do as I say, Mr. Arrow. The good guys always win!"

The guards stopped within arm's distance and demanded to know where we were assigned. Granger said, "I'm the head driver."

"For who?" the guard demanded.

I could see Granger's right hand strengthen its grip on the pipe. "I ain't driving for nobody," he replied. "Driving heads is what I do!" With that, he hit another home run, crushing the guard's skull and driving him into the other two. All three fell to the ground. "Run, Mr. Arrow! Run!" Granger cried as he began swinging his pipe overhead, threatening the other two guards, who were peddling backward while still on the floor.

I turned and was gone before Granger's words stopped echoing in the cavern. As I twisted and turned through the narrow pathways between the feeding tanks, Greys sat up abruptly, splashing liquid onto the floor behind me. Then I heard two quick shots followed a few moments later by a third. Granger had probably taken a couple of those.

Sooner than anticipated, I reached the first sconce and quickly opened the door beneath it. The passageway on the other side just didn't look right. Maybe it was the lighting, or maybe the desert brown color of the walls, or possibly the ominous smell of snakes, but I knew I had taken the wrong doorway. As I turned to retreat, I suddenly felt the grip of a reptilian on my left bicep. He hissed at me. I pulled the skinning knife from my belt and stabbed it into his wrist. He let out a squeal of pain and slammed me backward against the wall. But my grip on the knife was strong, and I tugged it downward with sharp pulls—one, two, three or more, each one ripping two or more inches through his flesh. He dropped me to the floor and fled back down the hallway, I assumed for band aids, and probably for more reinforcements.

I reached the exit and stumbled back out into the feeding area. Stopping for a moment to get my bearings and to catch my breath, I heard a commotion coming in my direction, but still maybe fifty yards away. The greasy liquid from the feeding tanks may have been slowing the progress of my pursuers. I followed the wall to a nearby corner and then another fifty feet or so to the second sconce. I opened the door beneath it, dashed down the hallway, and soon found myself back in the cavern of cages where Granger and I had first met. *You picked the wrong door, Granger*, I thought, *but you had the correct two eye-balled!*

I wound my way through the cages until I got to Granger's office. It looked as though nobody had been to visit him while he was helping me. Then again, how would I know since it was such a mess? The computer monitor on the workbench nearest his stool was flashing, so I checked it out. The message alternated between some alien hieroglyphic symbols and the word *NOTICE!* I assumed that both messages said the same thing, intended for different audiences. I touched the screen, and the flashing stopped. A message then appeared:

> *Disturbance at level six contained.*
> *Migration of his excellency relocated.*
> *Essential personnel remain Denver.*
> *All others report Livermore 2 days at 0200 hours.*
> *Dress uniforms.*
> *The Day is at hand!*
> *Cmsr. Nargas*

I'd have to think about the message, but who had time to think? I jotted it down on a piece of paper and shoved it into my pocket so that I could think later. Right now, though, I needed to find that shuttle schedule and figure out where they'd taken Mona.

The schedule was where we had left it, partly unfolded and next to a small pile of miscellaneous pieces of metal that resembled Erector Set components. I opened the schedule and ran my finger down the English side until I came to 0215. Dulce! *Mona is in Dulce!* That's all I needed. It was a no-brainer. Well, at least it was a best guess, and it gave me a plan of action: I would go get Nelson and McGarvey, and we'd head back to Dulce to find Mona.

The clanging of cage doors being opened began to break the silence of the morning. Along with the noise came various shrieks and howls. The door to Granger's office was still open, so I peered out. The noise was definitely coming from the direction of the door to the feeding area, so I figured that the NWO guards had followed my scent and soon would be on me.

There was no time to lose. I bolted out the door and headed toward the air duct that had served as my entrance/exit since yesterday. Along the way, creatures and half-humans reached out at me and shook the bars on their cages as I passed. Some cried for help, but I didn't stop. There was no way most of them could ascend the rungs to the surface, and having them tag along would only slow me down. Besides, most of the cages had some form of electronic locking device that I couldn't open. At least I rationalized that I couldn't, and I didn't feel like I had the time to try to find out. *God will probably judge me poorly for that.*

When I reached the air shaft, the vent cover still rested against the wall. I grabbed the end of the nylon strap that was still attached to the cover, then used the cover as a step to help me climb up into the shaft. Quickly, I lifted the cover upward to set it back into its intended position. The noise of opening cages was getting much closer and, looking backward I could see shapes moving in the dim light. *I'm going to be toast,* I thought. They would be on me in no time, and I felt helpless without my 1911.

As I turned to exit past the fan, the vent cover was suddenly jerked outward and clanged to the floor. Large human hands grasped at the floor of the shaft, and I braced myself for the worst.

"Mr. Arrow! Mr. Arrow! Are you still there? Can you hear me?"

It was Granger!

I scurried on all fours back to the hole in the wall,

grasped Granger's wrists, and pulled backward, helping him to get the upper half of his torso into the shaft. "Granger!" I exclaimed, "I thought you were dead."

"Not yet, I ain't!" he replied, breathing heavily. "They done tried to do me in, but this old man ain't done yet." He wrestled the remainder of his large frame into the shaft and rested his back against the wall.

"What about the shots?" I asked.

"The first two was shot at me," he said, pulling back his shirt and showing me a minor flesh wound on his right side. The bleeding had already stopped. "The last shot was sort of mine. I grabbed that fella's gun hand in mine and was turning the gun trying to get it out of his hand. But it went off, and I think it didn't do him no good."

"Thank God you're okay, pal," I said. "Do you think you can climb out of here with me?"

Granger took a deep breath and nodded. "None of them folks I let out of them cages can reach this high," he said, gesturing to the vent hole. "If any of them reticulans or draconians come into this area, them folks will cause them some misery."

"You're thinking like a soldier, Granger," I told him. "Diversionary tactics!"

Granger smiled.

"Come on," I said, tugging on his shirt sleeve, "it's this way."

We took a left at the main air vent and hurried, hunched over, toward the vertical shaft that would take us up to Nelson and McGarvey. Moving hunched over was hard on me, so it had to be extremely hard for Granger. He was a larger man than I am, and he had a few more years on him. I could hear him breathing heavily behind me, so I stopped once to let him catch his breath. Well, it wasn't all for his benefit. So far, it had been an interesting evening. I had been chased and shot at by NWO guards, knocked unconscious by some sort of alien device, stripped and almost dissected by one giant lizard, and then survived a wrestling match with another one. I could feel the toll that the evening's festivities had taken on my body, and I still had to climb out of this hole in the ground.

෨෪෨

I climbed the vertical shaft ahead of Granger, so his arrival wouldn't surprise Nelson and McGarvey. I knew I was near level four when the end of several cords touched my face. I brushed them aside, immediately evoking a voice from above. "Is that you, Dan?" It was Nelson.

"Yeah," I replied, "and I brought Granger with me."

"Granger?" he asked in surprise. "What about Mona?"

"I fucked it up. They've taken her to Dulce."

"You're shitting me!"

"I wish I was. I found her and freed her, but they discovered us and recaptured her."

"How did you manage to escape?" Nelson asked, offering me a hand into the level four side vent.

"Granger cold-cocked a lizard and helped me escape. They were planning to use me as an ingredient in their dinner recipe."

Granger emerged from the shaft, and Nelson offered him the same hand he had offered me. "So you've decided to come up to the surface for fresh air!" Nelson said.

Granger rolled onto his butt and nodded, breathing heavily.

"Thanks for saving Mr. Arrow," McGarvey said to him.

Panting, Granger simply gave the thumbs up sign.

"So what did you discover down there?" Nelson asked me.

"The most important thing I saw was U.S. troops walking alongside reptilians, Greys, NWO troopers, and Nazis. They're all in collusion!"

"No shit?" Nelson asked.

"It's all part of the NWO world domination plan,"

McGarvey chimed in. "Elite teams of specialists from all the armed forces around the globe have been trained in tactics to keep the populace under control when they take over."

"I can't believe that the US Marines or Navy would assist in an overthrow of our government!" I told McGarvey, knowing that he was going to lecture me.

"Only the elite forces, Mr. Arrow. The ones with the extraterrestrial or NWO insignias. All the other military personnel will be assisting the populace with basic survival during the aftermath of some calamity—probably a pandemic, or possibly a manmade mega earthquake that will change the shape of our land mass. The elite forces will be summoned by the president to maintain control through martial law. When he gives that order through the Department of Homeland Security, our country as you know it, including the government as you think you know it, will be history."

Nelson was speechless. I hadn't expected such detail, and I had already figured out the plausibility of what McGarvey believed.

"So how would they create a manmade mega earthquake?" I asked.

"People all around the USA and in some foreign countries have been calling authorities to report loud booms that shake their homes and rattle their dishes. Some report grinding metal-on-metal sounds that they believe may be the trumpets of the end of days. Google it. It is all there for you to see."

"So what does that have to do with a mega earthquake?" Nelson asked

"Although they continue to drill tunnels to create more and more pathways for the TAUSS, with alien assistance the NWO has been tunneling along fault lines deep underground. When their tunneling is complete, a single suitcase nuke will set the whole tectonic plate system in motion. Some theorists believe that California will slip into the ocean and that the Mississippi will flow northward after the plate movement ceases and the dust settles."

"You've got to be kidding me," I told him. "What about that Australian pandemic stuff?"

"Mr. Arrow, they need something like a polar shift, or a pandemic, or something really destructive in order to take control, and the population will be in such shock that anything that looks like help will be welcomed. That's when the railcars with shackles will appear to remove anyone who is aberrant, outspoken, or simply different."

"I've done heard about the drilling," Granger said, "and most of them Marines have shoulder patches with reticulans on them. Is that regular for the Marines? Could be some truth to what your friend here has to say."

"Listen," I said, "we've got time later to contemplate this stuff, and I've got some other stuff to share, but right now there may be a hundred lizards and Nazis climbing up this shaft to kill us. We've got to slow these Nazi bastards down, and you all know how." I looked at Nelson and asked, "Are the canisters all in place?"

"All set," he replied. "There's two at each fan vent, except by the guard desk, where I put three."

"And what about the fans? Did you reverse their polarity?" I asked McGarvey.

"They're all set, Mr. Arrow. It wasn't too difficult because they were standard Carrier units."

"Do we still have four gas masks?" I asked.

"We put fresh canisters in them while we were waiting for you, Dan," Nelson replied.

"Then let's get her done," I replied.

"What about me?" Granger asked.

"You stand guard here, Granger." I gave him the skinning knife that I still had in my belt. "If anything comes up that shaft, slash it in the face with this and push it back down—unless it's Mona."

"Gotcha, Mr. Arrow," he replied.

Nelson handed each of us a gas mask. Before we headed

in opposite directions down the air vent tunnels, McGarvey showed Granger how to put his mask on. When Granger appeared settled with the new apparatus on his face, we synchronized our watches and determined that we would begin opening the valves on the Zyklon canisters in exactly ten minutes. Then, I headed down my tunnel to the third fan vent, and McGarvey and Nelson headed down the opposite vent tunnel to the same relative location.

I got to the third fan vent with two minutes to spare. While I waited, I put the gas mask on and tightened the rubber straps to secure it in place. It smelled like an old tire, but it was better than the coming alternative. I looked through the fan blades into the cavern and could see Nazis stirring. It was morning, and they had duties to perform.

When the second hand on my analog watch hit the ten minute mark, I quickly turned the handle on the first canister lefty-loosey until it was wide open and I could hear the gas rapidly escaping into the cavern beyond the fan. I did the same with the second canister Nelson and McGarvey had positioned here. Then I back-tracked to the second fan vent and did the same. I could already hear coughing and shouts in German that I could not understand.

By the time I reached the first fan vent, pure havoc was reigning in the Nazi cavern. As I began turning the valve on the first canister, the fan system came on. As I had hoped, the fan blew gas into the cavern instead of sucking the gas out and away. "Enjoy this, you creeps," I shouted through the whirling fan blades. "This is for all the poor bastards you gassed in the death camps during World War Two!"

While all my canisters were emptying their love into the cavern, I scurried back to the vertical shaft. McGarvey and Nelson were already there.

"We'd better hoof it, fellas," Nelson said. "There's gonna be a mess of angry hornets after us pretty soon!"

I sent McGarvey and Granger up first, followed by Nelson, and I took up the rear guard.

Before he started his climb, McGarvey handed me his

snub nose .38 in case I should need it. He was right about that.

"Besides," he said, "I don't think I could hit the broad side of a barn with it."

A snub-nose couldn't hit anything you pointed it at if your target was farther than ten feet away, maybe less.

The climb back to level three seemed quick, probably because adrenalin was pumping excitement into every cell in my body. As close to death as I had been that day, I'd never felt more alive. God, I loved an adrenalin high!

The guys were all out of the shaft before I was. The forklift that Nelson had used to carry the Zyklon and to lift the steel grating from the shaft was right where we had left it. As we paused to celebrate the return to level three, we could hear some form of distant commotion coming from the direction of the ramp to level four, so we knew that we would soon have company on this level. "I think I hear your hornets buzzing," I said to Nelson.

I'm not sure who took the lead toward the elevators, but that's the direction we were headed when suddenly the door to the stairway burst open, and half-a-dozen Nazis popped out, looking a bit confused, but seeking their way out of the caverns below. Our group took a quick right and ran toward any kind of hiding place. As we did, we heard the word, "Halt!" We ran even faster.

As we raced past the pallets of Zyklon, I thought maybe we could open a few canisters to slow down our pursuers, but there really wouldn't be enough time before they were on us. My hasty thoughts were interrupted when shots rang out, maybe two, maybe three. I wasn't counting. But I turned as I ran and fired my .38 twice, just to let them know that we were armed. That would cause them to slow down a little and become more cautious. At least I hoped so.

"This way," Nelson shouted.

We followed him through a corridor with high ceilings, past two jeeps with NWO markings, and suddenly we were in a low-lit room with extremely high ceilings. Three giant pieces of tracked machinery stood like stone sentries guarding the entrance to some make-believe harbor. "Laser moles," Nelson shouted. "Come on!"

Ahead of us were the largest machines I had ever seen in my life. They were cylindrical in shape, at least thirty feet in diameter, probably more. At each end, hundreds of three-foot rods with glass eyes projected outward from a protective collar. It reminded me of a lamprey eel. The sides, also cylindrical in shape, included several built-in platforms where technicians or soldiers could stand.

Nelson climbed six rungs which were welded onto the recessed steel panel on the side of one of the machines. When he reached the level platform above the vehicle's large tracks, he opened an oval hatch and disappeared for a few moments. When he reappeared, he beckoned us to follow him. "The keys are in it!" he exclaimed.

We wasted no time climbing aboard. Out of breath from running so quickly, Granger had difficulty pulling himself up the rungs, but with McGarvey's pulling and my pushing from behind, we got him onto the platform, and he crawled on hands and knees to the oval hatch. Then he stood and ducked into the machine. I followed, and we were all inside together. Nelson told me how to lock the hatch. "We're safe for the moment," he told us. "These babies are high temperature impermeable steel. And, they're bullet proof!"

Nelson climbed into the driver's seat with McGarvey beside him as co-pilot. Granger and I strapped ourselves into luggage harnesses that folded down from the interior walls about eight feet behind the pilot stations. Nelson flicked a couple of switches on a control panel in front of him, and a large-screen television came on, showing us everything in front. Along the bottom of the screen were screens within screens, showing us the side and rear views.

"Here they come," Nelson exclaimed, pointing to the rear screen. I could see small figures moving cautiously on the rear screen. Then I heard a muted thumping coming from the quarter decks on the mole.

On one side screen, I could watch as men pried at the hatch in a futile effort to find a way in.

Without warning, our mole screamed like a jet engine coming to life. Nelson had turned this baby on! "It operates on nuclear power," he told us. "The rods on the end are called thermal stress fracturing penetrators. They project light beams which can melt anything on Earth. Beneath them is a muck remover. Along the sides are glass formers that press melted rock into the seams in the rock around them. They create the glass-like walls that you see in the tunnels and caverns."

"Does it get real hot inside when it operates?" McGarvey asked.

"Yeah, but it's air-conditioned, so it won't be too bad." Nelson turned to Granger and me. "Hang on!"

He pushed forward on a control stick, and the mole began creeping along the floor. As he turned a dial, the machine accelerated. On the rear and side screens, I could see Nazis jumping to the cavern floor from various points. I counted an entourage of at least twenty Nazis, and they were following behind us, waiting for us to emerge so they could unleash their anger upon us.

The large front screen suddenly became very bright. "What happened?" I shouted to Nelson.

"The lasers are now on. Gentlemen, we are now creating molten rock!"

We were moving forward through solid rock, and, on the screen, I could see that, behind us, the Nazis were standing at the edge of the cavern we had just exited. As we proceeded, I could see the circular shape of the tunnel behind us. Closest to us, the walls glowed red but quickly darkened, and, by the time we were thirty yards away, they had hardened and become black. I assumed that because of the heat, the Nazis had to hang back until the rock was cool enough to walk on and the air was cool enough to breathe. Then I saw a jeep enter the tunnel behind us. It carried five Nazis.

"We've got company," I shouted to Nelson.

"Yeah," he replied, "those are technician's vehicles. Their tires are made from alien material that can withstand molten temperatures. Can ya'll imagine what that technology would do to our rubber industry if it was commercialized!"

From the pressure of the straps that crisscrossed me like parachute belts, I could sense that we had begun to climb at an upward angle. A small screen in front of McGarvey indicated our angle of ascent. I guessed it was about thirty degrees, and I figured that it was going to take us the better part of two hours to reach the surface.

"How long before we get home?" I shouted to Nelson. "I've got to pee."

Nelson laughed. "We should surface in about fifteen minutes."

"That seems almost too soon," I replied.

"We're clocking six miles per hour, Dan," he said with a wide grin. It was obvious that he was loving his first time behind the wheel. "Comparing this baby to the moles I drive back in Dulce is like comparing a rowboat to a speedboat." I could understand the analogy. In my world, it was like comparing Davey Crockett's Old Betsey to Rambo's AK-47.

Granger looked uneasy. "What's the matter, buddy?" I asked him.

"I ain't been on the surface in a long time, Mr. Arrow."

"I'm sure that a lot has changed, Granger, but you'll be fine once you get adjusted to it." I patted his thigh. "You're going to be something of a celebrity."

"Why do you say that, Mr. Arrow?"

"The world is waiting for someone who has really ridden in a flying saucer and who has worked side-by-side with aliens. Millions of people are looking for the truth to be revealed, and you'll make history when you do. You'll get book offers, and movie offers, and you'll be the guest on dozens of television talk shows. You'll be richer than you could ever have imagined."

. "Sounds like something that ain't real."

"Well, it's different from the United States that you re- member, but it's still the USA, and it's definitely real."

We felt the mole lurch and then suddenly stop, throwing us harshly against our straps. Nelson jumped out of his seat and came back to me. "We've broken through the surface, Dan."

"Well, let's get out and go find Mona," I said, smiling.

"Well," he said, "we're nose up in the middle of a run- way."

"I guess you hadn't figured on that."

"Not exactly," he replied.

The sound of distant sirens led me to say the obvious: "Airport security will be on us in no time!" I looked around the cabin trying to think and then asked Nelson, "Can you put this thing in reverse?" I asked.

"Yeah, no problem."

"Well, good! I'll help McGarvey and Granger out of this buggy. You put this thing into reverse, and that will push the Nazis back into their hole. Then we'll figure out what to tell the authorities."

The sirens were getting closer. I unlocked the hatch and told McGarvey and Granger to come with me. "That was some ride!" McGarvey exclaimed as he exited the mole. But Granger had to shield his eyes from the intense bright- ness of the morning sun. He tried to go back inside the mole, but I told him that staying with the mole was not an option. I helped him find the rungs and McGarvey helped him to the ground.

No sooner was I on the warm tarmac than the mole lurched backward. Nelson appeared in the hatchway and waited until the hatch was at ground level before simply stepping onto the runway. Then, we all stood watching in awe as the mole slowly slipped into the ground. "I set it for two miles per hour," Nelson told us.

Two armored panel trucks and a security squad car stopped around us, blocking our exit in any direction, except if we decided to jump down into the glass lined tunnel left by the descending laser mole.

I heard a voice say, "Hands up." Without looking, we all instinctively raised our hands.

Nelson was the first to turn to face the security police. "Oh shit," he said.

McGarvey, Granger, and I then turned. The security police all wore NWO guard uniforms, and the insignia on the panel trucks bore the NWO logo. I heard the tinted glass rear window on the side of the squad car slowly descend. I looked briefly in that direction.

A blonde woman with black sunglasses shrugged. "Take them to Interrogation."

Behind her, I could see the shape of a reptilian face.

"We're in some deep shit," I said aloud.

"Maybe deeper," Nelson replied.

"We're gonna be in the soup," Granger told us.

I leaned toward Granger. "Granger, no matter what happens, we kidnapped you at gunpoint to show us the way out of the underground facilities. Understand?"

"But, Mr. Arrow—"

"No buts. We forced you to show us how to get out of the facility."

The shortest of the NWO guards saw that we were whispering. "Shaddup!" he ordered. I winked at him. He strode over to me like a DI approaching a new recruit. "Are you some kind of wise guy?"

"Are you some kind of pretend law officer?" I asked

He hit me in the gut with the butt of his TEC-DC9. As he did, I grabbed its long clip with my right hand. "Hey, bucko," I wheezed. "This assault weapon is banned under federal law."

"Fuck the federal government and fuck you," he told me.

I released my grip on the clip, which was a mistake because it enabled him to swing the butt of his weapon into my temple. The last thing I remember was my cheek frying on the gritty tarmac.

Chapter 26

I already told you, I came to Denver because I'm investigating a missing person's case. The name of my client is confidential."

"You were trespassing on federal property."

"I didn't see any warning signs indicating that the federal government has anything to do with the Denver airport, except to ensure that personnel adhere to FAA rules and regulations."

"And how did you gain entry into a secure governmental facility?

"Like I said, the door was open, so I walked in. Check your security camera videos, and you'll see me walking around in the dark, looking for anybody who could give me directions."

The tall blonde bitch in the sunglasses nodded to the goon in the NWO uniform, and he sent a right cross into the left side of my face for the umpteenth time since I had found myself in the interrogation room.

❧❧

Smelling salts. *Great,* I thought. *More questions and more pain yet to come. Maybe Granger should have let that lizard cut me to pieces. I think he's going to get the chance to do that, anyway.*

The questions began again.

"Who are your companions?" the tall blonde asked.

"The skinny geek came with me because he was looking for a friend who disappeared. The bus driver was in a cage in your zoo and asked me to let him out. I figured the zookeeper had a map and the keys, so I forced him to show me the way out."

"Is Granger Taylor a spy for your organization?"

"Who is Granger Tyler?" I asked.

"Taylor. Granger Taylor. He is a spy for your organization, correct?"

"I don't know anyone by that name."

"He is the large, older man who accompanied you when you trespassed."

"The skinny geek accompanied me into your facility because he is looking for a friend who he thinks you're holding captive."

"How did you gain entry into a secure governmental facility?"

"I already told you—the door was open, so I walked in. There was absolutely nobody around, and nobody answered when I knocked on the door."

"Why did you steal one of our drilling machines?"

"I didn't steal it. You guys locked the door, and we couldn't get out of the facility any other way than to dig out. I borrowed it, but I made sure that it went right back where I found it."

"You are a liar, Mr. Arrow."

Oh, she knows my name, I realized. This was the first time she had used it. "And you are holding a United States Citizen against his will," I replied. "I'll bet there are dozens of citizens being held against their will in that zoo of yours. When the government finds out what you're doing, they're going to shut you down big time."

"Mr. Arrow, your government already knows what is going on in this federal facility. It is a federal research facility not unlike Plum Island. Deadly diseases must be contained.

You trespassed into a restricted facility where you possibly came into contact with a deadly virus. You must be kept in quarantine indefinitely."

"The only viruses I came into contact with are you and your goon here, and I can't wait to shove some antibiotic up both of your asses."

I figured that her goon would punch my lights out again, and I wasn't disappointed.

ℯↄℯↄ

When I came to, I was lying on my side in a cage. My face was swollen, and my left eye socket felt like it might have been broken. But I could see, and that was a good sign. My head was pounding, probably due to the beating it had received, but also because I was hungry and cold in this dark space.

It reminded me of Granger's cavern. In fact, I thought it might well be Granger's cavern. And maybe I was just in some out of the way location that prevented me from getting my bearings.

"Dan! Hey, Dan! Are you okay?" It was Nelson. He was in a cage, too, about ten feet away from me.

I pushed myself into a sitting position. "Where are we, Nelson?"

"Are you okay?" he asked again. "When they brought us back down here, I wasn't sure you were going to be alive in the morning."

"Yeah, I'm okay. I feel like I did ten rolls and a couple of flips down the straightaway at Darlington. How long have we been here? How long have I been out?" I asked.

"You've been out about ten hours. We've been down here about nine. I don't know if it's day or night, but I'm thinking, it's probably about nine p.m."

"How about McGarvey? Is he okay?"

"I haven't seen him or Granger. They separated us at the

Interrogation Center. They shipped you and me back down
here in a military grade Hummer."

"Did they hurt you?" I asked.

"No, not bad. They roughed me up a little, but I think
they took all their frustrations and anger out on you."

"How did I get so lucky?"

Nelson chuckled. "To be their punching bag, or to be
alive?"

"I'm not so sure that being alive is lucky...Do you know
if we're scheduled for the food preparation lab?

"I overheard them saying something about migrating us
like that poor sap Powers, but it won't happen until after
some big shot gets migrated at some ceremony at Livermore. I think it's probably Hitler."

I knew Nelson was on target. As we had figured out earlier, it was part of the NWO's master plan to take over the
world. After some man-made, virus-borne Armageddon,
that bastard will get to govern the few humans who are left,
and the alien hybrids will come topside to live among us,
purportedly to help us, until there are no more of us and it is
only them. As Granger had told me, the newer, smarter hybrids would dominate the Earth for a few thousand years,
and then it would be their turn to be exterminated as yet
another newer, smarter hybrid is introduced. My head hurt
at the thought of it.

The loud squeal of metal on metal broke the silence, followed by a bang, as some large door was opened and closed
in the distance. Then the sound of approaching footsteps
filled the cavern. It was somebody in leather-heeled shoes,
and the peculiar clicking sound of the heels on concrete
made me nervous. It was probably that blonde amazon and
her goon squad. Was it time for more interrogation?

I had to blink several times to clear the blood and sweat
from my eyes before I could see who was approaching my
cage. One tall figure stood out, accompanied by two men in
suits and a cluster of smaller gray aliens. I groaned when I
saw that the goon who had used me for a punching bag was

leading the others toward me. The two men in suits were walking quickly to keep up with him. The aliens scurried about like children or small dogs. Make that Chihuahuas. As the small ensemble reached my cage, two of the Greys took the hand of one of the suits and pointed at me. Without warning, the goon grabbed the upper edge of my cage with his large hands and shook it sharply. I guess he wanted to be sure that I was awake.

Instinctively, I pressed against the back of my steel prison.

"Are you Arrow?" one of the suits asked me. He was the shorter of the two, about five ten. He wore his hair in a businessman's butch—short, but not so short as to look military. His shoulders were narrower, and his hands looked soft, like he had a desk job.

"I think I used to be," I replied. "Your goon may have changed my mind this morning."

"Where did you get that stupid last name, Arrow? Are you an Apache or something?"

I thought his line of questioning was odd. "It was French. They spelled it A-R-R-E-A-U-X until my grandfather landed at Ellis Island and nobody could pronounce it. I think he figured that the current spelling was more patriotic. Will that help you find me in ancestry.com?"

"You're pretty funny, Arrow," he told me. "I think I can see what Special Agent Casola sees in you."

"Do you know Mona?" I asked. "You'd better not hurt her."

The suit turned to the goon and motioned for him to leave us alone. The goon scowled and then lumbered across the aisle and stood beside Nelson's cage.

I hadn't noticed it before, but the Greys were now gripping the sides of my cage and staring at me like kids would stare at a monkey in the zoo. The suit tugged at one, looked it in the eyes, and all the Greys instantly released their grip and joined the goon. He must have ordered them away.

"You were tough to find, Arrow. But your little deed with the Nazis didn't go unnoticed."

"That's how you knew where to find me?" I asked.

"That, your poorly written email pretending to be Special Agent Casola—by the way, she always signs her emails with an M, not Mona—and your cell phone. You left it on, so we were able to track you through the NSA. I wish we could have gotten here a little earlier. Maybe we could have saved you from some of Pablo's punishment."

"And maybe you could have saved a few Nazis?"

"You took out two hundred thirty-six of them, and another five hundred are too sick to perform their duties."

"Too bad I didn't get more," I muttered. Then I pointed across the aisle toward Nelson's cage. "Is Pablo the goon?" I asked.

"That would be Pablo. He doesn't speak English."

I sensed that this suit wasn't here to cause me any more pain. "What do you want with me?" I asked.

"My name is McKinley Smith. Special Agent Casola calls me Mack. I'm FBI."

"You're Mona's boss," I replied.

"So she's told you about me?"

"She's mentioned your name once or twice. Mona thinks you're one of the good guys. Wait until I tell her how wrong she is about you."

Mack Smith motioned to the other suit. "This is David Keyhoe. He's CIA. David, this is Dan Arrow."

"Pleased to meet you, Mr. Arrow," Keyhoe said. "I've heard a lot about you." He stuck his hand inside my cage, as though he wanted to shake hands.

I just gave him a look of disdain.

"So what's next for me?" I asked. "If you plan to chop me up and distribute my parts across the desert, go ahead. I think I'm ready for deliverance."

"Listen, Arrow, not every spook is a bad guy, and not everyone in the FBI or the black ops community supports what's going on here. We've come to enlist your services for the good guys."

"You sure have some line of shit," I replied. "This place is crawling with all sorts of aliens, Nazis, and NWO creeps who plan to exterminate most of the population of Earth and then take over."

"You've pieced it together pretty well, Arrow, but you're missing some information. Not all of the aliens are bad guys. Some are here to prevent the very scenario that you've described. Keyhoe and I are working with them. You might say that we're double agents."

"Sure, you are. Look at where I am and where you are and tell me that you expect me to believe that. You're even traveling with the goon who gave my face this makeover."

"Listen, Mr. Arrow," Keyhoe interjected, "we're here under the guise of interrogating you. We're playing a dangerous game. If you would just cooperate, maybe we can get you out of here and put a stop to the extermination scenario."

I just looked at him in disbelief.

"Arrow, we know where Special Agent Casola is, but we need your help to rescue her," Smith told me.

That caught my attention. "Is Mona okay?"

"Yes, for now. But things are going down that we have no control of. We don't know what will happen after tomorrow."

"And what is happening tomorrow?"

"There will be a procedure followed by a ceremony at Livermore," he replied. "We need to interrupt that procedure."

"Are you talking about Hitler's migration into a new container?"

Keyhoe and Smith looked at each other. "So you already know," Keyhoe said.

"Yeah, I already know."

"If you already know, then what are you doing about it?"

"Well, my buddies and I were on our way to do some-

thing about it when we took a wrong turn and found ourselves back down here in the meat locker."

"Work with us, Arrow, and we can get you out of here,"
Smith said. "Maybe we can help you rescue Special Agent
Casola in the process."

"Finding Mona is my primary objective," I told them.
"Stopping Hitler will be collateral damage."

Mack Smith looked peeved. "If we don't prevent Hitler's
migration, there won't be any Mona—or Dan Arrow for
that matter. You'll both be in the feeding tanks for the
Greys."

"Mr. Arrow, your body would already be in the feeding
tanks, except that they have a backlog of Nazi bodies to
butcher before they get to you," Keyhoe chimed in.
"They're still working to clean up the mess you left them."

It was Mack's turn again, and these two were striking
chords. "There isn't much time left, Arrow. You're either in
with us or in the feeding tanks. It's a clear choice."

"What about Nelson?" I asked, pointing in Nelson's direction. "He's been a good friend, and he's sweet on Mona,
too."

Mack turned and looked behind him. Nelson was interested in what was going on, but I didn't think he could hear
what we were saying. "Okay, him, too," Mack replied.
"Was he the one with you in Dulce?"

"How did you know about that?" I asked.

"The NSA gave us records of your cell phone locations
for the past week. And the alien commander at Dulce reported the incident to the CIA. You've been to some interesting places, and we'd like to know more about what
you've uncovered."

"Mona took most of the notes, so if you really want to
know everything that we've uncovered, you'll have to wait
until we rescue her. My primary interest has been finding
the killer of my client, which I guess has been a wild goose
chase since he isn't dead."

"And who would that be?" Mack Smith asked.

"You know I can't disclose client information. Besides, you probably already have a good idea who it is."

"Yeah, I'm pretty sure we do. The NSA knows everybody you've talked to over the past month, and they gave us transcripts of most of the conversations. Nothing you do can be hidden for long, Arrow."

"Then I guess they know you're here right now."

"Yup. They know where I am at all times."

"Will they have a transcript of this conversation?"

"No, not unless somebody is wearing a wire. We left our cell phones topside, and this lab isn't wired for eavesdropping. They didn't think there would be a need for it."

"And I'm carrying interference," Keyhoe said. He reached into the breast pocket of his suit jacket and showed me a small device with a red indicator light. "Nothing we've said can be picked up electronically because of the signal that this baby emits. It makes the speakers on electronic ears squeal at an unmerciful pitch."

"Okay," I said, "I guess I'll have to trust you. Besides, I'm not interested in being the main course at some alien's picnic. Let me out of this cage and let's go get Mona."

Mack signaled to one of the small Greys. It approached my cage and ran its three slender fingers across a keyboard on the side. At the sound of a click, the door to my cage popped open, and I crawled out. Mack and Keyhoe helped me to my feet.

"You're looking pretty beat up, Arrow," Mack said. "Are you sure you're up to this?"

"I'll be good once I get out of this hole and get some fresh air," I replied. "Let me talk to Nelson for a minute."

I staggered over to Nelson's cage. He had a puzzled look on his face. "What's going on, Dan?" he asked. "I thought you were going into the soup."

"These guys want us to help them stop Hitler. In return, they'll help us free Mona."

"Are they on the level?"

"I don't really know. The shorter one is Mona's boss.

He's FBI. The other one is a spook. All I know is that they'll help us get out of this hole. Maybe it'll buy us another day or two. When this is over, I don't know if they'll live up to their promises. There's always something else, some hidden agenda with these guys."

"Count me in, Dan. Another day is another day. Down here, I'm just waiting until it's my turn to be sliced and diced."

"Yeah, that's how I see it, too."

I turned to Mack Smith. "Nelson's in. Get him out of this chicken coop."

Chapter 27

Mack Smith and Keyhoe led the way into the shuttle. Nelson and I followed. The cavern was surprisingly devoid of pedestrians compared to the last time I was here. It was like everyone was on spring break or something because we had the shuttle to ourselves. I commented about that to Mack.

"They're all already at Livermore," he told me. "The ceremony after the procedure is a major event. A crowd of more than ten thousand is expected. The Vice President may even be there."

"No shit?" I replied. "I never trusted that son of a bitch."

"Like many, he's only ensuring that he has a reservation in the caverns when the pandemic is unleashed."

The doors to the shuttle closed and Keyhoe suggested that we all sit until the shuttle reached maximum speed.

"How fast would that be?" Nelson asked.

"We'll arrive at Livermore in less than forty minutes. You do the math," Keyhoe replied.

The shuttle lurched briefly, and we could feel the acceleration in our cheeks, but there was no sensation of turbulence. "This is definitely Maglev," Nelson told me.

❧❧❧

Ten minutes into the trip, the shuttle slowed to a stop.

We were at another underground facility. The doors opened, and a giant of a man stooped down to enter the cabin. I estimated his height at ten feet. He had sandy-blond hair and blue eyes, and his complexion was as fair as a baby's. He smiled in acknowledgement of Mack Smith and nodded. Then he sat on the floor, maybe to keep from bumping his head on the ceiling, but maybe to be less intimidating.

"Arrow, I'd like to introduce you to Waam," Mack said. "He's from the planet Ummo."

I raised my hand as an Indian would do in an old-time western movie. Sitting down, this guy was as tall as Mona and maybe taller. If I could have, I would have contracted to be his agent for a position in the NBA. No such luck, however, because he was all business. I hadn't noticed it when he came in, but in Waam's hand was a duffel bag. He handed it to Mack, who handed it to me. Mack told me to sort out the contents with Nelson. Mack thought that the uniforms inside were the correct sizes, at least according to the CIA files on each of us. Go figure. Nothing, but nothing, is private anymore.

When I emptied the contents into Nelson's arms, it was clear that we were to be dressed as NWO guards, both of us at the same rank. They even had provided military style boots in the correct shoe sizes. "These uniforms identify you as Central Agency Interrogators," Mack told us. "They don't see many around Livermore, so you will stick out like sore thumbs, but nobody will question you. Central Agency Interrogators conduct all investigations into allegations of disloyalty and abrogation of duty. Nobody will want to talk to you."

It was a good thing, too, because I didn't want to talk to anyone, and I was pretty sure that Nelson was on the same page.

Mack asked us to change into the uniforms while he and Waam went over the details of their plan. Waam began by trying to reassure us. "Let me begin by explaining the recent history of your Earth," he said. "It has been visited by the inhabitants of many planets in the past. In fact, as it formed, your Earth was seeded by several races from Zeta Reticuli. The variety of your flora and fauna can only be credited to the formal seeding program, for no other planet has such abundance. But yours was not the first in your solar system. First to be seeded was the red planet, which was originally in your orbit, but which was forced into an orbit farther from the sun by a near miss with Nibiru, your sun's tenth planet, as it passed through your solar system on one of its ten-thousand-year orbits. Transport of plant and animal species from the red planet to Earth occurred quickly, as did the transfer of much of your water. A coalition of scientists from a half dozen planets carefully planned the maneuver and oversaw the development of life on what we now refer to as the garden planet.

"But the intergalactic coalition that spawned and protected life on Earth was overthrown by greedy leaders from other star systems, whose own technology was superior and whose purposes were more self-serving. They chose not to vacation on the garden planet but, instead, to mine its gold and other minerals, and to lay waste to its gardens.

"Your kind was created by the greedy ones to serve them as free laborers. In developing your species, they manipulated the DNA of primitive life forms and added elements of their own DNA. Thus, you look similar to intergalactic mankind, but you have retained your primate thumbs and the muscle mass to give you an advantage in lifting heavy objects. However, your creators limited your lifespan and your brain functions. Thus, you were denied the ability to communicate through telepathy or to learn effectively. Because they developed your kind quickly, and because you were not destined for jobs requiring high mental capacity, imperfections were tolerated. And, when discovered, those with higher brain capacities were terminated at birth.

"Eventually, as the most valuable mineral deposits were depleted, the greedy ones left the Earth, and for the last three-hundred thousand of your years, the intergalactic coalition has protected your planet from outside interference and even from some among your own species whose actions would harm the balance. Witness, for example, the many publicized sightings of coalition tureens above your nuclear arms facilities. They are permitted to be seen only to send the message that we cannot let you destroy this beautiful orb."

"So, what's the problem?" I asked. "You have the technology to destroy our weapons."

"Yeah," Nelson added, "y'all have already shut down the warheads in some of our missile silos."

"There exists an intergalactic agreement, a hands-off policy, which prohibits our interference with your evolution, unless your leaders agree to specific actions. We are permitted only to stop you from self-annihilation, because that would affect this experiment that you call Earth."

"Is that why we're going to Livermore?" I asked.

"Not exactly," Mack replied. "The greedy ones are back. Currently, there is an intergalactic cold war ensuing. The aliens are not too different from us humans in that regard. They have disputes and wars over resources and territories. Sometimes small skirmishes erupt even in our own skies."

"What's their agenda?" I asked. "The greedy ones?"

"It isn't clear, but I would guess it's no different from what we experience here on Earth—power, domination, and territoriality," Mack replied.

"Mr. Arrow, in an attempt to avert all-out war, our intergalactic coalition has tried to placate the greedy ones," Waam continued. "Our leaders have turned their eyes away from small transgressions, thinking that the greater good must prevail. Unfortunately, the greedy ones are back, and they are here, living among you. You yourself have already experienced interactions with them. And, as much as I hate to admit it, if forced to do so, our coalition leaders would rather lose the garden planet than to risk a war that would imperil one of their home planets."

"So you're saying that we are poised for a take-over?" I

asked. "Who are the greedy ones? How do we recognize them?"

"Mostly they are the reptilians and their Greys, Arrow," Mack replied.

"You mean the ones that accompanied you this morning?"

"No, the draconian grays have narrower, more elongated chins and an easily identifiable sinister appearance. The Greys you saw this morning are innocents who are with the coalition. If I could make a comparison, the draconians have created rottweilers, and the coalition has created golden retrievers."

"Created?" Nelson asked.

"They are all humanoids," Mack told us. "Mankind is the primary and dominating life form in our galaxy. Living organisms that are roughly fashioned, or hewn, from mankind's DNA are called hewn-man, or human. Those who are fashioned from humans are humanoids. The Greys are humanoids that have greater brain power than humans, but they were constructed from human DNA to serve mankind. They have no ego and will do only as instructed. They are robot-like, but are constructed of flesh and bone."

Nelson finally began to put it altogether. "No shit?" he said. "Y'all mean to tell me that humans aren't natural. That we're just some kind of fabricated animal?"

"In truth," Waam replied, "there is nothing natural in our galaxy. Those who created mankind and reptilians were several species from other galaxies who seeded our planets tens of millions of years ago. We don't know who they were, but we have evidence of their existence. We have no name for the prime creator of it all."

"Well, doesn't that beat all?" Nelson replied. "At least we have a name for our Johnny Appleseed. We call him God."

"Let's get back to the greedy reptilians," I said. "I hate those lizards, anyway. Who else is working with them?"

Waam stretched his legs, and then said, "A few of my

own kind, Ummites, have drifted over to the NWO. And a few Nordics, as well. But worst of all, many of your human governments have agreements with the reptilians through their Greys. At first, during the early encounters, your leaders thought that the Greys were the decision-makers. They didn't realize that they are simply humanoids. The Greys gave your governments small pieces of advanced technology, most of it minor and of little consequence to the greater agenda. In return, as part of a formal agreement, your governments have given the greedy ones permission to experiment on humans and animals, so long as not too many of any species are taken or are left to be discovered as dissected carcasses. But, the reptilians have broken their agreements and have abducted many more humans than originally estimated. Currently, they are working on a hybridization program that will enable them to dominate humans and capture your Earth as their home planet in this galaxy. Your Nazi government was the first to establish a mutual agreement with the reptilians, followed by the Chinese, the Russians, and your own USA. A shadow government now exists to oversee all subterranean activities. It is called—"

"Let me guess," I interrupted, "the New World Order. Our president has mentioned it in many of his speeches."

"And nobody blinked an eye, did they?" Mack replied.

"So what's the plan for tomorrow?" I asked.

"You mean today, Arrow. It's already today," Mack reminded me. "And, you already know that Hitler is going to be migrated to a new container today. It will happen in the early afternoon, and we have to stop that migration because doing so will throw a monkey wrench into the works for the aliens. Hitler's second coming is supposed to be the signal that heralds the beginning of the New Age and the rise of the New World Order."

Nelson finished tying the laces on his boots and stood up. "How do I look?" he asked.

"Like an NWO stooge," Mack replied. "You're going to fit right in." Mack turned his attention to me. My laces were still untied, but I stood up. "Fix your line, Arrow. The line of your shirt is supposed to lead directly to the line in the zipper of your trousers."

"I was never one for military protocol," I told him. "Too many regulations."

"Yeah, your personality doesn't seem to fit the military mindset. You're going to have to play the part, though, especially when we arrive at Livermore. If you act like an SS officer in a World War Two movie, you should be okay."

"What about you?" I asked Mack. "How are you dressing?"

"Just like this. Keyhoe and I are two of ten ambassadors from the FBI and CIA. We have a special invitation."

I was suddenly less than comfortable with Mack and Keyhoe. Maybe taking us to Livermore was part of some other chain of events that had now been set into motion. Maybe we were going to be sacrificed as interlopers in a subterranean world in which we did not belong. I shot Nelson a quick look, but he was still busy preening himself using the reflection in the polished chrome doors of the shuttle.

"What happens when we get there, Mack?" I asked.

"We'll pass through a security check point. We can have no weapons on us and can carry nothing in with us. No cameras or cell phones are permitted. Only official videographers and photographers are here to record the event. They have all been donated by the major networks, ABC, NBC, CBS, FOX, and Al Jazeera. This is a major global event.

"Once we're through the checkpoint, we'll have to find our way into the arena. Grandstands have been erected, and Nazi and NWO brigades will be marching in review. You two will have to lose yourselves in the crowd and find a way to stop the ceremony. You know that this may be a suicide mission. Once you've interrupted the ceremony, I don't know how you'll escape. You'll be six stories underground

and surrounded by NWO supporters who'll want to skin
you alive."

"That's it?" Nelson asked. "That's the plan? Y'all are
just dumping us inside, and then it's up to us to figure out
how to do the deed? Don't y'all have any weapons hidden
in the arena or some strategy figured out? How about some
sort of diversionary tactic?"

"Actually, we have no idea about the physical layout or
the schedule of events. It's all been kept above top secret.
Not even our inside folks have been able to communicate
with us about the schedule. All we can do is hope there is a
chink in their armor," Mack replied.

"Aw, fuck me," I griped in disbelief. "We'd have been
better off left in those cages in Denver. Why don't you just
shoot us both right now and get it over with! Every son of a
bitch guard in that place is going to be heavily armed. How
are we supposed to pull anything off without a plan?!"

"We're counting on you and your uncanny knack of
lucking into solutions to otherwise impossible situations,
Arrow. You are famous for it at the FBI."

"I'm not an NFL quarterback, Mack. I'm just a slightly
overweight guy with a basic sense of survival. But you're
pitting Nelson and me against incredible odds."

I rubbed my forehead and then asked, "So what are the
marching orders, anyway? Are you expecting us to kill or to
capture Hitler? Do we do that before or after he migrates
into his new container?"

"You need to seize whatever is your best opportunity at
the spur of the moment. Hitler is already deceased according to commonly held beliefs, so you can never be found
guilty of killing a dead man."

"I don't think capture is a viable option, Mack," I said.
"He'll have to be unconscious or else he'll resist all efforts
to be moved. Besides, he's going to be a mile deep in Nazis
and NWO guards who aren't going to let us take him out in
handcuffs."

"The important thing is to stop the migration, right?"

Nelson asked. "Let's focus on that and then damn the tor-
pedoes. I say we—"

I interrupted Nelson. "How do they migrate somebody
anyway?" I asked.

"It is done by polyconductor magnetic fields," Waam replied. "By immersing an entity in a powerful magnetic
field, and rotating the field in a counterclockwise direction,
the entity's connection to its container is broken and the
true entity, the conscious electrical self, is released in the
form of a small magnetic field. That smaller field is then
channeled into a circular storage unit, about the size of a
small suitcase. That portable unit is then moved by hand to
a migration unit that essentially pours the small magnetic
field into its new container, which is then motivated into
life by a brief series of mild electric shocks."

"It sounds like something out of Frankenstein," I said.

"Actually," Mack replied, "it's supposedly painless for
the entity that is being migrated. According to the few in-
terviews that I've read, post-migration entities recall a feeling of lightheadedness followed by black-out until they are
revived."

I made a mental note to ask Powers about his experience
with migration when I saw him the next time. If I saw him
again. Then my thoughts turned to Mona. What a shitload
of information I'd have to share with her. She was going to
find it incredible. Well, maybe. She would probably have
more to tell me, I reminded myself. I also made a mental
note to listen to her before I blabbered on about my own
experiences. She didn't like it when I talked over her or
when I thought my shit was more important than hers. I
kissed the first knuckle on my pointer finger and whispered
to Mona that I would soon be there to rescue her.

The sensation of my stomach pushing against my back
let me know that the shuttle had begun to slow down again.
To me, it felt like we had been traveling for only twenty
minutes, so I asked Mack why we were stopping.

"We're approaching Livermore," he replied. "When the

door opens, just follow Keyhoe and me and do what we do. When we enter the arena area, you're on your own. Remember, you're officials of the Central Agency of the New World Order. Good luck stopping the migration, Arrow. You, too, Nelson."

"Where is the Central Agency located, Mack?" Nelson asked. It was a good question, and I should have thought of it myself.

"Astana. Kazakhstan. Ten stories underground," he whispered in short bursts over his shoulder as the door opened.

Waam led the way. As an Ummite, his height was imposing, causing the crowd to part as he strode gracefully through the shuttle waiting area and into the main underground station area. Keyhoe and Mack kept close behind him, followed by Nelson and me. When I looked at individuals and small groups of humans, regardless of how they were dressed or who they represented, their eyes quickly descended, or they turned away, pretending not to have seen us. The uniforms were working like a charm, especially the two gold bands around our biceps under the NWO insignia that signified that Nelson and I could be trouble. This was one place where it felt good to be a badass.

In the distance, I could see four large double doors that were wide open, accepting the multitude that was flowing into them. This had to be the arena. As we neared the doors, the crowd closed in on us. The air was full of unfamiliar scents, an unpleasant mixture of strange body odors, some reminiscent of the pachyderm houses at the Bronx Zoo and others of reptile farms, unique perfumes and colognes, and simply poor oral health. Given where I'd been in the past twenty-four hours, my own musk must have added to the joy. Despite the use of air ducts and fan systems that exchanged carbon-dioxide-laden air with fresh air from the Earth's surface, there were simply too many beings for the subterranean system to handle, and the air in the arena was abruptly stale and humid.

We stopped briefly at an intersection of corridors that reminded me of the outer gangways around Yankee Stadium—the old one. Waam bent down and whispered that Nelson and I should follow the corridor to the left and see if we could find our way to the dais area. He, Mack, and Keyhoe were going forward to their assigned seats in the second tier. "If I never see you again, Waam, I appreciate all the info you've given me to chew on," I said. "It's a difficult story to swallow."

"It is not a story, Mr. Arrow. Someday your history books will be rewritten so your children will understand the truth about their existence on one of the smallest and newest planets in the galaxy. They will learn that the God of their fathers was simply a committee of scientists comprised of several species of mankind, and that they, as were all humans, were hewn of man. I wish you peace and good will, Mr. Arrow."

"Thanks, man," I replied. "Go buy yourself a beer and a hotdog and enjoy the ceremony."

Waam gave me a puzzled look and then turned and walked through Gate 14E and into the arena.

Chapter 28

Commissar Nargas entered the arena at Gate 2W. Behind him scrambled two Greys, each holding the end of a chrome chain. At the other end of both chrome chains, followed Mona, wearing a dog collar to which the chains were attached. She felt ashamed and humiliated to be paraded in front of thousands of aliens, humans, and humanoids who supported the agenda of the New World Order. The material of the dress that the commissar's aides had provided her for the event was scratchy, and she thought perhaps she was allergic to it.

The commissar greeted several dignitaries who were seated in the fourth row, directly behind his seat in row three.

"It is a great day, Commissar!" hissed a reptilian in a yellow jump-suit with an unknown solar system emblazoned upon his chest.

"Yes, his excellency's dream will be achieved today, and it will be our queen's finest hour," Nargas replied.

"Blessed be her majesty," said the reptilian.

"And may her days be long and fruitful," said another reptilian two seats to the left.

A small cluster of reptilians within earshot kissed their claw-like middle fingers and then touched them to their foreheads saying, "Glory to her majesty."

Nargas repeated the gesture and replied, "May all glory

be hers." Then, he turned and motioned to the Greys to sit Mona between them to his right. Mona stumbled briefly as her collar was pulled downward by her captors, but she caught herself on the arm of her seat, turned her body, and sat down awkwardly. The chains had become twisted around her, so the grays each tugged on their ends of the chains, causing the metal collar to turn violently, rubbing an abrasion onto her neck. When Mona cried out in pain, the commissar spat and hissed at the two Greys, who pulled back in fear. "Treat her with gentle dignity," he warned them. "She carries the fate of your own lives in her womb."

Both Greys slackened their chains, but only slightly, for they knew that if Mona escaped, they soon would be in the feeding tanks. One Grey caught Mona's eyes in his gaze and told her, '*We don't want to hurt you, but you cannot attempt escape. If you do, the commissar's justice will be swift and merciless.*'

Mona heard his words deep within her brain and understood. She nodded and looked around her. She and her captors were seated on the right-hand side of a large arena, something akin to a football field. The center portion was empty, its concrete floor gleaming as though it recently had been waxed. Center front was a large stage, probably one hundred feet in width. Above it hung a huge screen onto which was projected the NWO insignia. She couldn't tell if it was from a projector somewhere above her, from a rear-screen projection system, or if the screen simply acted somehow like a large television screen. It was certainly new technology.

Suddenly the air was filled with trumpet fanfare and the image on the large screen switched to two lines of illegible cyphers. Below them were another two lines of different, but equally illegible cyphers. And below them was something written in a Germanic language. Below that was French. Below that was English, which read: *Please be seated. Our program will commence in five minutes.* Mona realized that each cluster of words and cyphers conveyed

the same message, but in a different language. If she'd had
a camera or cell phone, she would have snapped a picture to
help with translating alien documents sometime in the future.

At the sound of the fanfare, throngs of NWO supporters
began pushing their way through the gates and into seats in
the arena. Similar to a major league baseball park, second
and third tier seats rose upward around the arena, tripling its
capacity and adding to the poor quality of the air. When she
heard several men shout orders and the sound of heavy
footsteps, Mona turned to look toward the rear of the arena.
More than a thousand military men had begun marching in
procession into the arena. All in uniform, they reminded her
of parades she had seen at Quantico during her FBI training.
Then her gaze focused on the reptilian seated directly behind her who was wearing a bright yellow jumpsuit. He was
looking directly at her, studying the female Earthling and
her movements. When their eyes met, the reptilian telepathically told her, '*You are indeed fortunate to witness today's
proceedings. You will be able to thrill your children with
the story of being a part of this event.*'

Mona squinted her eyes in anger. "Fuck you, and your
New World Order. Someday I'll be wearing your skin on
my feet!"

The reptilian raised his hand to strike her but stopped
himself because at that same moment the commissar turned
to look at Mona. Nargas's eyes quickly darted from Mona
to the reptilian behind her. His arm moved quickly, slashing
the elongated nose of the other as he grabbed at the yellow
collar that circled the other's throat. Blood spurted from the
gash, causing those seated on either side to leap to their
feet. Within seconds, a team of four NWO guards took control of the situation, subduing the bleeding reptilian with
stun guns and removing him from the arena. A few moments later, the empty seat was filled by an extremely tall
man in a pale blue jumpsuit. He smiled and nodded at Mona
and then greeted the commissar.

"It is nice to see you again, Waam," the commissar said into the giant's eyes. "You must join me for lunch this week. I would like to know how news of our occupation of the garden planet is being received on Ummo."

"Tomorrow I will call your chief of staff to arrange a good day, Commissar," Waam replied. "I will gladly rearrange my schedule so that we can chat."

"Excellent," Nargas replied. "Permit me to introduce my special guest. Her name is Mona, on special assignment to my office from the FBI."

"Greetings," Waam said to Mona. "It is a pleasure to make your acquaintance."

"You speak English," Mona noted aloud.

"Not as well as you, but yes. I have lived on Earth since 1948, first in Italy and then beneath Rendlesham Forest near Woodbridge, England."

"You should have stayed in Italy. They fought with the Nazis during World War Two. We're not as friendly to Nazis over here."

"So I've recently learned," Waam replied.

Mona gave him a quizzical look then turned to face the dais.

When the military band began playing, Mona could hear the echoes of the troops marching in cadence. Occasionally a single voice would shout a command, followed by a chorus of male voices repeating the phrase. The words were incomprehensible to her, but, in her mind, she could envision young junior school officers drilling at Quantico. *It's very much the same*, she thought. *Young heroes marching to some false glory, with no thought of the maiming and pain that many will endure. However, unlike the young men who fought so bravely to defend the United States, the men in this arena are part of a new military force, one not yet assigned to action on the surface of the Earth. These bastards are part of the plan to overthrow the Earth as we know it.* She refused to turn to watch them march in formation to their assigned positions within the arena. She also refused to turn to engage in further conversation with the giant man who was sitting behind her. What did he say? *'So I've recently learned.'* What does that mean? she wondered.

As she listened to the music, Mona's eyes explored the stage at the front of the arena. There was motion in the wings, probably assistants and technicians conducting last minute preparations and readying the main event. . Occasionally, an appendage struck the giant screen from behind, causing it to move and sending waves of motion through the NWO insignia that was still projected onto its surface. As she watched, suddenly the insignia disappeared and live action video of the advancing troops was projected for all to see. A round of applause moved through the audience.

While the companies of soldiers were marching into place, guests were still flowing into the seating areas. They came in an assortment of sizes and shapes. Many in uniform, but many more in civilian garb, and all wearing a look of excitement and wonder on their faces. None had been into a facility so large and so very far underground. Yet, once inside, there was no sense of claustrophobia because the ceiling was a football field high and well lit.

Mona watched the crowd surging into the arena, first observing to her left and then to her right. It was when she returned her attention to her left that she thought she saw him, although she couldn't be certain. The progress of guests was slowing, not due to there being fewer of them, but due to the lack of empty seats at each level. Ushers in NWO uniforms were busy urging those seated to move closer together to make room for those who were not yet seated. While the cluster of guests at Gate 1E stood waiting to be directed, a solitary head moved, pushing through the bodies, as if searching for someone.

The head looked like Danny Arrow, but it was on a body wearing an NWO uniform, an official of some sort. Her heart leapt at first, but then she realized that it couldn't be her Danny. Not here, not now. Oh, but if he only could be here!

The commissar noticed Mona's body motion when she thought that she had seen Danny. He quickly turned to the see who or what caught her attention. But by then, Dan was already gone, fading back into the crowd, seeking a better place to view the event and to try to discover a way to bring it to an abrupt halt. Nargas looked into Mona's eyes and asked her telepathically, '*Did you recognize someone?*'

Mona turned away from him. Nargas motioned to the Grey to Mona's right. The Grey took Mona's head in its hands and turned her face until she was looking into the commissar's eyes. '*My dear,*' he told her, '*there are many representatives here from your world, some from your own FBI. You will undoubtedly see a few familiar faces, but do not look to them for assistance. They are here by special invitation from Her Majesty Queen Igua, and they are all supporters of the New World Order.*'

Mona spit at him, but her spittle hit the Grey to her left on his cheek. The Grey squealed in disgust.

Nargas raised his finger toward the ceiling. '*If you would only adjust your attitude,*' he reprimanded, '*you could find yourself in better circumstances. There is no need for resistance. As has always been the case, when your container has completed its mission, you will be returned to your living quarters and to your way of life.*'

"I don't have nine months to give you," Mona replied. "I want this thing out of my body now!"

Nargas turned his attention away from Mona and toward the video being projected onto the stage area. A camera was scanning the audience and sending close-ups of guests to the projection unit. It was now focusing on the commissar, so he smiled and waved. The camera then panned to the left and stopped on Mona, displaying her full-face and with her metal collar. A small wave of chuckles and delight ran through the audience. Mona hung her head in shame.

Chapter 29

The crowd in front of me began to part, as though avoiding something ominous. It was Nelson coming toward me with his face full of excitement. "Dan! Dan! Did you see Mona? She's here," he exclaimed.

"Where? Are you sure it was Mona?"

"She was on the big screen about a minute ago. You didn't see it?"

"I haven't been watching the screen. Where is she?"

"Somewhere in the audience. She was sitting between two Greys. She had a metal collar around her neck, like she was a pet dog."

"We've got to find out exactly where she is so we can rescue her when this thing goes down," I replied.

"She's somewhere on the main floor, I think maybe on the right hand side. She's not in the bleachers."

"That's your job beginning right now, Nelson. You've got to scour the main floor until you know exactly where she is. I want to know which side, what row, and approximately which seat."

"What about Hitler, Dan? We've got to stop his migration."

"Leave that up to me," I replied. "You find Mona and try to let her know that we're here." I didn't have the foggiest idea of how I was going to stop Hitler's migration. I just knew that it had to be done.

"Shall we set a meeting time?" Nelson asked.

"Yeah, how about fifteen minutes. Meet me at the ramp to Gate One-E."

"Okay," Nelson replied. I watched for a few seconds as he strode boldly through the crowd and blended into obscurity. The uniforms that Mack Smith and that guy Waam had given us were still working well. I made a mental note to thank them if I ever saw them again.

I knew that Nelson would find Mona. He was like a dog in heat, and nothing would deter him from rescuing her. That should have been my role, but I also knew that somebody had to stop the migration ceremony, and I was probably the one who should give it a shot. I had a knack for stumbling into weddings and funerals and making an asshole out of myself. I was famous for it. Maybe that was what this ceremony needed, an asshole who ruined everything for the bride and her family. In this case, the bride would be Hitler and his family would be the NWO.

I made my way to the wings of the stage and looked behind it to see who was there. A tall lizard approached me, claw on his weapon. I pointed to the two gold bands on my arm. He nodded, stopped, and returned to his guard post. I peered beyond him, searching for anything that I could do to stop the ceremony. Then it struck me—this thing was televised! Hitler wasn't on the stage at all. Instead, he was in some other chamber, probably a lab of some sort, where the migration could be facilitated in a controlled environment. *Shit, I should have realized that earlier!*

As I turned to find an exit or corridor that had the appearance of being overly protected, the band music stopped, and the voice of an announcer spoke in some tongue that I couldn't understand. A teleprompter backstage had drawn a small cluster of NWO types, so I joined them to see what was going on. A female lizard had been introduced and had begun speaking to the crowd. At the bottom of the monitor, her prepared speech was scrolling across the screen in three separate lines: in some alien hieroglyph, in German, and in

English. She was babbling on about seizing the day, the great awakening of the New World Order, and the beautiful future where humans and celestial minions would work together to make the garden planet a jewel of intergalactic cooperation. *Yeah*, I thought, *you'll wipe out most humans, and with Hitler's help, you'll force martial law on the survivors. Liberty and justice for all would be out the door, and we humans would be slaves to your alien desires. Suck shit, komodo face!*

Before my thoughts could be read by any of the party-goers, I drifted away from the monitor and looked for a facilities map. There was always one of those posted on the wall. Well, at least there always was topside. Wasn't it some kind of federal law? I didn't drift too far, and I didn't see anything written that I could interpret.

As I was looking, a couple of NWO guards walked quickly in my direction from a corridor leading away into darkness. I stopped them and asked, "Where is the migration room?" They looked at me strangely and spoke to each other in German. I rephrased my question. "*Der Fuhrer?*" I asked. I thought that was how Colonel Klink talked about Hitler in Hogan's Heroes.

They both looked back down the hallway. Then, the older of the two raised both of his palms toward me. "*Darf niemand!*"

I figured out from his facial expression and body language that I couldn't go down that corridor which, of course, was exactly where I planned to go. I smiled and nodded. They continued toward the stage area. I gave them five seconds of lead time, and then I quickly marched down the corridor and into the darkness from which they had emerged.

Not far down the corridor, I saw the reflective yellow glow of animal eyes. I was being watched. I did not stop but continued forward as if I was on a mission. I guess that I was. Within a few seconds, a red dot of light appeared on my chest. Whoever belonged to those eyes had me sighted in for a quick kill. *Great,* I thought, *I'm already a target and this sucker is going to split me open if I don't know some secret password.*

"Tell *der fuhrer* that we've received a report of a bomb in the arena," I said. "He needs to delay his migration." I couldn't think of anything else to say.

"Identify yourself!" came the reply. It was female, and at least she spoke English.

"Central Agency," I replied, pointing to my arm.

Without warning, a flashlight beam burst through the darkness, blinding me briefly. It moved from my face to my arm and then back to my face.

"You look familiar. Have we worked together before?"

"Have I interrogated you for dereliction of duty?" I asked boldly.

The beam of light went out as quickly as it had come on.

"What was that about a bomb?" she asked.

"The Central Agency has received warning that a bomb has been planted in the arena. We must take precautions to ensure that *der Fuhrer* is safe from potential harm."

"His excellency is well protected."

"I must inspect the facility," I replied, pressing a little harder.

"There is no admission except for laboratory staff required to perform the migration."

"And the cameramen? Are you sure of their loyalty? Are the cameramen who are here today the same ones who were here during rehearsal? We believe that the incendiary device is small, perhaps disguised as a briefcase or a camera."

"Wait here," she ordered. She turned and marched up the corridor and into the darkness.

About a minute passed before she returned, bringing with her a tall blond gentleman in a black suit and a man in a lab coat. Even in the dim light of the corridor, I could see that the tall man's eyes had no whites, but were entirely black. The man in the lab coat could have worked in any laboratory in any university or research facility.

"This is the officer who brings the warning," she told them.

"Who is your superior?" the tall man asked.

"I report to the Central Agency to a woman whose name I cannot mention," I replied. Hell, I couldn't think of a good name that quickly, and I didn't want to come up with a name that was unrecognizable, especially if this guy was from the Central Agency.

"He must be referring to General Altarian," the guard said to the tall guy. I jumped at the opportunity and snapped, "Her name is not to be mentioned!"

"What is the problem, then?" the tall man asked me.

"We have received reports of a bomb in the arena area. I must inspect the facility to ensure that his excellency is safe from possible harm."

"The procedure is about to begin," the man in the lab coat said. "We really shouldn't delay the migration for fear of possible mitigating circumstances."

I shot a look at his I.D. tag. "Dr. Laskey, would *der Fuhrer* be happy with you if, after all these years, his brains were splattered all over the walls and ceiling of your laboratory simply because you didn't take a moment of extra precaution?"

"We only set this lab up yesterday morning. I don't see how anyone would have had the time to plant a bomb."

"We believe it to be small, perhaps a suitcase nuclear weapon or something even smaller. Possibly a device that could easily be hidden in a camera or small container. It could be detonated remotely, from as far away as an orbiting satellite."

"It is possible, Dr. Laskey," said the tall man, "that, if a bomb has been planted, an individual viewing these proceedings from anywhere on the garden planet could set the device off by simply bouncing a radio signal off of one of the thousands of satellites in orbit around this orb."

His words surprised me. It was like he was on my side. And, I could see that his comment had painted a look of concern on Dr. Laskey's face. "This is all too confusing," Laskey muttered. "I need confirmation."

"We don't have much time, Dr. Laskey," I replied. "There is another officer from the Central Agency here with me. He is currently inspecting the dais area. Will his independent confirmation be enough?"

"It would make me feel better about delaying any further. His excellency is anxious, and the audience will grow impatient if they are made to wait much longer."

"Then finish your preparations," I told him. "I will find Colonel Nelson and bring him to you for confirmation."

"I will accompany you," said the tall guy in the black suit. "You lead."

I turned and strode quickly down the corridor, followed by the tall guy and the female guard. When the corridor turned slightly to the right, the light from the back stage area formed a rectangle in the darkness.

The female guard stopped and told us, "I will remain here at my post."

I waved my hand in the air to confirm that I heard her, and the tall guy and I continued on.

As we approached the back stage area, the tall guy put his hand on my shoulder. "Your friend is not a colonel. Neither are you. The rank on your uniform is interrogator, grade four."

I figured that I had been made and that I was going to be cooked. I turned suddenly to try to break his grip, but he caught me with his other hand and squeezed my arm painfully.

"Ow!" I complained instinctively.

The tall guy released his grip slightly, but there was no way I was getting away from him. "I am with Waam," he told me.

"Waam?" I asked, pretending that I knew nobody by that name.

"You are Dan Arrow, aren't you?" he asked.

I didn't know whether to acknowledge his question or

not. "The Waam I know is three feet taller than you, and his eyes are not black," I said.

"Waam is older than I am," he replied. "Ummites grow slowly until we attain middle age. Then our bodies accelerate growth until we reach ten or more feet tall. Waam has fully matured and is nearing the golden age."

"If you are with Waam, why haven't you stopped the migration process yourself?"

"It is against our moral code to kill a human being. Hitler is a human."

"So you'd let the Earth be overrun with lizards before you would kill a human?"

"It is so."

I shook my head in disbelief. "You have a strange sense of morals, Jack," I replied. "We'd sacrifice any human being if it meant that a greater number would be saved."

"Yes, we know. Your kind did that many years ago to one who looked human but was not. It set your evolutionary development back by two thousand years."

This guy was talking in riddles. "So are you going to let me go?" I asked.

"Is there truly another here to help you?"

"Yes, like I said, his name is Nelson. He should be at Gate One-E."

"Let us find him before Dr. Laskey completes the migration process."

Chapter 30

When the audience applauded, Mona's attention returned to the large screen above the stage, where a reptilian wearing a golden cape lined in vermillion was about to speak. On its head was a tiara, so Mona guessed that it was female and some sort of dignitary. The reptilian cleared her throat and then touched her lips with her three claws. Mona noticed that her nails were shorter than the Commissar's, perhaps because of manicuring or perhaps because she had no need to slash other lizards the way the Commissar had a few minutes ago.

The crowd in the arena hushed, waiting for her words. The words *Her Royal Majesty Queen Igua* appeared on the screen, again below lines of hieroglyphs and other tongues foreign to Mona. When the queen began to speak, the sounds which emanated from her jowls were guttural tones and hisses and which conveyed nothing to Mona, so she began to read the line of scrolling English text:

"My loyal subjects, dignitaries from the galactic coalition, representatives from the New World Order, and friends from the governments of the garden planet, it is indeed my pleasure to welcome you today. This is a special day for those of us from the Zeta Reticulan system, for this is the day when the work of our scientists triumphs over that of the original creators. We will demonstrate today that we have solved the mystery of migration, which has so long eluded those before us. No longer will our fabricated containers reject their occupants after a few months or years. No longer will our own kind be forced to live underground for fear of the harmful rays of this system's star. Today, he who has helped us and who was cast into exile by his own kind will rise again in the eyes of hewn men to live among them and to govern their destiny. Through his leadership in the implementation of Agenda Twenty-One, hewn men and draconian hybrids will live and work together on the surface, our little children will play together, be educated together, and make this planet an island of peace and possibility for the galactic future."

The audience in the arena burst into applause. The queen smiled and nodded. Then, she took a sip of liquid from a long straw pointing rigidly out of the cap of a water bottle. A small amount of fluid dribbled from the side of her mouth, down her jowls, and onto her white blouse. She was too self-absorbed to notice.

"In a few moments," Queen Igua continued, "our cameras will switch to the temporary migration facility which was assembled for today's historic event, where we will meet Dr. Sigmund Laskey. It was Dr. Laskey whose work brought our dreams to fruition." The Queen paused for a moment. "Dr. Laskey, are you there?" she asked. "Dr. Laskey?"

A loud squeal of feedback split the air in the arena, causing many to wince in pain. Mona covered her ears and turned her head to the right. It was then that she saw Nelson. He was standing alone at Gate 1E, looking carefully at Mona's row. In fact, she thought, *he is staring at me!* She canted her head quizzically. Nelson gave a brief, but clear wave of hello, then he folded his arms and looked away. Mona froze momentarily and then turned to see if her captors had seen the exchange. Both Greys and Commissar Nargas were glued to the screen and her majesty's greeting. Mona then turned to see if those behind her had seen Nelson. The tall man in the blue jumpsuit looked her squarely in the eyes, then smiled, flicked his eyes briefly to the right, and nodded. Mona turned quickly toward the front again. *What does he know?* She looked to her left. Nargas was still watching the screen.

When Mona carefully returned her gaze to Gate 1E, she wanted to cry out but knew that she couldn't because to do so would jeopardize their safety. Danny was standing beside Nelson. He seemed to be introducing Nelson to a tall man in a black suit. The three were nodding and whispering to each other. Then Danny turned toward the arena. His eyes began to crawl along the third row of chairs until they met Mona's. Her heart leaped when their eyes kissed. "Oh, Danny. You're here!" Mona whispered to herself. Danny smiled briefly and nodded. He formed a fist at the level of his waist and tightened it. Then he turned and followed the tall man and Nelson back into the corridor and away from the arena. Mona's heart sank at first, but soon her mind began racing. *Danny is here. He's up to something. God speed, Danny Arrow!*

Another squeal of feedback sliced through the arena. Then a muffled thumping sound, followed by a humble, nervous voice, "Your Majesty? Hello, Your Majesty. Yes, I am here!" It was Dr. Laskey. He was dressed in his lab coat, and his hands were visibly fidgeting. Public appearances were clearly out of his comfort zone.

"Dr. Laskey, meet your adoring friends and comrades," Queen Igua said, raising her hands and encouraging the audience to respond. Loud applause erupted again.

"Thank you, thank you!" Laskey replied. "But it hasn't been all my doing. Many hands and many minds have worked together to bring us to where we are today."

While Dr. Laskey introduced several other scientists and lab technicians, Mona again looked toward Gate 1E, hoping to see Danny one more time. The Grey to her left noticed and yanked on her chain. Mona turned to look at him. He pointed at the screen and told her, '*Watch. This is history being made.*'"

Mona returned her gaze toward the screen. Laskey was explaining how migration was accomplished and how he would momentarily demonstrate step one in the process by freeing a willing participant from his container and transferring him to a small toroidal box, no larger than a briefcase. The camera zoomed in on the volunteer, strapped onto a metallic gurney which, according to Laskey, was being momentarily held erect for viewing pleasure. The audience chuckled. The captive stared into the camera lens and appeared panicked.

"Arthur!" Mona cried out in horror.

Chapter 31

After introducing Nelson to Doroo, nephew of Waam, I asked Nelson if he had located Mona. "She's about twenty seats out in row three," he replied. "She knows that I'm here."

I started counting heads—men, women, some I couldn't be sure of, a couple of lizards, a Grey—and suddenly there she was, and she was looking at me! I wanted to push my way down through the seats and take her in my arms, but I knew I couldn't. So, I smiled, briefly nodded, and then gave her the old atta-girl sign with my fist.

Doroo reminded me that we needed to get back to the migration chamber, so I said a mental farewell to Mona and followed Doroo and Nelson into the corridor. As we walked, I couldn't get past thinking about Mona in order to conceive of a strategy to stop Hitler's migration.

But then, halfway up the dark passageway, we were joined by the female sentry. That put me back into the proper mindset.

"Is this the one who can provide confirmation about the explosive device?" she asked, motioning toward Nelson.

"Yes, this is Interrogator Nelson," I replied.

"Follow me," she ordered.

We proceeded down the corridor in single file until we came to a door with a small red light flashing above. The sentry turned to us and held her finger to her lips.

"Shhh!" she reminded us.

I guessed that the televised program was in full swing.

Then she punched in a code number, opened the door, and we all quietly walked in.

The room was set up like a television studio. The walls and back of the room were dark, but blindingly bright lights were directed at those who were on camera. Other than the female sentry who took up a position at the door, we couldn't see exactly who was in the room, except for Dr. Laskey and an unknown creature that was strapped to a table but whose face we could not see. Implementing our excuse for being in the room, Nelson and I began to scour it, supposedly looking for a small bomb, but really looking for anything that could put a stop to the Hitler's migration.

As we searched, Dr. Laskey continued his monologue about the migration procedure. "Thus," he said into the camera, "when the magnets are rotated quickly in a counterclockwise motion, the electrical self is released from the container and is captured by the revolving magnetic field. The trick is to move the electrical self through a series of polyconductor wires and into the portable battery. From there, the porta-pack is moved to the main unit, where the charge is transferred into the new container. Often, but not always, a series of small electrical shocks are required to cement the electrical self into the new container and to reset the brain, similar to the way in which simple laptop computers reset when they are rebooted."

"When may we see the process in action, Doctor?" Queen Igua asked.

"Shortly, your highness, one of our technicians will prepare our willing volunteer for the procedure." Laskey nodded to his right. A heavyset figure stepped forward, holding a brown glass bottle in his hand. His motion caught my attention as he stepped from the dark edge of the studio and into the light. It was Granger! I waved my hands at him, but because he was blinded by the bright lights and I was in the darkness, he could not see me.

"Before attaching the electrodes," Dr. Laskey continued, "our technician will now clean the skin of our volunteer with acetone to remove body oils which may interfere with electrical signals."

Granger unscrewed the bottle cap, poured a small amount of acetone onto a cotton ball, and began wiping the volunteer's chest and sides.

"As he attaches the electrodes, the technician will ensure that the color on the sticky pads corresponds to the color on the wires, red to red, blue to blue, and so forth," Laskey said. Granger followed his instructions, holding up each wire to show the audience that the colors on the connecting wires corresponded to the colors on the electrodes.

"Because the wires are connected to ports immediately on the side of the table, they will not interfere with the rotation of the large electromagnets," Laskey said.

Granger demonstrated how the wires attached, moving his hands the way Vanna White showed a toaster to the television audience. It was enough to gag me, and I was sure he was performing under duress.

I continued moving along the walls, poking and prodding, forcing technicians and crew members to move their feet or to open their bags. They all looked annoyed. When I reached the end of my side of the room, I looked for Nelson. He showed a sign of relief when our eyes met. He mouthed something that I could not understand.

"What?" I mouthed back at him.

Nelson pointed at the volunteer on the table and mouthed, "Mc-Gar-vey!"

"McGarvey?" I mouthed back.

Nelson nodded.

"Fuck!" I mouthed.

A small lizard standing beside me looked up at me with suspicion. I pointed to the two bars on my shirt sleeve. He slowly stepped to his right and began moving in the direction of the sentry at the door. I was sure that he suspected something.

"And now, Doctor, could we please greet his excellency?" Queen Igua asked.

The camera panned toward me. A spotlight came on and was directed at a short, older woman who was standing directly in front of me, dressed in a hospital gown. As she stepped toward the front of the room, I thought that she had the gait of someone who was pushing eighty-five.

"Greetings, Your Majesty," the old woman said.

"And greetings to you, Your Excellency," the queen replied. "Honored guests, may I present the leader of the New World Order, His Excellency, Adolf Hitler!"

The roar of the crowd in the arena could be heard from inside the room as it resounded down the corridor from the stage area. After a few moments, as applause began to subside, the assembled men in uniform began chanting, "*Sieg Heil! Sieg Heil! Seig Heil!*"

The chanting continued for a full minute before the old woman raised her hand in Nazi fashion, saluting the guests in the television audience. Applause and cheers rang out again.

For a moment, my mind traveled back to high school, where a history teacher told our class that *Seig* meant Victory and *Heil* mean Hail. Hail Victory! *Hell no!* I thought.

The old woman began to speak. "My comrades, my generals, my friends, it is time for the great emergence and the second coming. The time is now. Seize the day!"

The crowd broke into applause again.

She held her hand up asking for silence and continued, "And it is an auspicious sign that this realization is today so deeply rooted in the subconscious of most nations that they participate in this redesign and reordering of the governance of this planet, either with open expressions of support or with streams of volunteers."

The crowd cheered, and many guests waved flags emblazoned with the insignia of the New World Order.

Hitler raised her hand again. When the applause trailed off, she said, "This female container in which I am dwelling is weak and tired. However, today I will emerge before you in a new container. Behold..."

The camera panned to a second table, propped up at an angle so that all could see. I was astonished, for lying still on that table was the body of a young man, probably in his early thirties, who was a dead ringer for the Hitler that I remembered seeing in photographs in history books. Right down to that stupid little mustache!

Hitler turned to Dr. Laskey. "Let us begin. Let this old worm emerge as a new and beautiful butterfly that can soar to the heavens!"

Nelson had heard enough. Pushing his way through two technicians, he rushed at the little old lady and tackled her to the ground. A reptilian guard touched his breastplate and sent a ball of liquid light volleying at Nelson, just missing him. It was a high shot, and as it ricocheted off the walls, it sent sparks flying in all directions. Screams and shouts erupted. Everyone dived for cover.

"Don't shoot! Don't shoot!" Dr. Laskey screamed. "You'll hurt *der fuhrer!*"

The lizard that was suspicious of me jumped onto Nelson, pulling him away from Hitler, who lay on the floor holding her ankle. Nelson struck back, and a fistfight ensued.

I hurried to McGarvey and began unstrapping his arms from the table. Before I could finish, a technician spun me around and sent a roundhouse into my cheek. I fell, crashing to the floor. Somebody tripped over me, managing to send the toe of a boot into my back. It hurt like hell, but I pulled myself to my feet and lunged at the technician who had struck me. We fell into several folding chairs, and he hit his head solidly on the concrete floor. Good night, Irene! I was lucky.

In less than two seconds, I was back freeing McGarvey, assisted by Doroo, who pushed away would be attackers. I noticed that he wouldn't hit any, probably because he was afraid of killing someone with his large hands.

Hitler was pulling herself across the room on her hands and knees, attempting to find safety outside of the room. But having disabled the lizard he had been fighting, Nelson grabbed her by the ankles and pulled her back into the center of the room. In front of the camera, he hoisted Hitler to her feet and put her in a full nelson wrestling hold. "They named this hold after me!" he shouted at the camera with a smile.

McGarvey joined the fray, exchanging punches with a woman in an NWO uniform. He wasn't much of a fighter but, then, neither was she. They fell into Nelson and Hitler, sending all four to the floor, but Nelson still had Hitler in his grasp.

I hurried to the camera, positioned myself directly in front of it, and shouted, "This is Interrogator Fourth Class Arrow from the Central Agency. Ladies and gentlemen, the Agency has received word that a small nuclear device has been planted in the arena and is set to explode in exactly four minutes. Evacuate the arena at once! Remain calm. Do not panic. Evacuate! Again, there is a bomb in the arena. It is set to go off in four minutes. Have a nice day."

The cameraman bolted from the room. I raced to the camera and turned it on Hitler, still being held on the floor in a full nelson. Then I rushed to help Granger, who was struggling with the female sentry. I pulled her off of him, said, "Sorry, lady," and punched her lights out.

I watched as Granger found his way to Hitler's new container and doused that beautiful young body with the entire bottle of acetone. A guard shot a ball of light at Granger, just missing him to the left. Granger toppled the table to the floor and fell prostrate behind it. The guard fired a second round as Granger hit the deck. It was a perfect shot, but Granger was behind the table, and the liquid light struck Hitler's new container in the belly, igniting the acetone and burning a six-inch hole clean through the container to the metal table.

That was one less future Nazi! The vapors from the acetone exploded into a ball of fire that filled the room, and flames leaped to the ceiling, driving almost everyone into the corridor, where they dispersed in two directions. The party was over!

Those of us who remained—me, Dr. Laskey, McGarvey, Granger, Doroo, and Nelson—stood breathing heavily while staring at the burning container. Well, except for Dr. Laskey who was weeping into both hands. Nelson was still holding onto a little old lady named Adolf.

"I guess we shook that bridge," McGarvey exclaimed.

I locked the door and sat down. My body had been through enough in the last twenty-four hours.

Chapter 32

Mona stared at the large screen in disbelief. An old woman had just been introduced to the audience as Adolf Hitler, and the crowd had gone wild, believing this bullshit. *They must be on drugs*, she thought.

As she read the text of what the woman was saying, in German, she thought that the scenario was even more preposterous. She turned to look at the tall man in the blue jumpsuit. He shrugged his shoulders when their eyes met. Mona rolled hers. The man smiled.

Mona turned to the Grey to her left and asked aloud, "You don't believe this bullshit, do you? You don't believe that old bag is Adolf Hitler, do you? He's been dead for seventy years!"

The Grey motioned for her to be quiet.

Suddenly Mona felt a hand on her right shoulder. It was the man in the blue jumpsuit. He shook his head. "Shhh."

The commissar turned to see what Waam was doing to his breeding stock.

"She was talking, Commissar, and I asked her to please be quiet, so I could hear his excellency."

Commissar Nargas turned to Mona. She returned his gaze. "This is bullshit!" she told him.

'Please refrain from loud conversation, my dear,' he told her. *'You are interfering with the pleasure of our important guests.'*

Mona huffed and sat back in her seat with her arms folded across her chest.

She watched the program for another minute, not really paying attention to the text, when suddenly a man ran in front of the camera, lowered his shoulder, and pushed the old woman off of the screen.

A ball of liquid light burst like fireworks on the wall inside the migration laboratory. The arena was absolutely silent for a moment, and then a thousand gasps of horror rose simultaneously when it was realized that this was not part of the program.

The camera swung wildly for a moment, giving Mona a rush of vertigo, and then it focused on the floor, where a small reptilian was pulling the man off of the old woman. It was Nelson! Mona jumped to her feet and squealed in delight with her fist held straight up in the air. The Greys beside her pulled on her chains and lowered her quickly to her seat. Commissar Nargas gave her a stern look and was about to reprimand her when the crowd erupted in screams. He turned to look at the screen. Fighting had broken out in the migration lab.

Mona watched the migration ceremony crumbling wildly out of control. She couldn't hold back her smile. Suddenly, Nelson was holding the old woman in front of the camera, shouting "This hold was named after me!" Mona didn't understand what he meant, but then it stuck her, and she broke into a broad smile.

The camera swung wildly again. Mona closed her eyes so she wouldn't feel sick. Then she heard Danny's voice. She opened her eyes, and he was full face on the screen. "This is Interrogator Fourth Class Arrow," he said. She didn't catch everything he told the audience, but she did hear him say, "There is a bomb in the arena. Evacuate."

The crowd panicked. Screams and worried cries rang out on all sides and from the seats above.

The NWO guards interlocked arms to try to keep the evacuation orderly, but the surge of guests trying to escape

certain death overwhelmed their few numbers. Chairs toppled. Smaller guests were trampled.

Mona rose to her feet when the Greys tried to pull her in
two separate directions, one toward Gate 1E and one following Commissar Nargas in the opposite direction. Mona
grabbed both chains and tugged against the opposing forces.
Without warning, however, the large hands of the tall man
in the blue jumpsuit took the chains and wrenched them
from the Greys, toppling them both to the floor. They rose
and charged the man, but he easily grabbed their necks and
smashed their heads together. They fell to the floor unconscious.

Mona cringed for a moment, expecting to hear Commissar Nargas's vicious hiss or expecting him to slash the face
of the tall man, but the only sounds were the panic in the
arena, the cries, and the rumble of quickly moving feet.
Nargas had disappeared! "That son of a bitch left me to die
when the bomb explodes!" Mona exclaimed aloud.

"There is no bomb, Agent Casola," the tall man told her.
"I am Waam from the planet Ummo. I came here with Dan
Arrow to rescue you."

"You came with Danny?" Mona repeated in disbelief.
Suddenly her interactions with Waam made sense. He had
been sitting behind her in order to protect her.

"Yes. Come with me," Waam told her. "We haven't
much time. The NWO will soon realize that there is no
bomb, and they will shut down this facility in order to find
those who are responsible."

"That son of a bitch left me here to die," Mona said
again, coiling the chains from her collar around her left
hand.

"Dan Arrow?" Waam asked, leading Mona quickly
through the scattered chairs and onto the stage.

The screen above them continued to project live action
video images of the migration room, now consumed in
flames, but nobody was watching.

"No, that goddamn lizard, Commissar Nargas."

Chapter 33

The doorknob to the migration facility rattled, and then the door shook, as somebody tried to open it. We all went into high alert. Doroo and Granger pressed against the wall to the right side of the door to avoid being killed if somebody blew the door open. Nelson still had Miss Hitler held in a full nelson and turned her toward the door so she'd receive the first bullet. "You are all dead men," Miss Hitler said.

I dropped to one knee and, out of instinct, reached for my model 1911. It wasn't there.

Then somebody knocked on the door. I had expected storm troopers to arrive to rescue Miss Hitler, but the knocking sound was just too polite to be storm troopers.

"Danny? Danny, it's me!" came from the other side.

It was Mona!

"Do you think it's safe to open it, Mr. Arrow?" McGarvey asked.

McGarvey had a point. What was Mona doing outside this door at this point in time? Could somebody be forcing her to call out my name?

Somebody kicked at the door. "Danny, you stupid jerk! Open this door, or I'll kick your ass!"

"Yeah," I replied to McGarvey, "she sounds just fine."

I rose to my feet and unlocked the door. Nelson pulled Miss Hitler back two steps just in case. The door opened cautiously at first, and then a head popped through near the top.

It was Waam, the tall guy that Nelson and I had met in the shuttle on the way here.

Miss Hitler squirmed in Nelson's arms trying unsuccessfully to break free and cried out, "Help me, Waam!"

Waam looked at Nelson and Hitler and then turned back into the corridor. I heard him say, "It's okay, Mona."

The door burst open and in she marched, wearing a dress that looked something like translucent green snakeskin. She glanced quickly around the room. "I see you didn't bother cleaning up for company!"

"We decorated it special for you, baby," I replied.

Mona rushed to me, threw her arms around my neck, and planted her lips on mine. "Oh, Danny, I was so worried about you!"

"I know, baby. So was I!"

"And we were all worried about you, Mona," Nelson said. "It's good to see that you're okay!"

Mona released me from her grip and kissed Nelson's cheek. "Who's your girlfriend?" she asked.

"Oh, she's just somebody I picked up," Nelson replied with a smile. "But I hear that a guy can learn a lot from older women."

Mona turned and looked at McGarvey. "Arthur, when I saw you on that table, I wanted to cry."

"Thanks, Miss Mona," McGarvey replied. "I think the cavalry got here just in the nick of time."

Waam and Doroo had greeted each other and were in their own conversation. Waam squeezed Doroo's shoulder. Then Doroo turned and left the room.

"What's he up to?" I asked.

"Doroo has gone to prepare our tureen. It will be necessary to leave soon."

"What about her excellency?" I asked, pointing at Miss Hitler. "We can't leave her here."

"No, that would not be wise, especially now that his excellency knows that Doroo and I are part of the resistance movement."

Without warning, Miss Hitler threw her head backward and smashed it into Nelson's nose and mouth. Then, in almost the same movement, she dropped to the floor and twisted free from Nelson's hold! She moved toward the open door but wasn't quick enough for Mona, who tripped her, straddled her back, and pulled one of Miss Hitler's arms up behind her.

"You're hurting me!" Miss Hitler squealed.

"Does anybody have handcuffs?" Mona asked.

Nelson's nose was bleeding, so he sat in a chair and tipped his head backward. "Kick that son of a bitch for me, would you?" he complained.

Dr. Laskey, who had been standing silent through all of the commotion, found a folded cloth on a small table near the migration device and handed it to Nelson. "Pinch the bridge of your nose," he said.

Waam appeared to be concerned. "What's bothering you, Waam?" I asked.

"My tureen is small and may not hold all who must escape."

"Mona goes with you," I replied emphatically. "There is no negotiation on that."

"I agree, Mr. Arrow. I think I can manage a total of nine passengers and crew."

"I count only nine of us."

"There are others," Waam said.

"So the question is who we leave behind. We can ask for volunteers."

"That would be unacceptable, Mr. Arrow. You know my posture on harming human beings. It would be certain death for whoever stays behind."

"How about Dr. Laskey?"

"He would certainly not be harmed, but I fear he would continue to refine the migration process, which would not be good for anyone."

"You're right," I replied. "Good thinking. Besides, may-be he could work for our government, the way Einstein and Von Braun did after leaving Germany."

"Do your trust your government? Wasn't it your gov-ernment officials who ushered in the New World Order when they made an agreement with the reptilians?"

Waam had a point. It seemed to me that any time the government gets involved in something good, they hide it from John Q. Public and find some destructive use for it. Atomic energy is just one example. But not just the atomic bomb.

I remember reading in Powers's notebook how free en-ergy sources exist, but the government does not permit those technologies to come to light in order to prevent big businesses, like the oil industry, from collapsing.

"Gentlemen," Dr. Laskey said, "perhaps I can suggest an alternative to your problem."

"What is your suggestion, doctor?" Waam asked.

"The problem seems to be one of spatial capacity and load." He pointed to me. "I was about to migrate *der fuhrer* when the process was interrupted by this gentleman and his friends. If you would permit me to complete the first stage of the migration, *der fuhrer's* electrical essence could be transported in a small, twenty-pound box."

"Listen to the doc, Danny," Mona told me, still sitting on top of Miss Hitler. "You could strap der Fuckhead down in the luggage compartment and not be bothered with him dur-ing our escape."

"Mona is correct, Mr. Arrow. It is a good idea," Waam told me.

Dr. Laskey's idea was a stroke of genius. Once inside the storage unit, Miss Hitler wouldn't be able to cause us any trouble. "Twenty pounds doesn't add too much to the load capacity of your tureen, does it, Waam?" I asked.

"It shouldn't be a problem as long as we distribute the weight equally around the cabin area."

"The electrical essence only adds less than an ounce to

the total load," Dr. Laskey added. "The twenty pounds of weight is all batteries and insulators."

Waam nodded. "This is all very interesting, Doctor. Would you consider spending some time on Ummo to help us with a problem we are facing that shares similar scientific principles?"

"Would *der fuhrer* be there?" Dr. Laskey asked.

"I think not," Waam replied.

"When can we leave?"

"Okay, Doc," I asked, "how do we set up the machinery to make this migration happen?"

Miss Hitler arched her back under Mona's weight and strained to look at Dr. Laskey. "Dr. Laskey, you must not be involved in this illegal kidnapping," she said. "You have been given the best of equipment and laboratories to conduct your work. Do not throw it all away to help these members of the resistance. They are all marked men."

"Yes, Your Excellency," Dr. Laskey replied, "you have given me excellent equipment, but you have not given me freedom." He pointed to Waam. "This gentleman did not order me to go to Ummo. Instead, he offered me a choice. Such freedom is something that you have never offered me. I am not sure where you are going, but it pleases me that you do not have a choice."

Dr. Laskey asked Nelson and McGarvey to help Mona put Miss Hitler on the table where McGarvey had been placed on display. They did so, strapping her by her ankles and wrists with the rubber devices that had held McGarvey. "Don't fight it, miss," McGarvey told her, "you ain't getting out of these."

"Where is my technical assistant?" Dr. Laskey asked.

Granger picked himself up off the floor and walked stiffly to the doctor's side.

"Is this the same as the practice drill?" he asked.

"Yes, except that it will be real. Would you please roll the magnetron here and place it so that it spins around the head of the table, but does not hit the legs."

Granger did as directed, pulling a large device with ten arms from a corner in the room and positioning it near Miss Hitler's head. Then he dragged an extension cord and plugged the unit into it.

"This here requires a two-hundred-twenty-volt circuit," he told us.

I nodded. All I could do was be an observer as the process unfolded. At least I wasn't watching it from a seat in the arena.

Dr. Laskey made some adjustments on his machine, flipping a couple of switches and turning two dials. Then he approached Miss Hitler, carrying a small handful of wires and electrodes. "Prepare the container for the migration electrodes," he told Granger.

"The acetone is all gone," Granger replied.

"There is some isopropyl alcohol in the magnetron. Second drawer down."

Granger found the alcohol and set it on the table between Miss Hitler's legs. Then he unbuttoned the top of her hospital gown, exposing what no young man should ever see— his wife at age eighty. Using a gauze pad, he began wiping Miss Hitler's chest and ribs with the alcohol. Miss Hitler, turned her head and sputtered, "You g—got some near my n—ose." Granger leaned over to wipe her face with a dry gauze pad. "Mr. Taylor," Miss Hitler whispered, "you do not have to be part of this conspiracy. Set me free, and I will ensure that you will be a very rich man."

"Uh-huh." Granger nodded, but he kept about his business, moving to Miss Hitler's ankles, where he scratched her skin several times with his nails, and then applied more alcohol. Miss Hitler arched her back at the pain.

Dr. Laskey placed the electrodes in the proper positions, peeling off their backing and sticking them in place. Then he attached the wires.

"What about her head?" Granger asked.

"Oh, yes, I almost forgot those. We wouldn't want to cook his excellency!" Dr. Laskey replied. He shook his head and smiled as his own forgetfulness. Miss Hitler gave him a hateful look.

Dr. Laskey stepped over to the magnetron and removed a small headband with pre-determined electrodes. He strapped it around Miss Hitler's forehead and connected two more wires. He then turned to Granger. "Would you please bring me the toroidal battery?"

Granger lumbered to a small metal cabinet that had somehow avoided damage during the fight. He opened the right side cabinet door then firmly shut it. Next, he opened the left side and retrieved a black rubber box that had four terminal posts on its top. "I forgot which side it was on," he muttered.

Dr. Laskey placed the battery on a small digital scale. "Twenty pounds exactly," he told us. I read the display, and that's exactly what it said. Then Dr. Laskey placed the box in a square aperture near the base of the magnetron. He connected one wire to each of the posts by clamps. "We are ready to begin!" he proclaimed.

Miss Hitler struggled against the rubber clamps at her wrists. I expected her to threaten us again, but before she could, Dr. Laskey placed a mask over her mouth and nose and said, "I suggest that you take a few breaths of this nitrous oxide, Your Excellency. It will ease your transition." Miss Hitler muttered something unintelligible.

Dr. Laskey then nodded to Granger, who began rotating the arms of the magnetron by hand. As he did, Dr. Laskey moved to a control panel and began turning a dial. Within a few seconds, the magnetron was revolving on its own, counterclockwise around Miss Hitler's upper body. Granger stepped back. We all stepped back, as well.

With the exception of the rush of displaced air, there was little sound. No sparks, no whining, no whirring. It was a well-greased machine. But the needles on the little meters on the control panel were moving, and Dr. Laskey kept his eyes on them. "We are almost there," he told us.

I looked at Miss Hitler. Her body was trembling, and her

eyes were full of fear. Then suddenly, she just went limp. It was like somebody turned off her lights and went out for dinner. I mean, how else could I describe it? One second she was trembling, and the next second she was gone. "Is she dead?" I asked.

"No, she is not dead, but her body no longer holds her," Dr. Laskey replied.

"What is this shit?" Mona challenged. "You've just knocked her out, and after we leave, she'll be as good as new."

"I assure you, miss, his excellency is in the toroidal battery and shall remain there until we relocate him to another container. This old container will enter rigor mortis within ten minutes. It is no longer capable of maintaining the appearance of life because the living essence is now gone."

"Do y'all mean to tell me that his excellency is in that little black box?" Nelson asked. "Is that what all this migration stuff is about?"

"His excellency has been migrated into a holding tank, if you will," Dr. Laskey explained. "True migration requires the second step in a two-step process. His electrical self must be transferred into a receptive container in order for true migration to occur. But, alas, you ruined the intended container."

He pointed at the burned corpse of the youthful body that had been intended for Miss Hitler.

"Bullshit!" Mona said.

"No, miss, come look at what has happened to the toroidal battery." Dr. Laskey removed the wires from the small black box and put it back on the digital scale. The display now read 20.0425 pounds. "The extra point-zero-four-two-five pounds is his electrical essence, waiting to be released into a receptive container."

"Well, I'll be damned," Nelson murmured. "So this is what happened to that poor bastard Bill Powers."

"I still don't believe him, Danny," Mona told me.

I looked a Waam. He nodded. "I believe it is time for us

to leave for my tureen," he told us. "We have already stayed much longer than we should have."

I pushed the magnetron away from Miss Hitler's corpse and did the only thing I knew to do. I poked her in the eye, the way a hunter would do to a recently shot deer. There's no sense in getting your leg shredded by the hoof of a deer that isn't quite deceased. She didn't flinch. "She won't be giving anybody any trouble," I told Nelson.

"One more thing, Dan," Nelson said, looking at the magnetron.

I understood, and he was right. Nelson pulled on one long arm of the soul catcher, and I pulled on another, tugging back and forth against each other until his broke free from its main shaft.

"That's an easy fix, gentlemen," Dr. Laskey told us. "Try the control panel."

He was right.

"So why are you telling us how to destroy your own machine?" Nelson asked.

"I can always build another one, but the NWO killed my research assistant when they discovered that she was with the resistance. They have no way to replace this machine. At least not for a few years. She was my only true friend."

Nelson picked up a piece of pipe that was lying near the wall and swung it into the monitor of the magnetron's control panel. Sparks shot out into the air. Granger stopped Nelson before he could take a second swing. "Safety, first, Nelson," he said. Then he unplugged the unit from the wall. "Like I told you, it's a two-hundred-twenty-volt circuit."

Before the plug could hit the floor, Nelson was swinging again and again. Then McGarvey stepped forward and pulled a circuit board and a few wires out of the hole that Nelson had pounded into the machine. "I'm taking this with us," he said matter-of-factly.

"Come on, Mona," I said, "Let's go home." I took her hand, and we followed Waam out the door and down the dark corridor, turning away from the arena, from which there were still sounds of panic. McGarvey was next, followed by Dr. Laskey, Nelson, and Granger, who was carrying Miss Hitler with two hands, like a bucket of fried chicken.

A few hundred yards down the corridor, Waam stopped us. We could see the motion of flashlights moving behind us. Someone was coming—and quickly. Waam felt the wall—touching here and there —until he found a sweet spot or something, because when he did, the wall began to shimmer and became translucent. "Come on," he told us. "This way to my tureen." Mona and I entered first, followed by the others. A shot rang out and then shouts and then another shot. Granger, who was still in the corridor, dropped the black box containing Miss Hitler and dived into the opening that Waam had created. His hand was bleeding.

I looked at Mona and then at the black box. I dived for it, feet first, sweeping my right leg into the corridor and pulling the box into the opening behind my calf. Another shot rang out. It missed me.

"They ain't aliens, Dan," Nelson said. "Aliens would have sent a ball of that liquid light at you." He was right.

Waam touched a place on the wall inside the opening, and its shimmering translucence slowed until it was simply rock again.

"What is that?" I asked. "How did you do that?"

"It's relatively new technology, something we captured from the draconians and back engineered. It works nicely, doesn't it?"

Mona was looking at Granger's hand, wiping it with the hem of her skirt. "I think you'll be fine," she told him. "Just put some antibiotic on it when we get home."

"I ain't sure I got a home," he replied.

"You can stay with me, Granger," McGarvey said. "We've got a lot in common. I don't have any family either."

Waam took the lead again, walking with confidence into the darkness of a new corridor. In the distance, I could see a soft white glow. As we walked, I could feel my muscles aching, but knowing that I would soon be above ground with Mona made it bearable. I could hear McGarvey huffing as he walked. He had discarded the circuit board and was now carrying Miss Hitler—the black box supported to a small degree by a dent in its side, put there by a single bullet and just the right size to enhance the grip of a single finger.

Soon we entered a small cavern with glassy walls which reflected the soft white glow of what Waam called his tureen. I would call it a flying saucer, classic shape, sort of like two Frisbees glued together, with a little dome on top. It was gunmetal gray in color, but the seam around its circumference was full of little lights, like those LEDs that they sold in the big box hardware stores outside of DC. Never liked them. That was why I bought three hundred sixty-watt lightbulbs when they stopped making them. I figured it was a lifetime's supply. But that was another story...

As we approached the saucer, a ramp descended, bringing Doroo down as it came. "You are all safe!" he remarked. "This is good."

He offered his hand to Mona, who took it and walked up the ramp into its lighted interior. I let Nelson follow her and then McGarvey, but I took Miss Hitler from him because he looked really tired of carrying an extra 20.0425 pounds. Granger went in next, then Dr. Laskey, and then I entered. Waam took rear guard, pressing a button and closing the ramp behind him.

The inside was incredibly clean and tidy, like my grandmother had already been there to prep it for company. The walls were some kind of molded composite from which the light emanated. Everything glowed, but softly. I had a brief conversation in a bar in DC with a guy from GE who was working on similar walls to light the homes of the future. I wondered if the technology that he described had been retro-engineered from saucers like this one.

There were no seats near the door, but seating areas followed the circular contour of the inner core. So, if you were seated, you faced the exterior walls of the saucer. Two of the seats had arms with depressions that looked like someone had pressed their hands into the plastic when it was still warm and soft and hadn't cooled to rigidity. I took them to be the pilots' seats.

"Is this a new model?" I asked Waam.

"I've had it since 1948 in your time," he said. "There are newer models, but this one has had a few upgrades."

As we settled in, Doroo opened the ramp again. Mack Smith popped in. "Did Special Agent Casola make it?" he asked

"I apologize for not checking in with you, Mack," Mona told him. "But I've been kind of busy."

"I know," he said, giving her a peck on the cheek. "Waam and I watched you come into the arena with Commissar Nargas." He turned to me and Nelson. "And great job, you two. It was quite a show. They've been scrambling out of here for almost half an hour. Hundreds of people in the Bay Area have called the air force to report UFOs. This will be a day that the NWO will never forget."

"I only regret that I didn't have a real suitcase nuke," I replied.

"Yeah," agreed Nelson.

"Keyhoe has taken care of that," Mack replied.

Nelson and I both raised our eyebrows.

Mack turned to Waam. "We probably ought to get going."

Waam and Doroo took their seats and placed their hands into the depressions on their armrests. Within two seconds, a low whine let us know that the saucer had been activated. As the whine turned to a hum, the walls of the saucer became translucent, and we could see the interior walls of the cavern in which we were hovering.

"Keep your eyes on the ceiling," Waam announced.

Above, the rock ceiling began shimmering. A few moments later, the saucer began to rise through the translucent rock. The process was almost exactly like the door that Waam had magically opened in the corridor, only this door was an airplane hangar wide, and it was above us. Suddenly, the sky burst into view. We were out of the ground, having emerged from a mile below the surface to a mile above the surface in less than thirty seconds. Yet there had been almost no sensation of motion, except for the visual effect on the cabin ceiling.

"Look in all directions," Waam instructed us, "and you can see everywhere."

We continued to rise until we slowed beside another saucer.

"We must sit in this holding pattern until we set our coordinates and have a clear pathway to our destination," Doroo announced. "The skies above Livermore are busy this afternoon."

Mona sat bolt upright. She rose to her feet, walked toward the outer walls, and stared through them at the passengers who were watching us from their own saucer, just one hundred feet away. "It's him!" Mona cried.

"Who, baby?" I asked, joining her at the outer wall.

"It's that motherfucking lizard Commissar Nargas! He left me to die when you announced that there was a bomb in the arena."

"It's okay, he can't hurt you anymore."

Nargas's eyes explored the tureen which hovered beside him. He recognized Waam at the controls. Then he saw her. Their eyes met.

Mona raised the middle finger on her right hand and flipped it at the commissar. "Fuck you," she screamed.

I put my right arm around her shoulder, and we returned to our seats. As we sat, Waam announced that we would be in Denver in four minutes. There was a slight sensation of motion, and the commissar's saucer simply disappeared behind us.

"You're going to be okay," I said again to Mona.

"I'm not so sure, Danny," she replied softly. "I'm pregnant."

Chapter 34

Mona was in the shower. She really needed it. Besides, we were supposed to meet Billy Powers and Marlene for cocktails and dinner at seven p.m., and she wanted to wash the smell of snakes off of her skin before we went down. Fox News in Denver was carrying a story that evening about an apparent earthquake and a large sink hole that had suddenly appeared in the hillside at the military facility at Livermore, just outside of San Francisco. They estimated its depth at one thousand feet. *Imagine that*, I thought. It had to have been a suitcase nuke, set off by Mack or some of his friends in the resistance.

❧❧❧

The ride back to Denver had been exceptionally fast. I estimated maybe three and a half minutes. Waam turned on the cloaking system, and we stopped briefly over the runway where we had emerged in the laser mole.

The hole was still there, surrounded by heavy equipment and barricades, and I figured that the runway was closed down for repairs. I hoped that somebody with some clout would send a company of troops down there to see what they could find, but then I realized that the military already knew what was down there, and they just wanted to secret it away under several tons of dirt and concrete.

Waam then dropped four of us off on a vacant piece of desert, about fifteen minutes outside of town. A limo was waiting for us, compliments of Mack Smith. Standing beside it was the driver, a tall guy with blond hair. It was no surprise that he was wearing a black suit and sunglasses. Granger, McGarvey, Mona, and I said goodbye to Waam, Doroo, Nelson, and Mack. Nelson was headed to Dulce and Mack back to DC. They kept Miss Hitler. Mack said he had plans for her. I suggested that he drop her black box into the ocean. He told me that he had a better idea, something about a voyage to the sun.

After dropping McGarvey and Granger off at McGarvey's apartment, the driver took us back to the hotel where we had started this leg of our adventure. Before he unlocked the door, he handed me a shoe box. "What's this?" I asked.

"Special Agent Smith thought you might need these things."

I removed the lid. Inside were two passports with our photos and new names, Ralph and Vera Arreaux. How thoughtful. He had also included a Visa gift card in the amount of $5000, ten one-hundred-dollar bills, and two Smith & Wesson Chief Specials in .38 caliber. I wasn't a fan of snub-nose revolvers, but they were a nice security measure. I assumed the one with the pink grips was for Mona. I also assumed that he anticipated that we might face some trouble.

"What's Mack trying to tell us?" I asked Mona.

"I hope he wants us to take a week's vacation, incognito. Frankly, I could use a few days off. I still owe my Ma a phone call, and it's going to take me that long to get up the nerve."

We got dressed and left the room at six-fifty-five p.m. We were both armed, but nobody could tell because the little revolvers slid nicely into small pockets.

When we found our way to the restaurant, Marlene and Bill Powers hailed us as we passed through the bar area.

"Over here, Mr. Arrow!" Marlene called out.

I introduced Mona to Marlene and Bill, reminding her that Bill's telephone call had opened up this new world to us. She smiled and thanked him. I think she was being polite, especially after being an alien's trick pony for the past few days.

After drinks, we had dinner. Marlene ordered surf and turf. Miss Powers opted to have another cocktail. "Eating doesn't mean what it used to," he told us.

I dived into a steak, and Mona opted for a mixed greens salad. I thought it was odd when she smiled and said, "Lizard food."

Our conversation turned to the New World Order and what we had discovered. "You were just too close to discovering what they were up to," I told Powers. "They've actually perfected the procedure that they put you through, but I wouldn't recommend going back into that snake hole to get a new container. Besides, their machine needs a repair job."

Miss Powers just nodded.

"If I see that guy Waam again, I'll ask him if he can help you get into a newer, more masculine container—" I realized that I was already speaking alien like a pro. "—I mean 'body.'"

Mona changed the subject. "Marlene, how are you handling renewing your relationship with Bill, especially since he's, well, not exactly what you had expected."

Marlene broke into a huge smile. "She doesn't look like my Billy, but she *is* Billy. And we had fun last night, Mona. Nobody can do what Billy does with his tongue."

Oh, jeez, TMI, I thought! That was an image I was going to have difficulty shaking out of my head: a middle-aged woman and a silver-haired granny engaged in... well, you've got the picture. As that flipped through my head, Mona smiled at me. "Maybe you can give my Danny some lessons, Billy."

Miss Powers smiled and nodded.

"That's okay, but I'll pass," I told her.

Marlene and her mother called it an early evening at nine. Billy needed to bathe, and I knew that meant he'd be submerged in that concoction of raw meat and Gatorade that Nelson and I had prepared for him. I hoped that it hadn't turned rancid, but that really wasn't any of my business. I had the feeling that Marlene would take good care of him during their time together, no matter how short it might be.

❧❧❧

Back in our room, Mona went into the bathroom and changed into a nightie. I stripped down to my skivvies and climbed beneath the covers. When she came out, Mona climbed into bed beside me. "You're my hero, Danny. Nobody would have gone into Hell to save me, but you did. You saved me from the devil himself."

We kissed. It was long, passionate, and promising. I had been waiting for that moment for what seemed like a lifetime. I was with the woman of my dreams, she seemed willing, and the night was young. I began to explore her breasts with my hand. She moaned and slipped her tongue into my mouth. I found the hem of her nightie and began to pull it upward. Without warning, Mona pushed me away. "No, Danny, I can't." she told me. "Maybe tomorrow, after I see the doctor."

"I ache for you, Mona," I pleaded. "Every part of my body is standing at attention."

"We've waited this long, Danny. Another night won't make any difference."

"You're asking a lot. A lesser man would leave right now and hire one of the girls in the lobby for the evening."

"Would you really do that to me now, Danny?" Mona snapped. "Would you really prefer a hooker to sharing this bed with me tonight?"

"I was just kidding, baby. You know I was."

"Yeah, right!" she replied in her usual annoyed tone. "This is the way it is—I'm pregnant, and the baby isn't yours. I want the doctor to tear this monster out of my body. When he examines me, I don't want any of you or your stuff glopping around inside me for him to see."

"Baby, I'm sure he sees that all the time."

"Not from a good Italian girl who isn't married."

I conceded with a gentle kiss on Mona's cheek. "We'll get that lizard out of you, Mona. You'll never have to give birth to that thing."

❧❧❧

The next morning, I drove Mona to the private abortion clinic where she had scheduled an emergency appointment. When we checked in, Mona gave the nurse her name and said that, no, I was not the father. We waited for fifteen minutes. I held Mona's hand the whole time. She was visibly nervous. The red splotches on her neck were a clear sign of anxiety.

"Miss Casola?" the doctor asked. He was standing at the entrance to a swinging door, holding a clipboard. The name on his pocket was Dr. Patel. Mona shook his hand and introduced me. He then escorted us to an examination room, down the hallway and to the left.

"And how long have you suspected that you are pregnant?" Dr. Patel asked.

"About three weeks," Mona replied.

The doctor listened to Mona's heart and then moved to her abdomen. "The baby's heartbeat is much faster than I would have anticipated," he told us.

Dr. Patel moved us to an adjoining room, where a technician was readying an ultrasound machine. Mona was instructed to lie on a table with her head resting comfortably on a pillow. The technician began her work, rubbing warm gel on Mona's abdomen and then moving a mushroom shaped wand across it until she found the fetus. We watched her progress on the television screen which was mounted on the side wall. "Babies go through stages, Mrs. Casola," she said.

"That's 'Miss,'" Mona replied firmly.

"Sorry, Miss Casola," the technician apologized, and then she continued with her lecture. "First, they look like fish, and then like frogs, and other animals before they take on our distinct human shape. See how your baby's head looks somewhat like a frog or a salamander?"

"I want it out!"

"I have to take measurements, first."

The technician carefully moved a cursor around the image of the fetus on her monitor, clicking at specific points. "Your baby is right on schedule for a two month pregnancy."

"I haven't been pregnant that long," Mona told her.

"Well, according to my chart you are at least two months pregnant, and maybe a bit more. But Dr. Patel will be able to tell you more. I'm not really supposed to tell you anything."

But you did, I thought. I wondered how long Mona really had been pregnant. I also wondered if Dr. Patel knew that his technician jumped at the first opportunity to tell his patients important news…well, probably only if it was good news.

The bad news would definitely be left up to the doctor. I thought that many technicians and nurses felt that they knew as much, if not more, than the doctors who employed them. But that was another topic for discussion.

The technician cleaned the gel from Mona's belly and ushered us back into the first examination room. A few minutes later, Dr. Patel entered and sat down. "Miss Casola, the good news is that your baby appears to be in excellent health, with the exception that its heart is beating twenty percent faster than normal. You appear to be approximately ten weeks along. I understand that you desire to terminate this pregnancy, correct?"

"Yes, absolutely. I want it out of my body."

"There are other options. You could decide against ending a human life by carrying the baby to full term and then giving it up for adoption."

"I want it gone, Doctor."

"I really must protest, Miss Casola. Your baby is a perfect specimen. Termination is the last thing that you should consider."

"I want this little bastard out of my body. It has no right to be in my body against my will."

Dr. Patel raised his eyebrows at Mona's comment. "Okay, then, we can schedule you for termination in ten days."

"No. Today!" Mona demanded.

"Miss Casola, there are others scheduled ahead of you."

"Dr. Patel," I said, "Special Agent Casola is assigned to a Homeland Security case that is vital to the safety of the United States. She is needed back on this case as quickly as possible. If there is anything that you can do to expedite her procedure, your government would be especially grateful."

"Agent?"

"Yes, I am a Special Agent on assignment from the FBI, Washington, DC. My badge is in my clothes on that chair."

I reached for Mona's clothing, but Dr. Patel stopped me. He walked out of the room and came back in about two minutes. "Okay, Special Agent Casola, I have cancelled a squash game for tomorrow afternoon. Can you be here at noon?"

"Yes, Doctor, thank you!" Mona replied.

Chapter 35

After scheduling Mona's appointment with Dr. Patel, we visited with McGarvey and Granger at a coffee shop in Centennial, just south of Denver. McGarvey told us that he and Granger had gone by Fritz Weiner's home to see if Fritz's daughter had come to claim his stuff. The house was completely empty, with no sign of any visitors. In fact, a small pile of newspapers, still in their plastic wrappers, lay on his driveway. "We took them," McGarvey told me. He and Granger had done the right thing. There was no sense in alerting criminals to the fact that nobody was home.

"The world has really changed, Mr. Arrow," Granger said. "Cars are so crazy looking, and so are the newer houses. It ain't nothing like I remember. I don't know most of the stores, and I hate the music they play."

"Except on the oldies station, Granger," McGarvey reminded him.

"Yeah, I guess that's so."

"We have scheduled a meeting with Denver MUFON for two days from now. Can you join us?" McGarvey asked. "We'd really like you to be there to help explain what's going on down below the airport."

"Unfortunately, we won't be able to be there," I lied. "Mona and I have been ordered by the FBI to go into deep cover for a few weeks. We can't call or write or anything like that." Hell, they didn't need to know that Mona was going to have an abortion.

"Arthur, I'm sure that you and Granger will be the best witnesses that MUFON has ever had," Mona said. "Both of you have ridden in UFOs, and both of you have had interactions with aliens of several varieties, both good and bad. Both of you know about the big event underground at Livermore and can explain the sink hole. They'll be infatuated with your story."

"You're right, Miss Mona. And we have proof. I already mailed them the memory stick from my camera. I mailed it before we went back down to get you."

Convinced that McGarvey and Granger were getting ready to set MUFON on its head with excitement, we said farewell and headed back to our hotel in Denver.

e⁄ɔe⁄ɔ

That evening, I didn't bother Mona with sexual pressure. I knew that she had the upcoming procedure on her mind, and that, after the procedure, it would be several days before I could try to show her how much I loved her, well at least in that manner. In the meanwhile, I held her hand, and we talked about a lot of personal stuff. She was still avoiding her mom, but I made her promise to call as soon as she had recovered from the procedure. I also made a mental note to call Hal and see how things were back in my office.

e⁄ɔe⁄ɔ

In the morning, Mona awoke sharply, smacking me on my face with the palm of her hand as she bolted upright. Realizing where she was after a moment of confusion, Mona covered her face with the palms of both hands.

"Jeezus, Mona, what's wrong?" I complained in surprise.

"Just a dream, Danny, I guess. That bastard Commissar Nargas crept into my dreams last night. What a nightmare! I can't wait to get him out of my head!"

"A nightmare?" I asked.

"Yeah, I can't remember all of it. I just remember lying on his table back in some cavern. He was standing over me with his shit-eating lizard grin and saying, 'Good girl.' All I could do was say 'Fuck you!' I guess that's all I ever told him."

"It's okay, Mona. We'll get by this in a day or two. He can't hurt you anymore. Besides, if he shows up, we'll put a bullet between his eyes and get you a new pair of boots."

Mona laughed. "That's what I told one of those lizards at Livermore. 'Someday, I'll be wearing your skin on my feet.'"

Chapter 36

Mona and I pulled into the parking lot at Dr. Patel's clinic about a quarter to twelve. As requested, she had showered but had not eaten so she wouldn't barf on the operating table.

When we entered the waiting room, Mona signed a few permission slips and presented her federal insurance cards, and then she was immediately escorted into the prep room. I was told to sit down and enjoy the afternoon. I wouldn't be able to see Mona until after the procedure, probably not until she was coming out of anesthesia. That was okay by me.

Training from my earliest days in security taught me never to put my back to the door. So I sat in the middle row of chairs, facing both the front door and the television. The tube was set on a channel where some guy was buying and restoring old houses so he could flip them for a profit. It was slow paced and somewhat boring, but at least it consumed time, and I anticipated having a lot of that.

However, about half an hour into the afternoon, a nurse appeared and asked me if I would follow her to Dr. Patel's office. He wanted to see me. *This can't be good*, I thought.

We walked through the same swinging door as yesterday, except this time we went to the very end of the corridor and into an office with cherry bookshelves and a large matching desk.

From the look of his digs, the abortion business must be booming.

Dr. Patel joined me within a few minutes. "Mr..." he asked, not remembering my last name.

"Arrow."

"Mr. Arrow, are you familiar with the term 'pseudocyesis'?"

I shook my head in the negative.

"Basically, it means 'false pregnancy.'"

"I don't understand what you're saying, Doctor."

"In clinical terms, pseudocyesis, is the belief that you are expecting a baby when you are not really carrying a child. People with pseudocyesis have many, if not all, symptoms of pregnancy—with the exception of an actual fetus."

"Are you saying that Mona is not pregnant? That she isn't carrying a baby?"

"That's exactly what I am saying, Mr. Arrow. Special Agent Casola's womb is empty."

"I don't understand, Doctor. Yesterday you heard the heartbeat of a child through your stethoscope. Your technician showed us a baby on the television. In fact, she took measurements of it on her monitor. She said it was two months along. And, so did you!"

"This is all very strange, Mr. Arrow. Clearly, it must be a form of pseudocyesis. That can be the only explanation."

"I can think of another explanation," I replied, "but you'd think I was a lunatic if I told you what it is. But I will tell you this: Mona was pregnant yesterday. You and I both know it!"

The doctor just stared at me, stone faced.

"Have you told her yet?" I asked.

"No, she is still under sedation, but I will tell her when she awakens."

"Can I be there when you do?"

"Unfortunately, the laws of the State of Colorado do not permit you to be there because you are not next of kin."

I gave Dr. Patel a look of complete aggravation and rose

to leave his office. "This is bullshit, Doctor, and you'd better be ready for a major verbal assault when you give Mona this news."

Dr. Patel's eyes descended to the floor, and his shoulders drooped. I marched down the hall to the waiting room. I knew that Mona was not going to be a happy camper in a few minutes.

❧❧❧

At two p.m., the door to Dr. Patel's examination room burst open, startling me. Mona emerged, being pushed in a wheelchair by the same nurse who had escorted me to Dr. Patel's office. Mona had a look of anger on her face that told me not to get too close too fast. "Mr. Arrow," the nurse instructed, "would you be so kind as to bring your car to the front of the entryway, and I will meet you there with Special Agent Casola."

I did as she said. When I pulled to a stop in front of the main entrance, I watched Mona push the nurse away, open the door, and climb into the Escalade."

"Have a nice day, Special Agent Casola," the nurse said.

Mona didn't respond to the nurse. She just snarled, "Drive!"

I pulled out of the parking lot and onto the main highway before I asked Mona how she was.

"That fucking low-life scum-sucking lizard!" was her response.

"So you're thinking what I'm thinking?" I asked.

"That son of a bitch Nargas is still interfering in my life. It wasn't a dream, Danny! That bastard kidnapped me last night, took me to some facility, and stole my baby."

I didn't know what to say. On one hand, Mona didn't want the baby. On the other hand, removing it should have been on her own terms.

"That fucker took a baby out of me without asking if he

could. I had no say whatsoever. Goddamn, I'm glad that
monster is out of me, but I've been violated again by that
bastard!"

She was right. I started to tell her so, but she didn't let
me get the first word out.

"This is America! We don't do shit like this in America.
We don't treat people like lab rats. I am not a lab rat! I have
rights, and they have been violated! My body has been used
as a breeding facility by some alien being who has no respect for human kind. Where can I go to seek justice? There
is no fucking place to get justice!"

"Mona?" I asked.

"What do you think, Danny? Do you think that baby is
alive, or do you think it's being used for dissection?"

My mind raced. How the fuck could I answer that question? I opted for the truth. "Mona, I believe that they're
working on a hybrid race, one that combines their intelligence with our ability to live on the surface of the Earth,
under our sun. I don't think that they'll dissect a hybrid that
they've created. I think they'll place it in one of their artificial wombs and let it grow to full term. Then they'll raise it
to be among those to inherit the Earth after the NWO plan
has been set into motion."

"I told him 'fuck you,' Danny. In the end, I'm the one
who got fucked. He flipped me off in my sleep, just like I
flipped him off from Waam's saucer. He's gotten the last
laugh, hasn't he?"

"We'll get through this, Mona. And, somehow, I'll find a
way to kill that lizard. Nobody takes advantage of my
wife."

"Wife! You said 'wife,' Danny! I'm not your wife. I'm
just some girl who gets fucked by the men in her life and is
left with nothing to show for it. Not even a goddamn baby!"

She was going places that I hadn't anticipated. "Mona,
do you remember what I told you in the shaft? I told you
that I want to marry you. I love you, Mona. I love you so
much that I already feel as though you're my wife."

"I never said 'yes.'"

"Promise me that you'll think about it, baby."

"You know what I'm going to say, Danny."

"I never know what you're going to say, Mona."

Chapter 37

It was almost dark when I turned onto Route 70 and headed west out of Denver. It had been a hell of a day.

"Will we ever be safe when we're sleeping at night?" Mona asked.

Hell, I couldn't promise that. I'd had a revolver under my pillow, but I had slept right through her abduction last night like nothing had happened at all. But I knew that it had. I'd seen the baby on the monitor, and I'd heard its heart beating like a little internal combustion motor on the speaker in the examination room. That baby had been there, and now it was gone. Only the reptilians would have done that.

As we climbed into the mountains, all I wanted to do was give Mona a break. Getting out of the hotel and getting some fresh air was a good thing. I hoped that our ride would help her to process the day's events, maybe to chill out and calm down a bit from the emotional upheavals that the day had brought.

When I saw an overlook, I pulled off the road and shut down the motor. We got out and took a blanket and a bag from the rear compartment of our Escalade. We then stepped over the small white barrier that kept cars from falling over the cliff. On the other side was a patch of grass about the size of our hotel room. It was all we needed to feel safe and free.

We spread the blanket on the grass and sat down. The air was warm, but not hot, and the slight breeze was just enough to keep the bugs away. I took a bottle of Chianti and two glasses out of the bag. "Nice," she said about the glasses. "Just like in the hotel room."

"Imagine that," I replied, opening the bottle with a cheapo corkscrew that was a freebie at the wine store. Mona then held the glasses, and I filled them both to the halfway mark. I held my glass in the air and said, "To a hell of a ride, Mona!"

We touched glasses, and I took a sip. Mona downed hers like she was doing shots and asked me to fill it up again. I complied with her wishes.

As we sat there quietly, the last bit of daylight gave way to darkness and the sky became a canvas of stars. Millions of them, twinkling and sparkling, and reminding me of how vast the universe truly is.

"Doesn't the sky make you realize how insignificant we are?" Mona asked.

"I don't believe that, Mona. If mankind is so insignificant, why are all those aliens so interested in us? Why do they want to merge with us to create hybrids? There has to be something special about humans."

"Danny, do you think the commissar took my baby, or did I just imagine it all?"

"You didn't imagine it, Mona. We both saw that baby when they did the ultrasound."

"At least it's gone." Mona sighed. "And I won't have to explain a bulging tummy to my father."

"When are you going to call them?"

"Tomorrow, maybe after breakfast."

We sat for a few minutes watching the skies. Mona turned and leaned her shoulder into my chest. I put my arm around her. A shooting star passed toward the north. It was beautiful. I kissed Mona on her forehead. "Things are getting better already," I told her.

"Danny?" she asked.

"Yeah, baby?"

"Danny, do you think we could be pawns in the hands of aliens, like aphids are pawns in the hands of ants? There are good ants and bad ants. Do you think they pluck us up all of our lives and do things to us that we don't remember? That maybe we find each other because they have programmed us to be together. And that we search for each other all of our lives?"

"It's all too crazy, Mona. I don't know whether it's alien intervention or Mother Nature but, somewhere deep inside me, I think I was searching for you all my life."

"Yeah, and when you found me—"

"Sometimes a guy like me doesn't appreciate fine wine because he thinks he only deserves cheap beer."

"Danny, you saved us all from the New World Order. You deserve a medal and a parade."

"Just a simple kiss from you would do," I told her.

"How about a hickey?" she replied.

"Sounds about right for a guy like me."

"You'll have to work for it, Danny. And you'd better be good."

Epilogue

The sound of Mona talking to somebody woke me up the next morning. She was in the bathroom, probably trying not to wake me. It didn't work. When I heard her say, "I'm sorry, Ma," I knew that she was finally calling home. God be with her. Italian mothers could be hard on their kids. But it is all out of high expectations and love.

In my sleep, I had been wrestling with something that just didn't sit right with me, and it kept running through my mind as I lay awake in bed. When discussing the termination of her baby, why was Dr. Patel so insistent that Mona keep her baby to full term? He was running an abortion clinic after all, wasn't he? And didn't he call Mona's baby a "perfect specimen"? Doctors didn't talk to their patients that way, did they? He sounded more like a laboratory scientist than a practicing physician.

Then my cell phone rang. I didn't recognize the number, but it was local. "Arrow," I said firmly.

"Mr. Arrow?"

"Yes."

"I must remain anonymous." The slight Indian accent made me pretty certain that it was Patel. Mona must have given his nurses my number.

"So? What's on your mind? "

"Special Agent Casola's baby is alive."

"I'd already guessed that. Where is it?"

"You will never be able to get there. I just wanted you to know that the baby is fine, and that it will have the best of care until it is able to play with the others."

"The others?"

"Hundreds of them. Clinics all over the world have given Star Children back to their galactic parents until the time of their return to Earth. Someday Special Agent Casola may actually meet her daughter."

"Where are they?" I asked, "The star children?"

"The physician who helped you did so out of duress. The safety of his family was at stake. Do not contact him directly because he is being monitored by the tall ones."

"Where are the Star Children?" I asked again.

There was a long pause, and then the voice said, "In the hollow moon."

The End

DAN ARROW AND THE HOLLOW MOON

Dan is told that by stopping Hitler's migration into his cloned body, he has not saved the world as we know it, but that he has only delayed Agenda 21. Now he must stop Agenda 21 if he is to save the world.

Dan and Mona travel on a secret mission to the dark side of the moon where they enter a world only theorized by a few scientists: The moon is actually a hollow artifact that was brought to Earth 50,000 years ago to serve as a space station from which aliens could monitor the development and evolution of human slaves. It is now the base of operations for the New World Order, which has scheduled a chain of events that will enable them to dominate mankind.

ↄ∞ↄ

If you enjoyed *Dan Arrow and the New World Order*, you will want to follow Dan and Mona as they continue to find more truth than fiction in conspiracy theories and the New World Order. *Dan Arrow and the Hollow Moon* will be available soon through Black Opal Books.

About the Author

Born in Massachusetts, Edward Baker traveled widely as a child because his US Marine father was transferred to new assignments across the USA on a regular basis. By the time Baker was twelve, he had crossed the United States three times. And at ripe old age of sixteen, he actually drove a stick-shift Ford across the USA, following his dad, who was pulling a small camping trailer behind the family station wagon.

An English major at Elon College, Baker earned a master's degree at Appalachian State University and a doctorate in Educational Leadership at the Graduate School of the Sage Colleges. After thirty-five years in higher education, and after retiring as the interim president of a public community college, he turned his attention to his first love, writing, while continuing to teach undergraduate and graduate courses on an adjunct basis at a private college in upstate New York.

During the warm months, Baker and his wife Edna reside in their cabin on Galway Lake, New York. During the cold months, they "hole up" in their winter quarters in Saratoga Springs, New York. When he's not teaching or writing, Baker is playing with his four grandchildren or working on a long list of renovations and construction projects.

Baker saw his first UFOs as a young man while camping out at Green Lakes State Park near Syracuse, New York. He saw his second while living on the beach at Emerald Isle in North Carolina, back when it was still a wild and undeveloped stretch of dunes. His first Black Opal release, *Dan Arrow and the New World Order,* is based on these experiences and on current conspiracy lore, combining the UFO mystery with national and international politics and the rumored agenda of the legendary New World Order. Baker says that the Dan Arrow books are fun to write because they permit him to delve into seemingly unrelated elements that mesh together into a fabric offering many clandestine possibilities.

39399750R00188

Made in the USA
Middletown, DE
21 March 2019